Five Sunsets by Franc

First Edition: Published June 2022

ALL RIGHTS RESERVED

Dedication

This is for all my holiday romances that didn't last so that I could have the one that did. The one that is still going, 4,453 sunsets later.

Introduction (includes possible spoilers)

Five Sunsets is a steamy contemporary romantic comedy. As with a lot of romance and comedy, tough topics are not ignored. Therefore, I'd like to highlight that among the things our main characters experience and talk about are grief, divorce, depression, suicide, and loss of loved ones. Specifically, there are first-hand accounts of losing a family member to suicide, losing a loved one to cancer, parental infidelity and neglect, suicidal thoughts, and addiction (alcohol and drugs). There are also references to queerphobia (biphobia). Please go steady if any of these topics are potentially upsetting for you.

There is also swearing throughout and more than a handful of steam-filled sex scenes, and not just because our main characters like shagging in showers far too much.

And if you like listening to book playlists, you can find the playlist the author used to write and re-write and cry and laugh and sweat over this book on Spotify if you search "Five Sunsets". Enjoy!

"When your world moves too fast and you lose yourself in the chaos, introduce yourself to each colour of the sunset."

- Christy Ann Martine

Prologue

Jenna

The first time I see him, he's checking out my brother's arse.

"Are your bum cheeks feeling hot?" I ask Jake, nudging my arm into his.

"Excuse me?" he asks, in longer syllables and a higher pitch than is perhaps necessary.

"There's an extremely good-looking young man eyeing you up right now, but don't turn around or he'll see. I'll tell you when it's safe."

I glance back to find the young man is still standing in the entrance of the resort's beach bar. He continues to look towards where we're standing at the circular bar in the centre. However, as I look at him for the second time, I couldn't honestly say he was studying my brother's backside anymore. In fact, did he just catch my eye and give me a lingering look too? I turn my head quickly before I can verify.

"Yeah, still not safe," I mutter before sipping my drink.

Objectively, thanks to an unhealthy obsession with elliptical trainers, Jake does indeed have a great bum, so maybe the young man was just trying to establish who I am to my brother. As I smile to myself, knowing he will soon see, I feel a warmth spread across my back, as though I can sense exactly where he's looking.

Or maybe that's just the light sunburn I acquired today by spending an hour or two too long lying on the beach. I wasn't even sure why I was there when I'm lucky enough to have my own private pool villa, a perk of my brother being the manager. It's not that I can't afford luxury like this, it's more that I'm reluctant to indulge myself these days. While a spacious villa with the most incredible view is stunning, beautiful, wonderful - all the adjectives - I'm still here alone.

Alone.

I thought I'd be better at being alone by now.

I push all this aside and return to the present moment, a moment that has great potential for not being lonely at all for my brother. And nobody deserves that more than Jake.

Not only is he my best friend and confidant, but my brother is also the person I leaned on most when my marriage was ending. Together, we've been through a lot, and it's nice to think maybe his luck is turning, even if mine is still firmly on hold. It certainly looks that way now he has his dream job managing this luxury adults-only resort on Crete's west coast.

Iliovasílema Villas is everything he's wanted in a job: high-end, independently owned by a local family, and in the ideal location. It's perched at the end of a peninsula that offers panoramic views of the blue waters where the Aegean meets the Mediterranean.

"My, my, my." My brother pumps his straw up and down in his pink gin fizz, the ice making a satisfying slushing sound. "That is interesting. Not that I can do anything about it though."

"Why not?" I ask before taking a nice long sip of my raspberry mojito. "It's your night off."

"But *I* am the Resort Manager and *he* is still a guest." He leans in closer. "It is a guest, isn't it? Not that having a staff member eye me up is any better. In fact, that's a lot worse."

"It's definitely a guest." I can easily recall how the man in question looked and how it told me he was a new arrival. There was his white cotton shirt with a very generous and confident three top buttons undone, tight jeans on long, sculpted thighs and the not yet sun-kissed pale white skin of his face crowned with dark hair that looked like it would curl if given time to grow. He looked fresh and perhaps a little lost.

"Well, he will have to lust at me from afar." My brother pretends to throw long hair he doesn't have over his shoulder. "Is it safe to look now? I'm dying to have a nosey at him. We don't get many here, you know, despite the Pink Pound prices, advertising in *Attitude*, and rainbow fucking flags plastered all over the website."

"You don't get many gays?" I ask, surprised.

"God, yes, we get plenty of gays. Just not the cute, young and single ones. Not the kind of twinks I could spend hours daydreaming about corrupting. I guess they don't quite have the budget yet... Oh God, I need to stop talking or thinking like this. But before I do, let my eyes just get hard for a second."

"Your eyes can get hard?" I ask in a whisper.

He either ignores me or doesn't hear and instead nudges me quickly. "Is it safe? Can I turn around?"

I tilt my chin to the side to check but quickly see that the young man isn't standing where he was before. Turning a little more, I still can't place him in the small group of bodies near the entrance, so I pivot and look all the way over my shoulder. That's when I see him sitting by himself at the table directly behind us, just a few metres away.

"Oh!" I'm a little taken aback.

It's not just his proximity. It's what he's doing.

Leaning back into the chair like it's the most comfortable place in the world, he's got a drink in his hand and his long fingers wrap around the glass like they own every inch of it. How he got a drink so quickly without coming to the bar is beyond me but there it is, and there he is. All of him. And he's quite a sight to behold.

It's not even the planes and angles of his body I now notice filling out his shirt, nor is it the way his legs are crossed, pulling the ankles of his jeans up to reveal soft dark hair, unapologetically on show thanks to a pair of black leather Birkenstock sandals identical to mine. It's his face, which I hadn't fully absorbed previously. With its square jaw, deep-set dark eyes framed by dominant cheekbones and a long nose with a noticeable bump in it, it's the sort of face that is both arrestingly handsome and intriguingly different looking. And then there's what he's doing. Because he's staring at me. And smiling. Smiling so broadly I can see countless white teeth and a matching set of dimples slap bang in the middle of each cheek. I blink at him once, twice, giving myself, him, and the universe time to get this picture back into focus. To get his eyes off me and back onto my brother's arse.

But he doesn't. He keeps on looking at me and smiling.

And I think my eyes get hard.

I can't stop the giggle that escapes me, nor the hand that rises to try and catch it, and this makes the young man chuckle too. I move my hand and pin my index finger to my chest. *Me?*

He stops laughing but keeps smiling.

I point at my brother. *Or him?*

He shakes his head then, looking down for a moment. His eyes all but squeeze shut as his smile broadens, opening up his whole face, a face that I am instantly persuaded was created to smile. Then he looks back up and very firmly points his finger at me.

"Oh," I say again, but it's barely more than an exhale.

I'm looking long enough to make Jake turn.

"Wow." He turns to look at him, and then whips around so swiftly that it snaps me into doing the same. "*That* is no twink."

"He's not?" I ask. Although I know it myself now, I play dumb. I need Jake to speak so I can figure out why I am currently rubbing my thighs together and doing Kegels at high speed. "But he's young and pretty and..."

"And masculine as hell," Jake adds. "Mark my words. That man is a cocky top."

"You always tell me that there are femme and soft tops," I say, trying to get my brother to talk more so I can feel less. Less heat in my body. Less curiosity in my head. Less anticipation in every cell of my being.

"True, but there is very little that's feminine or soft about that man," Jake says with a dramatic backwards nod before he sucks on his straw again.

"Isn't it strange how much information we can get from someone just from a few looks," I say, genuinely fascinated by it. I make a mental note to research this later.

"Not to mention the bucketload of testosterone flooding out of his youthful pores," Jake continues.

"How old do you suppose he is?" I ask, but I know the answer already. It's *young*.

But Jake's not listening to me, he's on a roll. "And that posture... far too confident and laid back. And did you see how big his hands are? You remember that article you sent me with comparative analysis of digit length and penis size? Did you see how long his thumbs were?"

"You noticed *that*?"

"Yes, I'm surprised you didn't," Jake replies. "Honestly, look at his thumbs. They're almost obscene."

"I'm not looking again..."

"Hmm. That's because he was looking at you, wasn't he?" Jake says in a slower, more deliberate voice. "That's the other reason he's no twink. Because he's not gay."

I don't speak and it's not only because I don't really know what to say. It's also because of the smile that refuses to disappear. My cheeks are pushed up so high I feel them brush against my eyelashes.

"I swear he was looking at your arse first," I mumble in something of an apology. "Besides, he's too young for either of us."

"Oh, he's young, for sure. But he's more than legal. And you..."

"Me?"

"You are not the manager of this luxury resort. You are on holiday. And you're single."

"I'm divorced," I correct him.

"Which is French for single, *n'est-ce pas*?"

"It's actually French for undesirable, Italian for soiled goods, and Spanish for don't-touch-me-with-a-bargepole."

"I'm not sure they have barges in Spain," my brother ponders, doing that ice-shucking thing again. "But you don't really mean that, do you? I thought you were feeling positive about it all. I thought you were ready for your *Eat, Pray, Love* moment. This could be it!"

13

"Oh, I'm always ready for an Italian to lick gelato out of my navel." I sigh.

"I'm pretty sure that didn't happen in the book." Jake frowns at me.

"Must have been the porno version," I shrug.

"*Eat, Gay, Cum?*" he suggests with a wicked smirk.

"Nice. But I think it was *Eat, Peg, Lick* that I watched."

"Ha!" He laughs with me.

"Anyway, the point is I *do* feel mostly positive about my divorce. We both know it was the right thing. But that doesn't negate the fact that a man who looks like *that*, is not going to look at a woman like *this*." I point to my chest again.

"Jenna Louise Forester, as a gay man and your brother I am both sorely unqualified and much too biased to tell you that you are a smoking hot snack."

I smile at him but quickly turn it into a smug pout. "Oh, I know. I have a shelf of an ass you could eat off, thighs that could keep any man's ears warm in the coldest winter, and of course, there are these delectably plump fuck-me-lips..."

"Too much, dear sister, too much." Jake covers his ears.

"However, I also know that *young* men don't always appreciate such things. And it's probably a good thing. I mean, I'm old enough to be his..."

"Don't say it!" Jake quickly glances over his shoulder. "Not until we have at least verified his year of birth, *or* that of his mother."

Before I realise what's happening, Jake is gone. He's waltzing off to the young man, his hand outstretched and his smooth voice carrying over the hum of the music and the growing number of guests in the bar. "Good evening, I'm Jake Forester, the Resort Manager."

Mouth hanging open, I watch as my brother walks straight for the man, who interestingly, does indeed have very long and curved thumbs.

Chapter One

Six Months (182 Sunsets) Ago

Jenna

I knew it was coming. I knew the envelope would land on my doorstep one of these days, and I knew I would have to open it and flick to the last page to see our signatures side by side for the last time. I'd been thinking about it for weeks and envisioning it for much longer. In some ways, I think I've been preparing for it for years, possibly always, which is as depressing as it is strangely comforting.

Even so, as I bend to pick up the envelope along with a bank statement and a local estate agent's flyer, I do so with shaking hands and short, unsteady breaths. My fingers don't stop trembling as I open it and flick through until I find one of Robert's signatures. I stare at the great loop and kick of his R and behold the peaks and troughs of his surname that follows.

The name I never took.

At the time, it was something I did as a small and probably pointless act of feminism, but recently I have been questioning my motives; did I always know? On the rear of the last page, I trace the imprint his pen left with his final signature and marvel at how familiar the shape of it is, and yet how it is now so very foreign, so very other. A single tear lands on the paper.

"Jesus, Jenna, get a grip," I say to myself because there's no-one else here. There's not been anyone else here for seven months, and I have become frighteningly comfortable talking to myself. Possibly because I'm still adjusting to both the silence of a single occupancy house and the noises that interrupt it. Noises I never noticed before like the foxes howling at night, the cranking of our

- no, *my* boiler - when it switches on, and the howl of the wind through every crack in the Victorian brickwork and window frames.

I carry the papers and post into the kitchen and sit at the small table in the corner, pushing the divorce papers to one side and picking up the paint swabs I'd collected the day before. There's a sunshine yellow I was thinking about using on the stairs, a pastel terracotta orange I would love in the guest bedroom, and a lush, earthy green that would make my bathroom look like a jungle, but they don't distract me. If anything, they make me feel worse, because I really shouldn't be spending any more money on decorating, not until I've figured out what I'm going to do about my job.

As a freelance sex and relationships columnist, I have never had a "proper job" as my father would say. Even aside from the topics I specialise in – intimacy, dating, sexuality, desire and pleasure – there are no set hours, no office for me to clock into, and I don't even have real colleagues, as in the same set of people I check in with regularly. Sure, I've often worked with the same editors multiple times over the years. But to them, I am one of many, and to me, they are people I have to be on my best behaviour with so I can never be my potty-mouthed, innuendo-loving self. And it suits me fine. At least it used to.

Because I don't think I can do this job anymore. How can I keep advising others on how to connect with their partners – physically, emotionally, sexually – when I lost all those connections with my husband? What kind of 'sexpert' am I when it's been nearly two years since I last had sex? How can I claim to know what makes love last, when it didn't for me?

A few of my friends who've recently become parents for the first time have told me how lost they felt at the beginning because there's no manual for parenting, no guidebook or road map to follow, and I can finally relate. Where's my map for this new journey? How do I navigate being single for the first time in over a decade?

With no guidebook and what feels like fast-disappearing hope, I do what I think any woman would do upon receiving their signed divorce papers. After briefly checking the time – 10:56 am - I stand up, move to the fridge and pour myself a large glass of wine. Then, I sneak my hands under my T-shirt and take

16

off my bra, followed by my earrings. I leave them all lying on the kitchen counter, as I take my wine back to the table. Finally, I pick up my phone and call my brother.

"Jenna, I was just going to call you-"

"Jakey," I interrupt with a deep sigh.

"What's happened?" he asks, panicked.

"It's done. My divorce papers just landed."

"Signed?"

"Signed, sealed, delivered. I'm not his. And he's not mine. Not anymore."

"Congratulations! That's fucking excellent!"

His words are like a slap in the face, and I don't know why.

"Yes, yes, it is. It just also hurts like hell." I bring my hand to my mouth to catch my sudden sobs.

"Oh, Jenna, what is this? What are you feeling? Is it regret? Is it guilt? Is it fear?"

I smile with blurry eyes. "Jakey, those are perfect questions. I should write you a report for your therapist."

"Don't deflect, Jenna. Tell me what's going on."

I pull in a breath and think about it for a few seconds before replying, "It's a bit of everything. But mostly, I just feel very sad and like I have lost something more than a perfectly decent enough husband."

"So, you *do* have regret?" Jake asks tentatively.

I pause again. I know I'm feeling regret, but I can't pin it on the divorce or losing Robert. Maybe it's from not doing it sooner? Maybe it's about my work? Maybe it's something else? I just don't know, and I hate not knowing.

"You know you can tell me, Jenna," Jake continues. "I know I've been Team D.I.V.O.R.C.E for a while now, but I will never judge you for however you're feeling."

"I don't know how I feel," I waver. "I just think I miss him sometimes. He wasn't all bad. I mean, he put the toilet seat down and never left dirty socks on the floor..."

"You're right, you know." I recognise his new tone of voice. It's defeat mixed with reluctance, wrapped up in his best hospitality voice; the one that is designed to make whoever he is in conversation with think that they're right. "Robert was decent enough, I suppose."

There's something about hearing my words in his voice. And not just his normal voice, but his people-pleasing, disingenuous voice.

"No." I sniff. "I don't want *decent enough*. And I don't want a man who can't talk to me about his feelings, or mine, no matter how well trained he is domestically. I don't want a man who is afraid of change. I don't want a man who is afraid to grow... or for me to grow."

"Well said, buttercup." Jake's normal voice is back.

"The thing is," I pause to take a deep breath, "what if I never find a man who is? What if this thing I tell all my readers to wait for, to work for, to have faith in... what if it just doesn't exist?"

My brother's groan reverberates in my ear. "You're asking the wrong person, Jenna. I'm the king of failed relationships."

"Maybe we're just doomed to lose in love, Jakey? Ugh. I never expected to be thirty-six and divorced."

"Oh, Jen. You know it's very trendy to be divorced these days. Everyone's doing it at least once, if not twice. You should really try to keep up."

I mumble out a quick laugh and then shake my head as I spot my divorce papers again, more tears still slipping down my cheeks.

"I'm so angry at myself for feeling this way. I tell people all the time to never feel any shame for doing what's right for them, and my brain, it *knows* this is right for me... I just hate not feeling it in my heart too. That's the part of me I normally trust the most and it doesn't feel very trustworthy right now."

"That's because your heart is still broken, Jenna. You need to give it time to heal."

I close my eyes. "It's been months, Jakey. Years really, if you think about how long it was since we... since we were in a good place."

"I'm so sorry you're hurting, Jenna," my brother says, and despite the physical ache in my chest, I feel a rush of love and gratitude for him.

18

"Thank you, that means a lot to me," I whisper back.

"Did you download the apps we talked about?" he asks with an upswing in his voice.

"The dating apps?" I shudder. I wish I didn't have such a vehement reaction to Internet dating. I know it may be the only way I do find love again. *If* I find love again.

"Yes, I wrote you a list in order of Dana's preferences," he says, referring to his friend who did indeed find her husband on an app. "And I've been mentally brainstorming a bio since you separated."

"Ugh, maybe. One day." I take a large swig of wine. "But not yet. First, I mourn, I grieve, I hurt."

"Sounds absolutely delightful." Jake groans.

I look at the kitchen shelves above my head and find the framed photo of Jake and me as children together, playing on the swings in the back garden of our childhood home. "We have to mourn our losses, Jakey, we both know that," I say softly.

"I know," he says, and then he coughs. I am not at all surprised when he then quickly makes light of what I just said. "No pain, no gain, eh?"

"I think it's more a case of no pain, no love. And no love, no life. We're not here to feel good all the time. We're here to love one another, and as so many have concluded, grief is love. They are two sides of the same coin."

"It's almost like you know what you're talking about," Jake says, and it makes me smile until he continues. "You should write a book about these things."

"That's a conversation for another day," I say quickly, not feeling brave enough to even think about work. I realise then that I've finally stopped crying. I jokingly toast myself in the reflection of the oven door. *Here's to wine and my brother!*

"So, back to dating apps," Jake says. "I'll send you that photo I took of you in Lisbon. Your tits look fantastic in that top."

"No, Jake, not yet." I chuckle with him. "Although please do send over that photo, my ego could do with a little boost right now. But seriously, I think first I

19

need to do some therapy, some crying, lots of reading, exercise, writing, and probably a lot more crying and then maybe I'll try to think about dating again."

"Well, could you keep a week free in that depressingly busy crying schedule so you can come to Greece next summer?"

I blink as his words land. "What!? You got the job?"

"I got the job!" he squeals.

And just like that, while I still feel my pain, my grief and my uncertainty, I also feel excitement and delight for my brother who has worked so hard for this opportunity. It's another helpful reminder that it's possible to feel good and bad things in the very same moment. It's possible for our heavy, breaking hearts to be buoyed and bolstered by the happiness of others.

"Oh, Jake! I'm so proud of you!"

"So, you'll come?"

"Sunshine, sand, sea and sexy Greek men? You try and stop me, baby brother!" I say, and I hope by then I'll have some of the mess that is my life tidied up.

Chapter Two

Six Months (182 Sunsets) Ago

Marty

I don't know how late it is, but I know it's time for a drink.

I lift my hand and feel the sand sticking to the side of my face. Rough grains line my tongue too and I try to wipe it all off on my sleeve but there's just more sand there. *Fuck.* Napping on the beach used to be my favourite way to pass the time before a shift or a meet up with new friends. Now there isn't a job to go to, nor are there many friends, old or new. And these days it's the only way I get any kind of sleep. Sleep, I find my body needs more and more.

Pushing up to sit, I brush off as much of the sand as I can and try to spit out what's left in my mouth. A quick look around helps me get my bearings. I'm at the most northern end of San Antonio beach, one hundred or so metres away from the hotel where I worked until they found me passed out in the storeroom mid-shift. Was that today? Yesterday? Or the day before? I have no clue and no interest in finding out.

I can tell it's evening because of the sun's position in the sky; dangerously close to sunset. Sometimes I feel brave enough to sit and watch it go down, but I already know today isn't one of those days, so I look away. It's become easier and easier to turn my back on the sunset, but it still hurts like hell.

As I push my body up to stand, the pain in my head intensifies and my mouth still feels dry. A nice cold beer will sort me out. I do a quick check of my pockets and I am relieved my phone, wallet and passport are all there. I haven't always been so lucky.

There are two messages on my phone. Both are from Maeve.

\<Call me back when you get this.\>

\<Seriously, Marty. Don't be a gobshite. Call me. I put money in your account.\>

"Yes, Maeve! You fucken legend!" I shout, trying to drown out the guilt I simultaneously feel. Knowing I have cash motivates me to start walking down the beach towards El Ocaso, one of the all-year beach clubs still open. I haven't been there in weeks but at this time of year, down season, I know I'll see a few familiar faces of other workers, even if they're not friendly ones. I'll likely find someone to drink with and if not, I'll drink alone. I'm not proud.

Stumbling across the beach to where a small crowd is gathered around the tables facing the water, I straighten up as much as possible and do a quick scan of faces. I don't recognise anyone. So far so good. There's nobody here who wants to kill me. Nobody here I owe money to. Nobody here I fucked then ghosted. Nobody here I pissed off in any other number of ways. Today really is my lucky day.

I'm also relieved when there's some generic house music playing rather than familiar melodies or lyrics that make me think of somewhere or someone I don't want to think about. For a long time, any song could be twisted to be about us, about places we had been. I knew so many things in my future would be ruined by what happened – sunsets, board games, beautiful bright eyes framed in kohl eyeliner – but crappy pop songs I don't even like? How did listening to bands I had only lukewarm feelings for suddenly make me feel like I could crumble into a million pieces? But no danger of that in this bar. This rhythmic thumping and unrecognisable, unimaginative tune is safe, and maybe after a beer, I could even nod my head to it.

I make my way to the bar and am grateful for the heat from the overhead lamps. Ibiza in mid-November is nowhere near as cold as Dublin, but there's a definite chill in the air at night. I really don't want to sleep on the streets or beach again tonight, but I also don't want to waste my money on a last-minute hotel room. I don't have it in me to be social enough to brave a hostel dorm. I should go to the bathroom and freshen up, see what I actually look like for the first time in... oh, I don't know how long. And I don't really care. First, I need that drink.

I order a beer and a shot of tequila to chase it down with and hold my breath as I hold my card to the pin machine. It goes through.

Thank fuck for that. I really do owe you, Maeve.

I know I should call her, but not now. If she hears the music and chatter in the background she'll go apeshit on me, and rightly so. I'll text her later when I have somewhere to stay... or rather, someone to stay with.

"Did you have a good nap?" a voice says beside me. I didn't even see them approach. My eyes were fixed on the shot glass I'd just emptied, waiting for the hum of the alcohol to melt some of the aching in my chest.

"Oh, you saw that?" I force a smile as I turn towards them. They're not bad looking and seem clean enough.

"Practically tripped over you," they reply, and I detect an accent, but I don't have the energy to ask about it.

"Had a late night," I explain, although I couldn't honestly tell them where I was or what I was doing.

"You've still got sand in your hair." A hand comes up and fingers rake their way against my scalp. I close my eyes to see if I feel something, anything. When I don't, it's a struggle to open my eyelids again.

"You don't remember, do you?" they ask.

I shake my head. "Have we met before?"

"I'll buy you another drink to see if that helps your memory." They wave at the barman.

My smile comes easily then, as do my short replies to their longer questions as we stand at the bar and sink another three beers each. I never do find out what it is I'm supposed to remember, but as we shuffle to the toilet and hide in a cubicle together and a small pill is placed on my tongue, I have such an overwhelming and heavy sense of foreboding déjà vu I almost spit it out and run away.

Instead, I quickly swallow it and follow them back out to the bar, where the music seems louder and there are more people on the small dance floor. Another beer is shoved into one of my hands while the other is pulled towards the dancing bodies that seem to move too quickly for me to focus on.

23

Thank God, it's still this crappy dance music. It's actually helping. The louder the better. The heavier the bass, the lighter my load starts to feel. Or maybe that's just whatever I took starting to work. That and the alcohol and the thumping of the music, it's all waking me up and making me want to move, to do what I came here to do; party, have fun, chase any and every high, forget what happened. Escape.

I start to move, tapping my feet and rocking my shoulders. I can't dance for shit, but I'm really good at not giving a flying fuck about that fact. I have a good smile, a great arse and I know how to flirt. I won't be dancing alone for long.

Out of the corner of my eye I see the pinks and purples the sunset has left in the sky, and it almost makes me stop moving. There's something magnetic in those colours and they're extra vivid and bold tonight, thanks to a near cloudless horizon. But then I feel hands come to sit on my hips and the back of my thighs brush against warm flesh. I step back into it, leaning into a body, and I reach behind me to see if I can hold a piece of it in my own hands.

Then I close my eyes to the sunset, to the world, and to whatever happens next.

The First Sunset

"Every sunset brings the promise of a new dawn."
- Ralph Waldo Emerson

Chapter Three

Jenna

For a few seconds, I turn sideways and do an awkward dance on the spot as I step one foot forward to follow my brother, then shuffle it back before trying again with the other. In the end, I can't move my feet any more than I can close my mouth or coordinate holding my drink in my hand with my clutch bag under my arm so I simply turn back to the bar, giving them both my back, which starts to burn as hot as fire, and it's definitely not my sunburn.

"Did you just check in? How was your flight?" Jake asks and I swear my brother doesn't need to talk *that* loudly. That said, my ears still strain to catch the reply, to hear the young man's voice, but I get nothing.

"Well, welcome, we're happy to have you here. I see you have a drink..." Jake is practically hollering.

I stretch back a bit, hoping that will help, but still hear nothing but a slight, deep rumble.

"Oh, yes, that's my sister, Jenna." I hear Jake say, even louder. My shoulders freeze close to my ears. "I'll try that again, shall I? Yes, that's my sister! Jenna!"

After a quick cringe, my features do an abrupt turn as I swivel to face them, smiling. Leaving my nearly empty glass at the bar, I grip my clutch like my life depends on it and make my way towards my brother, all the while wishing I was in something a bit more sophisticated than the bikini and oversized T-shirt dress I've been wearing all day.

"Hi." I hold out my hand. "I'm Jenna."

He's heard my name three times now. Are we trying to drill it into him?

"Hi Jenna," he says, and immediately I want him to forget it and ask me my name again so he can say it back to me because it sounds so good in his voice. A voice that is husky and ragged. A voice that has an accent. An accent that is very possibly Irish.

Lord help me if it's Irish.

"Hi," I say again, like a fool, as he gets up and leans forward to shake my hand with a firm, warm squeeze.

"Nice to meet you." He sits back down, leaving me standing there, resisting the urge to curl my hand in a ball to keep the heat he left there. "I'm Marty."

Yes, he's definitely Irish. Did my right knee just buckle?

"Oh, like in *Back to the Future*?" Jake says, with a hand splayed against his chest. Marty's kind smile tells me he has heard this approximately a thousand times, but he covers it up well with that broad, teeth-filled grin. Teeth that are all white and straight, apart from four at the bottom that overlap slightly, which I find adorable for reasons I can't articulate.

"Well, no. Fortunately, my surname is not McFly. It's actually O'Martin."

"Marty O'Martin? Are your parents alcoholics?" My brother's mouth drops open. He overdoes aghast best of all.

"No, but I am, possibly," Marty says, without missing a beat.

Oh, Christ. This conversation is like a landslide and I don't know how to make it stop.

"You're *possibly* an alcoholic, Marty O'Martin?" Much to my dismay, my brother is still talking.

"Possibly yes," he says. "And my name is Aiden, but everyone calls me Marty. It's a rugby club nickname that just stuck around."

"Hmmm, rugby players..." My brother rubs his lips together and closes his eyes. "Tell us more about *that*."

"I don't play much anymore."

Because I'm studying his face intently, I see a small dip in his smile, the dimples disappearing and his dark brown eyes losing their sparkle.

"And you just got here?" I ask, changing the subject because for some undefinable reason my urge to see those dimples again is sudden and strong.

"Yes, earlier today. I've already tested out some of the facilities. The gym, the pool and spa. All very impressive." Marty nods at my brother.

"I aim to please," Jake says with a quick flutter of his eyelashes.

"Dear God," I whisper, but I smile when I see Marty is unperturbed, laughing to himself.

"How about you, Jenna, when did you get here?" He turns to ask me.

"Two days ago. The whole resort is beautiful," I say, winking at Jake. "And the views from up in the villas are spectacular."

"The view isn't so bad here either," Marty says, staring right at me. I feel a single bead of sweat slide down the valley of my back.

"So, what do you do, Marty O'Martin?" Jake fills the space my stunned silence creates.

"I'm a chef... well, no, technically I'm training to be a chef."

This sobers me up quickly. It brings his youth front and centre of my mind. A trainee chef. Meaning he's a student or not yet qualified. Whatever it is, it means he's young.

Too young.

And yet earlier he pointed at me. And right now, he's smiling at me and kicking lightly at the chair I'm leaning against. "Are you going to sit down and join us? Or do you want me to get a crick in my neck from looking up at your beauty?"

My brother claps his hands together. "Oh, we have a live one here, Jenna! Quite the smooth operator!" He exclaims, easing a little of the tension in the air.

I feel myself blushing as I sit down and wish I had something equally quick and flirty to say back to him. Instead, I ask him a totally offensive and unsympathetic question.

"So, if you're possibly an alcoholic." I point at his drink. "Then what's that?"

If he's unnerved by what I just said, it doesn't show. "This? Well, yes, it's a mocktail. I asked your bar staff to make it for me," he tells my brother. "I like to call it Sex with Socks On. It's basically Sex on the Rocks, but no liqueur."

"What's Sex on the Rocks?" I say, without thinking it through.

"A cocktail," Jake says at the same time that the lightning-fast Marty leans towards me and says, "Maybe you'll find out one day soon."

I know my brother doesn't hear because he isn't doing what I'm doing, which is staring at Marty so intently my pupils feel strangely immovable in my skull.

Yep, my eyes are definitely hard.

"Sorry." Marty leans and brings his chiselled face closer, just a few inches away. I can smell him – it's spice and citrus and something else, not sweet, not floral, but still soft and fresh. He doesn't touch me even though part of me wants him to, just a tap on my knee or maybe a gentle nudge on my arm, just something to let me know if this attraction I feel is real. That it's not just made up of the evening's warm air, the cocktail I just drank and the magic-hour light that surrounds us now that the sun is a little lower in the sky.

"That was a bit forward, even for me. I apologise," he says.

As Marty sits back a little, I realise that I can't think of witty things to say because it's been a long time since I flirted like this. But I suppose I may have to try and learn again soon. This spurs me on to try a little harder.

"Don't apologise. I need telling sometimes. I only know about Sex on the Beach, you see, but everyone knows about that, don't they? You probably don't need reminding exactly how sweet and juicy and fun that is, do you?" I say, staying close but also ensuring no part of my body touches his.

Out of the corner of my eye, I see Jake being approached by a staff member and after a very dramatic eye-roll he's standing up and walking away, doing up another button in his shirt.

With him gone, I can unabashedly fix my attention on Marty, and I do, watching his Adam's apple bob as he swallows. I start to think I've left him speechless, and that makes me feel almost as good as when he pointed at me earlier. But a beat later he's composed, turning his head so our eyes meet. This close to him I can see how they're oak brown with flecks of other colours in them, green and gold maybe.

He holds my gaze as he speaks. "You're right. I'm not interested in Sex on the Beach, and I can't even say I crave real Sex on the Rocks but being sober does mean I miss the shit out of French Kisses, Screaming Orgasms, Sloe Screws and a good old-fashioned Royal Fuck."

His dimples are back as he smiles. Then he sits back and watches me react.

It's my turn to swallow hard and force myself to blink slowly, ensuring that when I open my eyes again, he sees the wide, playful grin on my face as I point my finger at him.

"Are they even all cocktail names? Because if they're not, you're cheating, and I do not tolerate cheaters."

His dimples deepen as he laughs. He puts his drink down, uncrosses his legs as if to ground himself, and leans towards me again. "I'm a lot of fucked up things, Jenna, but I'm not a cheater. And yes, they're all real cocktail names. But I can't even blame my alcoholism on that. I've worked in bars and restaurants since I was fifteen, and right now I'm working for my uncle who runs a cocktail lounge and restaurant in Dublin."

"Sounds fancy," I say, hoping I didn't flinch. It's just so strange to hear him say things like 'working in bars and restaurants'. It's like going back in time to my teenage and student years.

He seems oblivious as he continues to smile and stare at me. "It is. It's exactly the kind of place I imagine you would look very comfortable in."

He's not suggesting a date, and yet I feel like I've been accosted. This whole conversation feels like I'm being accosted. Part of me is desperate to dive in and bathe in it, but I also want to check first that the water is safe to swim in. I want to know that this banter isn't just a facade for something else. A joke. A dare. Simply put, I don't want to be made a fool of. I'm not strong enough for that yet. Perhaps it's this awareness of my own vulnerability that again makes me reach for a terrible joke.

"So, at the risk of being both racist and insensitive, what's it like being Irish and an alcoholic?"

His reaction is worth the risk because laughter rumbles out of him.

"I guess it's like being Italian and gluten-intolerant... Or French and vegan." I laugh with him.

"You are a funny man, Marty. Sobriety looks good on you," I say, although I want to suck the words back into my mouth as soon as they're gone. How do I know if it looks good on him compared with when he was drinking? I force myself to not think about what would lead a man who is surely only in his twenties, to call himself an "alcoholic, possibly".

"Can I buy you another drink so you can say more flattering things like that to me?" Marty asks as his laughter dies.

"As long as it's a Sex with Socks On," I say, far too swiftly. "I feel like sobering up too."

He gives me another dimple-framed smile, then pushes up to stand, and that's when I see exactly how tall and broad and *real* he is. The noise my throat makes is so much louder than I would like that I'm grateful when he doesn't seem to notice before striding away. I sit back and watch him, telling myself that if all I get this evening is the opportunity to watch him walk away from me like this, slightly bow-legged, thick in the thighs and shoulders, and narrow in his waist and ankles, then I'll be happy and grateful, and frankly, good to go for a marathon masturbation session tonight. This thought has me bringing my hand to my mouth to smother a giggle, which is how Jake finds me as he rushes back into my line of sight.

"Can you fucking believe it?" he exclaims, his hands moving as fast as his mouth. "My first night off in weeks and one of the mid-level villas added sodding bubble bath to their jacuzzi. It's like a naff Magaluf-in-2005 foam party up there! We have only minutes to stop it cascading over the terrace to the villa below, so it's all hands on deck. Just wanted to check you were okay and..." He trails off as he sees Marty standing at the bar, leaning against it and giving me a thumbs-up. A thumbs-up that gives myself and Jake a clear view of how long and thick and curved that digit is.

"Clearly, you are more than fine," Jake says, lifting his left eyebrow and studying me for a moment. "You know, if you weren't my sister, I would tell you that you have a moral obligation to yourself to screw his brains out..."

32

"I literally just met him." I shake my head at my brother.

"You've had longer conversations than seventy per cent of my hook-ups in the last few years."

"Well, that's on you and Grindr," I say.

Jake waves my comment away. "The point is, he's very attractive. You scrub up well enough. And my God, he seems very into you. I'm afraid there wasn't time for me to grill him about his age or that of his mother's, so yes, it may indeed be a weird Mummy kink, but who fucking cares if it means he gives you get the *Eat, Poke, Lube* night of your life?"

I pull my shoulders back. "Are you serious? Mummy issues? I'm hardly *that* much older than him."

"I said a Mummy *kink*, not Mummy *issues*. Two very different things. Says the man with a Daddy kink *and* Daddy issues but hey..."

"Oh, Jakey," I say wanting to pull him into a big hug... and to put a fist in my father's face even though he's currently 2,500 miles away. "But we have dinner tonight."

"No, we don't. Not if this works out. Just please... enjoy yourself. You deserve this," he says, before pointing a slightly concave finger at Marty. "You deserve *that*. Even if it's just for one night."

I feel a frightening number of different things in response to my brother's suggestion, so I take a deep breath and tell myself they will pass. With my exhale, I blow Jake a kiss.

"Don't worry about me. I'm a big girl. Haven't you got to go?" I say. Behind my brother's head, I see his assistant manager, Lionel, running across reception carrying a stack of towels. Jake turns to where I'm looking.

"Oh, Meryl-Streep-in-Mamma-Mia, Lionel! Not the guest linen!" He charges off in pursuit.

I turn back to watch Marty some more, hopefully, while he's not looking, so I can let my eyes roam his back and better, his backside, but then I see he's not alone. There's a woman standing next to him. There's a *young* woman standing next to him and they're talking together, *intimately*.

33

There's a young woman standing next to him and they're talking together, intimately, *and she's resting her hand on his arm.*

There's a young woman standing next to him and they're talking together, intimately, and she's resting her hand on his arm, *and she has the kind of beauty that only the young are blessed with* - the unspoiled, smooth and very symmetrical kind.

"Oh, fuck," I say out loud to myself, wishing I hadn't abandoned the last few mouthfuls of my mojito. "That sucks donkey balls."

Chapter Four

Marty

I'm standing at the bar trying to catch the staff's attention so I can order two mocktails for myself and a woman who is doing something to me. Something strange and brilliant and terrifying. I'm not sure how I got here, but I might be happy I'm here. Maybe.

Actually, I do know how I got here.

It all began a few months ago when I reluctantly agreed to accompany my parents on a luxury holiday to celebrate their thirtieth wedding anniversary. Then this morning my mother woke me at the arse crack of dawn, bossed me around until I was in a taxi on our way to the airport, where we barely spoke a word to each other until we'd all had coffee, and even after that our limited conversation had felt like a huge effort. It was no different on the plane when I grabbed the single seat across the aisle from the rest of them and shoved my headphones in my ears but didn't listen to a single song.

Music is still hard for me.

I felt a bit bad about ignoring them all, so once we got to the airport I collected the bags from the carousel and pushed the trolley to where we found our transfer car. But then my mother gushed about how helpful and strong I was and how happy she was that I was with them and that made me shove my headphones in again as soon as we were on our way. I still didn't listen to anything as I watched the island pass us by. The sunshine reminded me of a million places I didn't want to think about. The heat took me back to sweaty days I shared with someone I missed. And the blue of the sky taunted me with so many memories, I closed my eyes for the last twenty minutes.

As soon as we got here, I realised that Mum and Dad must have spent a ton of cash on this holiday. From the champagne offered upon arrival – which I insisted they all drank while I sipped an orange juice – to the way the receptionist called me 'Sir' even though I am almost certainly younger than him. This resort is pure luxury, and it made me feel an uneasy amount of guilt that my parents couldn't be here by themselves. I mean, they could have. I told them to, many times. But they would never have gone if I hadn't agreed to join. They would never have left me on my own.

So that's how I got here, to Crete.

As for how I got to be standing at this bar, well, that's a longer story, even if it took less time to play out.

It began by me walking into our villa and realising it was the most luxurious accommodation I'd ever stayed in, and for that reason and a hundred others, I couldn't stay inside it a minute longer. I couldn't hear my father boast about how many different types of coffee pods we had, nor could I watch my mother clasp her hand over her mouth at how "simply stunning" the view was. Not that she was wrong – it was a truly impressive panorama of the peninsula – but it hurt to have such beauty in front of me. And when Maeve started to do a video of herself standing by the pool – our *own private pool*, for Christ's sake – I knew I had to get out of there. I rushed to what was my room, dumped out the contents of my duffel bag and filled it with my gym gear, trainers, a change of clothes and a pair of swimming shorts. Then I yelled out that I was going to go find the gym and I ran out the door before anyone could stop me.

There followed nearly two hours of the treadmill, the stationary bike, the rowing machine and then far too many reps on far too many weight machines. When my legs started to shake and my hollow stomach grumbled at me for food because it hadn't had any since the sub-standard airport breakfast, I stopped and finally took in the view, too tired to resist its splendour.

The rugged beauty of the view appealed to me. It was breath-taking and memorable, but not in a pristine or lush way, rather in a very raw and rough way. I liked how the blush-red soil, arid climate and sun-filled days didn't seem to be a hospitable environment for much more than low-growing bush, olive trees and some cacti, meaning the volcanic mountains inland were a mix of muted greys, earthy greens and terracotta oranges. This contrasted with the sparkling sea that these jagged hills tumbled into. The water's bottomless blue was as calming and clear as a cloudless sky, as long as I didn't let any memories creep in.

I accepted then that this was probably one of the better things I'd agreed to do with - or rather, *for* - my parents in the last few months. Indeed, I had spent most of the last few weeks moaning profusely to Dad about bringing our race bikes to ride early every morning here but looking at the landscape, I suddenly couldn't wait. It would be good to explore the roads for the first time tomorrow morning, to feel a breeze in my hair and some more muscles ache in my legs.

"Hey, dickhead!" A voice snaps me out of my thoughts and back into the beach bar. A voice that is both angry and familiar.

"Shit," I say and close my eyes, not bothering to turn around.

"Yeah, I found you, you dope. Do you even know how many kittens Mum is birthing right now?"

I turn and watch my sister Maeve come to stand next to me at the bar, her hands on her hips. "Probably several and they'll be better sons to her than I've been so win-win, I'd say," I reply.

"You can't just disappear like that!" She swipes at my forearm. "And you definitely can't just go straight to the nearest bar and start drinking. Jesus fucken Christ, Marty!"

"I didn't!" I protest, feeling spikes of irritation climb up my neck. "First, I went to the gym, then I went to the spa where I had a very traumatising swim and sauna, and now I'm here, about to order a *mock*tail. Thank you very much for having zero faith in me."

Maeve studies me. "Seriously?"

I lean forward and breathe on her nose with a loud *Ahh*. "See, no booze," I say with a smug smile.

She pulls back and waves her hand in front of her face. "Ew, Marty! Why are you such a scabby spanner?"

"And why are you doing Ma's dirty work for her?" I snap back.

"I'm not. At least I wasn't going to at first. I was prepared to just let you go and be moody by yourself, and I told Mum as much. But then it was like four hours you'd been gone, and she was nagging at me about how we've got dinner reservations and..."

"And you thought the worst too," I say, but the spite has gone. Instead, I'm just disappointed. Disappointed in them. And, as always, disappointed in myself.

"I didn't think the worst," she says quietly. "I was worried."

My shoulders sink as I sigh. "I'm sorry I disappeared," I concede. "I needed some space."

"Save it for Ma." Maeve glances around the bar, her eyes lingering on the horizon where the sun is perfectly positioned in the centre of the sky. I estimate it's about an hour away from sinking into the sea.

"It's beautiful here, isn't it?" Maeve says and I go to reply, but she's already got her phone out, taking photos. I look away and manage to get the barman's attention.

I'm about to ask Maeve if she wants a drink but she's stepped further to the side and is now shooting a video, moving her phone in a full circle taking in the bar and the beach. I roll my eyes and order drinks for just myself and Jenna, who I then turn to look at. She's talking with her brother, who is so red in the face it makes my own cheeks feel hot.

Taking in Jenna's side profile, I shake my head when I think about how I first came to lay eyes on her.

That's also not much of a pretty story because when I first walked into the beach bar, I was focused on one thing and one thing only; getting a drink. Rightly or wrongly, I felt like I deserved it. I had all but convinced myself one would be acceptable. But as I searched for a space at the bar, my eyes had lingered a moment too long on a figure standing at it. Specifically, on a pert and firm bottom.

The owner of the backside in question had been leaning against the bar, wearing cotton shorts that were almost irresponsibly tight - although he had the legs and butt for them. The cream and beige hues of his clothes matched his colouring, all soft earthy shades - chestnut hair atop his head and lighter, sun-bleached hairs lacing his tanned calves – and I strained my neck a little to try and get a look at his face. When that failed, I went back to looking at his butt.

I knew what I was doing. I was waiting for the rest of my body to wake up, specifically for some heat to land in my groin, but alas, nothing. I knew I was looking a moment too long because the man with the nice arse had a companion who turned her head and clocked me.

I'm not sure if it was being caught out or if it was what I saw in her heart-shaped face, but immediately, I felt something.

Taking in her tanned skin, slim nose and warm brown eyes that sparkled in the sunlight - and, arguably best of all, a pair of full lips that were an almost unnatural pink - I felt restless but not unsettled. Watching her chubby cheeks bunch up below her eyes when she smiled, I felt something simmer inside me. And when, from even a few metres away, I noticed a sprinkling of freckles across her cheeks and nose, I felt that simmer rumble to a slightly alarming boil, but it wasn't unwelcome.

Illuminated by the sun's descending rays, her light brown hair framed her face with gentle waves that stopped at her shoulders. There was something about its volume and kinks that told me she had swum in the sea or pool today, and it warmed me that she was likely having so much fun on holiday she hadn't bothered to do anything with it other than just let it dry as it was. Studying her further, I took in her shapely brows, her dark eyelashes and the laughter lines crinkling the skin in the corners of her eyes and across her forehead. Something that made me want to laugh and smile and feel a skin-wrinkling kind of joy in my own face.

It would be too simplistic to say that those wrinkles told me she was older than me, and it wouldn't be the whole truth. I already sensed that she was older from the way she carried herself with her shoulders back, chin up, those lips moving into an astonishingly wide smile as our eyes met.

Almost as quickly as she made eye contact with me, she turned away. I waited a moment before also looking away, getting the attention of a passing server. I explained what drink I wanted and advised her on the quickest way to make it so she didn't even need a shaker, and sure enough, she was back with my drink after a few minutes, every second of which I spent looking at the woman who continued talking to Mr Nice Arse. Because yes, his arse was still nice, but I was undeniably more concerned with the curve and lift of the woman's bottom which stretched the fabric of her clothes.

As I quickly grabbed a free table behind them, I spent a few minutes trying to decipher what she and he were to each other. Their quick exchanges were full of smiles, nudges and giggles and this could have been friendly or flirtatious. Clueless, I let my gaze ride over the swell of her hips and the cinch of her waist where her hand was resting, and I noted how tanned her calves were and how lush her thighs looked where the hem of her dress kissed them. I also noticed she had a gold chain on one of her ankles, and it promptly made me think about biting it while holding her legs up against my chest.

"Oh, that's interesting," I had whispered to myself before taking a sip of my drink.

Because my dick had seen her. It hadn't gotten hard, not yet, but it had grown heavy. It wasn't down to fuck, but it was ready to find out more. And so was I. So when she looked back and met my gaze again, I smiled. Really smiled. Because suddenly it was not just possible to do that, it was easy.

"Who are you buying a drink for?" Maeve returns to my side, dragging me back to the present moment. I follow her gaze to where the barman is preparing two drinks.

"You know me, Maeve, I can't help but make friends wherever I go," I joke, rather than answer her. It's my default setting.

"Friends?" She cocks her eyebrow, but her eyes stay down as her fingers fly over her phone's screen.

"Yes, *friends*," I emphasise before quickly swallowing the distaste in my mouth. Defensive doesn't even come close to how I feel. Guilty too, because I wasn't thinking about Jenna like I want to be friends. The realisation is sobering, which is ironic considering how horribly sober I've been for months now.

"And why was the spa so traumatic? I can't imagine it would be a shithole. Not in a place like this, surely?"

What can I say to that? *No, it was amazing, but it was also where I had a near-panic attack in the sauna followed by a crying fit in the pool, in front of two plump elderly German women who kept giving me pitiful smiles and bouncy thumbs-up to check I was okay. And then, when I was in the showers, this totally gorgeous lean machine of a man came in and I said hello to him while I was lathering shower gel on my balls, which meant he pretty much ran away from me in horror. To top it all off, as I watched the muscles in his back and butt flex when he stalked off, I didn't feel anything. Not a single dick twinge. Not a single filthy, lusty thought entered my mind.*

No, I can't say any of that, not to my sister.

"It's not a shithole, not at all. I just…" I trail off as I run out of words. I suddenly don't have the strength to make a joke and swerve the question.

"It's today," she says and lifts her eyes to mine. "The date."

I nod and chew on the inside of my lip, the words still failing me.

"And you wanted a drink?" she asks tentatively.

Again, I nod. I wanted a drink so badly.

"That's why you came down here." She lowers her voice. She has our father's green eyes, but her current solemn expression is all our mother.

"Not exactly," I say. I find myself smiling, and it feels like a small chink of light in the darkness. "There was this cat…"

"What?" Maeve's brow wrinkles.

"I was just standing there outside the spa, and this small, scrawny cat appeared, slinking out of the bushes beside the path. He sat down a metre or so away from me and looked at me in that sort of judgmental way cats do. I started petting it and he let me do that for a few minutes until he decided he'd had enough and then he moved a bit further away."

"But what does that have to do with… well, anything?" Maeve is looking at me like I've grown a second head.

"He was just like Arnie," I say, my voice suddenly hoarse. "Small, strong, self-assured, and a little needy even if he would never admit it."

"Are you saying you think that the cat was… is… Arnie?" Maeve's eyes widen.

41

"No. Maybe. No. Oh, I don't fucking know." My short laugh is strangled. "All I know is that when I asked the cat what I should do next, he turned and walked away, down towards the bar here. And he kept turning around, checking I was following him. You know how much Arnie loved sunsets and a sundowner cocktail."

I try really hard to hold on to the smile this memory brings, but it fades like it always does. And Maeve notices.

"I can't believe it's been a year," she says, looking at me with open, sad eyes.

One year. One whole brutal devastating and destructive year.

"Yeah," I say.

We hold each other's gaze for a few moments and then she nods at the sun slipping lower in the sky. "But it's nearly over." She rests her hand on my arm, which is unexpected but welcome. "Today. The anniversary. It will soon be done. And you survived."

I can't respond to this. I start to chew the side of my cheek.

"You know that's why they booked it for today," Maeve continues, her voice slow and soft. "They wanted you to be busy and have something to look forward to."

I press down with my teeth a little harder. A second later I taste blood.

"And it's your birthday too, in a few days," Maeve says and while her hand stays on me, her eyes are back on her phone. She's never off it too long.

"Don't remind me." I groan. "What a sad state of affairs I am, celebrating my birthday stone cold sober with my parents and annoying little sister."

Maeve's fake laugh is deliberately loud and coarse. "Your annoying little sister who bailed you out how many times in the last year?"

"Yeah, yeah," I say. I know she's teasing me, but still, it's a kick in the gut.

"Do me a favour, Marty," Maeve's fingers apply a little more pressure on my forearm. "And you can't say no because you fucken owe me. Try and keep an open mind about your birthday, and this week. You may actually enjoy yourself."

"Jesus, Maeve, it's not like I got on the plane intending to have a shite time," I begin. "I'm not the one who…"

"Don't start." She holds her other hand up, the one still gripping her phone. "I don't have time to referee fights or to come and find you in bars you probably shouldn't be in. Just behave yourself, get a suntan and be proud of how far you've come."

I balk at her words. "Proud? What in the flying fuck do I have to be proud of?"

Maeve shrugs like we're talking about the weather. "Well, you're still here, aren't you?" she says, and it hits every painful, tight chord inside of me.

Chapter Five

Jenna

Where is my brother when I need him? I want him here with me, rescuing me, not saving the resort from a bubble bath tsunami.

I need him here to laugh at the ridiculousness of my thinking a man possibly ten years younger than me was interested in me. I need him to join me in snorting at how that young man is now flirting with the most attractive woman in the resort, a woman who could easily be fifteen years younger than me. Of course, men like him go for girls like her.

I'm not surprised. It's human, and I don't mean that flippantly. Most of us allosexuals are wired to look for aesthetically attractive people so that we, in the simplest terms, can produce attractive offspring. It's what we are wired to do. Throw in some very restrictive beauty standards exploited by capitalism and colonialism, and of course, this man is going to choose that woman over me.

With this in the forefront of my mind, my brain has a path it is comfortable walking down to explain away this rejection. And yet still my stomach sinks. Why do I feel like I have a bruise growing all over my body? Why is the rejection making my throat dry and my eyes sting with potential tears? Why do I feel like I lost a lot more than just a fun one-night stand with a man far too young to be anything more?

I quickly tell myself that I shouldn't feel so downhearted that the first real flirtation I've enjoyed since my divorce is now over. I should be happy I had a little fun for a few minutes and that even watching him walk to the bar - a visual I know I can and will mentally summon again, possibly along with the soundtrack of Donna Summer's *Love to Love You Baby* – is on hand for me later in my villa with my vibrator.

I nod once as I realise what else will help me feel a bit better; taking control of this situation. I don't need to sit here and wallow while this younger woman gets to hear the filthy things that I want Marty to say in my ear. I get up and head to the bar.

"Hi," I say as soon as I'm in earshot.

"Oh, Jenna, shit, sorry, I got distracted." Marty turns and looks genuinely surprised to see me, which only goes to confirm he'd either completely forgotten about me or he's now unsettled at the prospect of me interrupting his best lines for this young woman who is unbearably more beautiful now I'm standing next to her. Her naturally blonde hair – I know it's natural because I'm studying her roots far too keenly – floats down her back, almost to her waist, which is impossibly narrow and wrapped in a tight spaghetti-strap vest top that disappears into high-rise, high-cling and just, wow, high-impact figure-hugging jeans. While she has the proportions of a 1980s supermodel, her face is that of a 1940s movie star, with prominent cheekbones, a narrow nose, elegant dark brows and olive-green eyes which keenly measure whatever, or whoever, she looks at.

"Hello," she says, looking as suspicious of me as I feel of her.

"Hi," I say with my thinnest smile.

"Shit, sorry," Marty slaps his forehead. "Maeve, Jenna. Jenna, Maeve."

I blink at him in disbelief. Does he expect me to pull up a stool and chat *with* them?

"Nice to meet you, Maeve, but listen, Marty, sorry to interrupt." I wince at my apology because whatever I'm feeling, it's not sorry. At least not to him. Sorry for myself? Absolutely. "Did you already order that drink, because I think I'll just get a glass of wine and take-"

Marty cuts in, "Oh, yeah, I did order it but no problem. I'll get you a wine as well. Maeve, do you want a drink?"

My mouth falls open.

"Nah," Maeve says, now looking at her phone. Her fingers are moving quicker than my heart rate, which is lining up with the speed of my thoughts.

What a mess. Did I simply imagine the previous words we shared? Did I hallucinate the way he pointed his finger at me? What the hell is going on?

I've got to get out of here.

I place my hand on Marty's arm to stop him trying to get the barman's attention and I instantly regret it. Because it feels so good. He feels so good, and I wish he didn't. I wish his skin wasn't warm under my fingertips. I wish it didn't feel so smooth but textured with fine hairs, like the softest velvet. I wish I didn't feel his warmth transfer to my skin as I keep my fingers there a moment too long.

"It's okay. I don't need a glass of wine, and keep my mocktail too," I say, taking my hand away a moment after he looks down at it. "I'll just leave you both to it."

I turn to walk away because suddenly I feel so stupid, and ludicrously, like I'm about to cry.

"Wait." Marty grabs hold of my hand, and in the same movement he somehow manages to lace his fingers between mine. He gives me a pull strong enough to stop me walking. "Where are you going?"

I don't want to open my mouth and say something foolish or risk crying when I've only known him five minutes, so I don't speak, just slowly, regrettably, pull my hand away from his. I then look at him before I look at her, and finally back at him again.

"She thinks you want to ride me," Maeve says, still staring at her phone's screen. As I hear the slang, I also hear the accent. It's Irish too, the same silky vowels and swirling tone.

"Oh, Jesus, no," Marty says. "Fuck, no. This is Maeve, my sister."

Sister. Sister. SISTER.

Relief calms me from the inside out while embarrassment heats my cheeks. I close my eyes to savour the feeling that returns – hope – and at the same time, I try to think of a response that can wipe away the uneasiness that now hangs between us all.

"How was I supposed to know that?" I say, a small smile curling my lips. "You look nothing alike. She's way hotter than you!"

47

Everything about Marty creases into laughter, his mouth, his cheeks and his body too as he leans forward a little.

Maeve also takes it the way I'd hoped, looking up from her phone and studying me with a thoughtful grin. "You're funny, I could like you."

"I should hope so. I did just call you hot," I say, stepping closer to them both. "Unless you're under the age of eighteen, in which case I would like to apologise profusely."

"All good. I'll be twenty next month. And I get called pretty approximately one thousand times a day," she says without a hint of sarcasm, again looking at her phone. "Okay. Best go back to Ma and Da and tell them I found you alive and sober. Albeit *in a bar.*"

Ma and Da... He's here on holiday with his parents and younger sister. That's... interesting.

"You don't need to mention that part. Oh, fuck it, mention it. Whatever. They should know by now I'm not going to do anything," Marty says to Maeve and his tone is different, rushed and tense.

"Bye, Marty. Don't forget, dinner is in an hour." She taps his arm with her phone then turns to me. "Sorry, I've totally forgotten your name, but nice to meet you."

And then Maeve is gone, her long blonde hair and slender limbs winding their way around the tables until she disappears.

"Seriously, she's a stunner," I say to Marty as the bartender places two glasses in front of us. "God was clearly saving up all the good genes for her."

He laughs again and hands me a drink. "You have no idea," he says. "You still want that glass of wine?"

"No, this will do just fine," I say with a shy smile.

Marty glances back behind us. "Look, we lost our table. Fancy taking these to the beach?"

I nod and turn to walk there with a smile I don't really want him to see. I still don't know what exactly is happening. That panic I felt at him finding someone else - a younger, prettier, slimmer woman - while unpleasant, didn't exactly feel misplaced. It made sense. It felt logical. Part of me *wanted* it to make sense so I could stop walking the plank I feel I'm edging down again.

"Shit, there's nowhere to sit," I say as soon as I realise it.

All the tables outside are taken, which is understandable because the sun has begun painting the sky copper and gold as it slowly slips closer to the sea, a perfect circle of hot pink. I look around for the sun loungers, but they're already packed away, stacked high to the side behind the DJ booth.

"Shall we just sit on the pebbles?" Marty says from behind me. I like hearing his voice behind me.

"I'm up for it," I say with some trepidation but also a shrug that I hope compensates for it. When he walks past me, I follow. We find a spot on the slate-coloured pebbles and he drops down in a far too effortless move. I can't help but notice that his knees don't crack like mine do when I join him.

It only takes a moment to feel how uncomfortably lumpy and bumpy the pebbles are under my butt and thighs but I daren't say anything, nor do I risk looking at him to see if he's having the same realisation. Instead, I bring my sunglasses down from the top of my head, take a sip of my mocktail and look at the strips of fiery orange branding the sky. It's beautiful.

Maybe that's why silence descends because neither of us have anything to say that could top what's happening right in front of us. It's a strange kind of quiet because its presence only brings the noises around us into sharper focus; the soft crashing of the waves, the melody and rhythm of the bar's music, the rising and falling hum of other people's conversations, interrupted by the chiming of glasses. It's a silence that isn't heavy, but it's not light either. It's made of something that begs to be filled but at the same time, it doesn't give me any clue what I should say next. But I know I have to say something.

As it happens, we speak at the same time.

"Sunsets are like visual poetry, aren't they?" I say.

"My arse is really fucking uncomfortable on these pebbles," Marty says.

We laugh together for a moment, but he breaks off, looking behind me at the stack of loungers.

"Considering your brother is the manager and all, what do you think about grabbing a couple of those loungers," he suggests. "Because you're right, sunsets are awesome, and I don't want to not enjoy this one because it feels like I'm sat on a million LEGO bricks."

"Let's do it," I say. Balancing our drinks on the pebbles, we head over to the stack of wooden loungers. He hauls one off the top with very little effort and sets it down before getting another. I bend to grab the first and while it's weighty, it's easy to carry, albeit a little too wide for a comfortable grip. Ignoring onlooking eyes, I manage to carry it over to our drinks. The job is much easier for him and so he's there before I am, and he watches me straighten up with an amused smile.

"You're strong," he says, but I can't tell if he's impressed or put off.

"I lift," I say but don't wait for his reaction. Instead, I sit down on my lounger, adjusting the back so it's upright. I don't know why I feel compelled to explain more, to throw a potential obstacle in my own way, but when he says nothing in return, I start talking. "After my divorce, my therapist recommended lifting weights as a new hobby, a new focus, a way to get out of my head and back into my body."

I wait for his questions about the divorce, about what went wrong, about my ex-husband and about why our marriage failed.

Instead, he asks, "Did it help?"

This almost leaves me as speechless as his flirty cocktail names earlier, and I brave a quick look at him. The dramatic reds of the sunset give his cheeks a new rosy glow, and his irises now have even more colour in them, definite flecks of gold in pools of dark brown. My eyes are drawn again to the bump in his nose and the oddest questions fill my mind. *Was that a rugby injury? How did it happen? Is he self-conscious about it? Can I bite it?*

"Yeah, it did," I answer him. "Or rather, it does. It's a journey, I guess."

"Yes, it is," he says like he really does agree.

"Oh, you're divorced too?" I say in a light way to show I'm joking. He's too young, surely. Isn't he?

"I'm not. Now, do you want to talk about your divorce while the sun puts on this show?" He nods at the horizon with what could have been a sad smile.

"God, no," I say, turning my head back to look at the stretches of colour that have again rearranged themselves. "My divorce has nothing on this view."

"So, will we just go back to flirting outrageously with each other?"

"I'll give it my best shot," I say, noticing how the colours are also reflected in the sea, making it shimmer effervescently. "But I am starting to think this view is now considerably more attractive than you, I have to say."

I hear him laugh. "What about my sister? Is it more attractive than her?"

"Oh, God, no. She's still much hotter." I turn to him, ready to wink, but I don't because he's looking at me like maybe he's proud of me, which makes no sense at all.

"It's good to know where I stand." His smile reappears, dimples too.

I take in a deep breath. "I think you could be in a lot of worse places than this right now." I nod at the sunset and raise my glass towards him. He nudges his against it and together we turn back to look at the horizon.

The silence returns but this time it's transformed into something welcome and comfortable. Now it's something I can, and want to, hold on to. Even as it unfolds in front of us, the sun sinking lower, bleeding more gold into the sea, I long to stretch out this moment because of what it already is and because of its deep, delicious possibility. I can practically smell and feel and taste the undeniable potential for sex with a man I'm fiercely attracted to, something I've craved for the longest time. I smile into the silence and watch the sun fall slowly towards the Earth, thinking about how I too could be in much, much worse places.

Possibly a minute or two later, maybe longer, he finally responds in a much quieter voice, almost as if he's talking to himself. "Maybe I'm exactly where I'm supposed to be."

Chapter Six

Marty

The silence is nice. I know I should reach for a better word than that, but I can't, and honestly, I don't want to. Nice is underrated. Not everything in life can be *amazing* or *wonderful* or *incredible*. Life gets uncomfortably full when it's lived like that, not to mention the struggle that comes with always wanting it to be all those things when it just can't be. I should know. Awesome was my default mode for most of my life and although I didn't think it at the time, it was exhausting and not at all sustainable.

Nowadays, *nice* and *fine,* and sometimes even just *okay* are more comfortable to me, cherished even, because a few years ago my perpetual optimism was flipped on its head and I was forced to experience the superlatives on the other end of the scale; body-crushing pain, devastating loss, bottomless grief.

So, even though I just promised her some outrageous flirting and even though I itch to look at her again and to ask a million questions so I can find out more about her, I also want to enjoy the *niceness* of this silence too. I want to sit with this new feeling that's bubbling up at the end of a day that has felt so hard and so sad. A hard and sad day that concludes three hundred and sixty-five hard and sad days.

That being said, there is nothing just nice, fine or okay about the sunset. The sunset really is spectacular, even though I have to squint to look at the edges of it because I stupidly didn't include sunglasses in the bag I rushed to pack.

"Are they always this beautiful?" I ask because I suddenly want to know. I want to know if I have to prepare myself for this kind of beauty every night for the next six days, the kind that Arnie would have given his right testicle to enjoy.

Jenna turns to me and looks a little confused.

"The sunsets here," I explain. "Are they always like this?"

She turns back and nods. "Yeah, they're pretty special. My brother says sometimes it can be cloudy or stormy and that makes the view a bit different, but we've had clear skies the last two evenings."

"When do you go home again?" I ask. Did she tell me already? *Come on brain, retain information, please.*

"Friday," she says. The sunset is reflected in her sunglasses and I notice we don't have much longer until the bottom edge of the sun dips into the water.

"So, five more days."

"Five more sunsets." She rolls her head to the side, her chin staying low, her gaze on me. She reaches for her glasses. "Do you want to borrow them? You'll hurt your eyes if you keep looking at it without."

"No, I'm fine," I say, waving away the offer. "I'm not looking directly at it, and neither should you be, by the way, even with sunglasses. I actually prefer looking at the sky around the sun and its reflection in the water. It almost looks like there's glitter in the sea, or maybe a million fireflies buzzing away on the surface. Do you see that?"

Looking back at the water, I watch her swallow before replying quietly, "I see that."

"I love how far the colours stretch out into the sky, all those different shades of pink and red and orange, constantly changing. I know fuck all about art but it's kind of like watching a painting in real-time, don't you think?"

She nods.

When she doesn't say anything, I keep talking. "It's hard to believe that what we're looking at is this almighty ball of burning gas hanging in the middle of our galaxy. A lump of mass so big we're all committed to circling it forever. It's mad, isn't it?"

Jenna is still, eyes straight ahead but something tells me she's listening to every word.

"It's a prompt, I guess, to look at what's happening away from the sun," I continue. "It reminds me to look at the other smaller things surrounding the big thing."

"That's kind of profound," she says, her face back on mine. She slides her body down a little and rests her head against the back of the lounger. "And there I was thinking you were going to whisper more filthy cocktail names in my ear."

I bend one of my legs and bring my hand to rest on it so I can lean a little closer to her. "Oh, I can do that. I'm just waiting for the sun to go down because, as you rightly pointed out, there's no way I can compete with this kind of a performance," I say, nodding in the sun's direction.

We don't talk for a few moments after she also turns her attention back to the horizon, but eventually, she speaks, "It blows my mind that this happens every single day."

I nod. "You don't watch the sun go down often?"

"Not often enough. I think the last time was on my last holiday, which was... shit, nearly three years ago."

"On my gap year, after school, I watched the sun go down almost every single night." I pause and take in a quick, necessary breath. "We sort of made it a rule."

"Sounds like one of the better rules I've heard of," she says. "So this gap year... Was that last year or the year before or..."

"I'm twenty-four," I say, knowing what she's really asking.

I watch her side profile to check for shock or panic or something more subtle like a flinch or maybe even a flash of intrigue. But there's nothing on her face. Eyes fixed on the sunset, her mouth is slightly open like it can't decide what to say, and her face can't decide whether to smile or frown.

"Twenty-four," she says, and she does this cute little wriggle in her chair before un-crossing and re-crossing her legs, drawing my eyes again to their curves, their golden glow and that sexy anklet. "Interesting."

"Interesting how?" I ask.

"Just... interesting," she says, and a broader smile grows on her lips.

"Well, are you going to put me out of my fecking misery and tell me how old *you* are?" I demand with a laugh.

"I'm..." she starts, but then presses her lips together and squints at me, looking very, very mischievous. "I was going to say I want you to guess, just to have a bit of fun with you, but now I'm petrified you're going to say something ridiculous, and it could be ridiculously old, or it could be ridiculously young. Either way, it won't make me feel good."

"Why? Growing old is a privilege," I say without thinking. Feeling, yes, but not thinking.

She blinks at that and has no response.

"So, how about I don't guess," I offer, because I feel like I owe her this much. "And instead, you tell me what does make you feel good."

She laughs. "And you're back. I was worried the flirting spirit had left you completely."

"Never." I smile, shifting my body so I'm more on my side, facing her.

"Will you survive if I don't tell you how old I am? Like maybe we could just stick to flirting and watching the sun go down and then... well..." She looks down at her drink, and then up at me, her eyelids still low. "I don't know what happens next."

"Nobody knows what's going to happen next, cupcake," I say and all I get back is a full-body sigh.

I turn again to look at the sunset even though her side profile with her full lips, freckled cheeks and long neck is a view I could look at just as long. The bottom of the sun is now just seconds away from sinking into the sea and I feel a flood of memories rush in, all of them tinged with a persistent melancholy that I wish I could avoid, just once.

"It's happening," she says, her voice low.

"I know."

"It feels so much more epic than just the end of a day," she says, and I know what she means, why she's saying it, but I can't help but question if she's only talking about the sun.

"I know," I say again, and then, without speaking, we watch the sea start to swallow the sun. The bar DJ's song choice – a soulful, chilled-out dance track - matches the sunset's climax perfectly and I am also glad I don't know the song so there's no memory to pull me away from this moment. I wait until the sun is almost completely submerged and then I finally look at the space it took up just a minute ago.

"You know, someone once told me that immediately as the sun goes down, sometimes you can see a flash of green light."

"Really?" she says in a voice that's more air than anything else.

"Yeah, an optic phenomenon. Apparently, it's when the sun's light gets dispersed through the Earth's atmosphere, like a prism," I say, almost hearing Arnie's voice in my ear. "Look out for it."

"Wow, science is so sexy," she says and my smile comes easier than I expect. Out of the corner of my eye, I watch her head lift off the back of the lounger. Her lips pull into a pout and her chin pushes out, studying the view.

"Did you see it?" I ask, after a minute.

"No," she says but still she looks.

"Yeah, I'm not sure it's true. I never saw it and we watched like three hundred sunsets together that year. It's probably complete bollocks," I say and that earns me a soft swipe on my arm as she laughs.

"So, who did you go travelling and watching sunsets with?"

I close my eyes as if the sun is still there and still shining too bright. When I open them again, I'm happy to see all of her face again as she's moved her glasses back to the top of her head. Her eyes are big and the colour of wild honey.

"If you're not going to tell me your age tonight, then I'm not going to tell you about that," I say.

Her head jolts back a little in shock. Of course, it's not the answer she expects. Who says something like that about someone they went backpacking with?

"Okay," she says simply and then turns back to the horizon. "Wow, look at the colour of the sky now."

"Nah." I turn my body to the side once more. "I think I'd rather look at you."

57

Chapter Seven

Jenna

Where do they teach twenty-four-year olds to talk like that? Is there a school in Ireland where they go and learn how to flirt unapologetically in a way that is shockingly bold, teetering on cheesy, and yet so very, very effective? And since when do twenty-four-year olds *look* like this? All lean muscle, manly height and five o'clock shadow defining an arresting jawline.

Thirteen. *Thirteen.*

That is the number that pinballs around my head and has been ever since he told me his age. I'd been hoping he was twenty-nine or twenty-eight. I'd told myself I could be forgiven for twenty-seven, maybe twenty-six. But a thirteen-year age gap? That's quite a difference.

Of course, it had to be thirteen; the unluckiest number there is. I know that this myth is superstition and confirmation bias at their most stubborn, but still, it feels ironic, or maybe like a premonition, a warning?

Not that I'm a superstitious person. I trust science and research and fact-based evidence too much. But even so, I still believe that there are things out there that don't have clear explanations and yet still exist, love being top of that list.

But this isn't love, I am quick to remind myself. This is lust.

As for the literature on lust, we don't have a comprehensive or foolproof understanding of desire, but we do have some knowledge of what makes us feel it. The hormones testosterone and oestrogen, in all genders, drive our ability to feel desire, and indeed do things to our bodies to make us more desirable to others, including the creation of pheromones. The amygdala part of the brain, always hungry for new stimuli, upon meeting someone physically attractive and soaking up some pheromones, is quick to latch onto them or repel them, which is why attraction often comes on so quickly. Once intrigued, there follows a series of powerful hormone rushes that make us feel good, rewarding and encouraging us to mate. Those tiny but powerful hits of dopamine literally tease us about what's to come after an orgasm, when they will also be accompanied by a warm hug of oxytocin. Lust is a powerful thing because it has to be. It drives us to do the most important things of all – survive, procreate, continue the human race.

It's also powerful for other reasons. Lust doesn't need as much luck as love. Lust comes quicker and, in many ways, keener, readier, hungrier. Lust is more visible and lighter to hold but is still strong and overpowering. Lust is both a logical chemical reaction and a magical madness. Lust comes, and it also goes. I know enough from personal and professional experience to know that while it is real and worth enjoying for as long as it sticks around, it simply isn't designed to last forever, and that's okay. That's a good thing.

A thirteen-year age gap doesn't matter when it comes to lust, especially when I'm a divorced woman, on holiday on a Greek island and desperate to feel a man, this man, touch my body with his hands, his lips, his tongue, his mouth, his everything. If he's willing...

That decided, I feel the last remnants of confusion and doubt slip into the sea with the sun. Now I know where this is going – and his flirtatious behaviour suggests he's on board - I can shift all my attention to making it happen.

"So, Marty O'Martin." I roll over to my side and look at him again. "Tell me about yourself."

"Ooh, this sounds like a date now." He sucks on his straw. "Or a job interview."

"Honestly, I don't know what this is." I move my drink around in the space between us. If that wasn't the perfect opening for pursuing my goal, I don't know what is. "What is this?"

"Two people who just met having a drink together? Two strangers getting to know each other as the sun goes down? Two humans who may or not fancy each other?"

Despite the fireworks of delight that shoot off inside me, I simply nod at that. "I think I might fancy you," I confess.

"I think I might fancy you too." He smiles. "Does that mean I might get to kiss you?"

I'm torn when I hear the word *kiss* leave his lips. On one hand, it feels like a flower blooming in the desolate pit of my stomach. On the other hand, it's not a flower I love although it's undeniably pretty and fragrant. *Kiss* is too small and tame for what I want. Because what I really want to hear leave his mouth are different words, like *lick, taste, suck, bite, fuck.*

"I might need one more drink before that," I say, not because it's true - another sugary mocktail isn't going to get me any more pliant than I already am - but just because I want to make this last, this part of the experience; the talking, the flirting, the looking at each other under the now purple and grey hues of a twilight sky. Even if our destination is sex, I still want to enjoy the journey.

He jumps into action, launching his body upright and grabbing my glass. "On it like a car bonnet," he says before looking down at me, pulling his brows forward. "Do you want cock... or mock?"

I clutch my chest and giggle like someone's tickling me. "Oh, I want cock, but I'll settle for a mock to keep you company."

"Oh, Jenna." He shakes his head, looking at the ground. "I'm sure there's an opening for an equally filthy reply but I am too flustered to find it."

"I hope that's not a warning of what's to come," I say, with a deliberately appalled look. "Also, pretty sure that was already filthy enough. You did say 'opening', after all."

"You're right. I sometimes don't know how good I am... And *that,* pretty lady, was your warning. Don't go anywhere."

And I don't. I sit there, squeezing my legs together, doing more spontaneous squeezes of my pelvic floor muscles, and stretching my mouth into the widest grin that's physically possible. Suddenly self-conscious, I look around and see some of the other couples and groups have left, and I am relieved considering we've been sitting front and centre of them all. I adjust my dress and my hair a few times and find my phone in my bag to check my reflection with the camera.

I wouldn't say I look my best. I'm make-up-free, my freckles are darker than ever in the dusky light, and my hair is still all tangled thanks to not brushing it since I swam in the sea earlier, but I also like what I see because I look relaxed and I look excited, two looks I haven't seen much on my features recently. Before I tuck my phone back in my bag, it buzzes.

It's a notification from a dating app.

"Please not a dick pic. Please not a dick pic. Please not a dick pic," I whisper to myself as I open up the app.

There I see that someone has liked my profile, and after a quick glance at Marty at the bar, I look back down at Nathan, 38, from Surbiton, a Chartered Surveyor, Football Fanatic and Avid Skier. Yes, with the words all capitalised. I swipe past the obligatory suited-and-booted-for-a-wedding photo to try and gauge what he really looks like in his other photos, but there's only one more where I can actually see his full face and body.

And it's almost worse than a dick pic. It's a picture of him holding up a fish while topless.

I groan as I put my phone away. It's a horrible jolt from home and a reminder of what awaits me there. It's also a reminder that whatever is happening with Marty, I need to grab it - and possibly him - by the balls. I look up to see him getting closer as he walks back with two drinks that look different from our last.

"So, I figured it was time for a Blur Job." He hands me another glass that has three layers of colour — rich brown at the bottom, a layer of an off-white liquid, and then some whipped cream on top. "We have a shot of coffee instead of Baileys, a layer of coconut milk on top of that, and finally some whipped cream and of course, a cherry on top. It's not going to be as good as the real thing but tastes delicious all the same."

"Are you talking about the cocktail?" I ask, giggles eager to burst out of me.

"Or the cock?" he finishes.

"That was too easy." I laugh as I take the glass.

"I generally am." He winks.

I wave my hand around and try to slow my laughter. "Okay, I need the brakes back on. You move too fast for me."

"Oh, I can go slow if you want, Jenna." He sits back down and then lowers his voice as he leans toward me. "Really, really, really slow and really, really..."

"Hmm," I cut him off. I close my eyes as a shiver runs down my whole body and a small moan leaves my lips. Only as I open my eyes again do I realise that was a better response than any words because when I see how he's looking at me - lips parted, eyes dark and wide - he looks like he finally ran out of words. I revel in this small win that I suspect will only spur him on. Even so, I'm taken aback by what he says next.

"You're a fucken work of art," he says in that deep Irish drawl and from the expression he has, all crinkled eyebrows, matching dimples, and generous eyes, I almost believe that that's what he really thinks.

As if he's just realised what he's said, he turns away, muttering something under his breath that I don't catch. Because he's suddenly busying himself looking in his bag, I don't ask him to repeat himself but I do wonder if it's a quick apology. Not that he needs to apologise. He doesn't need to be embarrassed for flirting so outrageously with me. It's all fun and games - fun and games that are going to lead me to get exactly what I want later, I hope.

As he continues to search in his bag, I push up a little and look around us. Now the sun has gone, the crowd has dissipated even more. There are plenty of free tables and the music being played has shifted tempo to a quicker, heavier beat. I think about suggesting we move to a table but realise then I'm actually very happy where I am, pretending that the rest of the world doesn't exist.

I settle back into the lounger and look at him again. His bag is back on the ground and he's now staring out at the sea with a contemplative look on his face. With my mission firmly in mind, I pick up our conversation again.

"So, I asked you to tell me about yourself, Marty. Tell me your likes, your dislikes, and what you want to do with this one wild and precious life," I say. I know he's not going to get the Mary Oliver reference and I'm glad because it will make me sound a lot more poetic than I really am.

"Okay." He nods and straightens up as if he's just remembered where he is. He has a quick sip of his drink before replying. "My likes. Food, rugby, the gym, ABBA, cycling, my Dad's barbeques, Queen - the band not the monarchy - the Thai beef salad this one woman made at a roadside stand in Chiang Mai, Elton John, pub lunches, sunsets, my Ma's apple crumble, the Bee Gees, hot buttered toast, fresh Colombian coffee, gosh, that's a lot of food..."

"And a lot of Seventies pop," I add, but nod for him to continue.

"I think I'm done with my likes. No, wait." He holds up a hand. "I need to add one to the list. Ankle bracelets."

I follow the nod of his head and look down at the thin gold chain wrapped around my ankle, the one item of jewellery I never take off. Heat rushes down my body and makes me curl my toes. We both watch them flex.

Marty coughs. "Dislikes. Off the top of my head, cancer, watching or reading or listening to the news, One Direction, cancer, advertising, Bulgarian squats, stretching, wearing socks, cancer, stewed tea, people who don't recycle, and yeah, cancer again. Oh, and food snobs, which is tough being in my job."

"What did One Direction ever do to you?" I fake alarm. I didn't miss how many times he mentioned cancer – and rightly, I'm sure – but I don't really want to discuss it when I currently can't stop thinking about what his long fingers would feel like inside my underwear.

"It's a long story." He looks away again.

"I agree about Bulgarian squats." I steer us in a different direction. "And I stopped watching the news too, recently. Only ever had it on because of my ex-husband so when he left, I stuck to the documentaries and Nordic Noir shows I really wanted to watch."

"Not rom-coms? I used to force my ex to watch them all the time."

"That's just cruel," I say choosing not to dwell on how this talk of exes is unsettling me a little. It's hardly good foreplay. "Despite reading a lot of romance novels, I'm not a big fan of romantic movies. Love a romance subplot but prefer the main storyline to have me guessing rather than giving me a predictable HEA."

"HEA?"

"Happy Ever After? You clearly only watch rom-coms, you don't read them."

"Clearly. But also, I wouldn't know a HEA if it hit me around the head," he jokes, but his smile is dimple-free.

"I think most Happy Ever Afters don't do that. It's possibly what makes them HEAs rather than GBH."

He chuckles at that. "You're a funny woman, Jenna."

"And you didn't answer the last part of my question."

"Oh, what was it? I can't even blame the booze for forgetting. Sometimes my mind just drifts a bit..." he trails off. There's possibly more to this twenty-four-year old than an uncanny aptitude for flirting and good looks, but that's not for me to think about. Indeed, the less thinking the better. I want more doing.

"Your goals for this one wild and precious life?" I prompt him.

His eyes fall to his drink, and it's like his smile sinks into it too. "Mary Oliver," he says.

"Yes." I sound as surprised as I feel.

"You didn't think I'd know *Wild Geese*?"

"Holy shit, you know the name of the poem!" I don't even try to hide my shock.

"Now, now, Jenna. I know more than just how to make mocktails and flirt with hot older divorcées."

"I should thump you for saying that." I hold my fist up.

"Nah, you should thump me when I start calling you a cougar," he chuckles.

"True. But seriously, how do you know about Mary Oliver?"

"I honestly don't. Not much. But I know that poem. My ex studied English Lit, wrote a bit of poetry."

That word again is enough to silence me. *Ex.* I really don't want to talk about exes. I want to pretend that he materialised out of thin air in the hotel lobby and has no sexual past at all, only a present - with me.

But I know that's unrealistic, and I know I need practise at this side of dating, so I risk meeting Marty where he's at. "My ex studied economics, and never read a poem in his life. So, you win on the exes front."

"Maybe we should shelve talking about exes," he says, after blinking at the horizon a few times. "I mean, they should probably go in the fridge with my alcoholism, your divorce, and your age."

"And your backpacking pal," I say with a nod.

He dips his chin and gives me a different kind of smile, a little rueful and maybe even a little provocative. It's a look that says, *Catch up, Jenna.*

"Oh," I say as I do catch up. "Your backpacking pal was your ex. Sorry, I just assumed it was a mate of yours, like another bloke."

His chin falls lower, practically resting on his chest, but his eyes hold mine, serious and steady.

"Oh," I say again.

Chapter Eight

Marty

I study her face to gauge her reaction. She doesn't seem shocked, appalled, or even that confused. She freezes for a few seconds as her lips press together. Then her eyes soften, and she tilts her head to the side as if she's just noticed something new about my face.

"So you're..." I realise she's asking me to label it.

"Bisexual," I say. "To be honest, I've only had one proper boyfriend and before him, I thought I was straight, so I've never really had to label it or talk about it much with a..."

"Hot older divorced woman?" She finishes for me with a wink that is just as comforting as what she says next. "Cool."

"Cool? That's it?"

"Sure," she says, still with that thoughtful look on her face.

"And you're..."

"Pretty straight, sadly. Now and again, I think I'm possibly bi-curious, because, I mean, have you seen women? They're beautiful. But when I..." She stops talking abruptly.

"When you what, Jenna?" I lean a little closer.

She gives me a level look. "I don't want what I'm going to say next to cheapen this conversation. You just shared something vulnerable with me and I want to be respectful of that."

"Permission to speak freely," I say.

"Okay." She clears her throat again. It's an adorable short huff of a noise. "Well, I've only ever slept with men. And when I... when I touch myself, I mostly only think about men. And I'm not saying that's an all-knowing, science-backed indicator of sexuality, because it's not, and besides, a growing body of research suggests sexuality is inherently fluid, but I feel pretty confident that right now I'm heterosexual. It feels right, and from what I know about people who do label their sexual identities, that's enough."

Despite her great eloquence and insight, my brain fails me by getting and staying snagged on the way she said, "touch myself". So much so I have trouble responding, or even breathing for that matter. My dick is coming along for the ride too, pushing up against the fly of my jeans. It's a brilliantly familiar and yet foreign feeling, all at once.

Welcome back, buddy.

"Sorry, I probably waffled on a bit then," she says interrupting the silence that stretches out because I'm still unable to form a coherent sentence in my head. "I can go on a bit about these things."

"No, no, don't apologise," I say. "You clearly know what you're talking about. I'm just a bit stunned that you sort of seem to know more about being queer than me, and well, I am queer."

She laughs softly and re-crosses her legs. I glance again at the gold chain on her ankle and it does nothing to redistribute the blood flow in my body.

"It's my job, actually," she says. "Or it was. I'm a journalist and I used to research and write about things like sexuality."

My eyebrows lift. "But you don't anymore?"

Her mouth pulls down. "No, but that's sort of related to my divorce so we veto."

"Gotcha," I say, and we each take a sip of our drinks. I can't help but feel it's a shame I can't ask her more questions about her work. It sounds interesting.

"Well, my brother will be disappointed his gaydar isn't working properly," she says.

"I believe when it's for bisexuals, it's called a Bi-Fi," I offer and delight again in hearing the husky rumble of her laugh. I don't think I'd ever get bored of making her laugh.

"I knew you were checking out his arse!"

"Guilty as charged." I hold my hands up, one of them still gripping my drink. "It's a nice arse."

"I will pass that on. I'm sorry you and your ex didn't work out. Break-ups are tough," she says, and it should sound out of place, but it doesn't. But that doesn't stop it from making my lungs cave in a little.

"Same to you, Jenna. I can imagine divorces are rough too," I say eventually.

"Exes were supposed to be vetoed, weren't they?"

I nod. "Correct. I guess you should do your dislikes and likes because we're almost running out of things to talk about with all this vetoing."

She breathes in deep. "Okay, here you go. Likes. Well, I like lifting weights, writing, swimming, hanging out with my brother, seeing friends, researching weird facts and stories about sex, orgasms, long walks, watching the seasons change, any and every kind of noodle soup, more orgasms, going to the theatre, reading smut-filled romance novels, and yep, orgasms."

"I can't argue with any of that, apart from maybe the long walks. Unless there's a dog involved, I'd rather be riding a bike or chasing a ball than just walking."

She leans closer, eyes alive and sparkling. "But what if there's the most amazing pub lunch at the other end? Roast beef or lamb? With all the trimmings?"

"With a log fire? Maybe some board games?" I play along.

"Yes, of course. And sticky toffee pudding for dessert."

"With custard or ice cream?" I give her my most serious stare. "This is a very important question, Jenna."

Her lips pout as she considers and it sends my blood pumping south again.

"Both," she says resolutely.

"Correct answer! And your dislikes?"

"Unsolicited dick pics, unwanted advice about investments, overpriced fine dining that isn't very fine, and men who pose topless with fish," she says after only a brief hesitation.

"Good job I left my fishing rod at home."

She narrows her eyes at me.

"I'm kidding," I say. "And excellent restraint not making a joke about rods."

Chuckling, she draws her knees up to hug them with her arms.

"Are you cold? I think I've got a jumper in my bag," I say, reaching for it. I should also check my phone for the time again. Missing dinner would not be a good end to the day.

"No, thank you," she says but she does shiver a little. I look at the goosebumps that cover the skin on her forearms and I want to feel their texture on my tongue.

Jesus, I'm close to going from 0 to 60 with this woman. I need to slow down.

"So, you're from the UK?" I rush to find a neutral topic of conversation. "Where do you live?"

"Islington, North London," she rests her head on the top of her knees. "And you live in..."

"Dublin. Born and raised," I say.

"It's a beautiful city."

"Yeah, sure, for those three days of the year when it stops raining and the sun comes out."

"London's not much better." She shrugs.

"I've never been."

She opens her mouth as if in shock.

"I have travelled, you know." I lean over and nudge the side of her arm.

"You're right, and I'm sorry," she says, and I can tell she is. "Tell me about your travels, if that's not still vetoed?"

My travels. *Our* travels. It's not an easy topic for me to talk about.

My counsellor, Jill, tells me often that it's important I try to talk about the happier times with Arnie, so maybe I should try. Maybe it will be easier with Jenna because she doesn't know what happened afterwards. She's not waiting for my voice to crack or for pain to shadow my words. "We did about fifteen months in total," I say. "Mostly in Asia, Australia and New Zealand, and then on the way home, a few months in South America."

70

"Sounds amazing. I sometimes wish I'd done something like that when I was younger."

"Why didn't you?"

"If I veto this, we really are going to run out of things to talk about, aren't we?"

"Possibly, although maybe that was where we went wrong in the beginning. Who says we need to talk?" I say with a wink that feels harder to perform than I expect. Suddenly my body and my brain are at war. While the former desperately wants to fuck her, the latter is terrified at the idea because that's what I used to do. That's how I fucked up again and again and again.

"God, yes, talking is so overrated," she says lowering her legs and sitting up straighter, her hands by her sides. "Do you want to... go somewhere where we can *not* talk?"

Her implied meaning is as clear as the bright moon I can now see high in the darkening sky, and maybe that's why it takes me by surprise. Even though she made my dick harder than anyone else has in months, just sitting next to her and taking in the briefest glimpses of her tanned skin, the shape of her arms and legs, the curves of her neck and hips, I am still taken aback that she's telling me she wants it too, that she's feeling the same kind of heat I feel.

But I don't want it. Or rather, I don't want to want it. I suddenly and vehemently don't want to only indulge my dick and newfound libido. I definitely don't want that today of all days.

"Actually, I'm really sorry," I say, a slight croak in my voice. "I think I have to go in a few minutes."

"Go?" Her head pulls back.

"Yeah, I promised my parents I'd join them for dinner, and I shouldn't be late." I suddenly despise the sound of my own voice.

"Oh, yeah, sure," Jenna says, glancing at our glasses that are both still quite full.

"I'm sorry," I rush out. "I'm a fecking eejit and I probably should have told you that sooner. I tend to do this, you know, fuck things up."

Jenna looks at me, unblinking. "Don't talk about yourself like that, Marty," she says after a pause. A string of seconds long enough that I watch her search my face, looking for something I'm not sure she finds. "Am I allowed to ask why you're on holiday with your parents... and your smoking hot sister?" I can see what she's doing. Trying to make me smile again. I wish I could indulge her and make her think it's working but I can't. I'm fast running out of energy and focus and just any kind of clear-thinking.

"It's a long story..." Feeling guilty, I reach for my phone again and see I now have five minutes to get up to the restaurant. I look at Jenna as I ready myself to go, but her pout, her wide eyes, the constellation of freckles across her face make me stop. I'll go in five. I can be ten minutes late. That would be okay.

"So... veto?" Jenna asks.

I shake my head as I sit back. I've had enough of that word no matter the amount of trouble it's saved me tonight. "Honestly, it's a free holiday. I won't be able to afford to go to a place like this for a long time. They offered, I wanted to top up my tan, so win-win." I hope she goes along with it. I'm not technically lying, just being selective with the truth. "I also missed the sunshine. I was living in Ibiza last year and it's been hard being back in Dublin after six months in the sun," I add because that much is true.

"Lucky you," she says. "I love Ibiza."

"Yeah," I say, leaving it at that.

"But do you like being in Dublin? You're young. You could live anywhere."

I choose to only answer the first part of her question. "Yeah, I love Dublin. It's my home. It's where I grew up. It's where..."

It's where I met and grew up with my best friend. It's where I fell in love for the first time. It's also where everything fell apart.

"Home is home," she finishes for me.

"Is London home for you? Is that where your parents are too?"

It's Jenna's turn to flinch. "Don't you have to go?"

"I have five more minutes," I lie.

"Yeah... London is home now. But it's not where I grew up, although near enough. We're Home Counties babies, Jake and me. From Surrey, but there's no family there now and most of my friends have moved on too. I've lived in London for nearly twenty years now, so yes, it's home."

I soak up the information quickly and start counting down years.

"Stop with the maths!" she says with a pointed finger and a warning look that's still part smile. I like how much she smiles, even when I'm sitting here giving her all sorts of mixed messages and I'm about to disappear.

"Just wait, I think I have it all figured out," I say and close my eyes while holding my fingers up using them to count.

"Seriously, stop!" she says and grabs one of my arms, pulling it down. When her fingers leave my skin, the place she touched tingles for a long time, which I'm sort of focusing all my attention on until I hear her make the sound of the Countdown clock coming to a stop. "Time's up. No more calculations, and no, I don't want to hear what answer you came up with. Oh, God, wait. I hope you got that sound reference!"

I open my eyes. "Are you joking? My Nan watches that show every day."

"Now I feel *really* old." Jenna laughs. "Is she in Dublin too?"

"Yeah, in a nursing home. I try and see her once a week or so. It doesn't feel like enough but work and... other stuff keep me busy."

"How old is she?"

"You know, I don't know for sure. Eighty-something."

"Well, I can confirm that I'm younger than your grandmother," she says with a wink. "Now, you should go."

I wince. Now it's my turn to hear Jenna dismiss me, I get why she looked so hurt a moment ago.

But she doesn't look as disappointed as I feel now. With a soft smile on her lips and slightly dazed eyes, she clears her throat again. "Would you like to know my villa number? For later?"

"I would love to know," I say on a deep exhale, but then quickly add. "But I am going to ask you to put it in the fridge with all the other things we agreed not to talk about tonight."

Now I see real disappointment on her face. It's like gravity pulls down on the pertness of her cheeks and the corners of her eyes.

"Oh," she says.

"It's not that I don't want to-"

"No, it's fine, Marty." She shuffles forward as if to get up. "I just think I misread some messages."

"Jenna, you got nothing wrong, and you did everything right," I say and I see the old Marty approach, the one that likes to flirt himself out of an awkward situation, the one that's ready to say *Fuck it* and ask for the villa number, but I ignore him. "You misread nothing. Like I said, I want to know. But I just want to maybe do this again first. Maybe tomorrow night?"

"This?"

"Have a drink with you while the sun goes down?"

"Watch the sunset together?" She seems puzzled.

"Yeah," I say and I hold on to my smile tightly because I still haven't got the grin back on her face.

"Okay," she says, sounding unconvinced. I watch as she re-crosses her legs and I notice the muscle in her upper thigh tense. Instinctively I wonder how firm or how soft they are or if they are a heady combination of both. *Jesus, am I really turning her down tonight?*

Yes. Yes, I am. I must. I need to.

I stand up as if to punctuate my resolve.

"Have a nice dinner," she says, also coming to stand. There's something about having her ready to leave to that glues my feet to the ground. Even though I know now that I'm going to be late, I don't move. Even though there is already a scattering of glittering stars in the dark blue-grey night sky, I stay where I am looking at her. Even though I know I am going to be in so much trouble with my mother, I don't even think about moving. I just look at Jenna.

"Your dinner," she says and clears her throat again. I already know she does that before she says something she feels a little awkward or embarrassed saying. "With your parents."

I close my eyes. I really do have to go. "Yeah, that."

74

But still, I don't move. Not until I feel a hand pull on my chin and a wet warmth cover my nose, a sharp little nip accompanying it. My eyes open in shock as I see her pull back.

"Sorry," she says, as she comes down from her tiptoes, her fingers on her lips. "I just had to do that."

God, she's so fucking class.

"Save it for tomorrow, cupcake," I say.

"Tomorrow?" she says looking confused.

"Yeah," I say, leaning down to pick up my bag while also very quickly adjusting my jeans. "Same time, same place?"

"Okay." Her hand still covers her mouth so I can't see if she's smiling. I really hope she's smiling.

"Tomorrow," I say as I start walking backwards. I say it again before I turn around. And I say it one last time, over my shoulder, before I leave the bar.

Chapter Nine

The Next Day

Jenna

The sunrise wakes me up and it's so astonishingly pretty that I don't even mind it depriving me a few of the eight hours' sleep I try to get. My brother chose my villa especially because it sits on the top curve of the hillside the whole resort is pitched against, and I have a panorama-style terrace that lets me catch the soft silver-blue sky at sunrise as well as the deep pink glow of sunset.

I wrap a robe around my body as I make my way onto the balcony to watch the sky change colour. I stand there in awe of the promise-filled silver-pink-hued view for many long minutes until briefly, spontaneously, I wonder if Marty likes sunrises as much as sunsets. And then I push aside his name along with the sinking feeling of rejection which accompanies it.

As if to reward this effort, the doorbell rings and I rush to answer it, tightening my robe around my waist.

"It's a fucking disaster!" my brother exclaims as I open the door. Carrying a wide room service tray, he pushes past me.

"Good morning, dear brother," I say to his back. "What's today's drama?"

"I've been summoned for a last-minute meeting with the Bouras', all five of them. And before nine o'clock in the morning! I may as well pack my bags and hide in your walk-in closet until we can both fly home on Friday together." With the large tray balanced on one shoulder, he waltzes through the villa and out onto the terrace.

"Did you carry all of this up the hill?" I ask in awe.

"God, no. Lionel gave me a lift," he says as he sets the tray down. "You know I try not to sweat until at least 11 am. Haven't managed it a single day since I've been here, but as the wise man said, I gotta have faith."

"One of Jesus' wise men?" I frown.

"No, no. George Michael."

"Right. So, this meeting. Sounds like you're assuming the worst, Jakey." We both start unloading all the plates and bowls. My mouth salivates at how good all the food looks and my stomach starts to growl. It's a growl that sinks a little lower in my body when I recall why I didn't eat last night. Marty. Marty and the way I went home to my villa, dove under my sheets and with my hand between my legs, replayed our mysterious magical sunset together until I came… seven times. It was worth skipping dinner for and I blush at the memory as I listen to Jake.

"Well, the family are hardly going to drive halfway across the island to give me a pay rise. Not to mention how there is no money for a pay rise because of last year…"

"I don't know how many times I need to tell you this, but last year was not your fault. You weren't even working here then." I start pouring coffee in cups.

"It doesn't matter. I told the family I would turn this place around and that's what they hired me to do." Jake places the tray against the wall behind him before sitting.

While Jake is happily working in his dream role as manager of a beautiful, sumptuous destination, it's not without its challenges. Iliovasílema Villas suffered a terrible season last year after it was locked down due to a freak gastrointestinal virus that spread like wildfire through the staff and the guests. It seems even having the most spectacular sunset views on the whole island will do little to eradicate a resort's reputation for being a hotbed for a stomach bug that had people unable to leave their rooms for days. It doesn't help that more than a few photos of the makeshift tent hospital that was erected to treat the worst patients appeared all over social media and on many news outlets.

"And you are doing it, Jake," I say. "Look at how spectacular this place is. The facilities are incredible, the weather has been perfect, and bubble bath debacles aside, all the guests seem happy…"

"All one hundred and twelve of them?" He falls back in a chair. "Jenna, this resort has capacity for three hundred and sixty guests. I am less than half-full."

"It's early season," I offer.

"It's still summer. As you say, the weather is fantastic right now, and actually, this should be one of our busiest times as guests can avoid school holiday surcharges."

"Isn't it someone else's job to get people to make the bookings? Marketing? Sales? PR?" I pile granola and fresh fruit on top of a bowl of yoghurt.

Jake grabs a banana and points it at me as he speaks. "You'd think so but apparently not. All budgets were slashed after last year's fiasco, and the sales team don't get any commission for bookings made so there's no incentive to push hard. I did what I could with the website before I got here, and I asked for budget for social media and SEO, but they don't have it. Last year wiped them out."

"I would have thought they'd find some money from somewhere to try and turn it all around. Especially marketing and PR…"

"I don't blame them." Jake sounds resigned, and I hate it. "Those photos of the hazmat suits and the makeshift hospital tents with the beach in the background… Jesus, you can't unsee that, and you also can't remove the image from the thousands of sites it's stuck on. I know because I tried. Did you know someone even did a forty-two-minute YouTube video analysing an image and saying it was all a hoax? They claimed it had nothing to do with a gastro bug, but rather the resort was lying about the virus, holding guests hostage and then forcing them to spend more money because they had to stay longer. Unbelievable! They zoomed in on the tent and said that it was one we already used for weddings and parties. I mean, as if! What kind of savages do they think we are using a 'tent' for a wedding? They're called marquees, for one thing. We also ended up *giving* guests money as compensation, not charging them. Anyway, this video is all over the review websites and comes up on the front page of Google. It's a bloody nightmare and we can't do anything about it." Having peeled his banana during that short rant, Jake bites a sizeable chunk off the top.

"You keep saying *we*, but it wasn't you, Jake. What happened was unfortunate for the old management and staff, but you also said that they ignored the first few cases of sickness for four days, that they didn't even call a doctor. That's how it got out of hand. And you had nothing to do with that."

As Jake chews the momentum of his jaw slows. "It doesn't matter. This is a make-or-break season. They need to make a profit this year, or they'll have to sell. We need maximum occupancy to make a profit, and I'm not even close to that and currently, the bookings are dire. My budget is so tight. I don't know what to do. I've been waiting so long for an opportunity like this, I have to make it work, Jen. I have to."

I reach to squeeze his hand over the table. "I know, Jakey, and you will. Just give yourself time."

He pauses after munching more banana. "At least having fuck all guests meant I could squeeze you in for this week, and upgrade you," he says with a smile. "It's so good to see you."

"You too," I say and I beam back at him. I recognise so much of myself in him: the unwelcome lack of self-trust, the desire to be cheery and upbeat no matter what, the temptation to find your flaws first before someone else does. We both have good reasons for wanting to shield ourselves from the darkness of the world, but I've learnt in recent years that my shield wasn't as strong or solid as I once thought, and it's hard to see Jake maybe also coming to realise this.

"You know, when this season is over you should take some time off," I say. "*Real* time off. Not just a few weeks holiday at a mate's hotel somewhere."

"Some of us didn't get nice settlements in divorces recently," he says and it's like a light but definite kick in my gut. "And you know I was an idiot with my inheritance, unlike you."

"You weren't an idiot."

"I spent a year in Sydney taking too many recreational drugs, renting a Harbour view apartment I couldn't afford and sleeping with gorgeous men with commitment issues."

"Sounds heavenly," I say. "Maybe I'll sell my house and go try that."

"Don't you dare. That house is your pension, and you still need to add your colour and sparkle to the monochrome vomit Robert inflicted on it. Besides, I thought your plan was to go home and start writing your book. Have you firmed up your idea yet?"

My book. That's what I should be spending my time thinking about, not obsessing over a flirtatious Irishman's intentions.

"No." I swallow down my food. "Not really. Divorce memoirs are so 2010. Mid-life memoirs are even more dated, especially by middle-class white women. And honestly, what I want to write a book about is intimacy. Intimacy and love and sex and desire and connection. But I just don't feel qualified to do that right now."

"Because of the lack of sex," Jake adds.

"And connection, and intimacy, and love," I add, although I don't say desire. There was a lot of desire last night.

I spoon another large mouthful into my mouth, hoping I can then avoid talking more about this with my brother. As he focuses on adding sugar to his coffee, I'm confident I've got away with it.

"Quick question, Jenna?" he asks as he lazily tinkles a teaspoon against the side of his coffee mug.

"Yes?"

"Have you been fucked since Robert?"

I nearly choke on what's in my mouth. My body shakes as I start coughing, loudly.

"Good God, woman. Don't die on me." Jake stands to pass me a glass of orange juice.

I force down whatever is left in my mouth and take a big swig of the juice. "Jakey! What kind of question is that before eight o'clock in the morning?"

"One I've been thinking about asking you for a while," he says with a slight lift of his shoulders as he sits back down.

"Well, I..."

"You haven't, have you? That's totally fine. Heck, it's understandable. And you know I'm not here to judge in any way, shape or form – at least not in real-time in front of your face - but I just think you may feel better about yourself if you got absolutely, utterly, back-breakingly railed."

I am stunned for only a second. "I don't disagree," I say, before needing to clear my throat again.

"Good, so you'll go find this Irish rascal today and finish what you started last night."

Inwardly I groan as I recall the brief messages I sent Jake about the sex I wasn't having with Marty last night. After he'd made a technically inaccurate joke about Irish craic, Jake had asked me if I was okay. I'd told him I was relieved as I had wanted an early night although lying to my brother didn't feel good at all.

"Jenna, you owe it to yourself to have a little fun…" Jake's eyebrows are high and a little ominous.

"It really wasn't a big deal. It was a little flirting and a little talking and then I asked him to come back to my villa and he declined."

"You offered and he declined?" My brother leans back.

"Yes. Twice, actually." I throw salt on my own wounds.

"Twice?" Jake's face says it all. Normally I love how expressive his features are but in this very moment I am not enjoying his crestfallen frown. "What the fuck? Is he a virgin?"

"I highly doubt that as he was in a long-term relationship for a while. By the way, your gaydar was way off. He's bisexual."

"Really?" Jake rolls the R for a second too long.

"His ex was a man." I keep talking, processing the thought as it materialises. "And I think there's a story there."

"Well, there's a story with yours too," Jake says as he finishes his banana. "And I suspect there could still be a story between you and this hot Irish bisexual."

"Marty, his name is Marty," I say as much as an excuse to say his name as anything, as if I may not get another chance. "God, I shouldn't have told you his sexuality. That was very crass of me. Disrespectful too."

"He was disrespectful when he denied you a shag."

I chuckle with my brother. "You are saying all the right wrong things to make me feel better."

"I'm just being honest. Has he seen you? You are almost as lovely-looking as me."

"I'm just confused. What kind of twenty-something-year-old flirts like it's his job and then bails at the last minute? I really thought he was at least semi-attracted to me."

Jake's coffee cup clinks as it lands back on its saucer. "Why do I feel like we have swapped roles here? Normally, I'm the one asking myself unhelpful questions about men and you're quoting from your books and research and generally smart, sensible brain about not hyper-fixating, not giving somebody you don't really know more energy and attention than yourself. What's going on here, Jenna?"

He's right and I'm not going to argue with him but I am going to clarify, more for myself perhaps than him, why my mind is spiralling and why I think that's okay. And then I will move on. I'm determined not to indulge this self-doubt for much longer.

"This is the first time I've felt... certain things for someone else, since Robert, and even with him I didn't feel much for the last few years."

"But you've been on dates..."

"Yes to overpriced restaurants with average food and dull men that didn't flirt with me. With men who had receding hairlines and protruding nose hair and children from previous marriages and probably quite excellent free financial advice but that didn't make me..." I groan. "None of it turned me on."

"Really? None of that turned you on?" Jake fake exclaims.

Suddenly bored and deeply despondent about the state of my romantic life, I shake my head as I sip my coffee. "Can we talk about something else?"

Jake flamboyantly shakes his arm to reveal the watch on his wrist. "Lucky for you, I have to go now and find out if I will live to see another day or if the Bouras' want my intestines for a new lobby light feature."

"Oh, Jake, please let me know how it goes." We both stand and start loading the tray again.

"As long as you promise to do everything in your power to get laid tonight." I am relieved when he is too distracted by tidying up to notice I don't reply but instead lean in to kiss his cheek.

After Jake leaves, I feel an immediate and unwelcome rush of restlessness come over me. It's almost certainly because of what my brother and I were just talking about: my book. Or rather, my dream to write a book. It's been a dream for so long that I've started to think that is all it ever will be. All it ever should be.

As I just told Jake, I don't feel qualified to write a book about love or sex or connection or intimacy when all of the above have been so sorely missing from my life. How can I profess the importance of work and effort and patience in relationships when my husband and I couldn't give each other any of those things? How can I write about intimacy and connection when I let both die slow, painful deaths in my marriage, long before we divorced? How can I write about desire when the first real spark of longing I felt for someone last night was rejected... twice?

While this restlessness is unwanted, it's not an unfamiliar feeling and I have things I can try and do to ease it a little. It's why I quickly change into some clean gym clothes, splash my face with water, pull my hair into a high ponytail and with my room key and a bottle of water in my hand, and my phone and headphones tucked in my sports bra, I make my way to the outdoor gym. It's only a short walk from my villa, as it's also at the very peak of the resort. I'd almost like the walk to be longer as I enjoy filling my lungs with air that's still cool and fresh but I'm approaching the gym in minutes. I check the time and because it's still early I'm hopeful I'll be alone when I get there, just as I was yesterday morning.

"Shit," I hiss to myself when I see that there's somebody already on the only treadmill. I don't always run but when I'm feeling like this – antsy, in my head, a little unnerved by myself – it always does me good to mindlessly pound on the treadmill and feel sweat trickle down my back. The other machines are free, so I quickly decide to do a cycle to warm up before lifting and if I still have the energy after and the treadmill is free, then I'll do a...

"Fuck," I say when I see who is running on the treadmill. I freeze about ten, maybe fifteen metres behind Marty and watch him, trying not to let the way the muscles ripple in his back melt my insides.

Looks like I didn't work this attraction out of my body with those seven orgasms. Despite wanting to stand there and watch him for as long as I can get away with, I force myself to look away. The attraction is still there, absolutely, but so is my embarrassment and that's not the kind of heat I enjoy feeling.

I turn to jog away, but not before my bottle of water slips out of my hand and lands with a loud thump on the gravel near my feet.

Chapter Ten

Marty

I can't believe what I'm seeing.

Admittedly, it's a beautiful sight - her backside round and shapely as she bends down to pick up her bottle - but I'm still a little perplexed about what that beautiful backside is doing. Especially when it starts to sway as Jenna takes quick bouncing steps up the path away from the gym. I hit stop on the treadmill and jump my feet to the sides.

"Are you running away from me?" I call out.

Jenna freezes where she is, one hand raised as if in the beginning of a sprint. Finally, she turns, and I see that the front view of her in her workout clothes is just as good as the back, the shape of her body completely revealed to me in black clingy Lycra.

"Hi!" she says with a limp half-wave as she walks back up the path. The colour in her cheeks is undeniably not from the sun.

"Hey, Usain Bolt." I come off the treadmill and stand with my hands on my hips, watching her.

"I wasn't running away."

"Liar!"

"I forgot something," she tries again.

"Liar!"

"I was just annoyed that someone else was on the treadmill already," she rushes to keep talking. "And I really wanted to do a quick run, so I thought I'd just do it the old-school way."

"Liar!" I bark.

"It wasn't because I saw you," she says, now a few metres away from me.

"Liar," I say, softer, because I'm laughing now and so is she.

"Alright," she says, her hands on her hips, and it does nothing to make me stop wanting to stare at her body. Right now, it's the subtle narrowing of her waist above her generous hips that has me feeling things.

She continues to talk. "Okay, so I *was* running away. But it's also true that I did want to go on the treadmill and well, there's a great big six-foot piece of Irishman currently hogging it."

"Six foot *two*," I say and then I wink because it would be criminal not to. "And I'm sure you agree that two inches can make all the difference."

She shakes her head at me, but still she smiles. "It's not even eight in the morning. Are you really going to start saying things like that already? And," she rakes her eyes up and down my body, "while you're wearing that?"

I'll admit it's not my best look. I'm currently barefoot with only a pair of black cycling shorts and a baseball cap on. My top was discarded thirty minutes ago, and my cap is turned backwards on my head, a head that is probably very sweaty and red thanks to me running immediately after Dad dragged me around mountain climbs for ninety minutes. It seems I'll do anything to avoid a conversation with my mother these days, including burning 1500 calories before mid-morning.

"Unlike some people, I don't run away from a challenge." I point my finger at her. "I rise to the occasion!"

"Well, there's no chance of me missing that," Jenna mutters, but it's loud and clear enough. I watch her lower her gaze to my crotch and slowly lick her upper lip. It's impossible to take my eyes off the slickness it leaves behind, but because I can indeed feel other parts of me reacting - in the most painfully and deliciously ironic way - I turn away and give myself the excuse of reaching for my water bottle.

"I'm sorry. That was possibly a bit too much." Jenna makes that short, sweet coughing sound she did a lot last night.

"Are you done with it?" She nods at the treadmill.

"Your device of torture awaits." I step to the side and squeeze the water bottle above my head, letting the spray wash over me. She blinks her eyes open wider watching me do it, then she looks away. We fall quiet for a few seconds, her staring straight ahead at the view, and me gazing straight ahead at her breasts. I watch them rise and fall right in front of my eyes and it's an effort to lift my eyes to her face.

Not for the first time, I am sorely regretting my choices last night. In fact, I hadn't been able to think about much else for the first half of our dinner after Mum had lectured me about my disappearance. Dad had tried to turn the conversation around by letting me order for everyone, but that only made Maeve moan about not getting what she wanted, even though she hadn't once looked away from her phone to read the menu. More than once I questioned what I was doing there when I could have been licking my way up Jenna's leg, from that maddeningly sexy anklet to her inner thigh.

Thankfully, the meal did improve once the food arrived, because the dishes I'd ordered were all excellent. But then Mum had thanked me profusely as if I'd made them myself and it had almost given me a headache trying to ignore the irritation that itched at me as a result. After our dishes were cleared and teas and coffees were ordered, we'd played cards all together and it was almost fun, even if I kept losing concentration because I was wondering where Jenna was, imagining graphically if not confidently that she was in bed touching herself while thinking about me.

But something else also happened last night. After dinner, after cards, after my father lifted his glass of after-dinner whiskey and gave a brief toast to Arnie that made me smile and shed a few tears, I felt proud. Not proud that I'd turned down a beautiful woman, but proud that I'd given myself time and space to let my attraction become just that, a real, genuine, hope-filled attraction. Not that the now sober and celibate man I am has any idea what to do with it.

Part of me knows leaving Jenna alone in the gym now would be the smart thing to do. I probably need to eat something, and I should definitely shower, but then there's the other part of me that woke up – hard, hot, and hungry - thinking about the way she talked in that cute, clipped English accent, how her anklet

89

caught the last glow of the sunset, and that part of me doesn't want to go anywhere.

"You happy if I keep working out?" I say, moving over to the weights section. Out of the corner of my eye, I see her neck turn as she glances back at me.

"You don't need my permission," she calls out now I'm further away. Her words feel abrupt, but maybe that's just because she's a little out of breath from running.

"Not for working out, I suppose," I say, trying to make light of it because maybe it is a strange thing to ask. Am I treating her differently because I know she's older?

"You crack on," she says. "And yes, I deliberately set you up with that one."

When I hear the laugh in her voice, I feel relief. "I can resist temptation," I say as I choose a set of dumbbells. "Well, some temptation."

I hear a few more giggles and then somehow, we fall into an easy silence as we both work out. The thumping of her feet on the treadmill changes pace every few minutes and I realise she's doing a version of circuit training – sprinting for a few minutes, jogging slower for a few more - and I move through my arms, shoulders and back reps, before getting a mat out to start my stretches. Every now and then, I look over at her, sometimes without even knowing I'm doing it, and on occasion, I watch her for a long chain of seconds. I watch the muscles in her butt and shoulders move, watch her calves strain and her short ponytail swing. Sometimes when I do this, her head is turned over her shoulder and she catches my eye and we smile or laugh. One time she sticks her tongue out at me and I like it far too much.

When she's finished on the treadmill, she cleans the machine and then comes close to where I am on the floor, actually doing the stretches I normally skip. I realise she's lining up weights for some lifts and I watch as much out of curiosity as I do for the shine on her skin that the perspiration has created. I want to lick it off.

She does a few sets of squats and lunges with weights in her hands, and there's something about the ease with which she moves and the way her breath slows rather than speeding up that tells me it's easy, what she's doing. Possibly too easy.

"You can lift more than that, can't you?" I say, and I move to kneel up. "You want me to spot you?"

She smiles at me down there in that position and I entertain the possibility she likes this view as much as I do.

"I wouldn't mind doing some deadlifts," she says, and she stacks up the hand weights before moving to the bar. "Come on then."

We get her a total weight of 70kg including the barbell which seems a lot for her, if easy for me. She moves over to the ground just outside the concrete platform we're standing on, and she rubs her hands on the sand and rocks there.

"I forgot my gloves," she says as something of an explanation and she holds up hands that are now a pinky-grey, dusted with the sandy soil there. "And my barbelt, but I won't do too much."

"So where do you want me to stand?" I watch her get into position.

"I think you know," she says without looking at me. Instead, she gives the ground she's grinding her feet down into a wry smile.

"Behind your masterpiece of an arse, right?"

She looks up over her shoulder at me and her eyes are so golden brown they steal a breath from me.

"Something like that," she says. "But honestly, you don't need to stand that close. Deadlifts don't really need a spotter."

What if I want to? I think to myself, and I would have said it out loud, only she seems so focused on the task in hand right now. Maybe being sober helps me know when there's a time and place for flirting, and when there's not.

After rubbing her hands together again, Jenna bends down to touch the bar, and I force my eyes up and away from the curve of her butt. Keeping her knees bent, she slowly pushes up to standing.

"That was too easy," I say, expecting her to move and get some more plates.

"Five more reps." She bends down again, and I get back in position.

After those five, she does indeed move to add another 10kg, and after that another 8kg. As she does six reps of each, I don't just get to look at the curve of her backside, but the soft valley of her back, deep and defined even through her top.

I would never call her body muscular, but it's sculpted, it's toned, and it's all feminine strength. And her skin, it's the perfect shade of roasted peach, kissed with syrup-coloured freckles everywhere; on the backs of her arms, across her shoulders and even in a few places on her neck. I wonder if they can be found further up her legs, along her thighs, on her hips...

"You still with me?" She moves to get two 2.5kg plates and attaches them efficiently. "This will be my last round."

When her second-to-last rep is done, she seems suddenly out of breath and gasps a little.

"Too much?" I ask.

"Just tired," she says, but doesn't elaborate. Nor does she move to do her last rep.

"You can do this," I say, and I clap my hands together.

"What was that?" She laughs and hangs her head low, shaking it.

"Isn't that what I'm supposed to do? Cheer you on! Big you up!"

"Just stay close," she says.

Oh, I will.

"You got this!" I call out.

"And quiet, please."

"Right-oh." I bend low only half a second after she does. She does indeed seem to need more of her to lift the bar this time and at one point I worry she's not going to do it, or that maybe she'll hurt herself. I inch a little closer, close enough that the front of my thighs are lined up behind hers. A moment later, the bar is up and she's standing straight, the back of her - all of it - pressed against the front of me - all of it. She holds her lift a few seconds longer than she held the previous ones, then she drops it with a loud thud. But she doesn't move, and it could be my imagination, but it feels like she applies a little more pressure, leaning back against me, seeking me out with her back and butt and I'm there, I'm right there, ready and warm and hard and...

"Hey! Streak of piss!" I hear an instant mood-killer of a voice.

"Fuck!" I hiss.

"Why are you fecking hiding from us here?" Maeve is marching towards us. I step back as quickly as Jenna shifts forward. Maeve is close enough now to see Jenna. "Oh, hello. Again."

"Hi," Jenna says and then she turns to me and adds in a whisper, "Hot sister."

"What are you guys doing?" Maeve's nose wrinkles, like she's just come across a bad smell.

"Weights," I say at the same time Jenna says, "Lifting."

"You don't lift weights," Maeve says with a snort.

"No, but she does." I point at Jenna. "And she's strong too."

"That's cool." Maeve gives a shrug that will appear uninterested to Jenna, but I know it's a serious indicator that she's impressed. Maeve curls her upper lip as she gives me a once over. "Could you put some clothes on, please? I don't want to taste my breakfast again."

It's Jenna's turn to snort now.

"It's got to be over twenty-five degrees already and I'm covered in multiple layers of sweat, so no."

"Well, Ma wants you back at the villa," she says, as she starts fiddling with the exercise bike's seat which is much too tall for her.

"Bollocks," I mumble.

"I'm all done," Jenna says. She grabs her phone, headphones, and a bottle of water. She doesn't look at me when she speaks, "Thanks for spotting me."

"Is that what you call it?" Maeve snickers as she continues to mess around with the bike seat unsuccessfully. "You better head back, brother dearest. Ma is not happy, even despite a double yoga session with twenty minutes of silent meditative breathing. Dad wasn't even allowed to flush the loo during it. I mean, look at what I've resorted to so as to escape it. I am actually wearing all this gear I get for free, giving myself a savage wedgie and obscene camel toe."

"Jesus, Maeve. Do you have to?" I shake my head.

"She's right." Jenna walks backwards away from us, much too quickly for my liking. "Lycra is not a friend of all parts of the female anatomy, but also at the same time, embrace it, Maeve. You look amazing, camel toe and all!"

She turns and then shuffles off in a light jog.

"Jenna, wait!" I call out.

"Oi! Don't forget your manky sweat rag down here." Maeve points at my discarded top.

"I'll be back in a minute, for Christ's sake," I spit at my sister as I race to catch up with Jenna, all the while very pleased to have another chance to see her from behind. "Jenna, wait."

She stops at the peak of the trail that joins up with the pathway that takes you to either side of the hill. The sun shines down on her. When she squints at me, with a saluting hand shading her eyes, the sunlight glows around her like a halo.

"What's up with your mum that she needs all that meditation and yoga?" she asks when I reach her.

"It's a long, long story," I say. "And I really don't want to talk about my mother. I want to ask you what time we'll meet tonight."

She looks away. "You said sunset," she replies quietly.

"I did." I nod. "But what if I wanted to be all kinds of wild and firm that up with a pre-arranged time?"

Jenna looks at the ground. "I'll see you at sunset," she says, and then she turns and walks away.

I watch and wait until she's made it over the crest of the hill, presuming she's taking the path to her villa, which must be on the opposite side of the resort to ours, right on the top corner. It's a relief, if I'm honest. The thought of her crossing paths with my mother is not a pleasant one.

I head back to the gym area and see my sister still struggling with the bike seat. "Come here, you muppet," I say, nudging her out of the way.

"Jesus! You stink!" She pinches her nose. I tut and drop the seat so it lines up with her hip.

"There you go."

"Well, thanks, I suppose." Maeve climbs on and puts her feet in the brackets on the pedals, but she doesn't start moving them. "What do I do now?"

"Jesus Christ, Maeve, you cycle. You don't even have to steer, surely you can cope with that."

"Haha," she deadpans and slowly starts to move the pedals. "Go talk to Mum. Clear the air, for feck's sake. We're on holiday and I am bored of all this aggro when I'm supposed to shoot sunshine-filled happy holiday clips that make my followers just the right amounts of envious and happy for me. Speaking of which, you're still going to help me today, right?"

"Yes, I'm a man of my word. Unfortunately." I pick up my cycling cleats, my top and water bottle. "After lunch, right?"

"Yeah," she says. "Jesus, exercise is for dryshites."

"Enjoy," I say and give her a wave as I start walking off, taking a swig of water.

"You better not mention Mrs Robinson to Mum," Maeve calls out.

"Mrs Robinson?" I stop and turn back.

"*The Graduate*, you uncultured swine. A 1967 film about a younger man and an older woman. But I suppose it's not a 2000s Jude Law rom-com so why would you know about it?"

"Nah. I'm more of a Matthew McConaughey fan myself. Besides, Jenna's not that much older."

Maeve gives me one of her famous eyebrow raises. "How old *is* she?"

I hope my shrug looks more nonchalant than I feel. "I don't know. She hasn't told me."

Maeve grunts with amusement. "Hmm. And when was the last time you heard Mum tell someone her age in public?"

"Jenna is not the same age as Mum."

"But Jenna *is* older than you, Marty. You can see that, right?"

"Yes, I am aware."

"And Mum is not going to like that," Maeve adds, her eyes on me now. "I can kind of understand why."

"What do you mean?"

95

"You're supposed to be taking things slow, calming down, getting your shit together." Her words are blunt but there is a cautious kindness in her eyes.

I step closer, my shoulders tense. "I'm sober. I live at home. I do whatever she tells me to do, like coming on this bleeding family holiday. Isn't that enough?"

"The holiday is hardly a hardship, dickhead. And drinking was a symptom, remember? Not the cause," she adds.

"I fucking hate when you're smarter than me." I point my bottle at her.

"I'm not. Nowhere close. There's a reason all I can do is post videos of myself and flog athleisure wear to people who will never actually wear it to work out. Ha! Like me!"

"We'll have words about that attitude later, missy, but I suppose right now I'd better go face the music, fight the dragon, enter the torture chamber, whatever." I add hand gestures to every word.

"Ma does love you," my sister says. It's so unlike her to say something like that it gives me pause. I look at her, waiting for eye contact or just some kind of clarification from her side, but she's back typing away on her phone.

"Yeah, yeah. Tough love," I mutter.

"Love *is* tough, it's what makes it last, I guess," she says with only the briefest look up. "Now piss off, ya melter, I've got hundreds of DMs to work through."

"Tough love you too," I call out and jog home, taking the opposite path to Jenna.

Chapter Eleven

Marty

"Ma! I'm back," I call out. I want to get this over and done with.

"Aiden!" Mum walks through the double doors from our pool and terrace. She's wearing a floaty sort of dress over her swimwear and a wide-brimmed hat that all but drowns her small features. While quite a bit shorter than Maeve, Mum has the same slim figure and long hair, although it's the dark shade of brown mine is. "How was the gym? Did you stretch?"

"Fine, and yes," I say, walking to the fridge to get another bottle of water.

"Breakfast is out on the terrace. I managed to save three rashers of bacon from your father's greedy fingers."

"Where is Da?" I turn my back on her, busying myself making a coffee.

"Just finishing up after a shower." She reaches for a mug. "Shall I make you that?"

"No, Ma, it's fine. I can do it," I say.

"Your father said you had a great ride. I'm so glad you're here and able to do that with him," she says, but I don't reply.

As I push a button and listen to the coffee machine whir into life, I wonder, not for the first time, why her smile, her questions, her heartfelt concern for me aggravates me so much.

"I'm not sure why you had to go to the gym as well," she continues. I close my eyes. "Your father said you covered a lot of ground, and you need your rest, and I'd ordered breakfast specially, and... "

"I wanted to go," I say through gritted teeth.

"I know but it would have been nice if we'd all eaten together," she says, unperturbed.

"We had dinner together last night."

"The prodigal son returns," Dad says, walking into the room wearing swim shorts and a T-shirt. He has a newspaper under his arm and his hair is still damp from the shower. Giving me a quick wink, he reaches for an apple from the fruit bowl. It is funny how he can say whatever he wants to me – often much worse things than my mother says - and it doesn't come close to irritating me in the same visceral way.

"Want a coffee, Da?" I ask, hoping his arrival will end my mother's line of questioning.

"No, thanks," he says, walking to the fridge and grabbing a beer.

"But before dinner, Aiden," Mum says, edging closer to me. "You still didn't really explain where you were all yesterday afternoon."

I pull the cup out from the coffee machine and walk away, heading towards Dad now that I see him sitting at the table on the terrace. When I hear my mother's footsteps behind me I finally respond. "Ma, I need to be able to do things by myself sometimes. You can't expect us to spend all day every day together this week."

"I don't mind you doing your own thing while we're here. I just worry..."

"That I'll drink," I finish for her, sitting next to my father as if he'll provide protection.

"No," she says after a beat.

"And by no, you mean yes?" I uncover the plate she's made for me and fuck, it looks good. Bacon, two fried eggs, toast, roasted tomatoes and some fun-looking potato and feta dish that has spinach, oregano and rosemary in it. Yum.

"Okay, yes, a bit. And what about other things..."

I grab some cutlery while rolling my eyes. "It's a five-star resort for honeymooners and rich retirees, I doubt it's a hotbed for hallucinogenics and poppers."

"You'd be surprised," my Dad says from behind his newspaper.

"James, you're not helping," my mother says pointedly. "It would be useful if you could tear yourself away from the sports pages to support me a bit here."

My father's sigh is so dramatic in its force and volume that it gets a smile out of me.

"How do you need my help, my darling?" he says, folding up the newspaper.

"Can you talk to Aiden about what this week is all about? About our wishes?"

"Jesus, Mary, and the twelve disciples." My father's head droops like it's suddenly a lot heavier.

"Or explain how we're not keeping an eye on him, rather just wanting to spend some time together," my mother adds. Her hand reaches for mine across the table. Her touch isn't exactly unwelcome, but my skin still bristles.

"I know, Mum, but I also think you need to trust me. With the drinking thing, especially."

She sighs. "Honestly, you're right. I know it's more my problem than yours. I think I feel guilty for bringing you somewhere where alcohol is well, everywhere..."

"Mum, I work in a bar, six nights a week."

"I know, but your uncle is there, and everyone at work knows... about... about..."

"About me spending the final six months of last year absolutely wasted, shagging my way around the Balearics until I drunk-drove a scooter into a wall and ended up in hospital with a punctured lung?" I finish, and silence falls.

"Yes, that," Mum says eventually, her lips pursed.

"It *was* a bit irresponsible of you, son," my dad speaks up and I look at him. His eyes are straining to read the crossword clues on the paper now folded up some distance in front of him. I'm not sure if it's my exhaustion, grief, or the reminder of what a royal fuck up I've been, but his light-heartedness and defiantly upbeat sarcasm quickly morphs into something that infuriates me almost as much as my mother's interrogations.

"Well, it's not every day your boyfriend and best mate dies of a rare blood cancer," I say, and I'd almost be proud of getting the words out if I didn't sound so viciously bitter.

Dad doesn't say anything, but he does hold my gaze and give me a quick half-nod.

"We know why it happened." Mum ends the short silence. "Well, some of it. Can't say I would have done it, all the same."

"Mum, your version of rebelling is skipping a book club meeting."

She leans forward. "I only did that once and it was because I read the wrong book! You'd be amazed how many books were written about women on trains that year."

I groan as I swallow a mouthful of egg. "The point is, I know I fucked up in Ibiza and I think I also know why you invited me on this holiday, or rather, why you insisted I came," I say.

"Because we want you to have a holiday. We see how hard you're working. And it's your birthday in a few days," she adds, like it's an afterthought, which I suspect it is.

"And you think if I was at home, alone, I'd do something stupid like go and get drunk or high."

"No, darling, we..."

"Yes, that's exactly what we thought," Dad cuts in, his hands inching closer to the newspaper.

"James!"

"You always say we have to be honest with each other. So, let's be honest." He turns from Mum to me. "We do still worry you'll go off the rails again. And yes, we thought this week would be a trigger." Dad looks back at Mum. "Is that the right word? Trigger?"

"Yes, well done, darling." My mum drops my hand to pat his arm, but with her other hand she whisks the newspaper further away from him.

"Then I'll be honest with you," I say with a sigh. "I nearly had a drink last night, but I didn't. I didn't. And honestly, in general, I don't miss drinking. Really, I don't."

"Personally, I've never thought you had a drinking problem, son," my dad says.

"Says the man drinking a beer at nine o'clock in the morning." My mother points at the bottle in his hand.

"What? I'm on holiday and we rode nearly seventy kilometres earlier." He toasts me with the bottle and I jovially return it with my coffee cup.

"I get why you don't want me to drink," I turn to Mum, "and frankly, I don't want to drink for the same reasons. I know I have to feel all the shitty things that I was trying to run away from when I went AWOL. And I am. Sort of. I'm working on it. I may not always show it to you guys, but I am."

Mum takes a moment before she speaks again which should have been my first clue. "So last night, before dinner, where were you?"

"I was here in the resort," I say sounding like the smartass I'm trying to be.

"Well, that was assumed but you were gone all afternoon and no one can stay in the gym that long, and why didn't you come home with Maeve after she found you?"

I swallow before speaking. Do I tell her the truth? That I met this really interesting woman and she made me laugh, a lot, and I'm not sure I'll ever forget the way her skin glowed in the last licks of the daylight as the sun went down…

No, best not tell her that. Best tell a whopping great lie instead.

"I ended up meeting the hotel manager in the bar. Got talking to him. Had a few drinks - *mocktails* before your blood pressure peaks - I watched the sun go down, and then I came to dinner."

"The hotel manager? What's he like?" My mother's interest is piqued now, and I internally applaud my own brilliance.

"Nice. Gay. Arse looks great in linen shorts."

"Oh, okay," my mother stutters.

"I'm teasing. I don't fancy him."

"He must be too old for you too, surely," Dad adds, and I choke on my mouthful of coffee.

"You can't say anything about that," my mother says tilting her head back so her hat lifts as she looks at Dad. It's almost impossible to notice the ten years between them now, but I do remember some kids having questions when my dad's hair went grey a lot quicker than their parents' did. I never saw it as a big deal. They loved each other and they've always been good parents. In some ways too good.

"Fair enough." Dad gives her a wink that she blushes at, which I try to ignore.

"Anyway," Mum refocuses on me, "I wanted to also ask you about your meds."

My skin is suddenly a lot tighter all over my body.

"You said yesterday that you've stopped taking them," she continues.

"Yeah, I did," I say, recalling how I blurted that out in one of the few stressful conversations we shared on the journey to Crete.

"Why?"

"Because... because I hate taking them. They make me feel broken," I say, and I know I am, but I don't want the reminder every morning and every night.

"That's not what they mean. If anything, they mean the opposite," she says and she swallows, pausing. "Are you sure that's a good idea? It's not even been six months and often that's when they actually start to work. You know when I was on Prozac after your sister, it took a few months for me to start feeling better and then, when I came off it, I had to do it over a long period of time."

"I know, Ma."

"When did you stop?"

"Last week," I reply, my eyes on my plate even though I'm just moving the food around it.

"Did you bring them with you?"

"Yeah," I say, and I'm ashamed to admit that I did it so that I could have them on my nightstand for her to see and assume I was still taking them.

"Are you sleeping okay, since coming off them?"

"Yeah, I'm sleeping enough."

"That's bullshit. I saw your light on at two o'clock in the morning," Dad says.

"What were you doing up then?" Mum asks Dad as she takes off her hat and smooths her hair.

"Man's gotta pee," Dad says. "Especially an old man like me."

"Nothing to do with those nightcaps before bed," Mum mutters. "So you're not really sleeping properly. Why don't you keep taking the mirtazapine then? Just do a half dose, about an hour before bed."

"Isn't that the anti-anxiety one? I don't have anxiety." Depression, grief, addictive behaviour, a little bit of trauma, sure. But not anxiety. I know the worst can happen. It already has.

"Well, you could try the venlafaxine instead. A small dose of that every morning would help you have a bit more energy and bounce in your step during the day," Mum explains. I hate how she knows so much about this.

"My energy is fine. Dad could barely keep up with me this morning."

Dad comes back to life. "Absolute bollocks. I was dragging you up the inclines."

"Well, I didn't see you in the gym after when I was running a sub-30-minute six kilometres!" I know I'm inviting my mother to comment on my excessive exercise, but it's worth it to have this competitive banter with my father. This is what we've always done. It's one of a few things I'm happy to still be doing with him, even though so much has changed in my relationship with my parents.

Predictably, Mum interjects. "You need to be careful with your heart." She leans over, her tone more scared than scathing. "I've read too many stories about young men having heart attacks after running too fast or doing too much sport."

"My heart is fine," I say, and of course, it feels like a lie. Reverting to old Marty, I make my bottom lip turn down and pretend to wipe away tears from my eyes. "Well, the muscle part of it, anyway."

"Would you maybe try the pills again?" Mum shifts in her chair, uncomfortable with my dark humour as she always is. "Like I mentioned, you could try taking..."

"I heard what you said." I raise my voice. I'm bored of talking about this. It's eaten up most of the high I felt after the exercise and seeing Jenna again.

"So, you'll do it?" Mum asks, hesitant but still determined.

"Whatever. I'll do it." I ready myself to stand as a surprising bit of relief seeps in. Thinking about yesterday's tears in the pool, my need for a drink, and my fairly aggressive flirtations with Jenna last night, I realise I could do with having those extremes a bit more under control, especially if I am going to spend a bit more time with her. I really hope I do get to spend more time with her.

"Okay, one more thing," Mum says, and reaches for my hand as I come around the table, closer to her. I hold my breath until she speaks again. "What do you want to do for your birthday?"

"Mum, I'm really not fussed..."

"Bullshit," Dad says. "You love birthdays."

I used to love birthdays. But that was before.

On my birthday last year, Arnie had literally just died, and it was the first day my hours weren't going to be filled with the immediate aftermath of his death. I'd spent the previous few days with his family helping them liaise with the funeral directors and just staying with Arnie until they collected his body. My dad and I then helped his father clear out all the hospice equipment we'd been loaned, while my mum made sure his mother at least drank water and a little soup whenever she emerged from her semi-comatose state. I've never heard worse sounds than the ones Arnie's mother made sobbing in those first few days after his passing and I doubt I ever will. We had known it was imminent, but I knew from the web of pain that spread across my own body after he took his final breaths that no amount of forewarning or time can stop that kind of anguish. That was why it wasn't the noises she made that were so frightening, it was the knowledge I could easily have made them myself.

On my birthday last year, I began drinking at lunchtime. I think I stopped sometime in October during a very brief sober week in Ibiza as the season ended and I tried to get a grip on a proper job. As for the birthdays before last year, I was always with Arnie. *Those* were the birthdays I loved.

"I can't really make you a cake this year, of course," Mum continues. "But I bet the kitchen staff here could do a much better job of it than I can. Did you get the manager's name? Maybe I'll go and ask him."

"Ma, I don't want a fuss," I say.

"Then what do you want?"

"I don't know. An afternoon on the beach. Some good Greek food. And a couple of lines of coke and a magnum of champagne, of course," I say with an over-the-top wink.

"Not funny!" Mum swipes at me with her hat.

"It was a bit funny," Dad says. Somehow, he has the newspaper and the sudoku back in front of him. "And I'm up for it."

"Of course you are," Mum says, and she's got the pink back in her cheeks and a softness in her eyes. "We can certainly try and do the first part. Do you at least trust me to organise something nice for you?"

I wave my hand at our view. "Mum, we're in Greece. The resort is incredible. The sun is shining all day every day. You could literally stick a candle in a plate of *dolmades* and I'll be happy."

"That's all I want, Aidey." She leans over to hold my hand. "Jesus, would you go and have a shower though now. You stink!"

I give them the grunt of discontent they expect as I circle the table, lifting my arms and bringing my chest close so they can get a full nose of my scent.

"Oh feck off, will you." My father slaps my stomach as my mother pinches her nose and clamps her mouth shut, both chuckling to themselves.

I walk to the bathroom knowing I've made them laugh and it makes me feel better, good almost. With that in my mind, I feel duty-bound to the promise I made to my mum a few minutes ago, so I find my pills, pop one in my mouth and swallow it down with a mouthful of water from the tap. Then I strip and shower, because Jesus Christ, I really do fucking stink.

The Second Sunset

"A sunset is the sun's fiery kiss to the night."

- Crystal Woods

Chapter Twelve

Jenna

Sunset is less than an hour away and it feels like its magic is already close. My body and my hands are moving without me controlling them. I'm not thinking, just doing. It's nice to be out of my head and into my... heart? No, that's not it. That's not what's guiding me to step into the shower, wash the sun cream off my skin and shave more of my body than I have in years. It's not my heart that prompts me to moisturise every inch of my skin from head to toe, and then pull on the best underwear I brought with me. It's not my heart that chooses a floaty denim summer dress and sprays an intoxicating amount of perfume on my neck, between my breasts and on my wrists, which I then rub together. It's not my heart that has me smiling at my reflection in the mirror as I apply my make-up and brush my hair.

It's not my heart, it's my pussy.

I'm horny and my pussy is in charge, which feels glorious. We have always made a great team.

Because, yes, I'm going. I'm going to meet Marty at sunset.

Bumping into Marty this morning at the gym has done little to douse the flames of desire I feel for him. And perhaps more pleasingly, the way he was with me – playful, eager, as flirtatious as last night – makes me think that he will show up tonight.

So I'm horny, and very possibly onto a sure thing. A sure holiday fling. God, it's been years since I had a holiday fling and suddenly, I want it so very badly. So badly that I'm rushing to fill my bag with the things I need until a familiar lurch in my stomach stops me in my tracks.

"Oh, for fuck's sake," I say to myself as I run to the bathroom.

Because I'm not just horny and possibly onto a sure thing. I'm also very nervous. And when I have any kind of jitters, I have nervous poos. It's not my finest attribute, but nobody's perfect. At least it's happening now, I think as I go do what I need to do, all the while chuckling at myself. Once I'm sure my stomach is going to behave, I grab my bag and leave.

When I get to the bar, I allow myself to feel a slight pang of disappointment that Marty is not already there, waiting for me in that same position at the bar when he ordered me a drink and gave me an indecent thumbs-up. But then I lift my eyes to the horizon and see there is still time before the sunset.

With my confidence level somewhat intact, I rush to get one of the few available tables left and then try to get a staff member's attention. When I do, I don't order a drink for Marty, just in case. It is one thing to be sitting in a bar and possibly looking like you're waiting for someone when they don't show up. It's quite another to be in a bar, waiting for someone with two drinks on your table and one is untouched, confirming your sad reality.

But still, I order a virgin raspberry mojito for myself because I don't like the idea of drinking alcohol if Marty isn't going to. Also, if tonight is going to go where I hope it goes, I want to be sober; I want to feel it all.

It would be a lie to say that I haven't spent most of the day imagining the things Marty and I could do together. It would also be an untruth if I said the urge to touch myself hadn't dominated most of my thoughts since I saw him in the gym, the defined muscles of his torso on show and his tight buttocks frighteningly biteable in his cycling shorts. But I resisted temptation and am paying the price now as I feel the heat throb between my legs. Thirsty from all these thoughts, I bring my drink up to my mouth and suck on the straw, hard.

"Hi, Jenna." A man's voice says next to me. It's not an Irish accent.

"Hi, Lionel." My brother's colleague is standing awkwardly in front of me.

"Your brother wants me to buy you a drink," he says. "But of course, I'm not going to buy it. I'll get it on the staff tab. And I probably won't have one myself as I'm working until midnight and alcohol always makes me so sleepy, but he wants me to keep you company while you... while you..."

"Wait for the man who's probably stood me up?"

"He didn't... I..." Lionel's brow furrows in far too many places.

"Oh, Lionel, I'm sorry. Sit down." I tap the chair next to me.

Lionel sits next to me, and I take a moment to look at his face. He's a handsome Black man with soft features – a rounded nose, big dark eyes, a full-lipped mouth that breaks into the brightest smiles – and I wonder not for the first time if my brother finds him attractive. He should.

"Why are you sorry?" He frowns.

"I'm being rude to you," I say.

"I don't think so," he replies. "If I was being stood up, I'd be rude to everybody." His eyes open wide. "Not that you're being stood up."

I manage to laugh a little then, if only to reassure him. "It's possible I am, and if so, I will need you and my brother to help me avoid him at all costs for the following four days."

"You can depend on us." He nods and gives me one of his radiant grins.

"How do you like working with my brother, Lionel?" I ask, hoping we can talk about something that takes my mind further away from the fact that every passing moment, as the sun dips lower and lower, really does suggest Marty isn't coming.

He drops eye contact with me then and I can't help but read between the lines when he speaks. "I like it a lot. I've learnt so much from him already, and it's only been six weeks."

"He can be a bit of a ball-buster though, am I right?"

Lionel squints at me before he laughs too. "He's firm and direct. I appreciate that."

"I'm sure he appreciates you too," I say.

"You think?" His eyes open again and his lips part, waiting for validation. *Oh, Lionel, I'm on to you.*

Discovering this blossoming bud of attraction Lionel possibly has for my brother has me feeling things that are unexpectedly soothing for my current predicament. So, Marty and I are not to be, but who knows what lies in my future? If I felt attraction like this to Marty, who says I can't feel it again for someone else? It's a scrappy crumb of comfort, but a comfort all the same.

"You know what, Lionel," I say slowly. "I greatly appreciate you keeping me company, but I think I just want to watch the sunset by myself."

"You sure?" he asks.

"Yes, it's a beautiful night," I say. *And I'm feeling brave*, I want to add. I feel stupid, yes – for getting my hopes up, for feeling almost convinced he would show - but I also feel brave. Brave enough to be okay if he doesn't. Brave enough to sit here alone and watch the sunset, which isn't as colourful or as dramatic as last night, but is just as captivating, maybe more so because the colours are more subtle, a neat ombre blend of pinks and golds, forcing me to look closer for changes, making me pay attention and be more mindful. Glancing out at the beach area ahead, I see a couple have stolen our idea from last night and are reclining on sun loungers staring at the sunset. I feel strangely possessive, but still, I smile at them. The sun is minutes away from diving into the sea, and while part of me is ready to watch it alone, I know I will do so reminiscing about how that was Marty and I last night.

I have to get used to this. I have to get used to being alone. Alone. Not lonely, alone.

Lionel says goodbye and as he walks away, I allow myself one last look around the rear of the bar, scanning faces and searching bodies. But he's not there. Marty's not coming.

"It's okay," I promise myself, my ears needing to hear the words as much as my mouth needs to say them. "It's going to be okay."

Chapter Thirteen

Marty

I dream of Arnie.

There's no plot, no action, no vivid scene playing out but he's there. We're together. I can feel his hair under my hand, his skin on mine. I can smell him, a soft and spicy floral scent that I would breathe in by pressing my nose to his collar bone, the curve of his neck and the corners of his groin. I don't know where we are but it's him as he was, before he became ill. He's solid and strong and his skin is tanned, so it must be summer which will make him happy because he loved sunny days the most. I can hear his voice, a little lighter in pitch than my own, but just as husky because he was the only person who ever talked just as much as me, if not more. As I start to wake, I feel that plummeting realisation that it's just a dream and I do all I can to stay in it, to stay with him. However, lucidity continues to pull on me and I know it will be over soon. Before I go completely, I beg him to laugh for me. Please, just let me hear him laugh. Let me see him smile, I plead. I just want to know he's okay.

Are you happy, Arnie? Are you happy?

I wake up with an ache in my chest, the kind that makes you question if you can take another breath. It's dull and sharp at the same time, heavy and electric, pulling my ribcage in and pushing my heart out. I don't even open my eyes fully because I can't. All I can do is roll over, gather the sheets up in a fist that I hold near my sternum and wait for it to pass.

Eventually, it eases but I don't feel much relief. Crushed, exhaustion washes over me as I finally push up to sitting and then start to get my bearings.

I'm in my bedroom in the holiday villa. The curtains are closed, but I swear I didn't do that. Their blackout material keeps the room dark, but there's still a little light creeping through the gaps at the floor and in the middle where they aren't fully closed. There's also a glass of water on the bedside table and two paracetamols. *Ma.* And there's my phone. I reach for it and check the time.

"Shit!"

I jump up and pull the curtains open. The pinks and oranges in the sky make me feel sick. I can't see the sun from this angle, but I know that while it hasn't set yet, it's soon. Too soon.

"Fecking fuckface fucker!" I shout. I fell asleep. I fell asleep for a long time. Hours.

"What the fuck?" My sister opens the door and marches in. "You just ruined my audio recording with that outburst!"

"I'm so fucking late!" I yell at her as I stand and pull on my shorts and then can't find my T-shirt on the floor next to them. Just as well, I should probably wear a clean one. I rush to my suitcase which I haven't yet unpacked. I sniff my armpits quickly and while I'm not horrified, I'm still annoyed I can't shower or do my hair or not be the disaster that I am.

"Late for what?" Maeve asks.

I pause. "Doesn't matter," I say and find a different shirt to the one I was looking for. It will have to do.

"Are you meeting Mrs Robinson?"

"Where are Mum and Dad?"

"On the balcony. Gin o'clock." She nods at the sunset outside.

Pulling a shirt on, I run to the en-suite bathroom, squeeze a blob of toothpaste on my tongue and push it around my mouth.

"Listen," I say to Maeve after I spit. "You know how I literally got RSI recording all those videos for you this afternoon? Well, I need to cash in that favour. Right now."

"Are you meeting her? The older woman?"

I close my eyes and sigh. "Yes, and I'm going to be gone for a while. Can you tell Mum and Dad?"

"You want me to tell them that you're going on a date with a forty-something year old?"

"She's not forty-something. Or she could be. I don't know. And I don't care. Tell them I'm having a drink with someone and-" I pause. "Wait! Tell them I've gone looking for the hotel manager. For a drink. And I'm going to ask him about birthday cakes. Yes, say that. But tell them that I'll not be back for dinner so you can all eat without me."

"They're not going to believe that." Maeve crosses her arms over her chest.

"Right now, I don't give a flying fuck. I just want to get down to the beach before the sun goes down." I race back to the bedside table and shove my phone in my pocket, and as I do, I'm relieved to feel the card of the villa key. One less thing to look for.

"Jesus, you are like a man on a mission," my sister says as I rush past her towards the door.

"I'm a fucking mess," I say and rub a hand back and forwards through my hair.

"Yeah, that's not helping at all." She wrinkles her nose at me.

"Piss off," I say as I reach for the door. "Oh, wait. I need you to cover for me. I don't mean that. Don't piss off. You're great."

"I'll keep the parents sweet," she says with a smile that calms me, just for half a second before I race out of the door and start running.

"Fuck!" I call out to nobody when I realise I don't have shoes on. But I don't stop, in fact, I sprint a little faster.

It takes no time, not really, maybe just a minute, because I'm running downhill after all, but every second feels like an hour because the sky is changing colour all the time – from a blossoming pink to a glowing copper - and as the pathway winds down around the villas I start to catch glimpses of the sun itself, hanging just above the sea as if it's going to touch any moment now. It's only as I enter the indoor area of the lobby that I realise how ridiculous I look. I'm barefoot, half-awake, out of breath and wide-eyed in panic as I realise how likely it is that she won't be there.

I really fucking hope she's still there.

Chapter Fourteen

Jenna

A quarter of the sun is gone when I see a figure out of the corner of my eye, but I keep my gaze fixed ahead of me.

"Room for a big fat eejit?"

Marty's here. He came.

But he's late.

"You know what, I'm not sure there is," I say. My stomach is flipping in a way that doesn't feel unpleasant, it's almost wistful. I haven't felt this sort of nervous excitement since I was a child.

He's late. Almost too late.

But he came.

The next thing I know, there is a soft thwack as his body crashes into the chair next to mine.

"What are you doing?" I ask, looking at him now and hating how my body reacts to his chiselled face, the stretch of his shoulders, the veins I can see in his forearms and hands. I take it all in in seconds. How is that even possible?

"Sitting down to watch the end of the sunset," he says. "And then I'm going to apologise to you. No, actually I think grovel is more accurate for what I'm going to do."

Because I'm at a loss for words, I turn my head back to the horizon too, and without saying anything else, we watch as the golden globe melts into the sea and the surrounding sky lights up red and orange and pink, almost as if in protest. When the sun is completely submerged, I turn my focus to the space it inhabited, looking for a green light, all the while wondering if Marty is doing the same.

"So, funny story..." he begins, and I already know I'm going to listen. I'm going to sit and hear what he has to say and then I'm going to see how it makes me feel.

"Arnie," he says then stops. I blink and wait for him to continue. "Arnie was my best friend and then, for the last three years, my boyfriend. We fell in love while travelling together. Well, technically that's not true. I'm pretty sure we were in love long before that but he's a stubborn fool and I was still in denial about how boys gave me boners. Anyway, just over a year after we got back from travelling – he was studying English at Trinity and I was doing Culinary Arts at a tech college – he became ill. Out of nowhere, he was getting all these bruises and nosebleeds and his skin was itchy all over. When he started to get fevers and would often sleep for more than twelve hours, he went to the doctors. A few days after that, we knew it was leukaemia."

"My God," I say, the air feeling thinner.

Marty keeps his eyes on mine as he talks. "Yeah, massive great big pile of shit. But there was some hope and we did everything we could. After six months we thought he was going to beat it." Marty looks down briefly. "After a year, we knew he wouldn't and that was when we moved into his parents' place together. He held on for another long, painful but very special eight months. I was holding his hand when he passed... which was a year ago yesterday."

My head clouds with confusion. I don't know what I was expecting him to tell me, but it most definitely wasn't this. I shiver as waves of sympathy for him wash over me.

"Marty..." I say, and I hope it says more than his name. I hope it says, *I'm sorry*, and *I'm here* and *That's so fucking shit.*

"Not long after he died, I went on a holiday with some mates. I didn't even want to go, but Arnie wanted me to have something... something to look forward to, and so I went. And well, I never went home. I got on that plane to Ibiza, got far too drunk and took more than a few illegal substances and when the rest of the lads took a taxi to the airport a week later, I didn't go with them. I got a job washing pots in a bar and didn't go back home for nearly six months. I'll save you the details, but it was a horrible messy time. It's why I don't drink anymore. And it's why my parents dragged me on this holiday."

"So, they didn't let you come down this evening?" I say trying to connect some dots.

Marty shakes his head and squeezes his eyes shut. "Oh, no. That's still my balls-up. Because of all the aforementioned fuckery, when I did come home from Ibiza, I started taking anti-depressants and also some other tablets to help me sleep, but I stopped taking them last week and well, I then stupidly took one today after thinking it may help with some... some extreme feelings I've been having, and well, I think I took the wrong one."

My lips curl downward, and I hope it doesn't appear in pity. It's in empathy. I can almost feel his pain in my own chest.

"It knocked me out and I woke up like three minutes before I got here," he says and nods at his feet. "Didn't even bother to put shoes on."

I test a gentle laugh. "Yeah, I noticed that and was going to ask if that's what the cool kids are all doing these days?"

"Ha, not the cool kids, no. Rather the moronic idiots who keep fucking shit up," he says, and it snaps me to move, to take what feels like a risk. I reach for his face, cup his chin in my hand and squeeze a little to get his attention.

"Marty, stop. Stop talking about yourself like that, because your brain will be so far gone believing it there will be no turning back."

His eyes are pinned on mine as we stay like this long enough for me to see the fading light make the flecks of green and gold in his eyes glow.

"I still feel like a dick," he says in a whisper.

"You look like one, with those crushed pillow lines all over your face and some serious bed hair going on." I put my hand in his hair and he closes his eyes at the touch.

"Seriously though. It feels all kinds of wrong to tell you about Arnie now as if that excuses being late like I'm playing him as a Get Out of Jail Free card."

"I don't think you're doing that." I rub my nails against his scalp, and he pushes into my hand. It feels very inappropriate but somewhat inevitable when heat floods between my legs.

"And do you want to know what the best part of yesterday evening was for me? It was that I wasn't that guy. That guy who lost his best friend and boyfriend, the guy who reacted by going on the rampage for months on end. That guy who lets people down."

"You didn't let me down. You don't owe me anything," I say but it doesn't seem to help ease the strain in his features.

"Yes, I let you down," he says. "I said I'd be here, and I wasn't. Also, I just lied to you."

I drop my hand from his head. "You did? About Arnie?"

"No, not about any of that. Sadly, that sorry tale is true. I lied when I said that you not knowing about my background was the best part of last night. It wasn't."

"What was the best part then?"

"Just being with you," he says. Then he places his fingers over my hand and I slowly roll my palm over. He takes long seconds sliding his digits along my skin and letting them find their place in between my fingers. The way warmth spreads through my body, it feels like a kiss, or much, much more. I stare at our hands locked together as I try to figure out how I feel about what he's just told me.

I don't know if it's intentional, but he gives me space and silence to do this. Neither of us say anything, and our eyes turn back to the fading colours in the sky, our hands still intertwined. Just like last night, we watch the very last blurred lines of pink and purple recede into an ombre grey that reveals a sprinkling of tiny stars. Just like last night, we are completely oblivious of the rest of the resort and the world around us.

While what he's told me is unexpected, and in many ways startling, I don't doubt what he's saying because it makes sense. I see the loss in his eyes. I heard his pain when his voice cracked. I feel how disappointed he is in himself, and I can tell that the grief inside him weighs him down no matter how much he tries to shake it off, no matter how much he tries to smile it away. I know all this, because I know exactly what that feels like.

With this realisation, this new kinship we share, something shifts in me and my attraction to Marty takes on a new form. It's still physical, but it's now morphing into something that could also be called a friendship, or maybe a companionship. And selfishly, that works for me. It works better than if our connection was just lust. Lust and friendship are a good blend, possibly the ideal combination for a hot summer fling in paradise.

"You're not a dick. You didn't stand me up. You've been through some serious shit," I say, as if to summarise. "And I really am so very sorry that Arnie died."

There's something about hearing his name that lights him up, his eyes sparkling in the twilight as he looks at me and squeezes his fingers against mine. "Thank you," he says.

I don't know why I ask what I ask next, other than it's a genuine request. It's what I want in that moment more than anything else. For him, and for me.

"Will you tell me about him? If it doesn't hurt too much. I'd love to hear about your travels together. I would just like to know more about him. And you."

Chapter Fifteen

Marty

I tell her about him. I tell how we met at rugby club, a year before we joined the same secondary school. I tell her how we were inseparable by the end of the first year. I tell her how I was the first person he told he was gay, the day after his fifteenth birthday. I tell her how he came on holidays with my family, and how I had my own key to his house. I tell her how much he read - anything and everything - and how he would banish me from his room when he watched certain TV shows because I asked too many questions. I tell her how he would get so annoyed when I talked about girls and I always thought it was because he hated hearing about boobs, but really, it was because he was fiercely jealous, something I didn't know until years later.

I tell her about the night we first kissed. I tell her how he was the first person I told I was bisexual. I tell her how travelling with him was the best time of my life, how we made memories to last a lifetime, the bittersweet irony of that not lost on me. And I tell her about his favourite places, and about mine. I tell her how incredible the sunset was on Koh Lanta. I tell her how one night in Cambodia we watched the sun go down and then stayed in the very same spot, on a beach, and waited for it to come up again behind us. I tell her how we planned on returning to New Zealand to live for a few years. I tell her how we talked about that trip as if it would still happen, right up to the day he died.

And then I stop, and it's not just because I'm sad or struggling to talk, rather because I have shared enough. I have shared what I'm willing to, because some of it I want to keep just for me. I also wonder if I have shared probably more than she wants to know. I also stop before I get lost in the other side of our story, the one that involves hospital wards, long complicated names of drugs I eventually learned to say with ease, other cancer patients who became friends, and their ghost-like family members and loved ones rushing from the ward to the toilets to sob. I can sense that Jenna is a generous soul, but even she doesn't want or need to talk about this, not here, not now.

"Thank you for sharing that," she says when my words slow to a halt.

"Thank you for listening," I reply, and I mean it.

"You probably need a drink now," she says with a tentative smile. "A non-alcoholic one."

"Jesus, yes," I say, lifting my hand to my mouth, the hand that isn't still holding hers. "My mouth's as dry as a nun's fanny."

"My God, Marty," she says, and I can't tell if the way she covers her crumpled face with her hands means she's disgusted or amused, but regardless, I'm proud to have shifted the mood a little.

Then I stare at our interlocked fingers. "I want to get it, but I also don't want to move."

She does it for me, pulling her hand away and grinning at me. "Go get me a drink, you filthy-mouthed menace."

I head to the bar and find the same woman that was working yesterday and she asks me what I have in mind for her today, making my task much easier. Together we concoct two mocktails and I proudly carry them over to Jenna.

"Here we go. A Cuddle on the Beach," I say, putting the glasses down on the table. "It's fruity, fun, and won't get as much sand in your arse crack."

"Thank you," she says with a tinkling laugh before taking a slow sip. I try not to look too intently at her lips, surprised at how desire is bubbling up inside me despite being so lost in thoughts of Arnie just a few minutes ago.

But it also makes sense. There's something about telling her about Arnie that feels like I've undergone a cleansing ritual, a process that has very faintly lightened the burden of my grief. The sadness and dull ache is still there, but the heaviest load and the razor-sharp edges of my pain have gone. Maybe that's why looking at her lips feels better, almost safer, than it did last night. Maybe that's why I say what I say next.

"Now I have three questions for you," I say, then correct myself. "No, four actually."

"Go ahead," she says, pulling a face that tells me she's bracing herself.

"Firstly, am I forgiven? For getting here late."

She doesn't hesitate. "Yes."

"Secondly, can I have dinner with you tonight?"

She is shocked by that one. "Yes." She smiles after a beat.

"Thirdly, was that weird for me to just talk about my ex like that? It's heavy and tragic and sad, but also he's still my ex. It's still someone I had feelings for... have feelings for. Like, I still love and miss the shit out of him. Is that weird for you?"

Jenna starts talking while looking at her drink, but eventually her eyes pull up to find mine. "It's not weird. Love is not as prescriptive or as predictable as we like to think it is. We like to put rules on love, like we do most things, and we approach it with a binary mindset, but love will never bend to fit in binaries or boxes. Love doesn't care. Love will just grow wherever it finds the right conditions. Your love for Arnie doesn't stop your capacity to feel physically attracted to someone else, even if he were alive that would still be true. Missing him and grieving him doesn't mean you can't also take pleasure in being with someone else when you're ready to... physically, I mean." I sense she is being extra cautious with her words.

"So you still fancy me? Even though I still have feelings for a dead man?" I am a lot less careful with my words.

"Is that your fourth question?"

"No, it wasn't. Shit!"

"You can have another one." She grins and bumps her body against my arm.

"You need to answer that question first," I raise my eyebrows at her.

Her teeth sink into her plump lower lip, the lucky buggers.

"Yes, I still fancy you. And to clarify, I don't find it weird at all that you still have feelings for Arnie. Honestly, I would find it weird if you *didn't* still have feelings for him."

I stare at her as I process what she's just said. I realise in that moment that I've been resisting what I still feel for Arnie for so long since he died, because it hurt. Loving him hurt me, because it reminded me of his absence, of his death. It wasn't a conscious decision, but I recognise now that somewhere along the way, I've been trying to stop loving him so that I could stop some of the pain. But what if it didn't have to be like this? How much energy and effort would I get back if I stopped trying to switch off that love? What if I could find peace in still loving him?

I must have been thinking on this for longer than I realise because she nudges me again, her arm warm against mine. "Your final question, Irishman?"

Blinking, I glide my eyes over her face, once, twice, as if I'm trying to count every one of her freckles. A question does indeed climb to the tip of my tongue. It isn't the one I was going to ask, but it's the only one I want an answer for now.

"Can I kiss you?"

If she's surprised by that one it melts away in a heartbeat, as does the distance between us when she tells me *Yes* in the sweetest whisper. I lean in too and time starts to slow down, the background noise fading away, and I close my eyes...

"Oh, he showed up!" A man's voice calls out and Jenna pulls back.

Fuck.

We both turn our heads towards the culprit, and I see an attractive young man with big brown eyes carrying an ice bucket with a bottle of champagne in it.

"Hi, Lionel," Jenna says pulling back further from me.

"Sorry, did I interrupt?" he asks. "I did, didn't I? Fluffballs. Jake wanted me to send this over to you. He wanted to come himself, but we have a rather annoy-no, err... challenging guest at the front desk and..."

I try to contain my smile. Who is this adorable human?

"It's fine, Lionel," Jenna says, and I love the pink that is now in her cheeks. "It's really sweet of you."

"Super sweet, thanks a million," I say, and then I stand up and introduce myself. "Hi, I'm Marty."

"Oh, wow, you really are Irish," Lionel says as he shuffles the ice bucket to one side and grips my hand.

"Afraid so," I say. "It would be a pain in the arse to keep up the accent all day long otherwise."

His smile is wide and genuine, his laughter light and airy and I don't think I could hate him for interrupting our kiss if I tried. And for a moment there I was really trying.

"So, shall I just put this down here?" Lionel moves towards our table.

"Actually, we're grateful, but we aren't drinking tonight," Jenna says but immediately I interject.

"No, you should have some, if you want," I say to her.

"That's it, I don't want. I'm happy with our Cuddles on the Beach." I somehow know her well enough to know she's being honest. "Did you open it already?" she asks Lionel.

"Yeah." He shrugs. "Your brother was insistent you'd want it to drown your - sugar cubes! I mean, to take back to your villa."

"Then you should keep it on ice until the end of your shift and share it with my brother," Jenna says.

"Great idea!" I agree.

"Err, okay, although I'm not sure that's allowed," Lionel stutters and I resist the urge to give him a big reassuring hug.

"Please just tell my brother that Marty showed up, so there's no need for me to go drown my sorrows tonight and I therefore insist he drowns his instead. With you." Jenna leans towards Lionel, her back arching in a way that drags my eyes down to her butt.

"Okey dokey," Lionel says and there's a hint of excitement shimmering in his eyes as he turns away from us. "Have a nice evening!"

"Fuck me, he's too cute," I say after he's gone.

"The sweetest man. I sort of hope he and my brother discover they like each other."

"Get in there, Sweet Cheeks," I say.

"Did you just call my brother Sweet Cheeks?"

"Yes, and I stand by it."

"Why do I feel like..." she begins but I stop her.

I stop her by coming in close, sliding my hand along the side of her neck, tipping her chin up and pressing my lips to hers.

And then I freeze. My lips stuck on hers, unmoving, I'm suddenly terrified I've forgotten how to do this. How do I kiss sober? How do I make it special for her? How do I make this more than all the drunken snogs and clumsy fumbles I can barely remember?

As if she can read my mind, she takes over, bringing her hands to cup my face, and lifting her lips a little before placing them back down on one corner of my mouth. It's an almost innocent but plush peck - like a blessing – and after an achingly long second or two she does the same in the other corner. As if that was the key I needed to unlock something, my mouth falls open and I place her lush upper lip between my own, resisting the urge to immediately nip it with my teeth because of how full and plump it feels. I so badly want to open my eyes and watch her kiss me - to watch her closed eyelids and get a close-up on her sweet pink lips becoming moist from mine - but I daren't risk letting any other senses in. I want touch and taste to get all my attention, and they do as she brings the tip of her tongue out to lick my bottom lip as if asking for permission, for more.

I see now that the last one hundred or so kisses I had were rushed and senseless, they were a means to an end, they were a necessary starter before the main course. This kiss, this delicious slow kiss, feels like a 5-course meal with wine pairing, and our tongues haven't even touched yet.

She hums when I release her lip and gives me a soft grunt when I find her tongue for a quick battle, only to pull away a second later. She breathes out a moan when I then suck in her bottom lip.

"Jesus," I say, pulling back a centimetre or two to catch my breath.

"Don't stop," she says, and her hands slide down my neck and come to rest on my chest, grabbing at the material of my T-shirt and pulling my body closer.

It's a miracle we only kiss, but that's all we do sitting there in a dark corner of a bar at dusk. Even though my whole body - all of it - wants to touch hers and even though it feels like what our tongues are doing is obscene enough by itself, all we do is kiss. It's only when I feel an ache in my back from stretching so far towards her that I think I should pull away, but I don't want to. I still don't want it to stop. In the end, she decides for me.

"I have a question for you now," she asks when she pulls back an inch, her forehead resting on mine. She's breathing heavily when I look down and see her mouth looks different - her lips plumper and pinker, their edges red from my day-old stubble. If she wasn't putting her hand up to her lips as if to check them, I would just dive straight back in.

"Go ahead," I say. She could ask me anything and I'd tell her everything.

"Can we skip dinner? Or maybe…" She rubs her nose against the tip of mine. "We can order room service to my villa? Later."

"Later?" I ask.

"Yes, after," she explains, still breathless.

"After?" I question.

"After," Jenna confirms.

"Okay," I say, processing.

"Okay?" she checks.

"Okay," I say, agreeing.

"Then, let's go," she says and she's moving – fast - finishing her drink with a hefty swig, gathering up her belongings and standing. I move a little slower, so I have to jog a little to catch up with her as she charges out of the bar, through the lobby and onto the path to the villas, with only a few coy looks back at me behind her. I take in the way her light blue denim dress floats out around her legs, and how she's maybe a little bit more tanned than this morning, and I wonder again about those freckles and where they are to be found on her body. I stop briefly to check the time on my phone, and to see if Maeve has reported any blowback from my parents but there are no messages.

"There you are!" I hear a voice and I know it's for one of us. Luckily for me, it's an English accent.

"Oh, hey," Jenna says, and up on the path ahead of me, I watch her turn to face her brother who emerges from the walkway to someone's villa.

"Going back to your villa?"

"Yes, I-"

"Did you not get the champers I sent Lionel to give you while I sorted out this absolute ball-ache of a guest? Claimed his pillows weren't fluffy enough. I literally had to come and plump them up myself. I can't believe Marty O'Martin didn't show up. That slippery Irish cockle." Jake puts his hands on his hips, no clue I'm about to walk into his line of vision.

"Hi, Jake!" I say with a broad smile on my face.

"Oh!" Jake startles. "Oh, hi!"

"Pretty sure 'Irish cockle' is offensive, but I'll forgive you," I say.

"We're just..." Jenna begins but then looks at me with pure mischief, "... going to have dinner."

"Oh. Should I make a reservation for you somewhere? In the resort or down in the village?" Jake pulls a phone out of his pocket.

Jenna straightens her shoulders. "Actually, that was a complete lie. Marty's coming back to my villa."

"Oh," he says again, the hand holding his phone falls to his side. "Yeah, I don't think I can help much with that."

Jenna smiles and I laugh under my breath.

"Hopefully I've got this one covered," I say and put my hand on the small of Jenna's back. Her shudder prompts me to curl my fingers and apply more pressure.

The heavy second of silence between us that follows is interrupted by Jenna smothering a giggle with a cough.

"Yes, well, enjoy," her brother says and he's looking beyond us now, his professional smile and smooth forehead back in place. "Have a nice evening."

"Oh, that we will, that we will." I practically sing.

"Okay! Enough. That is my sister!" Jake launches forward with a finger pointed at Jenna who is still trying to hold her giggles in, possibly not helped by the fact my hand is now flat against her backside, my fingertips digging into her flesh.

I hold my other hand up in surrender to Jake. "I apologise. I'm just being my cheeky Irish cockle self."

"Did you just emphasise the 'cock' in cockle?" Jake squints at me then shakes his hands to dismiss us, addressing Jenna as if I'm not there. "I cannot with this one. Good luck, be safe and for God's sake, don't put bubble bath in the jacuzzi."

Then he turns on his heels and heads back to the reception.

"Love you, Jakey! Enjoy your champagne with Lionel!" Jenna calls out to him, and before waiting to see his response, she's off, her body moving away from my hand so quickly that I have to rush again to catch up with her.

Chapter Sixteen

Jenna

"Well, that wasn't awkward at all," Marty says, stepping up to walk beside me as I climb the hill to my villa. The light is that dreamy shade of silver-grey that somehow opens up the sky in a more mysterious, ethereal way than the blue of the day.

I don't reply, but I do pick up my pace.

"He cares about you," Marty adds.

I nod, but I'm not sure he sees.

"And I was just having a bit of fun with him. You know, it's what I do when I'm in an awkward moment. I make it more awkward. I crack bad jokes. I try to make everybody laugh but I forget that most people don't have my effed-up sense of humour."

I'm smiling. I know exactly what he means, because I have that sense of humour too.

"Is not talking a pre-match thing for you?" he asks. "I mean, we all got our game plans and things we have to do-"

I turn suddenly and step toward him, pushing up on my toes to kiss him. "I want you in my bed," I say when I have his bottom lip between my teeth, meaning it's barely audible, the M and The B impossible to say, but I think he gets the idea as I see a flash of something light up in his eyes. A beat later I feel his hands grip both of my butt cheeks, pulling me flush to him where I feel the hard ridge of him. It startles me enough to drop his lip and close my eyes, savouring it.

"Show me the way," he says but he doesn't let go, and his lips come down on mine again.

"Aiden?" A man's voice tears us apart. It's an Irish accent and it's coming from some way behind me, further up the hill.

"Feckity feck feck feck!" Marty says into my forehead before straightening up, lifting his hands off my butt. He pulls his head up too but leaves the bulge of his erection resting against my stomach.

"Aiden, what are you..." the voice continues, and I turn so I can see who it belongs to. I can't resist leaning back so my backside is pressed up against Marty again. "Maeve said that you were meeting the-"

He stops when he sees me, and I can't help but smile. There's no denying who this man is. He has the same height, broad shoulders, narrow hips, and five o'clock shadow. The lean definition in his chest and arms, and the way he walks - knees turned out slightly, a very subtle bounce in each step – are all undeniably made from the same DNA as Marty. His father. While an instant discomfort rises in me, it's doused a little by the fact I can see this man is at least twenty years older than me, which is a relief I didn't know I needed.

"Hi Dad," Marty says with clear reluctance in his voice. "Yeah, I did go to the bar to meet the manager but..."

He trails off, and I resist the urge to look up at him and question that blatant lie.

"But now you're here, and I'm assuming this is not the manager," his father says, looking at me. I see his hair is fairer than Marty's and his eyes are lighter, green maybe, like Maeve's. "Not because I'm a sexist pig and think women can't be hotel managers, but because Marty already told us the manager was a man, and we actually thought he may have caught Marty's eye but looks like we got that wrong, eh?"

"Dad, this is Jenna. Jenna, this is my father, James," Marty says through a clenched jaw.

Marty's dad steps forward and holds out a hand to me, giving me a warm smile. My palm is pulled into a firm grip. It moves my body slightly, enough to recognise that Marty is losing his erection, and I am inexplicably sad about that.

"Nice to meet you, James. I'm the hotel manager's sister," I say as if to explain.

134

"Oh. Well, that's an interesting plot twist."

"No plot, Da. Just me and Jenna had a drink and now we're going to get some dinner and... wait. What are you doing here?"

"We need more ice," he says holding up the metallic ice bucket he's carrying. "And frankly I needed a fresh air break from your mother and your sister, who have been painting each other's nails all evening while arguing about the pros and cons of veganism. So I offered to go get it myself, and of course, I accidentally on purpose went the long way. They've been bickering about which pulses are the best sources of protein for the last hour and there's only so much I can take now I've done both crosswords and all the sudokus I can find."

"Understood." Marty nods. "So, Maeve is a vegan now?"

"No, of course not, she single-handedly demolished the cheese platter we ordered with our drinks. But you know what she's like. She's watched five YouTube videos on something and now she's an expert."

I snicker at that. As if noticing my smile, Marty's father looks at me again then, his eyes softening even more.

"I'll let you go," he says, and he walks past us, before pausing a few steps down the hill "You have a nice evening now. Enjoy your dinner."

"Thank you," I say, hoping my smile is as normal as possible and not at all in the 'I'm-about-to-get-laid' category. "Nice to meet you."

"You too, Jenna," he says and gives me a half-wave. I turn back to Marty but then hear him call out, "Be safe, son... if you know what I mean!"

I crash my head onto Marty's chest. I haven't had to even think about parents giving sexual health advice since I was a teenager, and I want to wince, laugh and cringe. I do a strange combination of all three into his shirt. Marty's hands slide down my back and he laughs into my hair.

"Is it me, or is the universe trying to stop my penis from going into your vagina?"

I laugh a little harder, smile a bit wider and lean a little closer to him.

"No, not the universe," I say. "Just our families. But guess what?"

"What?"

"I have a lock on my villa door. And a Do Not Disturb sign. And also…" I pause, waiting for his eyes to find mine.

"Yeah?"

"Even if that were to be true, there are one hundred more things we can do besides P in V."

That gets me the reaction I want as I feel him harden against me again. As if to reward him, I rock my hips into him before I push out of his arms and start running up the hill again.

"Race you!" I call out.

"Oh, come on, that's hardly fair. Have you ever ran with a massive boner?"

"Oh, come on, Marty, it's not that big!" I call back but keep running.

Chapter Seventeen

Jenna

"Can I shower first?" he asks once he's in the villa. I hear the door click closed behind me as I walk straight for the bedroom.

"You didn't run that fast."

"No, but I did fall asleep in my sweaty boxers after three hours of being director, stylist and sound tech for my sister in the blistering sun."

"Should I ask?" I turn at the entrance to my room.

"Please don't." Marty steps up to me and slides his hands around my waist. "You could join me? In the shower, I mean."

I nod but don't speak. Suddenly the thought of being naked with this man terrifies me. Robert cherished my curves from the start, which I loved, but a small part of me always wondered if he was a fluke. That part of me is currently growing in size and volume as I think about shedding my clothes in front of this younger, taller and more physically sculpted man.

"Of course, you can shower." I head towards the en-suite bathroom. Through double doors, it opens up into a space that's almost as big as the bedroom itself. The walk-in double shower is on one side of the room, there's a free-standing bath close to the far wall and then a double sink on the side opposite the shower. The toilet is a separate small room just at the bathroom's entrance, opposite a small walk-in closet. I watch Marty take it all in, nodding at the bath as if to say hello.

I step into the shower and turn one of the heads on, waiting with my hand under the spray until it feels warm. I have every intention of leaving the room, letting him have his shower, but he's standing near the sinks pulling his T-shirt off and I know there's no way I'm missing this. I lean against the shower's glass wall and watch the waves of muscles rise and fall in his back and torso. It's undeniable that he's probably leaner than he should be, what with his broad structure and height, and the way his ribs stretch his skin, but there's also no denying how badly I want to trace every single dip and swell of his muscles and bone with my tongue. As if to tease me more, he turns so he's directly facing me as his hands go to the fly on his shorts, then they stop moving and that forces my eyes up to his.

"You look..." he begins. "Hungry."

I close my eyes, mildly embarrassed but too turned on to care. I keep my eyes on his for long enough to say, "Keep going."

He pauses, then obeys, and I swallow a smile when I realise he's going slowly as he pulls the zip down and then lowers the shorts. His tight grey boxers are filled out by his hard-on and I almost curse at the low light in the bathroom for not giving me a more detailed look, but there's no waiting, because just when I think he's going to wait until he's right at the shower's entrance to get rid of his underwear, they're off, yanked down and he's kicking them away.

I can't help it. My eyes study his cock; it's really long, plenty thick enough and curved, amusingly, just like his thumb. My eyes linger on the round head and its defined edge. As he walks towards me and the shower, I watch his dick, jutting out at an angle. It's a beautiful cock and that curve is like a promise and a pledge.

I have to swallow before I speak.

"Can I watch?" I ask stepping to the side.

"I think you already are." He walks past me, his penis bobbing and his thigh muscles flexing. He kisses the top of my head as he passes me and then he's under the water, the curves of his butt in my line of sight. They're all muscle, just enough to grab and hold on to. I want to tell him how lovely he is. How much his body pleases me. How I could look at it for hours - not touching, just looking - and I'd not get bored.

However, I stay silent as I sit on the tiled seat built into the wall behind me, directly opposite Marty. I sit there, feeling a gentle drizzle and the occasional splash of warm water land on my skin, and I watch him as he uses my shower gel to create a lather all over his body. He startles a little when he turns and sees me sitting there, breathing heavily. My back is pressed back against the shower wall and the coolness of the tiles is a refreshing contrast to the heat in my core.

"Do you mind?" I ask again, dragging my eyes up to his. His hair is now being flattened by the water and it looks so different, darkening his features. It makes him look a little older and I savour that.

"Not at all," he says, and he runs his eyes over my body, although it's completely covered compared to his. "I wish you were wearing less, but you still look fucking class."

His quaint, youthful choice of words makes me smile and I temporarily forget just how turned on I am. But I don't want to forget. I want to be consumed by this feeling. It's been so long since I felt this way.

I watch him wash his face, his chest, and under his arms. Then he turns away from me and squeezes more shower gel down his body and foams it up between his legs, his butt tight as his hands work for some time, and all I can do is imagine. And I do. Then he bends slightly and rubs more bubbles at his thighs and his knees. Finally, he does a figure-4 stretch to bring up his feet and washes them too, the soles noticeably dark. Recalling why they are so dirty melts something inside of me.

He raced barefoot to come and see me.

After he's washed his other foot, he turns around to face me and tilts his head up to the shower head, the water running down his shoulders and back. Then he's rubbing between his butt cheeks and giving me this playful smile that makes our eye contact a little too intense, so I look away. Just as well, I now have the perfect thing to stare at again. His cock. It's a little less erect now but still full, noticeably taut. I can see a vein on one side, a zig-zag that I want to trace with my tongue. The more I stare, the more it grows as he angles himself under the spray. My own body is responding in exactly the same way. I've long been aware of the pull in my nipples, the quick belly-breathing I'm doing and the way I can feel my wetness through my knickers.

"Jesus," he says to himself as he turns to the side, his dick undeniably closer to a full erection now as it sticks straight out. Shaking his head slightly, he turns all the way back around and I see him using my shampoo to wash his hair and I feel my insides tighten at the idea of him smelling like me. "You make me blush," he says.

"I like watching you," I say as if to explain myself or reassure him.

He tilts his head back to wash the suds out of his hair. "And I think I like being watched," he says, and his voice is smooth, almost sleepy.

With that soft, humble tone, and his cock now pointing skyward and the shape of his balls tighter and higher, I can't sit there any longer. I want to touch him. I *have* to touch him. Forgetting I'm even dressed, I walk towards him and under the water. I put my left hand on his neck and invite him to watch what my other hand is doing as it wraps itself around his dick and squeezes him at the base. Then I slide my grip up, loosening it a little around the sensitive head. He sighs and leans his chin against the side of my face. I do this a few more times before I reach down and gently take his balls in my hand, feeling how full they are. When he shudders, I apply a little more pressure before cupping them again and feeling them from a different angle.

"Jenna," he says, and hearing my name startles me.

My ex-husband never said my name during sex. He never said much at all during sex, and I thought I was okay with that.

I thought I was okay with a lot of things.

"What do you want?" I ask him, the water running into my eyes and mouth, no doubt smearing my mascara and make-up, but I don't care. I love the way my dress is sticking to my body now, giving me new sensations on my breasts and my thighs. All the places I love to be touched and caressed. "Tell me what you like."

"You," he says, and I wonder which question he's answering, but he clarifies quickly after his lips crash onto mine. "Right now, I just want you."

It's not the answer I want – I want details, instructions, a comprehensive guide to his body – because I want to get this right, even if it's only for one night. Or maybe that's the very reason I want to get it right.

"Tell me-" I pull back, but as I speed up my strokes on his dick, gripping a little harder, he takes my mouth again. We kiss with a hunger that I now know was just a seed the last few times we kissed. Now it's growing, wild and ravenous, covering all the ground it can, invading whatever part of me it hadn't already. When his hands move from my lower back to squeeze my arse and pull me against him, I gasp, slipping my hand out from between our bodies so we can press closer together. When he starts to rock against me, seeking out friction and rhythm against the wet fabric of my dress, I moan into his mouth. When the fingers of his right hand lean down and climb their way under the hem of my dress and his knuckles brush my thigh, I think my legs are going to give way, but he holds me firmly against him with his left hand. I still move though, opening my legs so he can find me, and he does, two fingers stroking the lace of my underwear.

"You're so hot and wet," he whispers into my lips.

"I'm standing under a shower. It's not all you," I say touching his nose with the tip of mine.

It's all you, I want to say but I don't.

"Can I take your underwear off?" he asks, his voice still quieter than usual, more breath and more depth.

"Fuck, yes," I say, and together that's what we do, me pulling up my dress and him ripping my sodden knickers down my thighs and calves. He's crouching down to do it and while I expect him to come straight back up, he stays there and kisses both of my legs just above the knee. I watch him lace kisses up my inner thighs, a little stunned. It's been so long since someone touched me in this way and it's abruptly overwhelming, too tender and too much. I move one of my hands to cup his chin and bring him back up to standing. But he grips the backs of my thighs with his hands and applies more pressure with his lips as his mouth climbs higher.

"You didn't think I was all talk, did you?" He leans back out of the spray and looks up at me.

"What?" My brain is dizzy with lust. I have no clue what he's talking about.

"The way I flirted with you the last few days," he says. "I am going to show you I'm not all talk."

Stunned and impossibly even more turned on, I don't have words to offer him in return. Instead, I take a deep breath and lose my fingers in his hair. With my other hand, I keep my dress held up around my waist but rearrange it so I can see more, so I can watch him as his tongue darts out and licks the full length of my pussy. I lean back to find the wall of the shower, convinced if he does anything else my legs really will give way.

But they don't. As he kisses my outer labia, tongues me open and then finds my clit, swirling the tip of his tongue around its peak, I close my eyes and concentrate only on the sensation and the building of heat and pressure. I focus on the lush roughness of his tongue, the tenderness of his kisses, and the power I feel having a man on his knees in front of me. Rocking my pelvis into his mouth, I am alarmed but not surprised when I feel the tell-tale squeeze that means I'm close.

"Stop!" I say and pull at his hair. He leans back and looks up at me. Beneath his dark eyes and now red, wet lips, I can see his dick is as hard as ever, the head almost purple in colour now. It's the most erotic sight.

"Are you okay?" he asks, running a hand down his face to wipe away the water that was falling on him.

"Yes, I just..." I stop, take a breath. "I just need you inside me. Right now."

"We should get dry and go to bed," he's saying and reaching up to turn the shower off, but I stop him.

"No, now. I need this now. I need you now," I say with little grace.

He's up on his feet in less than a second and he's pressing me against the wall, and we're kissing with all that hunger again, but this time I can taste myself and that just adds an extra layer of excitement to it all. His hands are inside my bra, pulling and stroking and gently twisting my nipples. My hand goes back to his dick, stroking, but with less control than earlier.

I'm breathless with how much I want him inside me, so I push him off so that he gets the message. I pull his hand and I shuffle the few steps to the seat I was sitting on and I put my right foot up on it. Feeling a little daring, I make sure his eyes are on my hands as I pull my heavy wet dress up my thighs. Then I glide my hands up and pull the shoulder straps down before reaching back and taking my bra off, dropping it to the floor. I must look a sodden mess. My mascara must be all over my cheeks, my hair is stuck in clumps to my face and neck, and my dress looks like a soaked bedsheet wrapped around the middle of my body, but I don't care. I've not felt this sexy or alive in years.

"Jenna," he says again, and he steps in front of me, looking down at my body. I close my eyes treasuring how he says my name in that low sexy voice.

"Marty, please," I say, an unapologetic beg. "Please fuck me."

"I will," he says, his hand combing hair off my face. "But first..."

"Now, Marty, I need you now." I sound like I'm crying, and I'm starting to scare myself.

He laughs a little, but his eyes are serious as they bear down into mine. "Jenna, I can't."

"What?" I would be less surprised if the ceiling came crashing down, yet his face is a picture of calm.

"I need a condom," he says simply.

"Fuck!" I yell out. I'm soaked and although I know I have some by the sink – a handful I packed in an act that felt fun but almost pointless at the time - I'm a dripping mess and I really don't want to have to walk across the room in a state of undress after I've put myself in this position that is now starting to feel anything but sexy.

"Do you not have any?" he asks, now looking more concerned.

"You don't?" I ask.

"I wasn't planning on this," he says.

What the hell does that mean? He didn't want to sleep with me?

I shake away these thoughts with a flick of my head. "I have some, over there." I point to the vanity case on the shelf under the sink. "In that bag."

"Stay right there," he says giving me a brief kiss.

I feel the warmth of his body leave mine and the urge to cry suddenly crashes into me. I close my eyes again - this time out of embarrassment - and wait. I feel foolish for forgetting about condoms. I feel foolish for being so needy.

I almost feel foolish for being so incredibly turned on, but then the woman in me that I've been nurturing and healing since my divorce starts to speak to me. I know if I have anything to feel embarrassed about it's not being turned on. My sexuality is never something to apologise for. If only feeling these things was as easy as knowing them.

"Are you okay?" he asks when he's back in front of me, opening my eyes with another kiss.

"I feel like a bit of an idiot not thinking about protection."

"Well, it's more for me to think about, isn't it?" he says.

I nod, again wondering why he then didn't bring any.

"You want to pick up where we left off?" He nuzzles my neck. I look down and see the condom is already on him and the site of the latex and the squeeze it has on his dick is still a bit of shock. For over twelve years, I haven't had sex with condoms and so this will take a bit of getting used to. Fear rises in me; fear that this isn't going to be the spectacular sex I expected. I want to face-palm myself for not having more realistic expectations.

But then his tongue is licking along my collarbone and one of his hands is on my breast. His mouth dips to my other nipple and he kisses, sucks and nibbles. It sends bolts of heat and tension between my legs and I'm rubbing my thighs together, almost as turned on as I was when I was begging him to fuck me.

"Yes," I say. "Yes, please."

He smiles against my breast, and I feel his hand tap my right leg. "Go on, back in that sexy as fuck position."

I try to contain my grin, as I lean back against the wall, prop my leg up and lift my foot. Then I pull my dress up again and show him where I want him.

"Say it again," he says, looking right into my eyes.

"Say what?" I ask, confused.

"Say you need me. Ask me to fuck you. And say my name." His voice is so sincere and sexy, I wish I could record it.

"I need you, Marty. Fuck me," I say, and I bring my fingers between my legs, feeling how swollen my clit is. "Please fuck me, now."

His smile shines out of every one of his features; his eyes sparkling, his cheeks high, his dimples deep, and his mouth stretched so very wide. In one single movement, he puts his left hand under my right leg, and lifts me up and against the wall. I look down and see his other hand guide his dick against my pussy. The slide of him, the slick latex and the heat of his cock as it rubs back and forth over my clit has me gasping in a rough but deep breath.

"Please," I say again, worried he's going to make me wait.

"Jenna," he says again, and I say his name back to him, repeating it, mumbling it, swallowing it until I feel the head of him find my entrance and in one swift, firm motion, he's inside me.

And I come.

I come so suddenly and so hard I dig my nails into his back and gasp out a loud, high-pitched "Oh!" that echoes in my ears. I come as he stays still, pushing me against the wall, holding my leg up and whispering my name in my ear.

Chapter Eighteen

Marty

"Jenna, did you just come?" I pull back to ask. "Or do you have extremely strong pelvic floor muscles that will likely destroy me?"

With closed eyes and her lips clamped shut, she turns her head, exposing the arch of her neck in a way that I know is supposed to hide her face from me but just makes me want to graze my teeth over the skin there.

"Yeah, I just came." Her body starts to shake in silent laughter. I think.

"Are you okay?" I ask. It's getting harder to keep still inside her because her laughter also squeezes my dick, not to mention how hot it is that she came already.

"I just had a mind-blowing orgasm. I'm more than okay," she says and her face tilts back down, her eyes on me. I am relieved when I can still see hunger in them.

"You want to stop?" I still have to ask. This is different from any other sex I've had. I'm not sure if it's because I'm sober. I'm not sure if it's because it's with an older woman. I'm not sure if it's because for the first time in over a year, I'm not thinking about Arnie and how it was with him. Some hidden part of me is aware of it, but I'm so far from focusing on it. All I am trying to do is not ruin this, for her or for me.

"Have you fucked me yet?" she asks with hooded eyes.

"Technically, not yet." I can't help the little jolt my dick gives, and I know she feels it because her eyelids lift.

"Have you come so hard you can't see?" She reaches behind and grips my butt cheeks.

"Not yet," I say, and my dick moves again but that's all me, rocking into her. She hums out a small moan.

"Have I screamed your name as I come?" She squeezes me again, but something tells me this is very deliberate.

"No, not yet," I manage.

"Then, no, I do not want to stop," she says, and she turns her head to nuzzle my earlobe, biting it softly, before panting in my ear. "Please fuck me, Marty."

So I do. I tense my arms as I hold her leg up with one hand and find balance on the shower wall close to her head with the other. I push against her with my chest, so close that we can't kiss anymore, and then I bend down and thrust into her deeper. I pull out then go back in again, going as slow as I can manage. She's warm and soft and smooth and it's so good, so good I almost don't want to come so I can stay here, but I need the release too. I have been feeling the swirl of desire for her for twenty-four giddy hours, which is no time at all, of course, but right now it feels like I have waited forever.

"You feel so good," she says. "So good."

"You're the one who feels good." I brush my lips against whatever part of her face is nearest to them, her cheek possibly.

"It's been so long." She whimpers.

"Since you had sex?" I ask. Maybe I should have asked this earlier.

"Yes," she says. "Especially sex like this."

I want to tell her I know exactly what she means, but I feel the build-up to my orgasm approach at a pace that shocks me. My sobriety is making me so much more aware of everything and leaving me more defenceless to delay the climax I am now chasing, rutting up into her faster.

"Jenna," I say her name again and her fingernails dig deeper into my lower back.

"Harder," she says. "More."

"Jenna," I say again, and I bend my knees, tilt my pelvis more and keep thrusting. Out of nowhere, I feel a heat in my left calf but I'm so close. It can cramp later.

"More," she says. "Fuck me."

"Yes," I say and it's more of a grunt than a word. The pain in my calf is taking the full shape of the muscle, and I feel the familiar pull begin, as if it wants to rip itself off my leg.

Not now, please not now.

I close my eyes, feel the tightness in my balls and feel my dick harden that little bit more. I'm so close.

And then my calf starts to spasm and the pain shoots up through my leg and into every other muscle in my body as I tense, terrified of moving as my calf muscle tightens beyond comprehension.

"Shit!" I call out and hold still, thrusting up into her one final, forceful time.

"Yes, Marty, yes," she's saying.

"Oh God, no, I... shit!" I hiss as the pain intensifies.

"It's okay," she says and she's stroking my back now, comforting me.

"No," I gasp out and lift my torso off her slightly. "I'm... fuck! Cramping!" I manage to say.

"Oh," she says. "Shit. What do you need?"

What do you need?

Even in the chaos of my pain, I feel the full weight of those words. Or rather their almost divine lightness. And I feel the clarity of realising that nobody has asked me that in a very long time.

As the pain continues, I'm almost certain my muscle is going to be permanently damaged. This cramp is so intense and wild. I know I have to move to try to find some relief. It's only then that I feel the ache in my balls, they were so close. I was so close.

"I need to move," I gasp. "Stretch."

"Okay." Jenna moves from underneath me. She quickly pulls her soaking dress and bra off over her head and naked, so exquisitely naked, she steps out of the shower and finds a towel for me which she throws over my shoulder. Then she grabs a robe and ties it around herself while walking back to me. I'm leaning against the wall now, trying in vain to move my left leg so I can stretch it out, but the pain is still too unbearable.

"I don't think I can move," I say with a weak half-laugh.

"Lean on me," she says. "Can you do that and just hobble over to the bed?"

"Yeah, I think so," I say and that's what we do. Me leaning on her and limping over to the bed in feeble hops.

"Put a towel down," I gasp out at her as we approach her perfectly made white sheets. "I'm wet."

"It will dry," she says quickly. "Just lie down."

I crash down on my front, as much to hide my shrinking erection than anything else.

"Flex your foot, if you can," she says, and I try but it's too painful.

"Fuck, it fecking hurts," I say.

"It will pass. It's your left calf muscle, right?"

"Yeah," I groan. "Does it look like it's about to rocket jet out of my body?"

She laughs gently. "No, but it does look tight. Can I touch it, to try and ease the tension?"

"Sure," I say. "But if I scream obscenities at you, I apologise in advance."

"I'll start with your foot," she says and she bends down at the end of the bed and I feel her hands wrap around my foot, one at the heel and the other on my toes, she slowly pushes my toes down so my foot is at a right angle. It pulls on the cramp and deepens the ache but almost in a good way. Almost.

"Shit," I whisper.

"Just hold it here for a while," she says. "It will pass, I promise."

It will pass. It will pass. That is something that I have heard so many times over the last year. *The grief will pass. The pain will pass. The hangover will pass. The depression will pass. The self-loathing will pass.* I've rarely believed it.

But when her hand makes a V-shape, presumably with her thumb and index finger, and she runs that up against my spasming muscle, I start to believe her. *It will pass. This pain will pass.* In fact, it's fading already.

"That almost feels good," I say as she does it again. Again and again, until the sharp pull has gone and even the ache left behind starts to dull.

"Is it better?" she asks eventually but she doesn't stop. With my eyes closed, face down in the pillow, I feel a dip in the bed and then I feel her come to sit on my backside, her robe plush and soft on my naked arse cheeks, and her hands

150

now going back to both of my calf muscles and massaging with the same V-shape but in the opposite direction. I can imagine almost perfectly what she must look like going back and forward from her waist to do the movement. It makes blood return to my cock, and I quickly slide my hand under my body to remove the wasted condom that has all but rolled off completely.

"I really want to lie and say no," I admit, my voice muffled in the pillow. "Because this feels so good."

"You should stretch more after you exercise," she says. "Or the bike rides with your dad."

The warmth I feel at her remembering that is a soft surprise.

"I did stretch this morning. I stretched for twenty minutes more than I usually do just so I could watch you run."

She chuckles. "I guess sprinting down to the bar didn't help?"

"Or running after you to get back here," I point out.

"I was a woman in need."

She moves to apply pressure through her knuckles now which burns my calf muscles, especially my recovering left one, but in a satisfying way. Every now and again she stops at the skin behind my knees and strokes me there with feather-light touches. It sends shivers up my whole body.

"You're good at this," I tell her.

"I did a course," she says.

"To become a massage therapist?"

She hesitates. "Not exactly."

"Then what?" As much as my cock is warming up again, I suddenly want to ask her questions and hear her answer them.

"Tantric massage," she says.

"What?" My eyes dart open.

"It's a kind of full-body massage technique that can be used to elongate and intensify sexual pleasure," she says.

"I know what it is," I say. "I'm twenty-four, not fourteen."

"Well, I didn't know what it was at your age." She sounds a little sad.

"What did you learn?" I am suddenly fascinated.

151

She clears her throat lightly. "I learned that my husband thought I was crazy for going."

"Serious?"

"Yeah, so after a few weeks, I never went back. I couldn't be interested enough for two of us. But I learned that no matter what tricks and hacks you may learn for sex, none of them will ever be as effective as just good old-fashioned desire. At least for me, that's what matters most and it's one of the things that makes sex amazing for me. And my ex-husband, I think he just stopped desiring me, and we couldn't get it back. No matter how many hours I tried to spend giving him hand jobs." She forces a laugh.

"What are the other things?" I ask.

"Other things?"

"You said, one of the things that makes sex amazing for you. What are the other things?"

She sighs. "How long have you got?"

"Look, I'm a simple man with blue balls who is enjoying the feel of your hands a little bit too much. Give me the shortlist."

"Everything," she says. "Everything has the potential to make sex amazing, if it's done with enough intention and connection."

"Intention and connection," I repeat. "You should write about this shit."

"I do!" She laughs louder. "Or rather, I did. I had a sex and relationships column in a Sunday newspaper, another in a woman's magazine and I wrote lots of other pieces for magazines, papers and blogs." She goes back to massaging my legs.

"You did? Shit, I didn't realise I was getting into bed with an expert. Jesus, a 'sexpert'" I say, sounding just as nervous as I'm abruptly feeling.

"A sexpert who just came the second you entered me." She laughs at herself and I suddenly want to see her face. It's been a few minutes since I have, and I miss it.

"Ah, I know you just did it to make me feel better in case I blew my load too soon. What with me being so young and all."

"No," she says. "That was just me being a very horny thirty-seven-year-old woman who just watched a criminally good-looking man undress in my shower."

I hold my breath and a beat later she stops moving.

Chapter Nineteen

Marty

"Shit," she says in a whisper.

"Thirty-seven, hey?"

"Yeah."

"Fuck, that's hot," I mumble to myself. And it is.

"Really?" Her voice has far too much doubt in it.

"Lift up a second," I say and as she does, I roll over underneath her. Then as she sits back down, still not looking at me, her body still curved forwards, her pussy lands perfectly on my groin and my dick instantly starts to harden against her warm flesh and soft curls. I sit up and put one hand behind me so I can hold my weight. The other I place on her neck, clearing her hair out of the way.

"I know it's old, Marty," she says, unmoving apart from her hands gripping my shins in a way that I find so sexy for reasons I can't put into words.

"It's older than twenty-four." I lean forward to kiss her neck.

"Too old?" she asks, and it could be my imagination, but she wriggles as if to place my hardening cock exactly where she wants it.

"Am I too young for you?" I push up more so my chest is flush with her back. I bring my hands to where her robe is tied at her chest.

"Probably," she mutters, and I wait for a laugh, but it doesn't come. Instead, I hear her gasp as one of my hands slips inside the soft towelling material and finds her nipple. Her breasts are that delectable mix of firm and soft, modest but still enough for a handful, and they're warm and smooth under my touch. My other hand starts to slowly pull down the side of her robe and she shudders as her skin is exposed to the air-conditioned room. I take my other hand off her body to pull the robe down as far as I can before putting my fingers back on her. I am still for a moment, letting my eyes take her in. The lack of bikini straplines tells me she's been doing some topless sunbathing, and this has me growing harder by the second. As does the way her bronzed skin is decorated in a pretty pattern of freckles and moles, the way her frame narrows at her waist, and how there are dimples in her back, and they wink at me as I sit there just looking at her.

"You're beautiful," I say as I stroke her back.

"I daren't turn around," she says, and she does indeed sound scared.

"Why?" I ask, my fingertips applying more pressure.

"I am pretty sure my make-up is all over my face and my hair needs a good brush, and..." She sighs. "I haven't been completely naked with a man in a long time. Especially one who is thirteen years younger than me."

I have questions but I know it's not the time. I also hope I can reassure her of my desire for her with my hands and mouth more than I could with my words.

"Turn around," I say, lying down flat on my back again. "I want to see you."

She lifts her hands and smooths down parts of her hair, wipes under her eyes quickly, and this only accentuates the curves and muscles in her back.

When Jenna doesn't move, I wonder if she's going to protest or insist she turns the lights off, which I will absolutely fight her on, but a moment later she begins to move, first taking off the robe, and discarding it. This gives me the most perfect view of her arse, and then, for a collection of heady seconds, she leans forward and I can feel my dick slide in between her lips there. But then she pushes up and pivots, putting her hands on the bed, and turning around so she is facing me. I almost want to stop Jenna there and keep her in that position - on her hands and knees - but I don't and instead I offer up a small prayer that maybe I'll get a chance to see her like that another time before this holiday is over.

As she shifts her weight so she can throw her other leg over my body, I feel the urge to inhale as deeply as I can, to drag out this moment for as long as possible, because fuck, she looks magnificent. Tousled and fucked and glowing and fucked and vibrant and fucked, fucked, fucked. Her cheeks are pink, her eyes are bright, and her lips are pressed together, plump and inviting. And that's just her face. When I glance down and see those breasts I want to lavish attention on, nipples already pebbled, I think about sitting up to suck one into my mouth, but I don't because there is more for my eyes to feast on, and they do. I see the curve and rolls of her stomach, the small smile of her belly button and long silver stripes of stretchmarks on her hips, lines that I move to stroke, delighting in their smoothness and silky texture. My eyes follow my fingers as I trace the shape of where her bikini has been, a shape I suddenly, desperately, want to discover with my mouth again.

"Sit on me," I grunt out as I grab hold of her backside, nudging it towards my face hard enough to jolt her forward. "Sit on my face."

"Marty!" She laughs, so unnecessarily and prettily embarrassed.

"Please," I say, and my grip and nudge are firmer still.

When she still doesn't move of her own accord, I bring my hand up and wrap it around her jaw and chin.

"Earlier, you asked me what I like," I say. "Well, that's what I like."

"You don't have to." She won't look me in the eye.

"Look at me, Jenna," I say, applying a bit more pressure with my fingertips. She finally locks eyes with me. "If you remember one thing about me, make it this. My job is all about flavours, textures and taste, but I have never, ever wanted to eat something as much as I want to eat you right now. Please let me taste you."

With her deep exhale, it's like all the fight leaves her body and she smiles at me in that way she did when she was watching me in the shower; a mischievous look drenched in longing and curiosity and just the right amount of apprehension. I give her bum another squeeze and finally, she starts travelling up my body. I tuck my arms and shoulders under her when she's close enough and then my hands are back on her butt, pulling her down and on top of me, which she does only to then lift up again.

"Sit," I say.

"I am," she replies.

"No, you're hovering." I pull down again.

157

"I'll suffocate you."

"It'll be a grand way to go," I say, with another pull.

"Marty, seriously," she says with more nervous giggles.

"I am *very* serious right now. I'm so fucking hungry for this. Feed me. Give me what I want." I yank her so hard she sinks down.

And I get to work.

I start slow, exploring, mapping her out, inside and out. I kiss, I lick, I suck, and I use my tongue, making it firm, making it soft. When she moans, I stay where I am, circling her clit until she starts to rock against me, then I stop and move down to push my tongue inside her and curl it as much as I can. Her taste is intoxicating – salty like the ocean, musky like the air on a hot summer's day – and I eat it all up. I want to go further, lower, deeper – eat all of her up - but I daren't when she just showed me how even this is not something she is used to. When I go back to licking up and down either side of her clit, she makes the sweetest strangled noise and I look up. Her eyes are closed, one of her hands is playing with her right nipple and she's biting that full bottom lip.

"Keep doing that," she mumbles. "It feels amazing."

I do as I'm told, closing my eyes again and digging my fingers into her backside harder, pinning her exactly where she is. My mouth is impossibly wet now, the air hot and full, but I don't want to move. Her hands come down to find my hair and they grip my scalp as she grinds down into me.

"I'm going to come," she says, breathless, pupils blown dark and wide.

She thrusts her hips hard against me and if my hands weren't happy on her backside I would lift them up and applaud her on, but there's no way I'm going to stop squeezing all her solid warm flesh while she comes on my mouth, which happens only seconds later as she rides out her orgasm and I get to taste more of her.

"Fuck," she gasps and what is probably my favourite word in the world has never sounded better. "Fuck."

When she pulls up to float above me, I let her. She looks down at me over the tanned mounds of her breasts and stomach, and she smiles. Then she reaches down and wipes my mouth, nose and chin with her hand.

"Still alive?" she asks.

"Absolutely. Not even close to being suffocated, sadly," I say and then I almost come myself when I see her put that hand of hers to her mouth and she licks herself off her fingers.

"I taste good on you," she says pushing back to lie flat on top of me. A beat later she's kissing my mouth and face, hunting for more traces of herself. I ready myself to pin her body against mine, roll her over and God willing, enter her again, but then she pushes off me and the absence of her smooth sun-kissed skin feels all kinds of wrong.

"Where are you going?" I say, the panic audible.

"My turn to be responsible," she says, walking to the bathroom, and I get to watch her butt sway as she does, delighting at the sight of red marks where my finger dug into her skin. While she's gone, my hand grips my length and strokes it, but I stop when I see her coming back into the room. She's completely naked and all curves and all woman and all things I want to touch and hold and feel. But the sexiest part of Jenna right now is that she's not covering herself up or feeling nervous. She's walking with her head high, her shoulders back, and a condom in her hand that she's carefully opening.

Kneeling on the bed beside me, Jenna has the condom out but doesn't put it on. Instead, she looks at my cock, almost inspecting it. She is anything but neutral about it because her tongue is licking her lips and her hands are both gentle and deliberate as she gives me a few rubs, moving my foreskin up and down. Then she bends down and swirls her tongue around the head, once, twice, then comes off leaving a kiss on the very tip. I suck in a breath and find my thoughts banging into each other because I want her to do that again, but I also want to fuck her and at the same time I need to taste her again because it's already been too long.

"Marty?" she says, talking to my penis.

"Yeah," I just about manage to reply.

"I don't want you to guarantee me anything about tonight, but I do want you to promise me one thing," she says, and she licks the small bead of pre-cum that we both watch emerge at the top of my cock.

"What?" I ask on a sigh. Whatever it is, I'm pretty sure I'll do it.

"Promise me I can suck this cock of yours properly before we're done tonight?"

By dipping her head down again and taking me in her mouth once more, she doesn't give me time to reply or ask the many questions that rush in, which is just as well because I don't even think they're questions for her. They're questions I need to answer, because in my mind, we are so far from "done" - not tonight and not tomorrow - although I have no clue what that means.

"Yes," I finally reply as that tongue of hers is tickling the underside of my cock.

"Good," she says when her mouth is off me. And then with considerable concentrated effort, she rolls the condom onto me. Seconds later, her legs are astride me and her hips are raised above mine.

"Jenna," I start, because now her tongue has stopped serving up slices of heaven, I can think a little clearer, and I want to tell her that there's a hundred things I want to do with her before tonight is over, but she seems to take my saying her name as an invitation because with her hand still on the base of me, and my hands sliding up her thighs, she moves to get herself lined up with my tip and in a single breath, she sinks down and takes all of me into the warm slick heat of her.

"God, that's the fucking best," I say and it's the truth. I almost want to hold her down like this, stay sunken inside her, but Jenna has other ideas. She rises just to sink down again, stretching her legs out so I slide in deeper. Giving me a contented look, she does it again and again and again.

As I watch her, feel her, out of nowhere a realisation hits me. This is what it was like with Arnie. Eye contact, dreamy smiles, sparkling eyes, and breaths we can't keep hold of. I am here in body and mind, nowhere else, and so is she. This is why it's so fucking good.

"Marty, I want to ride you until it hurts," she gasps out and I react by gripping her hips, tight.

"Yes, Jenna."

Jenna starts to move quicker. Rising and falling, she strokes me, she rides me, she fucks me. Then a few minutes later, when her breathing is hurried and rough, she shifts forward and rocks back and forth. Then she pushes up on her hands and does this combination of both that almost finishes me, not least because I get to watch her breasts swing right in front of my eyes. When she sits back again moments later she opens her eyes and looks at me like she is thinking about doing something else.

"Do what makes you feel good," I say.

"I believe I've had exactly two more orgasms than you," she replies, and her hands are on her hair again, pulling at it in a way I suspect adds something to sex, one of her things.

I want to know all her things.

"I am but a mere penis owner. I could and would never compete with someone who has a mighty clitoris. Come as much as you want. Come as much as you can. I want all your orgasms."

"I want you to come," she says but I see she can't stop herself from rocking on top of me again.

"I want you to come again, and I will bet you fifty fucken Euros it will make me come too." I move her hips faster, digging my fingertips into her as hard as I hope I can without hurting her. She arches her eyebrow for a moment, as if questioning or challenging me, but then she leans back and it's like I hit something inside her that makes the challenge just melt away as she grinds in earnest against me. Her hand comes down to join us and I can feel her rubbing at her clit in a way that makes me want to yell out because it's so hot, but instead, I lift my head off the pillow and kiss her neck.

"Come for me, Jenna," I say, and she nods and doesn't stop nodding although it slows while her finger picks up pace and she starts to moan and gasp. Somehow managing to hold her body up, parallel from mine, she reaches back with her other hand and her fingers graze my balls and along my perineum and it sends new jolts of tingling pleasure up my dick. Her hand stays there, searching me, playing with me, until she throws her head back and I watch her mouth make that same circle it did earlier and then she slams her hips back in five short and sharp movements that ride my dick so hard it almost hurts.

"Oh, fuck," she says. She sounds breathless, shattered. She brings her hand up to my side to hold herself up.

"Stay exactly where you are," I say into her ear, and I grip her butt, holding her as I thrust up and into her hard and fast and desperate until I too am orgasming everything I have into her.

As the pleasure washes over me I feel the very things I chased for months in the Balearic Islands. I feel the undiluted bliss, the briefest but deepest seconds of peace, and I exhale as my body completely surrenders to an overpowering physical pleasure that seems to warm my bones. It reminds me why I chased it so hard, so desperately, but what I also realise, as my orgasm subsides and heart rate starts to slow, is that I never got it. It was never like this. I already know the thrill of this high will stay with me one hundred times longer than it did with those brief encounters. Even though I used to pursue it like it was oxygen, I never actually got it and so I think I forgot how good sex could be. Or maybe I was actively trying to forget. Maybe by not caring who it was, where it was, how it was, I was actually trying to obliterate the memory of how good sex can be.

But now I remember. Now I know exactly how good it can be. And I have no idea how I feel about it.

Chapter Twenty

Jenna

Fuck, I've missed good sex.

I've missed feeling like my insides are on fire. I've missed feeling this full and satiated. I have a sudden urge to thank Marty for how I feel, but as I open my eyes to look down at him, I see his eyes are still closed, his breath still shallow, and there's a slight frown on his forehead.

"Are you okay, Marty? Was it good for you?" I ask in a quiet voice, suddenly panicked it was all very one-sided.

His eyes pop open.

"Good? Good!?" His frown disappears as his dimples emerge. "I just saw stars and comets and planets and green little aliens on those planets high-fiving each other because of how good that was."

I collapse on him and bury my laughter, and my relief, in the few hairs he has in the middle of his chest. His arms come around my body and hold me there.

"So good," I say, and it feels like I'm revealing too much but also not using words that are close to adequate.

"Yeah, that was pretty fucking special," he says, and I can't stop my smile at first, but a second later I bite it back into my mouth. Special must be one of those words Irish people use like "grand" and "mighty" which have so much more power to us unassuming British folk who rely far too heavily on middle of the road adjectives like "nice" and "fine".

Hoping, therefore, that I'm not saying too much, not exposing too much of myself, I risk agreeing. "Yeah, it was." I give him a kiss of thanks, right in the middle of his ribcage. We stay like that until his dick slides out of me and he taps my arse gently.

"Better deal with this," he says, and I move to the side so he can stand up. "Is there a bin in the bathroom? Can I put it in there?"

"Yeah." I think how strange it is I can't ever remember being asked by a man where to put a condom after we had sex but surely it must have happened. Now alert for more unpleasant feelings, I wait for the hormone crash that should follow that incredibly satisfying trio of orgasms, but it doesn't come. Not yet, not when I can still see him, and he is still naked. I pull my eyebrows together as I lay face down on the bed and watch his delightfully muscled backside walk away from me. I then watch his swinging dick walk back to me after I hear the toilet flush and the taps run. I should go and do the same, but I can't move. I can't do anything but lie prone on the bed and smile at the sight of him walking back to me.

"You know you have the most amazing arse," he says as he joins me lying on the bed, and his hand is on it.

"Better than my brother's?" I suddenly want him to smack it, berate my cheekiness with a hard slap, but he just buries his face in my shoulder and laughs.

"Well, I haven't got to know your brother's as well as I have yours, and now I never will, but still, I really can't imagine it would beat this."

"You know you can smack it," I say pressing my shoulder against him.

He nods as he swallows that information, but he doesn't move his hand.

"I'm serious," I say in low voice.

"Do you *want* me to smack your arse, Jenna?"

"Maybe later," I say, embarrassed all over again. It doesn't help when I realise what I just said. *Maybe later. Assumptive, much?*

"Can I stay? For a bit longer?" he asks as if reading my mind. He sounds almost as fearful as I am to invite him to spend the night here. To ease this unwelcome new awkwardness, I reach for what has worked best between us so far; humour.

"You just made me come three times," I say. "You can stay as long as you want. You and your dick and your talented tongue can move in."

He laughs but it doesn't sound as hearty as usual. "The three of us appreciate that. But I will go back later. I'm getting up early to ride with Dad."

"To do *what*?"

"A *bike* ride, Jenna, get your mind out of the gutter." I feel a light slap on my left arse cheek.

"Hmm," I say with great satisfaction. "You were listening."

"Tell me more about your work," he says out of nowhere as he rubs very gently at the exact spot he just hit. It shouldn't feel as good as it does - sore, hot, prickly, tender.

"What do you want to know?" I ask, pushing up to rest on my forearms.

"Did you like study sex or something to become a sex writer? After that performance, I can kind of believe it."

"I wasn't just a sex columnist. Actually, sex was a very small part of what I wrote about. Really what I was writing about was people, and relationships, and love. Sex is just a big part of that for some people, but not everyone, of course."

"So, tell me about it." I feel him shift a little closer, the hairs on his calves, thighs and in his groin tickling the side of me in the most delightful, teasing way.

"I always wanted to be a writer. I love books and reading, and was convinced that I would end up writing the steamy romance novels I used to smuggle out of the library as a teen, but then, in my last year of school I had this horrible break-up and got really angry with those kind of books giving me completely false expectations about men and love, so at the very last minute, I pulled out of my combined creative writing and English Lit uni course, and switched to sociology with creative writing."

"And that helped you learn what makes relationships work, and what doesn't?"

"No, of course not. That can't be taught. If it could then I wouldn't be single, divorce wouldn't be a billion-pound industry, and half of the television shows we watch, books we read, or music we listen to wouldn't exist. Of course, there are some things that definitely enhance relationships that research proves and experience confirms - good communication, honesty, being self-aware, being forgiving and open-minded - but truly, there's no winning formula and it's my experience - professional and personal - that luck and timing play as big a role as anything."

He props his head up on his elbow. "But how did you start writing about all this?"

I find myself smiling as I recall a fuzzy string of memories I'd not thought about in a long time. "Once I knew I wasn't going to be the next Danielle Steel, I thought about maybe going into journalism, so at university I joined the student newspaper, doing all sorts from film reviews to local job listings - really thrilling, ground-breaking stuff - but then they wanted someone to do an anonymous advice column and I put my name forward, and it took off. This was back before social media and blogs, when Dear So-and-So agony aunt columns were really popular. To my mind, I was just giving very obvious answers to very obvious questions - about how to ask someone out on a date, how to go on said date when you had next to no money, how to talk to a fuck buddy about contraception, how to tell your parents you're queer - but people apparently needed the advice, and others liked reading it. In my second year, I was asked to do a weekly one-hour show on the uni radio station answering anonymous questions, and I also ended up interning at a national newspaper for a summer, doing research for a features editor. After I graduated, I was all set up to do a journalism MA, but that summer I was bored working in a clothes shop so I just sent out some examples of my columns to a women's magazine in London and they got me in for work experience. After a few weeks doing that, they hired me to support their D-list celebrity agony aunt, by which I mean, I wrote her column for her while she partied six nights a week, filling tabloids with paparazzi pics. When she very publicly had to go into rehab about a year later, they took some headshots and I took over, officially. Ask Jenny, it was called, because they thought Jenna was too weird a name." I laugh at how I didn't even put up a fight then. I was so young. "God, it was so cheesy, but I was so proud, and it was really rewarding helping people. I never did do my MA, and instead started freelancing for women's and teen magazines, and even the gossip rags when they were popular for all of five minutes before social media took off. Once I had a decent portfolio, the broadsheet and tabloid editors came knocking and I was able to pitch articles wherever I wanted."

"Wow, the big guns." He kisses my shoulder which makes me shiver. "Are you cold? Should we get under the covers?"

I nod, not cold but suddenly desperate for that.

"But you said you've stopped. Why?" Marty asks once we're under the sheets. This time I'm lying on my back and somehow that makes me even more aware of the length of his body lying on its side beside mine, and how his dick rests against the curve of my hip. It is only too tempting to reach my hand and play with him, take us away from this conversation.

"You don't want to know about that," I say.

"I asked, didn't I?" His eyebrows lower.

"Okay." I give him a smile that I hope apologises for doubting him. "Well, because it's sex and sex is, well, always interesting to a lot of people, I was often encouraged by editors to answer more sex-related questions than the general questions about relationships and intimacy and that's fine, because, yes, I'm an allosexual who loves sex so I was happy to do it most of the time, but then it became more of a struggle, and more than a little ironic because..." I squeeze my eyes shut.

"Because?" he prompts, and now I'm also holding my breath because his hand is on my stomach, his fingers stroking and searching. I am a second away from tensing my muscles to pull it a little tauter, but I don't. I am who I am. He's seen me, and now he's feeling me, and by the feel of his hardening cock at my side, he's enjoying it. I will not let misogynistic beauty standards even get close to ruining this for me.

The answer to his question comes quickly and easily.

Because I was hired to help people have better sex and improve their relationships and how could I do that when I was having the worst sex of my life - if any sex at all - and my marriage was dissolving in front of my eyes?

But I don't say it out loud.

"Because I needed a change. I needed some time away from work to grieve after my divorce." That much is true.

"Oh," he says, and the way his features fall has me wondering if he can see through my lie, but then I realised what I just said.

"Shit, that was a really insensitive thing to say after what you shared about Arnie."

Marty's hand, which was cupping and gently squeezing my breast, stops moving. "Grief is grief," he says with a half-shrug. I don't feel relief, though, until his hand starts playing with me again.

I'm so convinced we're warming up to round two that I start to move my hand to find his dick, but then he speaks again. "Why did you and your ex-husband get divorced?"

"There is no way I can go into it while you play with my nipple like that," I say, closing my eyes as the warmth and humming in my body picks up again.

"I can stop," he says but he doesn't. My answer to this is to wrap my hand around his cock, which is now hard and hot against my hip.

"Don't you dare stop," I say as I move my fingers on him, applying pressure in a fluttering motion, one digit at a time. I keep doing this as I move my grip up and around his head, playing with the skin that glides around it so brilliantly. Robert was circumcised and while I had thought that was my preference, now I'm suddenly not so sure, which is now a strangely comfortable feeling - just not being sure.

"Same to you, cupcake." He lifts his hips and bends a leg up, giving me a bit more room to play with him.

And then there are, blissfully, no more questions, and no more lies. There is no more talking at all, apart from single breath-filled words, at most a couple at a time, and moans. We moan for each other as pleas, as orders, as praise, as warnings and as rewards. When I come up on my knees and push him down on his back, his moan becomes a growl. When I bend my body so I can take him in my mouth, his growls are grunts. When I tell him his cock is beautiful, he hisses and brings his hands to hold my hair so he can see more of what I'm doing.

"Those lips of yours," he mumbles. "You look so fucken pretty putting them to work on me."

That spurs me on, and I lick him until he's wet all over. I suck him into my mouth and take him as far down as I can. It's nowhere near as far as I would like, my gag reflex kicking in and making me choke. But then I recall an old trick I read once and I pull off to yawn, and this means I can go back and take more of him down my throat. It's still not enough – for me and probably him too – but I bring my hand up to cover the rest of him as I suck and start moving up and down, twisting my head a little as my lips ride over the head. I keep doing this until my jaw aches and then I drop my head lower and play with his balls in my mouth, only to then return to kissing, licking, and sucking his penis. When I feel ready again, I take him back into my throat. I repeat this until I'm so lost in what I'm doing, his voice is almost a surprise.

"You need to stop if you don't want me to come in your mouth," he says, and I look up at him, pulling off for a second, but keeping my hand going.

"Do it. Please, do it. I want to taste you too," I say before plunging down onto him. The curiosity I have about what he tastes like when I drink him down has me pushing harder against my gag reflex, and squeezing my eyes shut when the tears come. I feel his hand stroke the side of my face, while his other fingers are still tangled in my hair, and I grip his hips harder as they start to tense and rock into me.

"Jesus, Jenna," he says, and he jerks once, twice, three times, and his cum fills my mouth and throat.

I keep my eyes closed, tickle my tongue against the underside of him, and suck, swallow, suck, swallow, suck, swallow. Only when I look up and see his smile, do I pull off, leaving a peck of a kiss on the tip of him that is now red and glistening with my saliva.

Then I lay my body down between his legs and place my head on his stomach so he can't see the incredibly smug grin I have on my face.

"I kinda want you to sit on my face again," he says, his fingers back in my hair, or maybe they never left.

"I am not sure I can," I say. "I'm old and I need a lie down."

169

He sighs. "I'm young and I need a lie down."

I laugh into his stomach then, feeling his abs tense when he joins me. I reach down and find the discarded covers we kicked to the side, and I cover us. I can't stop my eyes closing as I nestle back down into his torso, feeling the hair and warmth of his groin against my breasts. I am almost asleep when I hear him talk again.

"Jenna," he says, and his voice sounds quiet, probably sleepy too. He probably has to go soon, and I brace myself for the stab of disappointment that will bring. I tell myself that it's just my hormones. It's only what the post-orgasm hit of oxytocin in my body wants me to do, to attach myself to this virile young man.

I lift my head to look up at him. "Do you have to go?"

"Soon, but first I want to ask you something."

Oh, Jesus, I think. *He wants to go back to that conversation. He wants to know what went wrong with my marriage.* I brace myself accordingly.

He comes up to rest on his elbows and I like how it brings his face closer to me, that strong jawline, his dark eyes, and that adorable bump in his nose.

"Can I take you out for the day tomorrow?" Marty asks. "Like... on a date?"

Chapter Twenty-One
The Next Day

Marty

It quickly becomes clear that unlike me, my father didn't come three times last night.

After our fifteen-kilometre or so warm-up getting to the foot of the small Kalathenes mountain range, Dad races off up our first serious incline without a glance back at me, until he's confident the gap between us is sufficient. Then he looks sideways for the briefest moment, just so I can see his shit-eating grin. Well, fine. I know I'd much rather be trailing a sixty-one-year-old man after incredible sex than have legs full of beans for a dawn mountain climb. Besides, I want to save my energy for the day ahead, my day with Jenna.

I'm not sure why, but she took some persuading to come out with me. In the end, we agreed if I could make her come again then she would go on our date, and while I had been ready for the challenge - the competitive streak in me always hard and eager - even I was pleasantly surprised when it had taken mere minutes once I'd settled between her legs. But then I'd become impossibly hard and she told me there was no way she wanted me wasting my erection. She promptly flipped over onto her hands and knees and I got to see exactly how fantastic her arse is in that position, and we rocked, thrust, slammed into each other until we came, at almost exactly the same time.

She was just as astonished as me about that and I think her words were "a happy fluke". I wasn't sure it was a fluke, but I wasn't going to tell her that when she is the one who knows more about these things than I do. She has words for all this sex stuff, I just have a new fascination at how it's so good with her. That was what I had been thinking about as I cuddled her to sleep - which took no time at all - then I wrote my phone number, a time and location on a piece of paper by her bed, kissed her head once – maybe twice - and left.

And now I'm getting my arse kicked by my father who is taking great pleasure in gaining the lead on me. But my competitive edge - and legs and cock - are still recovering from last night, so I'm going to let him go ahead, and leave him thinking I'm busting my balls to keep up with him by closing his lead here and there. That works for the whole of our seventy-kilometre ride, during which we watch the sun climb high above the horizon. I think briefly about some of the sunrises Arnie and I watched together, and I smile.

I smile and that's it. Now that feels like a very happy fluke.

Back in our villa, Dad goes straight to the fridge for a beer. Mum and Maeve are at a yoga class, so I know he's going to sneak one in before Mum gets home, probably while he dips his feet in the pool, which she'll also kill him for if he's not yet showered.

"Hitting the shower, Da," I call out.

"Son," he says. I stop and turn because my father so rarely seeks out my company without a sporting activity or game we can play together.

"Yeah," I say but don't walk back into the room.

"Thanks for doing that with me. I dare say you may have had a better offer last night and maybe this morning too, but I appreciate you coming back and riding with me." He gives me three winks during that little speech and each one makes me feel a little queasy.

"Sure, Da."

"Your mum appreciates it too," he says. "I'm working on her, you know. I know it's not been easy, but she's... honestly, she was a fecking mess when you were gone and we didn't know where you were for a while. And then when we got the call about your accident, we really thought the worst. It was like... Well, you can imagine. When Colm and Sheila lost Arnie, we couldn't help but think about what it would be like if we lost one of you. Your mother holds on to those kinds of feelings a lot tighter than I do. We all know what she's like when she gets her claws into something."

"I get it, Dad," I say, and I do. I have thought about this a lot over the last year or so. They loved Arnie too, and they are close to his parents. I know it's been hard for them, Mum especially, but it's harder for me to admit that sometimes my own pain and loss made anyone else's feel like a mere graze in comparison. Mine was an open stab wound, bleeding profusely. And I didn't have any capacity to stem the flow of my own blood loss let alone find plasters or bandages for theirs.

"Just go easy with her," he says. I pull the inside of my cheek between my teeth, then turn and walk away because I'm done with this conversation now.

Twenty-five minutes later I return – showered and dressed - and Mum and Maeve are there in their yoga gear.

"Aiden!" Mum calls out. "You want a coffee? Breakfast will be here in fifteen minutes."

I walk to the door and slide my Birkenstocks on. "Nah, Ma, I'm heading to the breakfast buffet, and then I'm going to be out most of the day."

"What?" I see her head pop out from the side of the open fridge door. "Where are you going?"

I take a deep breath. In between reliving some of my favourite views of Jenna, I went to sleep last night thinking about how this conversation would go, so it's time to find out which of my many hypotheses is correct.

"So, here's the thing... I have a date," I say.

"Such a dirtbird," Maeve mutters without looking up from her phone.

"A date, Maevey, not an orgy," I say with a roll of my eyes.

"Wouldn't put it past you."

"Is that who you were with last night?" Mum closes the fridge and walks towards me. "Wasn't that a date of sorts? Or is today with someone else? Surely not!"

"Yeah. Kinda. And no. Not someone else. It's the same person. But last night wasn't a date, so..."

My father coughs and I want to throttle him. I haven't asked him if he told Mum about bumping into Jenna, but something tells me now, if he has, he has withheld some information. Well, I can do that too.

"We had *non-alcoholic* drinks together last night," I say with emphasis. "But today we're going on a proper date."

"Aiden, we've only been here two days. How have you possibly met someone who you want to *date*?" my mum asks with the deepest frown she allows herself.

"*She's* very pretty," Maeve says, stressing the pronoun.

"I'll agree with that," my father mumbles, confirming that he did indeed tell Mum about Jenna.

"Will *I* get to meet her? Seeing as everyone else in the family already has." Mum holds her hands up in a very dramatic move that makes the rest of us look anywhere but at her.

I see an easy way out of here and I take it, shifting into first gear eagerly. "Sure, Ma. You can meet her. But not today, okay? Let me have today with her, then I'll introduce her." I step over to my mother who has her hands on her hips. I give her a kiss on the cheek, then turn and rush out of the door as quickly as I can because I'm not sure I sounded anywhere near convincing enough.

Introduce Jenna to my mother? Not in a million years!

Ten minutes later, I'm in the resort's lobby armed with the banana and croissant I grabbed from the breakfast bar. My other hand is knocking on the door that has a sign that says, "Resort Manager".

"Come in!" a voice calls and I do so while plastering a big grin on my face.

"Good morning, Resort Manager!" I say to Jake, who is sitting behind his desk, his eyes narrowing with suspicion when they see me.

"Hello, Irishman who snuck out of my sister's villa in the middle of the night!" He leans back in his chair as he signals for me to sit down opposite him.

"Wow, you're one of those managers. Eyes and ears everywhere?"

"Nah, she texted me this morning with all the juicy details," he says. "Bravo, Marty O'Martin, bravo."

"Bravo? Juicy?" I arch an eyebrow. "Tell me more about this text message."

He crosses his legs and wags a finger at me. "Never. Besides, I'm more curious why you're here?"

"I need your help," I say.

He groans. "If it's about the smell coming out of the drains in the beach toilets, or the wasps' nest in the herb garden, I am aware of these issues and could really do without a reminder."

"No, it's more about taking your sister out on a phenomenal date."

He looks only momentarily impressed.

"Considering her ex-husband once took her to Paris just for macaroons, the bar has been set very high." Jake gives me a pointed look. "But he was also an emotionally unavailable workaholic who made her miserable towards the end, so I'd say there's some wriggle room."

I store all of this away for another time and press ahead with explaining what I have in mind. He listens and nods and, when I've finished, he claps his hands together.

"Easy," he says. "And a very lovely idea, Marty O'Martin. All very simple, but very effective. Jenna will love it. Let's make it happen." He's about to reach for his phone but stops. "On one condition."

"Name it," I say, curious.

"Will you write the resort a review when you get home? Or better than that, before you leave. Long story but I've got to try and encourage some more word of mouth reviews and fast."

"I can do that. Will get my sister and parents to do the same." I nod and it pleases me to see Jake smiling as he picks up his phone and starts making some calls.

I eat my croissant while he talks. When he's done, I thank him at least five times and then stand to leave.

"Hold up a minute, Sonny Jim," Jake says, also standing. I have more than a couple of centimetres on him, but he holds himself well and he has the kind of personality that leaks through his pores and fills any space he's in. It's the same charismatic quality Jenna has - quick-witted, sparkly eyes, an upbeat but realistic view of life - but unlike Jake, hers doesn't leak out of her, it's more something that is drip-fed to you the more time you spend together, something I fear I could become addicted to.

"I'm not sure what Jenna's said about our parents, and of course, at our age it's sort of irrelevant, but as her nearest and dearest I feel something of a duty to ask you to be gentle with her," he says and then he winces. "Not in the bedroom, I mean. You can be as rough with her there as she wants you to be, but rather, with all these activities you have planned today..."

"Our date?" I add for him. What's with these thirty-something-year-olds and their shying away from that word? I thought we were the ones who were supposed to be immature.

"Yes, that." he nods. "Jenna didn't exactly have her heartbroken by her ex, it wasn't like that at all, but she is quite... bruised. A lot more bruised than you may think. I know that this is just an insanely fortuitous holiday fling for the pair of you, and all power to you both, but please, just go easy on her.."

"Thanks for the pointers." I start to peel my banana. "I'm kind of into her."

"I can tell. And I think that's exactly *why* I'm asking you to be gentle with her." His quick pout and the way his eyes assess me from head to toe are just as cryptic as his words.

"Message received," I lie, because I really have no clue what he's warning me to do or not do, but I already know I have no intention of hurting Jenna. "And thanks a million for your help."

"My pleasure." His expression has softened and I see his eyes look tired, his skin a little flushed and peaky.

It's my turn to squint at him. "How was champagne with Lionel?" I ask.

His eyes widen briefly. "None of your business," he says with a pout.

"That good, huh?"

His eyelashes flutter. "Should I call Yiannis back and cancel that booking?"

"No thanks," I say quickly and bite into my banana again. "I'll put my spoon away and stop stirring now."

"Appreciated. As is your... err, discretion," Jake adds glancing at the door again to check it's closed.

"Don't worry about me. I'm easy like Sunday morning," I sing but when I see his face turn to thunder, I hold my hands up and back away.

"Oh, shit. One more thing," I say, after opening the door. "It's my birthday tomorrow and I promised my parents I would ask you about a cake. Are you able to possibly organise something? I could make it myself if you let me have an hour in one of your kitchens. I don't want to cause any bother, but I thought it best I ask rather than my mother, who will almost certainly give you a migraine in the process."

Jake smiles. "Birthday cakes are easy, and your mother is welcome to come and talk to me about it. I have a lot of experience with migraine-inducing guests," he says.

"I don't doubt it, but you haven't met my mother. I really wasn't joking about the headache. My father, sister and I sometimes take co-codamol with breakfast just as a precaution." I take a final bite of banana.

"I bloody hope not if you're planning on taking my sister around the island in a car! But for the cake, just let me know where you'll all be dining and I'll have something arranged," he says.

I nod and give him my broadest smile. "Thanks, Jake. And thanks again for your help for today."

"Not at all," he says and then he waves me off like I'm bothering him. "Be gone. Go and whisk my sister off her feet, but like I said, put her down safely afterwards." He pauses, his eyes looking up at the corner of the room. "Or not. Throw her on a bed, tie her wrists together and rip her clothes off, for all I care."

I blink and swallow slowly. "Wow. You and your sister share a lot of things I don't share with my sister."

"Oh, we don't share stuff like that at all. That's just what I wish a tall, dark and handsome stranger would do to me." Jake smacks his lips as if to punctuate the end of that line of discussion. "Have a great day, Marty O'Martin."

And before I can stop myself, I say, "You too, Sweet Cheeks." And walk away humming *All Night Long* by Lionel Richie a little louder than is necessary.

Chapter Twenty-Two

Jenna

It's strange being more nervous about putting clothes on for him than taking them off. But here we are. And by here, I mean washing my hands in the bathroom after my third nervous poo of the morning and it's not even nine o'clock yet. Goddamn my sensitive bowels. Considering I skipped dinner again last night and couldn't eat much of the breakfast that my brother sent to my room – this time unaccompanied by his lovely self as he had a wasps' nest emergency or some other implausible drama to attend to – I have no clue where this is all coming from.

And yet I do, because it's the first time I am going on a date with a man I have a real attraction to. It's hard not to make it into a big deal when I've spent the last year questioning if such a thing was even possible again for me.

I comfort the nerves by reminding myself about last night. About how good it was. About how hard I came. About how he looked in the shower, between my legs, on top of me.

These thoughts are what keep me going as I pull out most of my clothes and try them on in rushed, stressed movements that make me sweat despite turning the AC temperature down. I realise quickly it's going to have to be a case of choosing something that makes me feel comfortable even if it doesn't make me look my best. I wonder when exactly the balance tipped in that direction, because ten years ago I would have gladly suffered blisters on my heels, rib-compressing underwear and an all-day wedgie for a date with a man who looks like Marty. But not today. Today I want to be comfortable, so my final outfit choice is another oversized T-shirt dress with Breton white and navy stripes paired with my sexiest black halter-neck bikini – the one that makes me smile at myself in the mirror because of the way the top cinches my cleavage and the bottoms accentuate the roundness of my butt – and I pull up a pair of denim cut-off shorts over the bikini bottoms just in case he has me doing anything more active than lying on a beach. Then I blow-dry my hair, run some product through it, and make sure I have a hairband on my wrist because I rarely get through a day without wanting to tie it back.

As for make-up, I make do with my industrial strength waterproof mascara that costs more than a week's worth of take-away coffees, a light dusting of bronzer and a generous coating of SPF lip balm for my lips because I hope to get at least ten kisses today. Maybe twenty.

I look at my reflection as I brush my teeth and a rush of unexpected questions charge in. *Am I trying to look younger than I really am? Am I dressed too casually? Or not smart enough? Will this dress show sweat marks? Should I pack another bikini in case we do go to a beach and this one gets soaked? Does Marty prefer my hair up or down? Would Marty rather see more skin, or less?*

As I spit and rinse, I laugh at myself because I didn't worry half as much as this about any of the few dates I've been on in the last year, and maybe that should have been my first sign. I make a silent promise to myself that when I get home I will not go on another date until I have a swarm of butterflies in my stomach like I do now.

When I get home... Fuck. *I really don't want to go home.*

I blink that thought away and fill a beach bag with a towel, my sunglasses, deodorant, sun cream, my purse and not at all as an afterthought, a couple of condoms. I spray far too much perfume all over my body and rub my wrists together – just like my mother used to. Doing this, I catch the time on my watch and see I should have left five minutes ago, but now I need to go to the toilet again. I groan and rush there. Once finished, I wash up quickly, check my reflection again and then do something I started doing once I left my husband. I talk to myself.

"You look good, Jenna. Just have fun, Jenna. If in doubt, drag him back to your villa and ride him until you get friction burns, Jenna."

With a nod of agreement to myself, I walk out and hurry down the path towards the main entrance, with far too much of a bounce in my step. I'm just deciding what I will do if he isn't there, but Marty is exactly where he's supposed to be outside the main building's entrance, looking up at me as I walk down.

"There she is! Looking fucken edible!" he says, so loudly a couple walking out of the main entrance turn and give him and then me a disapproving look.

"Hi," I say. I want to say the same thing back to him. He looks like he was made to be on holiday, with his simple white T-shirt and khaki shorts that end above the knee, making his lean and sculpted legs look at least a foot longer than they really are. He's wearing the same style Birkenstocks as me – although mine are gold and his are black – and I smile at this because it's like another brick in that bridge that connects us over our age gap.

As I approach him, I have no idea if I should shake his hand, lean in for a hug, or push up for a kiss. I'm grateful when he decides for me, grabbing my hands and pulling me against him where he pushes his lips on my forehead.

"I'm sorry I'm late," I say and I suddenly really, really am. I want any second with him that he will give me.

"I'm glad you are. We're still waiting on..."

"Well, bugger me senseless, that was hard work." I hear my brother's voice and turn to see him marching out of the building's double doors, two phones in his hands. "The sooner I can speak Greek, the better. Good morning, Jenna. You look nice. Ish."

"Ish?" I give my brother a look.

"Well, you could have made a bit more of an effort." His index finger wags up and down in time with his eyes as they assess me.

"She looks great," Marty says.

"You clearly have sex tunnel vision," my brother says. "Anyway listen, Yiannis fucked up, royally. They thought you wanted a scooter, not a car. I've called and their last car just got picked up so it's a scooter or nothing. How do you feel about that?"

"We're going on a scooter ride?" I am suddenly very grateful I put those shorts on. But a scooter will be fun. With a grin on my face, I look up at Marty and see he looks a little ashen, almost shocked.

"There's really only a scooter?" he asks.

"Yes, I'm pretty sure it's their mistake but when they're communicating with me in English and I'm the bossy foreigner I don't really feel in a position to complain."

"A scooter's fine," I say.

"Actually..." Marty begins and his eyes lower to mine. "I'm not sure I'm comfortable driving a scooter."

"I can drive then," I say. I don't know what's going on, but I hope my smile is comforting.

Marty turns to Jake. "Are there any other hire car companies you can call?"

"I could... But the chances of you getting anything in the next hour are as good as my hangover magically disappearing."

"Right..." Marty bites the side of his lip between his teeth.

"I don't want to be a pushy dick, but I think this really is your best bet because I've already sent Lionel off with the..."

Marty holds two straight fingers up in front of Jake. "Ssshh, Sweet Cheeks."

"Huh, so that name is staying, is it?" I say with a small smile.

"I shouldn't like him calling me that, should I?" Jake says and then one of his phones starts ringing. "That's Yiannis. I'll go meet him."

He walks down towards the main entrance talking into his phone like the caller is a long-lost, much-loved friend.

"Hey," I say and give Marty a little nudge. He still looks lost in thought, so I wait for his eyes to find mine. "Are you okay?"

His hand comes to the back of his head, rubbing. "Yeah, of course," he says, then closes his eyes. "Actually, no, not really."

"Never ridden a scooter before?" I ask.

"No, it's not that. It's just I...when I was abroad..."

"Oh, is it a you and Arnie thing?" I say wanting to kick myself that I didn't think of it sooner.

"No, well, yes it was, but no... I just. I had an accident once and now... now..." He trails off, his cheeks hollowing as he bites them in his mouth.

"Well, then we can just skip the scooter ride and we go back to my villa and we..." I bob my eyebrows, almost pleased. One whole day with this man in bed. What could be better?

"No," he says, and he shakes his head roughly. "No, I want to do this."

"Then great! We'll do it." I find his hand and give it a squeeze.

"Fuck me, I'm such an eejit," Marty says and he's looking away, out in the direction of the sea, like he wants to run away there.

I smile and push up on my toes to press my lips to his. "I *will* fuck you, you eejit. Later. But first, we scooter!" I smile against his mouth when I feel his lips do the same.

"But could you... would you mind driving? I think that would help a lot," he asks.

"Of course, I can." I sound a lot more confident than I am.

"Grand," he says quietly.

Our heads turn in sync when we hear the approaching roar of an engine and we turn to see a muscular dark-haired man wearing aviators driving towards us with my brother's arms wrapped around his waist, like he genuinely fears for his life... or maybe, like he wants to grab handfuls of that stocky torso. I bite back my smile.

"He could have your brother arrested," Marty mutters under his breath to me and it's good to hear him making a joke again.

Just over ten minutes later, we are ready. We look ridiculous on a battered old scooter together, wearing helmets that my hair is not going to enjoy. Marty has his thighs flanked against the back of mine and my bag is wedged in between us on his lap. The feeling of Marty's firm legs against the back of my own is the one sensation that has me keeping my laughter under some control because it feels good; grounding and sexy, and just good. So good it makes me realise just how touch-starved I've been in the last year. My fat cheeks are squeezed tight in the helmet and I am grateful Marty can't see me, until I realise he actually can, catching a glimpse of me in one of the side mirrors. I hear him chuckle and he tells me I look like "a cute little hamster storing food for winter." I swipe at his leg, which makes him squeeze his thighs around my butt. We descend deeper into laughter together. We haven't even switched the engine on.

"Are you sure you'll be okay?" my brother asks as I turn the key. "And Jenna, if you must crash make sure it's a total and you end up in hospital so you can claim it on your insurance rather than me having to pay off Yiannis in free meals for his family for the rest of the season. Please, and thank you."

"Thanks for the vote of confidence, brother dearest," I say and then I rev the engine once, twice, and give myself a moment to feel a sliver of fear about driving this thing. And then I do what I've been doing with all my negative thoughts in the last year, I push it to the side and focus on the good.

"It's going to be okay," I tell myself again.

And I believe it. How could I not? I'm on a scooter, with a sexy young man who has his hands on my hips and a plan for a day together. A day in the sunshine. A day on a Greek island. A day in paradise. A day I never expected to happen. But it's happening…

I'm at the road entrance to the resort when I slam on the brakes, and this forces Marty's body to shift into mine in a way I don't mind at all. I make a note of that.

"Sorry, just testing the brakes," I call out.

"Fine with me," he says, and I feel his arms snake around to grip my waist.

"But also," I say. "Which way? Where are we actually going?"

He laughs and then tells me to turn left and to follow that road until he tells me otherwise, and while part of me hesitates at not knowing where we're going or what we're doing, I lean back against his embrace, turn left and wait for him to show me the way.

Chapter Twenty-Three

Marty

Our first stop is a Greek coffee place that Jake confirmed is where many locals go to get their morning caffeine fix. I don't know much about Greek coffee, other than it's very similar to Turkish coffee which I have made before, but I did a little research last night to get the basics. This is what I enjoyed about travelling; discovering other places and finding out their flavours, their foods and their drinks. Discovering their morning rituals, and the traditional drinks and dishes that bring joy and comfort. It's these that the chef in me always wants to seek out.

Receiving a sceptical but warm welcome from the man behind the bar and the fellow patrons inside, I order a *metrio* for Jenna, a coffee with sugar, and I opt for a *sketo* myself, the same drink without sugar. As Jenna finds a table just outside the front, I watch the man make our drinks and take the deep breaths I still need after Scooter-gate this morning. I never imagined I would react like that to the prospect of getting on a scooter again, but Jenna's reassuring smile, the promise of the day ahead and a firm internal pep-talk to myself all helped steady my shaking legs as I climbed on.

And now I feel something like pride take root in me, because I did it, even though I was scared. Even though I was on the cusp of panic, I didn't fall over the edge.

The man mumbles something to me as I move to take our small cups of night-black coffee from him, and with little fanfare he follows me and plonks a plate of pastries that look like baklava on our table before rushing away again.

After advising Jenna to wait a little longer for the coffee's 'sludge' to settle, I watch how she nods and reaches for a pastry. Taking a bite, her full lips are momentarily covered with flakes of pastry. When she uses her tongue to sweep them up and pull them into her mouth, she also closes her eyes to savour the sweetness of the honey and I swear my heart skips a beat. A beat that my dick catches, swelling in my shorts. It's not that I've forgotten how sexy she is but part of me is actively trying to ignore it so that I can make today about something more than sex. But then she does something like suck the honey out of a piece of baklava, her eyelashes flickering, and sex is all I can think about.

"How did you find out about this place?" she asks, snapping me back into the moment.

"Dad and I have passed it on our ride the last two mornings and it's always busy with locals, so I was curious. Also, the hotel breakfast is great and all, but it's far from a real Greek or Cretan experience. I wanted to at least try and find out what that looks and tastes like," I say, handing her coffee to her.

She takes a sip and her nose wrinkles.

"Do you like it?" I ask.

She blushes. "Honestly, no. I rarely drink coffee without milk, but I appreciate the authentic experience." She lifts her cup to her lips again. "Really, I do."

I smile and we drink in silence, both of us watching the road traffic pass us by. At some point, the Greek man from behind the counter swaps our empty plate for a full one and while Jenna protests she couldn't eat another one, she waits less than a minute to put another small roll of pastry in her mouth and I have to use all my energy to yet again remind my cock today is about more than sex.

And yet again, my cock ignores me.

"This one has walnuts in!" she exclaims, and I moan inwardly. There is nothing sexier than a sexy human excited about food.

"There are walnut trees all over Crete," I say.

"You know what a walnut tree looks like?" She is startled.

"You don't?" I ask, faking shock back at her, and we both laugh.

186

Coffees finished and back at our scooter, I can't help myself. I reach for her hand as she goes to grab her helmet. I shove her hand in my mouth and I suck all the traces of honey off her fingers. Before letting her middle finger go, I bite it gently between my teeth and smile at her wide eyes and slack jaw.

"Marty," she says, and it could be a reprimand, or it could be admiration, something related to awe.

"Sorry," I say. "Had to."

I sense she's trying to contain her smile but still it kicks up her lips. Then she turns and puts her helmet on. I wait for her to get in position then I take her bag, swing it over my arm, and slide in behind her, not giving a fuck that my erection is now pressed up against her firm butt cheeks. I could be imagining it, but it feels like she rolls back into it before she turns the key in the ignition.

"Where to now, Harry?" she shouts over the engine.

"Harry?"

"And I'm Lloyd. Like in *Dumb and Dumber*!" She calls out.

"What are you talking about?" I'm baffled.

She switches the engine off and turns slightly to me. "Oh, God, don't tell me that cultural reference fell into the void of our age gap. The movie, *Dumb and Dumber*? It has a scooter scene in it."

Laughter bubbles out of me as it clicks. "Oh, Jesus, yes. That's exactly what this looks like. Ha!" And just like that, I now have another scooter memory that can maybe, possibly, hopefully, eclipse the other one.

"Phew, thought I was going to have to write you a list of problematic early Nineties comedies to watch."

"You can still do that. We can watch them together," I say and she waits a beat before turning on the engine.

"Okay, where to, Harry?" she shouts again after clearing her throat.

"Still trust me, Lloyd?" I call back.

"Yes," she says, and it makes me smile more than it should.

"Then let's keep going left," I say as I place my hands on the tops of her thighs, close to where they meet her hips. I think about the stretchmarks she has there, and I want to feel them under my tongue again.

A moment after we set off, I can no longer fight the urge.

"Mock!" I call out into the warm air that rushes past.

"Yeah!" She sings back, after only a second.

"King!"

"Yeah!"

"Bird!" I holler.

"Yeah!" Our laughter drowns out the noise of the few vehicles that pass us.

We weave our way around a coastal road that takes us through a few small villages, past garages, hotels and one or two other luxury resorts. Then the road turns up and climbs away from the shoreline, which is when I start looking for the turning. As soon as I see it, I squeeze my hands on her waist and lean forward as close to her ear as our helmets allow.

"Take that road on the right," I say.

She does, but slows down when she realises it's little more than a gravel path.

"Are you sure?"

"Yes." I squeeze her again. "Trust me."

As we descend the bumpy, uneven path that is littered with potholes, I relish how her body moves, bouncing and jiggling under my hands. When the low-lying trees and shrubs lining the path start to dissipate, I crane my neck above Jenna's shoulder and see the deep azure blue of the Mediterranean because we are now on the western coast of Crete. A moment later, the path reveals where I am taking us.

It's not the prettiest beach in the world. The sand is a dusky yellow and is littered with boulders and rocks. The water doesn't rush in and there are no crashing waves, thanks to a natural sea barrier created by the incisive curve of the mountain we just turned off. Instead, the water smoothly laps against the sand, making just enough noise so a gentle swooshing rhythm can be heard. But it's that stillness that I noticed and craved when I was up on the mountain path with Dad yesterday morning. That and the way the beach is only accessible by that long makeshift road, and being low season and mid-week, there aren't any of the locals I suspect keep this beach a secret for themselves.

We have it all to ourselves.

"We're here," I say as Jenna parks before a dilapidated wooden fence that marks the beach's beginning. I scan the sand in front of us and see exactly what I want to see. I climb off with her bag.

Jenna is silent as she takes off her helmet and looks around her. I can't tell what she's thinking but her shoulders are low and relaxed and when I move to get closer to the sand, she climbs off and follows me.

"Where are we?" she asks, approaching me from behind.

"I'm not entirely sure, but I can show you on a map. That's how I showed it to your brother."

"Jake? Why did you show him?"

"Because of this," I say, and I nod to the blanket and parasols arranged on the sand. Under one of the large umbrellas that have the resort's white and blue stripes, is a picnic hamper, a cool box, four towels rolled up, and a sports bag. I grin at how perfect it looks, even better than I expected. I really do owe her brother and I'm still not sure how I'm going to pay for it all, but I will worry about that another time.

"What's that?" Jenna says as she comes up to stand by my shoulder.

"You know, I have no idea! None in the slightest! I am completely confused!" I wave my hands around in a dramatic fashion before turning to her and gripping her hand in mine. "Let's go find out!"

We half-jog, half-skip across the sand towards the blanket.

"Did you do this?" Jenna says as she lifts the lid on the hamper, and I see bread rolls, plates, glasses, cutlery, and napkins inside.

"Who, me?" I say pressing my hand to my chest, my expression and tone possibly a little camp.

"Oh," she says when she frees the top of the plastic cool box. "Champagne."

"Well, actually I didn't organise that," I say because for obvious reasons I'd not mentioned booze.

"There's water and orange juice too," Jenna reassures me. "What's in that?"

She's pointing at the sports bag which I am unzipping, knowing already what's inside.

"Snorkels!" I say and show her.

"Wow!" She says as her mouth stretches into a smile. "How did you organise all this?"

"Have you met our Resort Manager? Ever such a helpful fellow. Fantastic arse too," I say as she steps in close and slides her arms around my waist. It's then I wonder how I have spent nearly an hour with her this morning and not kissed her yet, not properly. As if reading my mind, she pushes up and presses her lips to mine, and I am quick to open my mouth, tasting coffee, honey and a little mint too. I sigh and hum as our kiss deepens and I instinctively rock into her when she grabs my butt. I am ready to take her right now and I sense she is too, but I'm not going to let that happen. Not yet.

"I'm afraid this is not on the date's itinerary," I say.

"It's not?"

"I don't see condoms in that bag, do you?" I nod to the snorkel gear.

"Well, knowing my brother, it's entirely possible."

"Nothing wrong with being prepared," I add. "But I would like to get wet in other ways first."

"Oh, that was bad," she says, and she loosens her grip, stepping back.

"Wordplay doesn't do it for you, eh? And I thought you were a writer." I chuckle as I bend down and reach for the bag.

"Not that kind of wordplay." She pulls her hair back into a ponytail, giving me a far too tempting look at her neck and shoulders.

"Come on," I say handing her a pair of goggles with a snorkel attached. "Let's go find some fish."

She looks at the gear with a squint in her eye. "Why do I feel like you're trying to make me wear the least attractive headgear possible today? Don't you want me to look remotely sexy?"

"You look plenty sexy enough, trust me." I peck her on the cheek before pulling my T-shirt over my head. I hear her inhale of breath as the material drops into the sand.

"Now you're just trying to distract me," she says, her eyes trailing down my torso.

"No, asking you to put some sun cream on my back and chest is how I'm going to really send you to distraction," I say before realising. "Oh, shit. I didn't bring any."

She rummages in her bag. "Voila!" She retrieves a bottle and then drops her bag and turns me around. "Don't move."

"Ah!" I yell out when the cold spray of the lotion smacks into my back, again and again and again. I am practically dancing with the shock of each spray.

"Hold still!" She starts to rub it in.

"It's your turn next," I warn.

"Shit," she says in a quieter voice. "I really did a number on you."

"What do you mean?"

"There are scratch marks all over your back," she says. "Must have been from the shower. We didn't even do missionary last night."

It's almost like she's talking to herself, remembering. I wonder if she's done lots of remembering. I know I have.

"Is missionary your usual position of torture?" I ask.

She doesn't reply, but then I feel her lips touch down on various places on my back, accompanied occasionally by the wet warmth of her tongue.

"Jenna," I say as I tilt my head back, so close to surrendering. "I really do want to get in the water."

"I'm sorry," she says and it's suddenly an apology I don't want. She has nothing to apologise for. I only wish I could see the marks she left on me.

As the scent of coconut fills my nostrils, I watch Jenna walk around to face me. She sprays my chest and stomach at least five times too many and we laugh again as I jump in shock at each one. She studies every inch of my skin that her hands rub across, smoothing the lotion in, and I don't understand how this is both so sensual and so caring. I also don't know why I want to fight the desire I have when I see her eyes dart around my skin like I'm her favourite food and she hasn't eaten for a week. I just don't want today to be only about sex. And I think I'd like for it to be the same for her.

"Your turn," I say when her fingers are a little too close to the waistband of my shorts.

She reluctantly hands over the bottle and holding my eyes with hers, she reaches down for the hem of her dress and pulls it up over her head. Allowing myself a long look at her breasts in her bikini top, I then notice the shorts.

"Off with them! Offensive denim!" I insist. She rolls her eyes but goes to undo the buttons and slides them down her thighs. Those thighs. Thighs my head belongs between.

Later, Marty. Later.

I then step back and position the bottle like a gun and spray three times on her stomach. She squeals.

"Fuck! That is cold!"

I start massaging the cream into her skin, marvelling at how warm and smooth she is there. When it comes to applying the lotion to her chest and arms, I spray it into my hands first.

"Now you're making me look like a bully," she says after I spin her around. But I don't put my hands or the cream on her body for a moment, because I'm too busy looking down at the flare of her arse.

"Marty?" she says, as if checking I'm still there.

"Sorry, your butt was talking to me," I say.

"Oh." She laughs. "What was it saying?"

"Something about how it has plans for me later." I start to spread the lotion around her back, feeling hard muscle, soft fat, and the ridges of her ribs and shoulder bones, all wrapped in luscious freckled skin.

"It does? What kind of plans?"

"Oh, it was all a bit vague but there was something about squeezing, something about biting, something about spanking. Your arse is going to keep me very busy."

Jenna doesn't say anything, but I see her move, her hand disappearing and then her fingers are back and her body is turning. She lifts her middle finger to my lips, which are already opening for her.

I taste her. Her heady musk and the sun cream she just applied and maybe even still a bit of honey from the baklava.

"You make me so wet," she says in a whisper.

And that's it. I've had just about as much temptation as I can stand. I drop the sun cream to the blanket, scoop up the two snorkel goggles and as I straighten up, I wrap my arms around her waist and lift her up and over my shoulder.

"You need to cool off, woman!" I yell as I run to the water's edge, her body bouncing against mine, her laughter-filled screams the sweetest sound in the world.

Chapter Twenty-Four

Jenna

There aren't any fish. Not really. But I don't say anything, I just keep swimming, enjoying how clear the blue water is, how it's cool but not cold, and how we are alone in a small cove that is completely out of sight.

I've always loved swimming - even got into the habit of going to a swimming club at London Fields Lido for the first five or so summers I lived in London - but then like most things when work became busier, I stopped making the effort.

Effort. Too often I find myself chewing on this word and the questions it makes me ask. Why did I not make more effort with the things that mattered most - my marriage and my career? Was there more I could have done? Did I become complacent? How much of the marriage's failure was my lack of effort? How could I have made more effort to keep doing my old job? Why am I so scared to put in the effort and just write a book like I've always dreamed?

I'm drifting away with these thoughts, not really looking for fish anymore and certainly not looking where I'm going, when I feel a quick pull on my ankle. I jolt up and lift the mask onto the top of my head.

"Oi!" I say looking at Marty who has also emerged. We tread water together.

"Oi yourself," he says with a grin. "You were halfway to Turkey."

"Wrong side of the island, genius." But I look back to the beach and realise that we are much further away than I thought.

"Still, you were speeding off, Little Mermaid."

"I'll do anything to avoid going home," I say, and it's a joke, but possibly not a lie.

Marty cocks an eyebrow but doesn't respond. "So," he says instead. "Snorkelling is a bit shit. I'll file that under things I also got wrong today along with the car-slash-scooter false start."

I shake my head and smile. What on Earth has he possibly got wrong today? It's all been so very, very perfect.

"Race you back to the beach?" I kick off before I can even hear his response after I bring the goggles of my mask back down but not the tube. I'm surprised my body slips easily into freestyle, breathing every three strokes, and I have no doubt the lack of significant waves help as I swim for more than a few minutes before I realise Marty hasn't caught up like I expect. I can't see him swimming beside me, so I stop and look around, wondering if I've gone in the wrong direction again.

But he's behind me, bobbing up and down as he swims towards me in a haphazard breaststroke. I think I may have found the one thing he can't do with charm and flair; swim. Twenty years ago, that would have been a turn-off but today, with everything I know about him and everything he's done to make today special, I am aware of something wrapping its claws around my insides with such a stranglehold it's almost uncomfortable.

Waiting for him to catch up, I float on my back and do lazy frog kicks to take me towards the shore, keeping my eyes closed to the bright sun that is now high in the sky. Then I feel another tug at my ankle, and I'm pulled into the hard chest of Marty, who can now just about stand up. I quickly swipe the mask off my head and hold it in one hand as my other arm wraps around his waist.

I don't know who moves to kiss who first, but I know I am hungry for him as our lips collide. Salt touches down on my taste buds as my tongue touches his and it makes me thirsty too. Thirsty for him even though I am neck deep in water. It makes no sense, in the same way he makes no sense. This man who came out of nowhere with his sex appeal and his witty banter and his love of sunsets and his desire for me. None of it makes sense but it's the best kind of nonsense in the world.

Without me really knowing what I'm doing, I'm sliding my hands in his shorts and finding him rock hard and ready and long. As I stroke him, I

196

remember what he felt left like in my mouth last night and I groan. I want to go down on my knees for him. I want to taste and swallow him once more. This thought speeds up my strokes and he responds by bringing his hands to my backside, kneading, kneading and kneading like I'm a dough that demands endless attention. I think briefly about his job. His hands making food, his body running around a kitchen, sleeves rolled up, and that image - him cooking, him making food, him creating dishes people love - makes my pussy clench and more disconcertingly, that hold on my heart squeeze tighter.

"You do something to me," I tell him. It feels like a safe, ambiguous way to say, *I fucking love how you touch me and how you make me feel and how you took me to this secluded beach where I could feel young and carefree again.*

"It's all you, cupcake," he says bending down and pulling me up so I can wrap my legs around him and even though it makes me lose my grip on his dick, I have it back in a second, reaching between my legs and having the perfect position to rub his hard-on against my clit through my bikini bottoms. It's his turn to groan when he realises what I'm doing.

"I wanted today to be about more than just sex," he whispers between kisses as I continue to rub us together.

"We're not having sex," I tease.

"You know what I mean," he says, but I don't. I don't know why he doesn't want to just give in to the desire. It's not like we have forever. "Besides, we don't have condoms."

"I do," I say and glance quickly at my bag on the beach.

"Jesus, I should have thought of that." He shuts his eyes.

"It's okay. I did..." I begin.

"But I should have," he says, sounding frustrated. "Just because you're older doesn't mean you have to be *more* responsible." He tilts my head up to look at him. "I am old enough to be responsible for myself, and when it comes to sex, for you too."

His voice is different when he says that, different from the Marty voice that cracks dirty jokes and utters endless filthy innuendos. His new seriousness makes me lean in to kiss him again, this time slower, this time with my hands on his upper arms, exploring the dips and dives of his biceps and triceps. When I pull away, he blinks a few times, and I see it too. He wants me.

"Wanna try something?" he asks, and I nod. I want to try so many things with him, if only I could tell him about some of them.

He takes a few steps, moving us to slightly shallower water so I can stand. Marty reaches under the water and cups my pussy through my bikini bottoms. My knees buckle when the heel of his palm starts to make small circles around my clit. Then his hand is gone, and he leans back from me only to then step closer, bending his knees and I feel the head of his dick glide where his hand was.

"Open your legs, just a bit," he says, and I do. Then I feel his dick slide along the full length of my pussy and stay there, hard and straight. "Now close them."

My thighs move to close around him and then I squeeze them tighter around his cock and he hums into my hair.

"Your thighs, they could rule my world," he grunts out, and I have never loved my body more.

Needing to keep my feet on the bottom of the ocean floor and my grip around him, I am only slightly disappointed I can't lift myself up and kiss him. But then he starts to move, and I feel how his extra height is forcing his cock to push up against my pussy and pleasure ripples through me. I close my eyes, lean into his chest and squeeze my legs closer together.

"This shouldn't feel so good," I say as the pressure starts to build and while I want him inside me, filling me, stretching me like he did last night, I also don't want to change a single thing.

"The water helps a lot." He rocks into me a little harder and I gasp. "But fuck yes, humping is not just for teenagers."

"You can come like this?" I ask.

"What do you think?" he asks with a smile, but I also see the way his eyes roll back a little and his jaw is tense.

I pull back, so my breasts bounce and he watches as he continues to rock against me. A moment later, Marty puts a hand on my breast, squeezes through the fabric before his fingers crawl inside and find my nipple. I close my eyes and thrust my body into his hand and against his shoulder as I pull back up, trapping his fingers where I want them, teasing me.

I then slide my own hands inside the back of his shorts to grab his butt and play with that. I start pawing at his arse, really grabbing as much as I can of the muscle there, but because he's so lean, there really isn't that much there. But when I pull his cheeks apart a little, I hear a grunt come from a place deeper than the previous noises he's made.

I lean back again so I can catch his eye. "Can I?" I ask.

He nods hurriedly. "Please."

I take one hand and glide it down the crease of his cheeks until I find what I'm looking for and then I apply a little pressure. Marty nods again and I smile as I move the pad of my finger in little circular motions, before then tapping softly. When I then go back to stroking his entrance, he makes that same grunting noise again and I'm so relieved he can't see my self-satisfied expression because my face is buried in his chest. His arms come around to grip my back, one hand on the back of my neck, the other around my waist. He's thrusting now, charging into the soft warm space my thighs create and I have to squeeze harder than ever, trying to cross my ankles over one another to keep my legs in place. All the while I continue to play with his hole, little taps, little rubs, little pushes of pressure, until I finally feel brave enough and I force the tip of my middle finger a little harder and it breaches him only slightly.

"Oh, shit," he hisses out and he jolts up and back a little too much that his dick gets free.

"Did you..." I ask, keeping my finger where it is, unmoving.

He shakes his head. A vein throbs in his neck. "So fucken close."

I move quickly, finding his dick with my free hand but keeping my finger where it is. I stroke his length, twisting my hand around his head, as he positions his body at a slight angle so it's easier for me to have my fingers exactly where I want them on either side of his body. I also have the perfect view of his head thrown back, his Adam's apple bobbing up and down, and his eyes closing shut as he comes barely a minute after I've taken him in hand.

He calls out with a string of curses that only my name interrupts and I don't stop stroking him until he goes quiet and still. But even then, I don't take my hand away from his hole, not until he dips down and wraps his arms around my waist to pull me up, so my legs are cinched around his body and our lips are touching again, kissing.

"Too fucking good," he says to me. "I love that you just did that."

"I love that you let me."

"Why wouldn't I let you do that?"

I shrug.

"Your ex?" he asks. "He didn't like it?"

"He didn't *try* it," I clarify.

His eyes run up and down my face before he says, "His loss. His big fat stupid loss. What else didn't he try?"

"A lot of things..."

"Give me an example."

"Spanking... Tying me up. Any kind of kink."

"You like that?"

I turn my head from the sun's heat, my cheeks warm enough now. "I think I'd like to try it. But I never really have."

"What else?" Marty asks.

"Ropes. Restraints. Breathplay, maybe."

"Dom, sub type of things?"

"Maybe. Do you think that's weird?"

"I think it's wonderful. Kink is a wonderful thing."

I look up at him, a little surprised if not shocked. "You have experience?"

"Sort of. Well, I have a funny story about a BDSM club I got lost in in Ibiza once but also with Arnie... Jesus. We tried a lot of things."

I feel suddenly in awe of him, the possible inexperience of his youth an illusion I now know was only in my mind. "How... how did you get so confident about sex by this age? About what you like? About trying new things?"

Marty nibbles on my neck as he talks. "I think being bi helped. It flipped everything I thought I knew about sex on its head. My eyes were literally opened to so many endless possibilities."

"I can imagine," I say. "I feel like I knew about these things, have read about these things, but I never applied it to my own life. I never really asked myself what my kinks could be, until I found myself bored and restless in my marriage and I realised the other ways I wasn't satisfied. But then it was too late. I scared him off."

He squeezes me a little tighter. "No, Jenna, no. I don't know him or your situation, but there is nothing wrong in wanting to try new things. I'm so sorry he didn't want to explore this with you."

"I actually feel sorry for him too," I say truthfully. "But maybe he's just happy being...vanilla."

He chews the corner of his lip in his mouth for a moment before speaking. "Vanilla is indeed a beautiful flavour and very few desserts are complete without it, but I think it's more than okay, good even, if you want to enjoy other flavours."

I nod and kiss him. I don't want to talk about my ex. I want to kiss this man, the man who put a lot of effort into today. I want to hold onto him and commit to memory what his bumpy-nosed side profile just looked like as he came. But Marty has other plans.

"Float on the water," he says, and he tilts in my direction so I can. Then he pulls back, keeping his body between my legs and one arm on my hip to keep me tethered to him. He smooths his other hand up my body, barely any pressure or weight in his touch so I can keep floating. His palm ghosts over my nipples in turn, and I close my eyes to the bright sun that is now immediately above us. I think momentarily about the snorkel mask that is still fixed to the top of my head and how ridiculous that must look and how ridiculous this whole scene is but how glorious it is too. Then Marty's hand slips my bikini bottoms to the side and I push my stomach up a little more, making my pelvis tilt towards him. He searches for a few seconds before finding my clit and then he's circling so gently I can almost feel each individual tingle of pleasure.

"More," I say. The light of the sun is dazzling even through my closed eyes. But I don't care, and I don't move. I couldn't move if I wanted to because then I would go under. It therefore, takes great focus to contain the shudders and shivers as he continues to stroke and I wonder if he knows what he's doing, if this control he's exerting over my pleasure is something he's doing consciously, but regardless, I'm soaking it up. This is exactly what I needed. Someone to push me. Someone to test me. Someone to play with me.

When he speaks again, it's clear he has no clue, but in the best possible way.

"Tell me how to touch you," he says. I lift my head slightly to hear him. "I want to get it right. It's been... I've not... It's been a while since I..."

Arnie, I think. Arnie was different. This breaks me and not only because of what I know about Arnie and Marty. It also breaks me because this is the question I begged my husband to ask me. This is the question I answered for him when he didn't. So what I give Marty is one of those unrequited speeches I gave him, words he mostly ignored.

"Stroke me," I say. "Up and down, up and down. Around my clit but also move away from it too. Tease my entrance, go lower too, if you want. Then go back to my clit, rub around it in circles or figures of eight. Increase the pressure slowly, and then take it away. Do that again and again. Tease me. I'll tell you when it feels really good and then just keep doing that."

He follows my guidance almost to the letter, and it gets harder and harder to stay still. So hard, I feel it encroach on my pleasure a little, but I welcome it. It matches how overwhelmed and conflicted I am feeling in my body and mind.

"Inside me," I pant. "I need a finger inside me."

He obeys, and when he moves his hand to put his thumb on my clit I thrust up - instinctively and uncontrollably - and get a mouthful of water as my head sinks under. I quickly correct myself and lie as still as I can, my arms outstretched, surrendering because there is nothing else I can do.

As if to reward me, he slides another finger inside me and I moan. Now I can feel him inside and out, the pressure builds even quicker and I feel my orgasm hurtle towards me so quickly I don't have time to pull in a breath as I rock my hips against his hand.

"Stay there," I gasp. "Don't stop."

And he doesn't. The circles on my clit, the stroking inside me, his tight, tight hold around my body.

"So fucken beautiful," he says and it's the last, missing piece of the puzzle that is my climax.

As the surges of my orgasm crash into one another, my whole body convulses. I clamp my legs around his waist to try and keep me up, but I know it's no use and the water thrashes over my whole body. My eyes open under the water, the sting of the saltwater not painful as much as a shock that dulls the bright edges of my orgasm. But then there are strong hands around me, pulling me up and against a chest that I am far too comfortable returning to.

"I didn't mean to drown you," he says as he slides my mask off and strokes my wet hair away from my face.

"Worth it," I say in barely more than a whisper because it feels like that orgasm took my voice from me.

We stay there for a while, the sun beaming down above us so hot and so big and so elevated in the sky it seems impossible that it could ever go anywhere else, that it would ever want to leave this perfect height where it can see everything, warm everyone and touch every living being on this planet. But the sun will go down later, and I feel the same sinking realisation with a peaceful acceptance even if I can already taste the grief my body will feel.

Because it's the truth. It's just the way life is.

All good things must come to an end.

Chapter Twenty-Five

Marty

Back on the blanket, with our tummies full of water, cheeses, bread and fruit, I pour her a glass of champagne and drop a strawberry in the glass, explaining how the dry bubbles will complement the fruit's sweetness.

"So, why a chef?" she says as she takes the glass.

"You can blame my uncle, Dermot. I grew up working in his restaurant, just as a part-time job to begin with. First washing up, then food prepping and cleaning, basic sous-chef work eventually. He gave me time in the bar after I was eighteen, and then service too, once he realised I was a cocky shit who can charm anyone with a pulse. And I liked all of it, but I felt the magic was really happening in the kitchen." I smile as a flood of memories dance in my mind. "My ma has always done the cooking at home, and she always did it in a way where meals would sort of just appear out of nowhere. Like it was magic. She didn't really share the process or get us involved, partly because she's a Type A control freak and partly because I was always too busy doing something else, riding my bike out around the neighbourhood or at Arnie's house annoying him and his family."

She reaches over and squeezes my shin then and it immediately dulls the edge of the wave of sadness that lands.

"When I was seventeen and due to work there full-time for a summer, I asked Dermot if I could work in the kitchen properly and he and the head chef were stupid enough to agree. I think it was punishment for his juniors to have to train me up, or maybe I was just cheap labour. But I bloody loved it. It was like coming home to myself. I feel a peace in a kitchen that I don't feel in many other spaces."

She squints at me. "But don't you all shout at each other? Restaurant kitchens are so busy and noisy..."

"My uncle's place isn't really like that. I mean it is. We shout, and we swear a ton. It is noisy and chaotic. We get stressed and bollock each other when things go tits up. But there's no bullying, there's no malice. We're all on the same team."

"It still doesn't sound very peaceful." She fishes out the strawberry and sucks on it in a way that is possibly illegal in some countries.

"You're right. It's not peaceful in terms of being quiet or calm, but it's the kind of chaos that makes me feel good. When I can find my rhythm and feel part of something, that's like peace to me. Maybe I'm not explaining it very well."

"You find your flow," Jenna says with a nod. "It's like when I write or get deep into researching something. I get in a zone and it all just flows."

"Yeah, that's it. I also like being part of something with other people. I would find writing too lonely. I like being around others. It gives me more energy."

"You're an extrovert," she says.

"I am," I say and take a breath. "Arnie always said that."

"Was he an introvert?"

I smile to myself. "Yeah, he was. Said he hated people, but that wasn't true. He just needed time alone now and then. I found that hard sometimes."

Jenna picks up another strawberry and I find it weird that even though I'm talking about Arnie and that feels normal – a miracle in itself – I'm also watching the red fruit go between her lips and I want to taste its sweetness on her lips – and that feels very normal too.

"I'm an introvert too, and so was my ex. We were really good at giving each other space... probably a bit too good." She shakes her head as she swallows the strawberry. "So, do you want to have your own restaurant in the future?"

"Maybe. One day. Truth is, I find it hard to think about the future. And there's still so much to learn. And well, even though I've never stopped working in kitchens, I did drop out of my degree."

"Because of Arnie being unwell?"

"Yeah, but I'm not even sure I should have gone to start with. I just panicked when Arnie had his uni place and so did everyone else. I thought it was what I was supposed to do. I mean, you may not believe it, but I do have a few brain cells. I guess I thought a degree in Culinary Arts was one way I could prove that."

"And now?"

"I don't think I want to go back." I sigh, and the relief of being honest with her, and myself, is immediate. "I dread the idea of going back. It's hard to tell if that's because of Arnie, because I'm grieving, or just because it's not where I'm supposed to be."

"You don't have to go back," Jenna says simply. "I don't know much about being a chef, but I can't imagine it's something you need a degree for. A kitchen sounds like much a better place to learn, especially for someone like you."

"I think I know all this. But my parents don't. I know you're going to think I'm a sap still caring what they think but they pretty much pulled me out of a gutter at the beginning of this year, and even before that, when I dropped out to spend more time with Arnie, they supported me through it all, both financially and emotionally. And I know they want me to go back, to have that structure and that degree to be proud of. Part of me feels like it's the right thing to do, like I owe them that much."

Jenna nods and takes another sip of her drink. "You know one of the few blessings my parents gave me was a lot of freedom, and I guess, the ability to carve out my own life. At the time I didn't see it like that, but I have never felt like I owe my dad anything, or like I need to prove myself to him. I can't imagine how much pressure that must be." This perspective makes my breath lodge in my throat. She's not telling me I'm wrong or right to feel that way, she's just acknowledging that it's hard.

"What do you think I should do?" I ask, feeling like she has the answers I need.

"Oh, I can't tell you that. But I think you can. I think you already know. And," she pauses and looks out to sea, "I think you need to remember that your parents will love and support you no matter what."

"What were you like when you were my age?" I ask, even though it feels like a risk, bringing up our age gap. "Did you know what you wanted to do with your life? Did you know where you wanted to be by the age you are now?"

Silence falls and I can tell she's really thinking about this and I can't explain why but it excites me. I'm suddenly desperate to know her thoughts. I wait and eventually, she speaks. "You know, when I hear you say it like that, it reminds me how I used to be obsessed with milestones and key chapters in my life. I really did think that life was going to be a sort of treadmill of working towards one goal after another. First, there's getting through childhood, teenage years, schools and maybe university. Then your professional life begins and somewhere along the way you meet someone, maybe marry, have kids. But life is just not like that. The milestones come and go but they are not what makes you who you are. You are not who you are because of what you do or don't achieve. You're shaped by the shit that happens along the way. The real life-changing events. And those things are never what you expect or can plan for. Like...like..." She trails off as her eyes go back to the horizon.

"Your divorce?" I offer.

"Yes, and no." Jenna turns to look at me. "I was thinking more about how it must be like that with Arnie. Your life must be very different now compared with before."

I nod and chew on the inside of my cheek so I can feel something other than the stab of nauseating pain as I relive the moment he left us. "Yeah, there is definitely a before and after, but there was also this whole other time that existed in between. The me that was in it, with him, during his treatment, and then his palliative care. But after... after, yeah, I just knew life was never going to be the same again."

"Like another world," Jenna says, lifting her sunglasses so I can see her honey-brown eyes that are almost the colour of liquid gold in the hue of my own shades. "It's like being on a different planet when the rest of the world just keeps going."

Our eye contact after she says that is different to any we've had before. She isn't guessing when she says that. She knows.

"My mother died when I was a teenager," she explains.

"Jenna," I say and my fingers twitch to reach for her. "How old were you?"

"Fifteen," she says. "By suicide."

"Jesus."

"Yeah." She looks down and finds something to pick at on her dress.

"That must have been so very hard. It must still be hard."

She breathes in deep before speaking. "It was, and yes, sometimes it still is. But it was over twenty years ago. That's a lot of time, Marty. Time is not a healer itself – like they so annoyingly say – but it can still be kind to you as you heal. It can still bring you joy and happiness."

"Can I ask what happened?" I speak cautiously.

"She was very depressed for many years before she died," Jenna says with an ease that surprises me. "Very severe depression. The kind you wouldn't wish on your worst enemy. So, even with all the loss and sadness and grief when she did die, I still remember feeling relieved. I still feel that relief baked into my sense of loss when I think about her. That can't compare to what you and Arnie and his family experienced."

I shake my head. "We are not going to do the Grief Olympics. Please, no."

"No, I'm not doing that." Her smile is kind and her eyes soft. "I'm simply acknowledging the irrefutable tragedy of Arnie's death. He wanted to live. He was young. He had so much ahead of him." Her hand is on mine as she says this. "But my poor mother. Life was unbearable, sometimes. I'm not convinced she always wanted to die either. But I know that life was very, very hard for her. And that was hard on my brother and me too."

"What about your father? Were they still married?"

She rolls her eyes but it's anything but flippant. "Yes, but barely. Their marriage was a shambles. My father had something of a double life." She pulls in another breath. "He had a long-running affair with the woman he is now married to, Carol. I'm still not sure exactly when they got together, but I know it was for a long time before Mum died, and we all knew about it. She would even tell us when he was 'at Carol's' although they didn't explain what that meant to us. It just was. And then, after Mum died, I understood much clearer. Him and Carol were married within six months. She became my stepmother."

"My God," I whisper.

"Yeah. It's a bit fucked up, isn't it? Honestly, I'm just grateful it happened when I was fifteen and not five. Carol didn't want kids, so we were a big inconvenience, messing up this fantasy life she wanted with my dad. The thing is, what makes it a bit easier to look back on now, I do believe she and my father genuinely loved and still do love each other, so yes, they should have always been together, but that's not easy to think about either. I think I'm at peace with how my mum and dad weren't in love at all, but it was still hard to not see my father really grieve for the mother of his children. And of course, Jake and I have always wondered how much of a role my father played in Mum's depression. Not that it was his fault, we understand that. But did he support her enough? Did he even understand it? Was it his affair that made her feel so utterly hopeless? I don't think it was just that." She pauses and looks down at the sand, and I let her take her time. "I know she loved us, but I also always felt like there was somewhere else, or *someone* else, she'd rather be. I've always wondered if we could have managed it better if she'd had more support and more..." She sighs but this seems to create space for a small smile. "I guess what I'm trying to say is that I wish my mother had had more love in her life."

I let silence fall so I can also lock those words away somewhere, although where I don't really know. Then I ask her the one question that I always want people to ask me when they find out I've lost someone I love.

"What was her name?"

"Catalina. Cathy," she says, and her dazzling smile makes me so glad I asked. I commit the name to memory. "Her mother, my grandmother, was Spanish. I never met her sadly, but I always loved my mum's name."

"Jake's older than you?" I ask.

"No, two years younger. It was much harder on him," she says, picking up a slice of watermelon.

"It must have been hard on you both."

She chews for a while before replying, thinking. I like how she does that. "I think at fifteen, I already knew quite a bit about myself. I knew I wanted to be a writer. I knew what I liked - boys, clothes, books, boys, music, my friends, and did I mention boys? - and so I had those things to focus on, and I really did." She sits up straighter and laughs at herself. "I was obsessed with having a boyfriend but then I got bored pretty quickly and would dump him and try another one, and repeat. I kept myself busy and even had fun, despite what was happening at home. Dad gave me a lot of freedom and honestly, for a few years after Mum died, life felt easier. Carefree, almost. Now, I know I was just postponing my grief, and that caught up with me once I hit my twenties. But even then, I was okay. Jake wasn't so lucky." Her smile drops completely. "Jake and Mum were really close. He didn't mind being around her when she was in her worst episodes. Me, I wasn't so good at that. It drained me. I'd rather be reading alone, with my boyfriend at the time, or out with friends. But Jake would often just curl up in bed next to her and stroke her back or comb her hair. He'd stay there for hours and hours listening to *The Archers* or reading the *Radio Times* listings to her."

"Shit. He was what, thirteen?"

"Yeah, when she died. Jake always had more patience than me. But he also needed more from my parents than I did; reassurance, validation, encouragement. And sadly, Dad wasn't the best at giving that."

"What's he like now? Your father?"

She rolls her eyes again. "Living in Edinburgh with Carol and three sausage dogs. I haven't seen them for over two years."

"And Jake? He seems to be so well put together and sort of larger than life," I say, thinking about all the banter I've had with him in the last few days. "Does he see your dad?"

"Jake's amazing. He's my best friend. I'm so lucky to have him," she says, her smile firmly back. "But no, he also hasn't seen them for just as long. I think he'd like to change that, actually."

"So that's your big before and after, the first big dividing line in your life." I nod, understanding now what she means. I can't help thinking how her having this, that grief, is something we have in common. It maybe explains why I feel so comfortable with her.

"Yeah, it is. But you know, the older I get, the more the before feels like a dream. Not a totally unpleasant one, I have to say. I think I've put those memories through a heavy rose-tinted filter, but I also know that who I am now is not defined by that single event and for a long time in my twenties - when I finally did grieve my mother - it felt like it would be the axis my whole life would turn around. But now, it isn't." Jenna tilts her head up and pushes air through her nose and then it stops, as if a thought has just popped into her head. "Maybe that's because of my divorce. Maybe all it takes is another dividing line to appear for the other one to fade in comparison. My divorce certainly didn't feel as dramatic or tragic or confusing - it was what I wanted - but it definitely felt like it had just as much, if not more power. It really stopped me in my tracks, made me question everything."

"You were the one who asked for a divorce?" I ask, unsure if I'm surprised or not.

"Yes," she says but she doesn't elaborate.

"You didn't want to be married to him anymore?"

"No, I didn't. He was, *is*, a good man. He took great care of me and supported me in lots of different ways. But..." She stops. Shaking her head, Jenna finally puts the watermelon slice in her mouth and sucks so hard I can hear the juice get pulled out of the fruit.

"But..." I prompt her after a few seconds.

She nods as she quickly chews. "I wanted things he didn't want."

"The sex things? The kink?"

"Not only that, but also..." Jenna looks up at me then as if remembering something she forgot. "Oh, Marty, this is not a great first-date conversation."

"Who said this was a *first* date? I think when you've shagged like rabbits like we did last night and done some excellent wet-humping in the sea together, well, then we've already moved on from that. Also, we've had two sunset dates together," I point out. "I would therefore say this is at least a fourth or fifth date."

"Sometimes I feel like you just say more words than is really necessary so your accent distracts me from thinking up counter-arguments," she says, with more head shakes.

"That wasn't what I was doing, but I can't promise you I won't in the future." I wink at her. "You like my accent, huh? I like yours too. All those prim and proper English sounds."

"You're doing it again." She points the watermelon rind at me.

"And you're hoping I forget my question, but I haven't. Tell me."

She narrows her eyes on me. "You really want to know?"

"I do." I nod.

She puts her sunglasses back on then but stays looking at me. "It wasn't just the kink." She sighs, and it sounds almost guttural. "I changed my mind about children. I decided I *did* want to have children with him."

I don't mean to fall silent. I'm just noticing how her body is different, her torso bent forward over her legs, her shoulders sloped and her hands stroking her shins, almost as if to comfort herself.

"And he didn't?"

"No," she says and stares out at the blue sea again. "We always said no to children. From one of our first dates, actually. And that's how I felt then, and it was how I felt for a long time. But a few years ago, I changed my mind."

"Why?"

"Why did I change my mind?" She scoffs, looking at me. "All the usual reasons. My friends started having kids, and my goodness they were cute. Well, some of them were. Some were ugly little buggers, but others... I mean, have you ever cuddled a helpless little newborn baby, or heard them sneeze, or sniffed the top of their head? You probably haven't, actually. But it will happen, and you better be ready for how that makes you feel. So yeah, I guess my ovaries woke up. I also found myself looking at my life and realising the only thing I had to focus

213

on was my career and that was getting harder and more conflicted as my own relationship – and specifically, our sex life - stagnated quite a bit. Also, at the time, I still loved Robert. He was a good partner for a long time, so I thought he'd be a brilliant father. And stupidly, stupidly, part of me even thought that having a child might bring us closer together... but he was firm and resolute about not wanting children, no matter how I felt."

I swallow and have to ask the only question that seems to matter after all that new information. "Do you still love him?"

Jenna looks back to the sea when she speaks again. "A part of me will always love him. In the same way part of me will always be in love with Jonathan Kennet and Tomas Dobrowski, the first and second boys I fell in love with. In the same way I'll always be the eleven-year-old girl sitting in the corner of a library learning about erections for the first time in a Judy Blume book. And I will always be the fifteen-year-old who read a Christina Rosetti poem at her mother's funeral. I'll always be the sixteen-year-old losing her virginity in the back of Liam Crowe's VW Polo. So yes, I'll always be the woman who fell in love with Robert. But right now, I am not his, and he is not mine, and my heart..." Jenna lies back then, stretches her hands above her head and turns her head to look at me. "My heart has never felt as free as it does now, which is so bloody exciting but also, utterly, utterly terrifying."

I clear some of the plates and then lie down on my side next to her. I have every intention of lying back and staring up at the few clouds that decorate the blue sky but before I do I realise there is another question I am curious about. It's nowhere near as important, but I feel like I need to ask. "And... kids? How do you feel about them now?"

Again, Jenna takes her time to answer. "Can I say that I really don't know? Because that is my honest answer. I think maybe I do still want them, but I'm definitely not ready to do that alone. I'm also not ready to rush into another relationship and get pregnant immediately. So, yeah, I just don't know."

I wait a moment before responding. I suddenly don't want to say a single thing that could make me sound so much younger than her wise and informed years, but I also want to be honest, and I think what I have to say could help her.

"I think not knowing is okay. I don't know how I feel most of the time." I smile down at her.

"You know more than you realise," Jenna says and her hands come up to comb my hair. "And you're right, not knowing is totally okay."

I lean over to kiss her lips, tasting champagne, watermelon and strawberries - all the sweetest, juiciest things in life.

Then I turn and lie down on my back, my head touching the side of hers, and I close my eyes. The calm that washes over me as I feel the sun's heat tightening the skin on my body is enough that I feel almost like I could fall asleep. Just after I remind myself that I probably shouldn't because then I'll burn as red as a boiled lobster, a very clear thought slices into my mind waking me up.

Startled and alert, I can't let go of it, but nor do I want to hold on to it too tight because it unsettles me as much as it soothes me. Because if Jenna hadn't got divorced and Arnie hadn't died, I wouldn't be lying where I'm lying now, beside someone I want to know for much, much longer than the days we are going to share on this island in the sunshine.

Chapter Twenty-Six

Jenna

The ice cream is what nearly undoes me. It's not just the ice cream, it's the way we eat it; walking hand in hand along the short waterfront promenade of Gialos, a fishing village further down the western coast of Crete.

More than the scooter, the snorkelling, the way he asked me how I liked to be touched in the ocean, more than talking about losing my mum and in a very different context, losing my husband, more than all that, it's the simple act of strolling along the water's edge together, my hand in one of his and the other holding a raspberry ice cream. I am stunned by how good it all feels, by how peaceful and affirming and downright comforting it is to have someone want to hold my hand; to be seen with me, as mine, and for me to be seen as his.

Even if it's not true.

As it happens, Marty isn't in a talking mood either and so we walk and lick at our ice creams, sharing each other's with little more than nudges and nods. He went for pistachio and salted caramel and it works brilliantly together.

"Want to walk back, or sit here on the bench?" He lifts our joined hands to point out a wooden bench looking out over a small harbour of fishing boats, a few metres away from where the promenade ends.

"Let's sit," I say, and we do. Then the race to finish our ice creams before they melt is on, and even though I give it my best shot, I still end up having to lick most of my fingers clean. I give our surroundings only a quick glance before I lift Marty's arm and do the same to his hand.

"And here I was thinking I could go an hour without an erection," he says, watching me.

"Not if I have anything to do with it," I say. When I let his hand go, I place it on my thigh because that feels like where it should be. I rejoice a little internally when I notice that the heart-shaped lump in my throat has sunk again, and my pussy has stepped up again, throbbing between my crossed legs.

We don't talk again for a while and I find my eyes focusing on the bobbing up and down of one faded green boat. I close my eyes behind my sunglasses, wondering what Marty would say if I suggested going back to my villa now so we could...

"Jenna?" Marty says, and I turn to see him also looking out at the water, but not in the same direction, more straight ahead and further into the distance.

"Yeah?" I lean my head against his shoulder. A second later his arm is around me and I hope he's about to ask what I was about to ask because I need to move away from this dream-like place. I need to see him naked. I want to straddle him. I want to gasp as he enters me or maybe hear him grunt as one of my toys enters him. I want to be consumed by these filthy thoughts so no other thoughts can-

"I feel all kinds of stupid saying stuff like this after two days..." Marty begins.

"Then don't," I whisper and turn my head to nibble on his neck.

Maybe he didn't hear me because he continues. "I just want you to know how much fun I'm having and how I don't take any of it for granted. The sex is amazing. You're so easy to talk to. And I just think you're fucken awesome."

My limbs loosen and I smile then. Because they're the words I think I want to hear. 'Fun' 'amazing' 'easy' and 'awesome'. They're young words. They're words free from any connection or connotation other than exactly what they mean. I smile and yet I feel a small splinter of disappointment lodge itself inside my stomach. But what else did I expect? He's twenty-four, he lives in a different country, and he's still mourning the loss of his first love and best friend.

I kiss his neck again before lifting my head up. I look at him for just a moment before I change the conversation's direction completely. "Can we go back to my villa now and fuck until we break each other's backs?"

"Only if you beat me back to the scooter." He darts up and is gone before I'm even standing.

"Marty! It's like twenty-seven degrees!" I shout, but he's not stopping, and I realise I'm going to have to run for my orgasms. As I do, the sweat trickling down my back, I feel young and free. I feel like I am living in the moment and in every one of his young and free words.

*****

We don't make it to my bed when we're back in the villa. We don't even make it to the shower I so desperately need. We don't even manage to take off each other's clothes - his shorts are around his ankles and my bikini is still on, the bottoms moved the side - and he takes me hard from behind as I feel the cool of the floor tiles on my knees and palms just inside the entrance of my villa. As he fucks me, he slaps me ten times on each butt cheek, checking in with me every few strikes and the only thing I say is, "Harder."

After, as I lie on top of him, enjoying the chill of the air conditioner above me and the heat of his body, he strokes my tingly and sore butt cheeks. I let him do it until I feel things swirling in my stomach and up into my chest, things I know are logical to feel after a day like today, but feelings I could really do without right now.

"Thank you for spanking me," I say, and it hurts to talk because my throat is sore from the noises I made when I came.

"Those are five words I thought I'd never hear, but you are very, very welcome."

"Shower time." I stand up and hold my hand out for him to take but he doesn't.

"Go ahead," he says. "I need a minute."

I arch an eyebrow at him but walk away, hoping he's watching my arse.

After switching the shower on, I go to the mirror to brush my hair, which is once again hopelessly tangled. I think I hear him talking to someone, presumably on the phone, but I resist the urge to move closer and listen, and instead brush my teeth and take my bikini off, laughing a little at the visible skin colour difference where it was. Then I walk into the shower.

Less than ten minutes later, Marty comes in, his shorts on but still not done up properly. He sits on the bench I sat on last night and he looks at me.

"My turn," he says, and I turn my back to him so he can't see my smile. I continue to lather up my body and then wash the suds off. When I go to shampoo my hair, I turn around and lift my arms so he can see my body like this, my breasts raised, my waist more defined. When I lean back to wash the shampoo out of my hair, eyes closed, I want to bottle up how I feel; sexy, sensual, confident. And spanked. It is the very tip of an iceberg I want to discover, but it is my iceberg and I am now not ashamed of it. I still have my eyes closed when I feel his arms circle my waist and press his naked body to mine. I feel the heat rise, thinking we are about to fuck in the shower again, not in the least bit angry about that, but then he gently turns me around, pressing my back to his chest, and I see him reach for the conditioner bottle.

"I normally shampoo twice," I say hoping the tease in my voice is clear.

"And here I am thinking you'd be impressed I even know how to use conditioner." He laughs, and he does know. He squeezes it onto his hands and then rubs his fingertips through the ends of my hair, before snaking them along my scalp, giving me a head massage. I close my eyes again and lean back, the shower spray to our side, warming my arm and hip.

"You're good at that," I say.

I hear some strained noise in his throat — a swallowed cough or a pained grunt - and when he speaks, I know why. "I used to wash Arnie's hair a lot. It was kind of our thing," he says. I think about that for a moment and wonder if he means before Arnie was sick, or during. Was this how Marty took care of Arnie when he didn't have energy to wash himself? The thought pierces into my heart which has been growing fuller and heavier in my chest all day.

"Like sunsets?"

"Like sunsets," he replies with a smile I can hear. He leans me under the spray to wash the conditioner out, raking his fingers through my hair, and I love how silky soft my hair feels as it lands on my shoulders.

220

"Thank you," I say when he's done.

"You're welcome," he replies and kisses my forehead. Then he grabs my shower gel, hands it to me, and promptly turns around and presses his hands to the wall, spreading his legs like I'm about to strip search him. "Over to you! Wash me good! I fucken stink!"

And I do. I put my hands all over him – everywhere - taking my time to lather up bubbles and maybe linger a little longer on places that I now know he likes, and then I switch the shower spray to come through the shower head and I take it and rinse him down. He shampoos his hair as I do this, and then switches the spray back to the rain shower above us so that when he is rinsed clean, we come together and kiss and the clean water washes into our joined mouths. Even though I feel him hardening against my stomach and I feel like molten lava between my legs, there's something about the kiss that stays lazy and long and lingering, keeping us where we are and no closer to fucking. We have hunger but the pace has changed, and it's why I'm not remotely surprised when neither of us makes a move to take our arousal a step further.

"I don't know about you, but I'm fucking starving," he says. "Shall we order in?"

"You can stay?" I ask and turn the shower off.

"Unless you want me to go?"

"Well," I begin and then move away from him, stepping out of the shower and grabbing some towels. I wrap mine around my body as I speak. "I do have another twenty-something year old on their way to come service me."

Instantly, upon seeing his face, I regret my choice of words.

"Service you?" He blinks, slowly moving the towel to go around his waist.

"You know what I mean," I say as light as I can make my voice. I turn away because the heat in my cheeks starts to burn.

"No, Jenna, I don't think I do," he says, his voice hard. "What did you mean?"

This. This is the problem with spending so much time with someone you have great chemistry with. It inevitably leads to feelings moving faster than communication, and now even humour - our fail-safe since the very first moment we met - is failing me.

"What food do you want?" I ask and pull my robe around my still damp body. I need to get out of the bathroom.

"Jenna," he warns, and even this tone of voice – this stern, warning air – thrills me as much as it scares me.

I turn to face him and rush out an apology, knowing he is owed that much. "Marty, I said a stupid thing. I'm sorry. Can we just forget I said it?"

"I asked you what you meant by it. Are you going to answer me?" His face has changed. His eyes are sunken, his cheeks hollowed out.

"Of course, you're not servicing me," I say. "Like I said, I'm sorry I said that."

"Then what is happening here?" Marty steps closer to me.

"No," I say out loud although it was only supposed to be for my ears. "We're not doing this. We're not ruining this perfect day with an awkward conversation about what we are and what we're not."

"Then don't," he says, unblinking. "Don't ruin it."

Exasperation floods me. "You are too quick for me. Your words... Your comebacks. And your fucking optimism!" I don't mean to shout – it's the last thing I want to do with him – but still I do.

"Me? Optimistic?" He places his hand on his chest. He's not shouting but his words are loud and big. "I'm a mess. I'm a world of pain, Jenna. I'm not optimistic, I'm just so fucken desperate to feel anything other than pain."

"Marty," I say taking a deep breath. "I didn't mean you're not in pain. Of course you are. You've been through so much..."

He interrupts me. "And do you want to know something about that, Jenna?" He steps closer to me and I freeze in the doorway through to the bedroom, leaning back against the door frame, suddenly exhausted as he stares down at me. "You are the first person I've met who seems to just let that be what it is. You're not trying to fix me like my mother. You're not ignoring it like my dad. You don't try to joke about it like Maeve does, and you don't want to dissect every sordid detail like my therapist, but you will listen if I want you to. You're the first

222

person who just lets me feel what I need to feel. You're the only one who has come close to making me feel like myself again, or better, actually, like somebody I actually want to be."

I shake my head and look down, confused but not surprised by my disorientation. I had been ignoring my own feelings all day and then I started to ignore his. How did I get that so horribly wrong?

"I'm not asking for your hand in marriage, for fuck's sake. I'm not asking for anything. I just want to be able to tell you how much I like you, and how this is more than just sex for me," Marty continues. "And if it is just sex for you, that's fine. I get it. But just have the courage to come out and admit it so I know where I stand."

My eyes warm with the urge to cry. I open my mouth, but words don't come.

"Jenna, please," Marty says and he comes closer still, so close I can feel his heat and I wish he'd put a shirt on or a bag over his head and that thought is what makes me smile and laugh a little to myself as I look up and into his eyes.

"Marty," I say and surely the way I say his name is enough, enough for him to hear and know the want and need and admiration I have for him. But it's not. His eyes still search mine.

"Tell me what this is for you," he urges and while I hate how he doesn't let me off the hook easily, I can't help but admire how he holds me accountable.

It's the vulnerability in his seeking eyes, and the faintest lines between his eyebrows and the hard edge to his chin as his jaw repeatedly flexes that has me reaching for his face, stroking and cupping it with both of my hands.

"Marty, I don't know what it is and maybe I should because I'm older and more experienced, and for Christ's sake, I'm the one who is supposed to be an expert in sex and relationships, but I really don't know what it is. But like we said earlier, I'm trying to be okay with not knowing. And I do know this much, it's more than just sex for me too." I wait for the ground to disappear from under me, but it doesn't.

"It's more," Marty repeats, as if to confirm for us both.

I nod.

"Okay," he says, and he bends down to kiss me on my forehead, ease and lightness back in his tone and movements. "Now let's go order some food. I could eat the front *and* hind legs off a scabby horse."

"Okay," I say a little breathless as I watch him walk away. "You go ahead. I just need a moment to get dressed, and... " I don't finish but he doesn't seem to mind as he's already calling out from the living area.

"No problem, just hurry up. We have another cracker of a sunset to watch together too."

Then I'm left alone, leaning against the door, feeling like it will take more than a few minutes for the room to stop spinning.

The Third Sunset

"Don't forget, beautiful sunsets need cloudy skies."

- Paulo Coelho

Chapter Twenty-Seven

Jenna

We eat outside as the sun moves lower in the sky, readying itself for its final blaze of colour today.

At first, I thought we'd ordered too much food, but as I watch Marty using the last piece of bread to soak up the remaining pasta sauce lining his bowl, like he doesn't know when he'll eat again, I realise we both needed it. It's yet another thing I'd forgotten about companionship; the joy of satisfying an appetite with good food shared with good company. Sharing a meal with a lover feels almost as intimate as sex. There is certainly something sensual about the way Marty's mouth works chewing his food and the satisfied grunt he makes as he swallows his last mouthful.

"So," he says once he finally stops eating. "I have to confess something."

"Oh, God," I say, leaning back in my chair. "You're actually forty-eight, just with an excellent skin care routine."

"No." He winces. "It's my birthday tomorrow."

I nearly choke on the sip of water I take. "What? So, you're actually twenty-five?"

"No, I'll be twenty-four tomorrow," he says with a dimple-dipping grin. "Surely you know by now I'm a rounding-up kind of guy?"

"You're actually twenty-*three* right now?" I ask, my voice and eyebrows high.

"Yes."

I don't know why my stomach plummets so dramatically, but I try my best to rein it in as a flash of disappointment or frustration, or something not at all good, momentarily lines his brow. But just as quickly as it appears, it's gone and he turns his attention to the view ahead.

"There's some clouds in the sky tonight," he says. "That will make the sunset look different."

I take in Marty's side profile, my eyes hitching on that bump in his nose and the dainty curl in his eyelashes. I see traces of his youth all over him, but I also see a man. A good man.

My stomach rights itself, and so do my thoughts.

I'm just about to tell him how his age doesn't bother me, to reassure him and ask him what he wants to do for his birthday, but he's standing up and stripping off his robe. Then, naked, he runs and jumps into the pool like the big kid he also is. The big kid I strongly suspect he will always be regardless of his age.

"Get in," he calls to me when he surfaces.

"I just got clean," I say.

"I'll have you dirty in no time again and you know it." He splashes me.

I squeal at the shock of the water, but a moment later shrug my robe off. Following his footsteps, I run and jump, rolling my also naked body into a ball in the air. When I hit the water, I feel the smack, hear the splash, and love how the water caresses and cools the sting of the harsh landing.

I can't remember the last time I jumped into a pool like that, but I instantly promise myself it won't be the last. In fact, as I surface, I swim to the side and climb up the ladder to get out so I can do it again, this time scissoring my legs and arms open in a star jump, grateful the terrace isn't overlooked. The next time I leap up as high as I can and twist my body around like a corkscrew. On my fourth jump I try to touch my toes and when I crash into the pool, the slap of the water is hard and sore against the back of my legs. I emerge laughing so much I swallow a mouthful of water and end up coughing so hard I can't talk. It's then I realise Marty is leaning his back against the infinity edge of the pool watching me, laughter wrinkling his face in all the right places.

"Jesus, you're a riot," he says. "Are you okay? That was loud!"

I laugh more then and that does nothing to stop me coughing. When I finally feel like I can speak without spluttering, I swim the small distance over to him. "God, that was fun. Why haven't I been doing that all day every day since I got here?"

He snakes his arms around my waist, pulling me closer. "Because you've been doing me instead?"

"Can I do you again?" I ask after a moment's hesitation, suddenly nervous after that terrible joke I made earlier.

As if he reads my mind he says, "Are you asking me to service you?" He leans back so I can see his eyebrows bobbing up and down and his stupid, beautiful lips are pulled into a stupid, beautiful pout.

Buoyed by relief, I play along. "Yes, I'm asking you to service me so good I forget my name." I wrap my legs around him.

"You'll never forget your name. Not when I'm growling it in your ear as I enter you."

Looks like he can play this game too. I pout as I stare at him.

Game on, Marty, game on.

"And I'll say your name as you push inside me," I begin. "I'll say your name every time you pull out only to go back in, filling me up, stretching me so good. I'll say your name when you hit that perfect spot deep inside me, the one that makes me so wet, the one that makes me come so hard."

He hums in his throat as his teeth nip at my neck. "Jenna," he says my name, full of want.

I continue, "And you know what happens when I come. When I squeeze you so hard and hold you so firmly inside me. I grip all around you because it's where I want you, where I need you," I say then drop my voice even lower. "I need you inside me, Marty. I want you to fuck me."

He pulls back to look at me then and I think he's going to say something back, but he doesn't. There is a second or two where he looks at me like he's seeing me for the first time and it's unnerving and I wonder if I pushed him too far, if my dirty talk was too much, but then his mouth dives down and takes mine and I can't breathe. I can't breathe because his mouth is claiming mine and he is

229

doing it with so much force, my nose is squashed against his and all my airways are blocked, but I don't care. Our teeth clash and our tongues fight, and I can't remember the last time I kissed like this. Maybe I never have. I add that to the growing list of things that have surprised me this week; you can kiss with teeth and really, really enjoy it.

"Marty," I say pushing him a little so I can breathe and speak. "Condom."

"Stay here," he says and moves to the other side of the pool to get out, giving me the most perfect view of his arse and back muscles. "You still want to do it here?"

I turn my head and nod at the horizon. "Yes. Let's fuck as we watch the sunset."

And I get one of his stupid, beautiful grins before he runs off. Seconds later he's jogging back, the foil square in his hand, and a beautifully semi-erect penis between his legs. His feet slide on the wet tiles a moment after I yell out not to run, and we both laugh as he jumps back in, holding the condom up out of the water. I meet him in the middle of the small pool and back him up to the metal ladder. I reach down and stroke his cock, play with his balls, hear him say my name again as he kisses the side of my head.

"Climb up a bit." I nod at the metal steps behind him. He does, looking perplexed but when his penis is out of the water and my mouth is on it, licking and flicking and sucking, he relaxes and leans back against the side. When I feel confident that he's fully erect and ready - his hips thrusting into my mouth - I pull off and take the condom from his hand and open it. After I roll it on, I hold the base and squeeze, loving how hard he is for me. I keep my hand there as he moves back into the water and his fingers cup me between my legs, rubbing as he backs me up against the infinity wall again.

"Marty," I say, hoping he remembers what I said.

"Jenna," he says as he takes my mouth while my hand moves his cock to where I want it.

"Marty," I say as he pushes forward and his head crowns into me.

"Jenna," he grunts as I hold him there, my hand around his base still, not letting him go any deeper yet.

"Marty," I whisper into his ear as I slowly remove my fingers and he slides all the way in.

"Jenna." He gasps as he bottoms out.

"Marty." I moan as he rocks inside me.

"Jenna." He laughs as his hands come up and play with my breasts.

"Marty." I giggle as I lean back and stretch my arms out parallel with the skyline and sunset.

"Jenna." He groans as he puts his hands on the pool's edge on either side of me and then thrusts up inside me, harder, deeper.

"Marty!" I call out as he hits the exact spot I was talking about.

"Jenna, Jenna, Jenna," he says, rolling into me, pushing me back against the pool's edge so hard I know I'll have bruises there tomorrow and I don't care. I want them. I want any kind of mark or scrape or graze that reminds me of this.

"Marty," I mumble when he takes one hand off the pool's edge and finds my clit with his thumb.

"Jenna," he says when he starts to rub me there.

We stay like that for the longest time. Him playing with me as he rubs me slow and fucks me fast. Us repeating each other's names. But then he stops and slows the pace right down, even taking his hand off my clit, leaving me wriggling and writhing for more.

"Jenna," Marty says. "You need to see the sunset."

In a single movement, he pulls out of me, grabs me by the hips and turns me around so I can see the sun hanging low above the horizon, turning the sky and all its clouds varying shades of pink. Some of the fluffy swirls are pastel shades of rose, and those closer to the sun are a vibrant hot pink. The sun will be gone in the next twenty minutes and I have half a mind to ask him if we can just stay how we are fucking in the pool until it is completely descended, but when he slides back into me from behind, tilting my hips slightly and sweeping his hand around to cup me from the front too, I know I won't last that long even if he does.

There is something about the clouded splendour of this particular sunset that guts me, making me feel empty even though Marty is making me feel so very full. This sunset, more than any other we've shared, seems to have a very clear message for me. It's a reminder that there will always be clouds. There will always be days when clouds block the sun, but that doesn't mean the sun isn't still shining, still burning its gases, being the pull we all need to stay exactly where we are, where we're supposed to be. It's a reminder that sometimes, clouds can be beautiful too.

"Jenna," Marty says again, and his hand moves up to my neck, wraps around my throat and turns me so I can kiss him.

"Marty," I say when our kiss breaks and I bend over lower and hold my body as steady as I can, pushing back so he can fuck me deeper.

"Yes, Jenna," he says, and I hear the strain in his voice, a tone I now know means he's close. I put a hand in the water and find my clit so I can meet him. It takes no time at all.

"Yes, Marty." I gasp as my orgasm charges through my pussy, my stomach, my thighs. "Marty, fuck, yes!"

Just as my body stops shuddering from my release, I feel Marty shiver behind me as he gives a series of short, hard thrusts. He grunts out my name as he stops moving and I lean back against him to hold myself up. I close my eyes to the golden pink hues that now fill the sky. Wincing at the dull but so sweetly satisfying ache in my pussy that comes as he slips out of me, I welcome the warmth of his body when he wraps his arms around my waist.

"Jenna," Marty says his chin on my shoulder. His lips are kissing my skin, soothing the sunburn I know I have there despite our best efforts today.

"Marty," I say back because his name is the only thing that fills my mind right now.

"Jenna?" he says again and it's a question now.

"Marty," I reply like a *Yes*.

"Can I stay the night?" he asks in a voice that is more hesitant than usual.

Stay forever, I think as I drift into a post-orgasmic haze. *Stay forever, like this, here with me.*

"Yes, Marty, stay." I turn my back on the very last minutes of the sunset and close my eyes against his warm wet chest, knowing happily that he will watch it for both of us.

Chapter Twenty-Eight
The Next Day

Jenna

When I wake the following morning, he is gone.

The panic rises in me and while I am quick to quieten it, I am not as effective as the note I find on the bedside table.

GONE FOR MY RIDE WITH DAD. BACK FOR COFFEE AT 10. CALL ME IF NOT GOOD. P.S. YOU ARE FUCKING AWESOME.

Again, he leaves his number below the message. I didn't put his number in my phone yesterday, but I did keep hold of the note he left, folding it into my purse behind one of my credit cards. I hold this piece of paper, staring at the slightly forward slope of his handwriting, not at all surprised that he writes in all capital letters, and I know I'll never throw the note away.

After glancing at my phone and realising I've slept in later than I have all week - until 8:45 - I sit up and acknowledge the sharp ache between my legs and a light sting on the skin of my butt cheeks as I slip out of bed. I smile about both as I brush my teeth and scroll through other notifications that have come up, including five new messages from my brother checking I'm still alive.

I look lazily at the bath, thinking a soak would do my aching pussy good, but I realise I have too much nervous energy for that and before I can talk myself out of it, I'm changing into a clean set of gym gear and pulling my hair into a ponytail. I grab a banana from the fruit bowl and eat it as I march up the path to the outdoor gym, my headphones on and my tried and tested playlist filling my ears. I get my phone out and send Jake a quick message to let him know I'm still breathing but if he doesn't hear from me again by the end of the day it's because I have died and my cause of death is to be listed as "Fucking A Young Irishman".

Focused on my phone, I'm already in the gym when I spot who else is there. It's Marty's sister, Maeve, with an older woman that has the exact same colouring as Marty. And when she stands up straight, coming out of a yoga position I'm not sure I could do, I see her side profile on full display complete with a familiarly commanding nose, albeit bump-free, and a very recognisable angular bone structure.

"Fuck," I say under my breath but keep walking, albeit a little slower.

They appear to be doing stretches on the mats together and by the look of Maeve's slightly pinked cheeks, I have a small hope that they're cooling down rather than warming up. Maeve is the first to spot me and I hit pause on my playlist as she lifts her hand in a meagre wave.

"Oh, hi," she says, and I see her glance at her mother once, twice, before putting her eyes back on me. She has a careful but impish smile on her face, as if she's considering what would be the best outcome in this scenario for me but at the same time, she also can't resist contemplating the most fun outcome for her.

"Hi," I say, and keeping my head down, I walk past them to the machine section. I hope Maeve receives my brevity as the invitation it is to absolutely not introduce me to her mother.

I am standing on the treadmill and finally breathing somewhat normally when I hear muttering behind me. I make the mistake of glancing back and I see Maeve's mother - Marty's mother - looking directly at me with her hands on her hips.

I smile at her, possibly a little disingenuously, then turn back to my workout, punishing myself by increasing the incline and the speed a little. I hit play again on my music.

"Let's go, Ma." I hear Maeve's voice clearly despite my playlist. I patiently keep my eyes forward and wait for the song to finish before I look back, relief sinking my chest when I see they have gone.

"Thank fuck for that," I say to myself and then, lowering the incline, I increase the speed and my music volume. I start to jog.

After a surprisingly easy twenty-five minutes of running – possibly a consequence of my boosted levels of endorphins after all the many orgasms I've enjoyed the last few days - I switch the machine off and turn around to go take my position at the weights.

That's when I see her walking back up the path.

Marty's mother.

I cover my face with my towel, wiping away the sweat and hoping against all hope that it will also wipe away the image of his mother walking towards me with a very severe frown on her face, but when I drop the towel I see she and her scowl are still very much on the approach.

"I forgot my water bottle," she says, a little too loudly.

I nod and smile as she goes to retrieve a purple bottle I hadn't noticed on the floor. I pick up a pair of 5kg dumbbells and stand in front of the mirror.

"So, you're Jenna?" She looks at me using the mirror's reflection.

I sigh and I know she will have seen my shoulders sink. But surely she can't expect me to want to have this conversation, even if she does.

"Yes," I say.

She nods and her lips curl up more on the right side than the left. It's definitely not a smile. "I'm Cynthia."

"Nice to meet you, Cynthia," I say and nod at her in the mirror. Then I start to pump my arms. I may as well use up all this nervous energy.

"You were with Aiden yesterday," she says and then lowers her voice. "And last night."

"Yes," I say simply. I remind myself that Marty is twenty-four. I don't need to apologise or be ashamed of sleeping with him.

"I have to be honest and say I'm a little surprised," she begins but I'm not about to wait to hear what she has to say.

"Because I'm older? Yes, I can understand that." And it's the truth. It's been surprising me since I met him.

"And you're English," she says, and my spine straightens, tingling a little. I hadn't even thought of that being a problem, and my oversight is as sobering as it puzzling.

"I am," I say, and square my shoulders.

"Where do you live, Jenna?"

"London." I slam down my weights, swapping them for 8kg ones. I need to feel more of a burn.

"What do you see in him?" She crosses her arms then, her stare hardening. "Apart from the obvious."

"Excuse me?" I turn to look at her, stopping my reps.

"He's too young for you," Cynthia snaps at me, her eyes just as fierce.

"With all due respect, Marty's an adult, and so am I-"

"Marty? You call him Marty?" she interrupts.

"Yes, that's what he told me his name was." I try not to sound spiteful but it's near-impossible.

"That's the name his ex gave him. His ex who *died*." She emphasises the last word with heavy eyebrows and an unforgiving glower.

"I know about Arnie." This conversation is moving from places I never expected to topics I wouldn't have dreamed of discussing with her, at least not like this.

"Then you'll know Aiden's been through a lot this last year. And even before that. He spent months with Arnie, looking after him. Nobody should ever have to watch someone they love die like that. Especially not a twenty-two-year old boy."

I bristle at the word 'boy' but I know nothing is to be gained from highlighting just how far from a boy her son is.

"I agree with you on that. And I truly wish it hadn't happened."

"Then maybe you'll also agree that this is not a good idea." She nods at me.

"There is no 'this'. We spent the day together yesterday..."

"And night," she adds firmly. "You spent the night together."

I shake my head and move to return the weights. "I don't think either of us really wants to have this conversation."

Cynthia shuffles to keep close to me, her arms folded across her chest. "And yet we are having it. And I'm asking you to stay away from Aiden. You don't know what he's been through."

238

"He's told me all about Arnie," I say again. I take a moment to look at her, really look at her. I know it's fear making her say what she's saying, but fear of what?

"Did he also tell you about what happened after that? How he disappeared completely for months after Arnie died. How he went on this drink and drugs binge around Ibiza, Majorca, and the other smaller island there that I can never remember the blasted name for."

"Formentera," I say with a sharp inhale.

"Yes, that's it, thank you." She gives me a quick nod. "Anyway. We barely heard from him for nearly six months until we got a phone call that he was in hospital."

"Hospital?" I ask without thinking.

"So, he didn't tell you," she says, and she can't contain her satisfaction. Her dark eyes sparkle like his do when he comes up with a quick and witty retort for me, but it's brief because as she continues to talk it completely disappears and there is nothing happy or triumphant about her expression. "He was in a scooter crash. Punctured a lung. Broke seven ribs. But if you'd seen the state of the scooter, you'd know that it was a miracle he walked away with just that."

A rush of different impulses fill my mind, but the one that is loudest, strongest, is the one to defend Marty. "People get in accidents all the time. I'm sorry that happened to him but I don't really understand your point."

Cynthia is quick to reply to that although the way her voice cracks makes me think it pains her to do so. "There were multiple witnesses and they all said he was speeding up as he approached the wall he crashed into. He wanted to do it. He did it on purpose."

A chill snakes its way down my back, like one of the many beads of sweat now pooling at the base of my spine.

No. Not Marty. Marty who is full of life. Full of pain and loss and grief too, yes, but so very full of life.

"He didn't tell you that part, did he?" Cynthia asks and while her tone is sly, her voice still cracks, like maybe it's actually a great effort for her to sound so mean.

I drop eye contact with her, feeling increasingly out of my depth. Cynthia continues to talk and I sense her trying to catch my gaze again but still I look away, listening, processing. Or trying to.

"That's what Aiden does," she continues. "He rushes into things. He goes full throttle. He did it with Arnie. When they went travelling, when they fell in love, and when Arnie got the cancer. Aiden was all in, straight away. And then when Arnie died, he was all in on self-destruct mode. He drank, he got high, and I'm sorry to be the one to tell you this but he slept around too, shagged his way through..."

"Ma." Maeve's voice silences Cynthia and makes us both twist our heads towards her. "That's enough."

Maeve's shoulders and her jaw are squared in exactly the same way Marty's was when we had the small confrontation in the bathroom yesterday.

"She should know," Cynthia says.

"Her name is Jenna, Ma." Maeve steps forward to create the third point in a triangle between us. "And you're meddling."

I could pick Maeve up and spin her around in circles, I'm so grateful for her presence and solidarity in this moment.

"I'm not meddling! Not really. Not when it's my responsibility to look after Aiden and make sure he doesn't get hurt."

"I would never hurt him," I blurt out. "I care about him."

Cynthia snatches hold of my words. "If you do, then you'll leave him be. Let him have a holiday with his family. Let him have this week with us before he has to go back to reality again." Her tone is softer now, but still not calm. There's still tension in every sound, as if she's truly begging me to do as she asks.

When I don't reply, Cynthia tuts out a sigh that I feel in my own lungs. Then she turns and walks past Maeve and back up the path, one of her hands on her face and her shoulders shaking.

I exhale as I turn to Maeve.

"Thank you," I say to her with a slight nod.

"Don't thank me," she says, shrugging as she takes half a step closer. "What she said was true."

"What?" I pull my head back.

"All of it. It's true. He did get in that accident, and people did say it was deliberate. And he did drink and shag his way around the Balearics. He was a massive dirtbird man whore."

"Right," I say in a whisper, and nearly chuckle to myself because part of me is wishing the context was different so I could address her slut-shaming and being derogatory to sex workers.

"But wouldn't you have too?" Maeve asks pulling me back into our conversation.

"What do you mean?" I ask.

"Wouldn't you have done the same, or something just as unhinged, if you were twenty-three and you'd just buried your first love and best friend?"

Maeve doesn't wait for my answer. She is gone as quickly and quietly as she arrived, leaving me standing there under a hot sun, its rays toasting the already pink patches of sunburn I got yesterday, any energy I had for my workout now completely gone.

Chapter Twenty-Nine

Marty

Coming four times in twenty-four hours doesn't improve my pace on our morning ride even though my father isn't pushing quite as hard as he did yesterday. It surprises me further when he stops close to the peak and pulls over, pretending to admire the view. It's possible he does enjoy the panorama for half a minute or so, but I know my dad. He's not a standing still and staring out at the horizon kind of guy. He needs to keep his hands and his brain busy, so I know this is an excuse for something else. And it doesn't take much to make a guess.

"Are you going to bollock me?" I ask.

"And take that fun away from your mother?" he jokes, then takes a swig from his water bottle. "Nah. You know me, I don't have the energy."

I nod and stare out again at the view. Unlike my father, I'm a man who could stare at a beautiful view for a long time.

"Well, for what it's worth, I am sorry," I say. "It wasn't my plan to skip dinner or stay out. And I did call to let you know."

"You did, but in some ways that made it worse for your ma. It was like you were choosing to not be with us rather than just letting time run away with you."

"Well, that's sort of what happened. I didn't plan to be gone all day. We just..."

"I don't need the details." He holds his hand up.

"It's not like that," I say quickly.

"Sure, son. I mean, I was your age once."

"Da, seriously. It's not." I wait until he looks back at me, squinting into the sun behind me, and then I speak slowly. "I really do like her."

He raises his eyebrows, high. "It's the woman I saw you with the other day?"

"Her name's Jenna."

"Jenna. Well, she's very attractive and I dare say an older woman can have a lot of..."

"No, Da. Seriously, it's not just sex. I feel this weird connection with her. I can't really explain it, but I think she feels the same way and..."

"Oh, Jesus, Aiden," he says and he's either trying to laugh and failing or trying *not* to laugh and failing because the noises he makes are just strangled chuckles and stifled snorts. "What are you like? You realise you can't be saying any of this shite to your mother?"

"It's not shite, Dad, it's how I feel." My chest tightens with the strain of trying to explain something that feels incomprehensible.

"I believe you, son. That's the thing. *I* believe you. I don't think you're bullshitting me or that you don't have feelings for her. But it's not that simple. I mean, how old is she?"

"Thirty-seven," I say in a quiet voice.

"Wow, you see now, that's quite a bit older." Dad seems surprised. I also would have said Jenna looks younger, but now I feel like I don't know anything about what people should look or be like at any given age. More importantly, I don't care.

"Do I need to remind you that you're ten years older than Mum?" I ask.

"I wondered how long it would take for you to say that." He is laughing for real now. "I shouldn't even say it's different, should I? What with her being a woman and all?"

"No, you shouldn't. I mean, I get why you would think that, but it's not different. I'm not a teenager. I'm twenty-four now and the only reason you guys know so much about my business is because I have to live at home while I pay off my debts. And then you went and dragged me on this holiday because you deemed me too irresponsible to stay home alone."

"Oh, it's our fault now that you shacked up with an older woman, is it?" Dad laughs louder and I know he wants me to laugh with him, but I won't.

244

"By the way, twenty-four is three years *older* than Mum was when you met her."

"Yes, but we didn't meet on holiday. It's really only been a couple of days, Aiden, are you sure..."

I interrupt him again, "You know me, Da, when I like someone, I like them. We have a spark. You say you remember what it's like being young. Didn't you have that spark with Mum? Didn't that all happen really quickly?"

I'm asking questions I already know the answer to. I've heard them tell this story too many times to forget it. My parents were married within six months. It was love at first sight, my mother always says when she has a glass of wine in her hand and a table full of eager listeners. Dad is always happy to sit back and watch her tell the story, a misty-eyed smile on his face.

Dad sighs, and I suspect his mind is also winding down memory lane, but then he straightens up. "But your mother didn't live in a different country. She lived three streets away from me, for Christ's sake."

"Her living in England doesn't bother me, not at all," I say and it's the first time I've acknowledged that to myself. Of all the things that make me wonder what the future holds for Jenna and me, the geographical distance we have to navigate is of no concern.

"So, you really want to see her again after this?" My father waves his hands around referring to the island, our holiday.

I bite the corner of my lip and think about what to reply, not because I don't know my answer but because I don't want it to be met with more challenges. I'm suddenly very, very tired and I want to go back to the resort, back to Jenna.

"We haven't talked about it, but I think I want to try. Or just stay in touch. Something." My father is looking at me in a very measured way. "Life's too fucking short, Da." I choke on the words, knowing I don't have to explain it further.

I don't. He rolls his bike closer and puts a hand on my shoulder. "You're absolutely right, Aiden. I'll never argue with that. And I'll never stop you from wanting to be with whoever you want to be with. I promised you that once before, and I'm promising it to you again." He smiles at me, the same warm, delighted smile Maeve has on the rare occasions she lets a natural grin shape her mouth. It's contagious and I smile back. That's when Dad's eyes sharpen. "Just go easy with your mother. Let me talk to her first."

I nod as he squeezes his grip on me then drops his hand.

"Actually," I say as he climbs back onto his bike. I smile when he groans. Heart-to-heart conversations are like good views for him; he gets his fill pretty quick. "Could you do it today? Like when we get back to the villa? I'd really like Jenna to join us for dinner tonight."

Eyes snapped shut, his head falls back. "Holy fuckballs, Aiden, are you trying to give me a heart attack and your mother a brain aneurysm?"

"No, I just want to spend my birthday with her, as well as with you all."

Dad's laughter is back. "I'll do my best, but seriously, you better warn Jenna what she's in for."

"Jenna will be grand," I say, sounding more confident than I am. "Thanks, Dad. And really, I am sorry that I didn't make it to dinner last night."

"I believe you are. Now, race you to the bottom, birthday boy!" Dad says and sets off before my cleats are even clipped in.

*****

It's just after nine when we get back and the villa is empty.

"Looks like your mum did drag Maeve to yoga." Dad heads straight for the fridge for a beer. I like how he doesn't even give it a thought in front of me. I also like how I don't crave the cold fresh smack of a beer on a sunny day. I haven't all week, not since meeting Jenna. I look around at the sound of a vibration and see Maeve's phone on the side jiggling with new notifications.

"Nah, no way Maeve would be able to sit through another yoga class, not without her phone. I bet they just went for a quick walk or something," I say and head to the coffee machine. Dad slides a cool bottle of water my way.

"Drink up," he says as he walks to go sit outside with a book of sudokus he must have got somewhere yesterday. "That was a hot one."

I smile and take a swig as the coffee machine kicks into life. I then take my drinks and go shower, standing under the hot water much longer than I usually do.

The bathroom has a different layout to Jenna's, albeit much smaller, but the décor is the same and it's impossible to look at the tiles and not think about what we've done in her shower together. It's also impossible to think about that without my dick getting hard and needy. But I do my best to ignore it, knowing I'll be back in Jenna's villa and hopefully in her arms and between her legs within the hour. This thought stamps a smile on my face that is impossible to shift as I dry, get dressed, and brush my teeth. I run the smallest dollop of product through my hair, using my hands to work it in, and then give up when I'm bored, returning to the bedroom to look for my sunglasses, wallet and some condoms as I had noticed yesterday Jenna was running low. That's when I hear the voices.

"She's practically my age, James!" my mother shouts.

"She's not," Dad says in a hiss. At least he is trying to keep his voice down. "She's thirty-seven."

"That's not even fifteen years younger than me!"

"So what, Cynthia? Relationships like his happen all the time. Look at us," Dad tries.

"That's different!" My mum is too quick to bite back, which tells me she's not thinking, only arguing.

"Is it really that different?" My father sighs.

"I just don't understand it. Why can't he just focus on himself and get better? Why can't we just have a family holiday and spend time with each other? After the year we've had, don't we deserve that?" I hear the tears in my mother's voice, the scraping of a chair and the swishing of my dad's Lycra as he no doubt moves to comfort her. I'm almost ready to push off and walk into the room, but then my dad speaks again.

"Maybe this is part of him getting better?" he says. "Maybe he already *is* getting better? Maybe this is just Aiden living his life and we have to let that happen?"

Thank you, Da.

"Then why do I feel like he's still somewhere else? Why do I feel like I haven't got him back?" My mother says.

Jesus, Ma.

I can't walk in on that. I can't deal with my mother in this kind of mood, so I turn to go and hide in my room for a little longer but stop in my tracks when I see my sister in the doorway to our shared bathroom, looking up at me.

"You'll have to face her eventually," she says in a whisper, her arms crossed, "if you're going to ask Jenna to dinner tonight."

"How do you know about that?"

"Dad just warned Mum about it, which is why she's having a mini meltdown." Maeve turns her fingers on one hand up, inspecting her nails.

"I'll come back later and talk about it. It's my birthday after all," I say.

"And you're not going to spend most of it with your parents, which is fine. I wouldn't want to either," Maeve says. "But you shouldn't actively try to ignore them on your birthday."

The need to not be here, to be in Jenna's villa, is so strong as it rises in my body, I feel like I could choke on it. I turn my head back to the living area.

"Want to run away?" Maeve asks, her eyes on me when I turn to look at her.

"Yes." I laugh with the relief of being honest.

"I get that," she says. "But sometimes you have to stick around and face the music."

"What do you know about that?" I ask crossing my arms now too.

"There's a lot you don't know about me, Marty. I grew up a lot in the last year too."

I lean my head back against the wall and study her. I always think of her as my little sister, the youngest in our family, but truthfully, sometimes she acts like the most level-headed of us all. She's so like our father with her calm ways, her preference for few words, but there's also this exhibitionist streak that I know is more like our mother, which is how she's built this ridiculously successful career for herself as an influencer. And in the process she has indeed grown up, a lot, not to mention how she was there throughout the whole of Arnie's illness and passing, and then afterwards.

"I am sorry about how hard the last year has been, and I know I've said it before, but I will say it again. I appreciate how you looked out for me while I was... away."

Maeve nods, quiet for a moment before shrugging. "I just didn't need the hassle of a dead brother," she deadpans, but her eyes are soft and warm.

When the idea comes into my head, I don't fight it. "How about we all spend the afternoon together? You, me, Ma and Dad? We can go to the beach, go on some pedalos or maybe rent a jet ski like we did in Dubai that time."

I can tell she's trying to contain the smile that comes from the memories of that trip. It was the first and only really big holiday we did, just after Dad sold his first business. We were fifteen and eleven and we persuaded Mum and Dad to let Maeve come on a jet ski with me where I did everything I could to shake her off, but it didn't work. And then once we were out at sea, away from our mother's stare, I let her drive and she went off so fast and hard I fell back and straight off the jet ski.

"You want to do that?" she asks.

"Yes," I say and suddenly I do. "But no phone, okay?"

She rolls her eyes, possibly annoyed or belligerent at even the suggestion she couldn't do an afternoon without her phone. "Depends on how boring you are," she replies.

I nod in the direction of our parents. "You think when I suggest it to them it will get me some favour about Jenna?"

She shrugs her eyebrows. "Possibly, although I don't want to think about what you're going to have to do to get Jenna to agree."

"Jenna will be grand," I say, her name making my heart rate speed up and temperature change. It may not be what she wants to do on her holiday - have dinner with my barely functioning family - but I hope she will feel the same as me, as long as we're together, sitting next to each other, and enjoying a sunset, she'll find some good in it.

"I'm not so sure. Mum and her had a nice chat in the gym," Maeve says.

"What? When?" I've suddenly cooled right down, although my pulse beats quicker.

"Just now."

"What did she say?"

"I didn't hear all of it. Mum snuck back after our workout, left her water bottle there." Maeve uses air quotes on the word 'left'. "But Jenna may not *want* to be at dinner tonight, just to warn you."

"Christ on a motherfucking bike," I say, rushing into the living area.

"Aiden!" My mother says as she steps out of my father's embrace. Were they really hugging for that long? "Happy birthday, sweetheart!"

"Thanks," I say as I race for the door, pushing my feet into my Birkenstocks. My teeth are gritted, and I want to have words with her, I will have words with her, but first Jenna.

Jenna, Jenna, Jenna.

"Where are you going?" My mother is fast on the approach towards me.

"To Jenna's," I say giving her a quick but firm look.

"Ah," she says. "Yes, I introduced myself in the gym and..."

"Ma, I'll be back after lunch. We'll spend the afternoon together, okay? All four of us. We'll go to the beach, or stay here, or whatever you want to do."

"Oh, Marty, I'd like that, very much," she says and clasps her hands together, holds them against her chest.

"Good, and *I'd* like it if Jenna joined us for dinner tonight." I turn the door handle, ready to go. "And I'd *really* like it if you could not make it a fucking nightmare for everyone."

I walk out of the door before slamming it behind me.

Chapter Thirty

Jenna

I'm in my robe when he arrives, and it's not at all deliberate. I wanted to be dressed and composed, because that conversation with his mother has sent my thoughts spiralling so much that everything is clouded in doubt, even the many hours we've shared together over the last few days. It shouldn't be that way, but it is.

The tides of doubt only rush in quicker, wilder when I see him.

Maybe it's the way his still damp hair is sticking up at all angles. Maybe it's the way his chest stretches his T-shirt as he breathes hard. Maybe it's the way his height takes me a little by surprise as he steps close and towers above me. Or maybe it's the way his eyes search my face, looking for answers to silent questions.

Whatever it is, I now feel utterly torn.

"Marty." I move to the side so he can come in, but he just steps into the space I left and wraps his arms around me, pulling me in for a kiss. A kiss that moves so quickly I place my hands on his chest and push our bodies apart before I get lost in it. He stubbornly keeps his hold on my waist.

We open our mouths to speak at the same time.

"I heard what happened with-" he starts.

"Your mother," I manage to say, before I stop because I know he will win this race.

He groans. "I'm sorry for whatever she said. I don't know exactly *what* she said, but I bet it wasn't... pretty, and I'm sorry."

I sigh. Despite it all, flames of attraction, hunger, need come alive inside me when he leans back and rocks his groin into me.

"Come in and let's have that coffee," I say. "And I need to get dressed so we don't get distracted."

He pulls his lips into his mouth, a guilty glint in his eyes, but he releases me and follows me into the villa.

"Do you mind making it?" I nod at the kitchen. "I'll be five minutes."

I take a little longer than that because I need a few moments to figure out how best to navigate this conversation. I think about it as I slide on my underwear and glide moisturiser over my arms and legs. I think about it more as I pull on a dress and brush my hair. I think about it as I put minimal make-up on and gold hoops in my ears.

I walk out in a white floaty sundress that cups my breasts and flares out and down to mid-calf. It's the kind of dress I would normally save for a dinner, but my vanity wants to at least have this conversation while feeling like I look good.

"Wow," he says in response, his eyes widening when he sees me. He is sitting on the sofa and our coffees are on the low table in front of him.

I point a playful finger at him as I sit next to him. "Marty," I warn. "I put clothes on so we can try and have a conversation without distractions, so don't distract me!"

He covers his eyes with the palm of his hand. "Well, this should do the trick," he says. I tap his arm so he drops his hand. We smile together, and it's as much an acknowledgement of the awkward conversation we're about to have.

"So," he leans down to take a cup and hand it to me, "milk, one sugar. I had to guess based on what you said yesterday. I hope that's okay."

"It's perfect." I can't help it, when I bend to get the cup in one hand, another reaches up and rakes through his hair.

"Jenna," he warns me.

"Sorry," I say, putting my hand over my eyes. We laugh again.

"What did she say, then?" Marty asks. "What sort of collateral damage am I looking at here?"

I pull in a deep breath. "She told me to keep my distance," I say, watching him closely for his response.

"Well, that's a given, but *why* did she tell you to stay away?"

I need another hard inhale already. "She thought I didn't know about Arnie. She thought I wasn't aware how hard it had been on you," I say.

"And?" he says, still waiting.

"I told her I did know. But then she told me about you leaving and travelling around the Balearics, and... and ending up in hospital."

He stares straight ahead. His mouth is closed, and he rocks back and forward a few times.

"She said you drank too much, did a lot of drugs, and," I cough because my throat suddenly feels thick, "that you also had a lot of sex."

That makes him smile, but because he's not looking directly at me, I can't tell if it reaches his eyes.

"Well, it's all true." He exhales so hard his chest dips down. "I can't deny it."

There is something about his honesty that prompts the same response in me.

"I don't really care," I say in a whisper and I really, really don't. I was only shocked to have *his mother* telling me these things.

"You don't?" He turns to me.

"Why should I? That's what many twenty-something-year-olds do, and they don't even do it because they've suffered the heaviest, heart-crushing loss," I say. "I'm not surprised you wanted to run away from it all."

He blinks, several times.

"You want to tell me how it was for you? In your words. That's what I think I'd like to hear now," I ask softly.

He sighs. "It was so far from being a good time. I was broke before I even got there. After my mates left, I had to get money and find places to stay so I did shitty kitchen jobs, worked in some bars and clubs too, and slept on people's couches, and yes, in their beds. It wasn't like I was always looking for sex with just anyone and everyone. I actually liked many of them, I just wasn't exactly good to them. Honestly, some people weren't very good to me either. It was messy. And yes, there was a lot of booze and drugs too."

I nod, listening, hoping he'll keep talking after he has a sip of his coffee.

"I was a ticking timebomb. I would fuck up in one way or another every few weeks - being late to work too often, sleeping with the wrong person who stole something from me or just kicked me out, I ended up owing people money too - and that's when I would jump ship. Literally. I would go to another town and then a few times, a different island. If it wasn't easy to be somewhere, I moved on. And then towards the end, I just stopped working and maxed out a couple of credit cards doing whatever the fuck I wanted. Or Maeve would send me a couple of hundred Euros to keep me alive. It was as chaotic as it sounds. I can probably never go back to Ibiza, to be honest."

"Or maybe you can just wear a really good disguise," I say, my need to make him laugh momentarily stronger than my desire to just listen.

"I like your way of thinking. I'd look good in a wig and glasses."

"And the scooter accident?" I say, steering him back because of course Marty would grab hold of an invitation to make a joke wherever he could find it. We really do have more in common than I first thought.

His throat moves as he swallows. "That was probably a long time coming. And yes, I was lucky to be alive after it happened. Honestly, I was glad when I came to in the hospital and they told me my parents were on their way. Even though I knew Mum would be going out of her mind, I'd never felt so relieved. Like finally, I could stop running."

I open my mouth to ask the only question I feel I need an answer to, but I close it when Marty reaches over and places his hand on my leg.

"That was nearly six months ago. I've been sober ever since. I've been working hard to pay Maeve back, as well as the credit card debt which Ma and Dad paid off. I started seeing a grief counsellor, Jill. I'm pretty sure I'm her favourite client, you know. And I meet up with Arnie's parents to talk about him and cry and just try and fucking work through this grief like I'm supposed to. I live at home, because I have no choice financially, but also because I know I need to right now. I do ninety per cent of what my parents ask me to do. I never go out on the lash, obviously. And I hadn't touched another body," he says and lowers his chin before looking at me, "until you."

I shiver with those words.

"I'm sorry I didn't tell you everything. I just didn't want you to realise how broken I was," he says, and the way his eyes are fixed on mine is brave and determined.

"You have always been yourself, Marty." I really do believe it. So much so I am now wondering if I can say the same about myself.

He levels a firm look at me. "And please don't think that this week is an extension of that episode, because it's not."

"I would be lying if it hadn't crossed my mind." I want to match his honesty with some of my own, even if I know there's still one question I would like to ask him and I suspect I'm not going to, not now I can see the relief blossom in his eyes. Besides, my body is already melting under his touch as he turns towards me, both of his hands on my legs now, sliding them up and under my dress.

"This is different, Jenna," he says. "So very different. I told you that yesterday, didn't I?"

"Pretty much," I say, holding his stare. "And I believe you."

"God, that gets me hard," he says, and he crashes down on me as if to prove his point, forcing me back against the arm of the sofa.

"What does?" I ask as he hovers above me.

"You just believing me. You *trusting* me," he says.

"I thought it was my body?" I say as I push my breasts against him and give him my neck to kiss.

"Oh, yes, that too, but when you've spent months having to constantly prove yourself, it's just so good to be believed, to be seen, just as I am," he says.

"I believe you, Marty, and I see you," I say, my voice low. "And I like what I see."

He grunts as he thrusts up against me, through our clothes. I feel a new dampness in my underwear.

"Good," he says, then he stills. "Because I'm about to ask you for a very big favour."

I pull back. "What is it?"

"Will you join me and my family for dinner tonight?"

My teeth clench together as my eyes roam his face, looking for the joke. "Are you serious?"

"Deadly." His dimples pop in a smile as he looks at my lips briefly.

"But your mother..."

"She will behave," he says and then he dives back into my neck, one of his hands burrowing further under my dress to cup my pussy. I gasp at the delicious pressure. "But I may not."

"Oh, Marty, you are such a fucker," I say. "I'm not sure it's a good idea... I don't want to gatecrash and-"

"You'd be guest of honour," he says, and the heel of his hand makes slow circles against me. "Come on, it's my birthday."

"Shit." I close my eyes and roll my head back. "I didn't even say happy birthday to you yet."

"You can say it after I make you come." He slides his hand into the top of my underwear and starts to pull them down.

"Seeing as it's your birthday, I would like to make *you* come," I say but my hands are lifting my dress, giving him more room.

"It's my birthday so I decide who comes first." He slides down, his knees on the floor, as my underwear is discarded and he positions his face between my legs, his mouth inches above me. "Besides, I haven't had any birthday cake yet."

"I'm not your birthday cake," I say wriggling as I feel him blow on me once, twice.

"Jenna," he says, serious. "That's exactly what you are. You're the best birthday cake I've ever had."

When he dips down and licks me open, I sigh and let my legs fall further apart.

"Marty," I say, my hand finding his head as he kisses all around my inner thighs.

"So will you come?" he asks before he laps at my clit once, twice.

"Well, yes, soon enough if you keep doing that." I put the knuckle of my finger in my mouth and bite into it.

"I mean tonight," he says and looks up at me, even though his tongue is on me, slowly stroking me back and forward. "Will you come to dinner tonight with me and my family? For my birthday?"

"Fuck, yes," I say when he sucks on my clit so hard my belly quivers. I press his head closer to me as my hips rock up into his mouth. "Whatever. Yes, fuck. Just keeping doing that."

He does. And as he does, he looks up at me and I look down at him and we stay like that until my body explodes in his mouth.

Chapter Thirty-One

Marty

We have our afternoon on the beach. It starts with Maeve, Dad and me riding in doughnut-shaped inflatable rings behind a speed boat, bouncing over the wake, while Mum stands on the beach taking photos on her phone that are terrible, but we all laugh at them. After, we get a round of drinks - cocktails for them, a mocktail for me - and we toast each other before all lying back on our sunbeds. Maeve whines at me long enough for me to relent and hand her phone over to her, and it's only minutes after that that I hear snoring and look over at my father asleep, his head pointed up and his mouth open. I shake my head and smile. Despite how the morning started and regardless of how the day will possibly end, I am glad we've had this time together and I know my parents are too.

"It would do you good to sleep too," Mum says to me from her lounger next to Dad's.

"I'll sleep when I'm dead, Ma!" I say with emphasis.

"Just make sure that's long after I'm gone."

"You'll outlive us all." Maeve snorts while staring at her phone, hands busy. "Look at Nanna, for Christ's sake."

"She's not *that* old."

"How old is she?" I ask.

"Ninety-one," Mum replies.

"So she was like forty when she had you. That's old for her generation," I say, looking at Mum who is staring out at the sea.

"Yeah, I asked her about that once," she says. "She said she was never much fussed by men growing up, but then she met Pops and they fell madly in love and I was a very happy honeymoon surprise. Or not. I possibly could have been a pre-honeymoon surprise."

I pause, thinking, calculating. "Wait, so," I begin. "Pops was sixty-odd when he died, wasn't he?"

"Fifty-nine, actually," Mum says with a quick glance at my dad's snoring body. "Much too young. But that's what smoking all day, every day will do to you."

"And he died twenty years ago?" I check.

"Yes, in September," Mum says thoughtfully.

"So he would be seventy-nine now, if he was still alive?"

"Yes, Aiden. Why are you so... oh," she says as the penny drops.

"Pops was Nan's toy-boy!" Maeve chimes in.

"It wasn't really like that, you know. I mean, I was never really aware of the age difference..."

"You weren't *aware*?" I say, audacity seeping into my tone. "That's interesting."

"Aiden," my mother cautions.

"It's just good to know it didn't bother you. That it wasn't a problem for you."

"I bet you wish he was still totally banjaxed most days now," Maeve says, thumbs still moving in a manic fashion. "He's almost clever now he's sober."

I don't say anything but close my eyes and tilt my head to the sun, something like triumph also warming me. I'm surprised my mother has stayed quiet but then I feel my lounger dip beside my legs. I open my eyes and see her sitting there.

"Aiden, I appreciate what you're trying to do," she says looking at me over her sunglasses. "But I'm not sure *why* you're trying to do it. Surely this thing is just a harmless holiday fling? I can't say I'm completely comfortable with it, but I can at least understand if that's what it is."

"Ma," I say, both in warning and with exasperation.

"I've already told you I'm okay with her coming to dinner," she adds.

"And..." I prompt.

"And I will apologise for... accosting her in the gym," she adds. "But can we just keep an open mind about how unrealistic this is. It's not like you have a future together."

I still stiffen at her condescending tone, but am too busy thinking about the point she raises to respond. I'm stuck on those two words. *The future.* It's the one thing Jenna and I haven't talked about.

"Sure look, there's nothing wrong with having a 'holiday fling' Aiden." She uses air quotes. "You don't have to invest yourself in a future with Jenna. You don't have to go all in so soon." Ma moves her hand as if to touch me but then thinks twice, probably because she can see the thunderous look on my face.

"You thought Arnie was just a fling at first. What was it you called it, an exploration? Me being curious?"

"And I'm not ashamed to say I was wrong. That was a steep learning curve for me."

"Well, maybe that's how you need to approach 'this thing' with Jenna." I wave my own quotation marks in the space between us.

She opens her mouth, then closes it again and her chin pulls down, the air emptying out of her lungs.

I look over at Maeve who has stepped away from us and is on her phone, holding it up and talking into it, waving at it occasionally and doing far too many pouts and V-signs with her fingers. She must be recording or live-streaming or something. So much for her having a phone-free afternoon, I think grumpily. I spare a quick thought for why my parents don't question Maeve's behaviour as much as they do mine, but then I don't have the gumption to pursue it. Not when I have to do something to improve my mother's mood before dinner tonight.

I sigh before sitting up and leaning towards my mother whose face is still sullen as she picks at the hem of her kaftan or whatever the fuck it is she's wearing over her swimsuit.

"Let's go for a walk," I say. "Let's go get an ice cream. Just us."

She lights up like pure sunshine. "Okay," she says, trying to swallow her grin.

"On one condition," I say. "We talk about anything but Jenna and my problems and the future and just well, anything that makes me want to run for the hills."

"Okay," she says. "I think I can do that."

"You better, because I will run for those hills, Mother. I'm quite fit at the moment, no matter what Dad has been saying." I swing my legs to the side and stand up. I reach out a hand for her and pull her up, noticing how petite and slim she is. It's strange seeing your mother's physical fragility so clearly.

She brushes sand off her legs. "He's been saying you've been too shagged out to keep up, which I probably shouldn't repeat considering those conditions you just set."

"Yeah, but that's nothing to do with my conditions. That's just not something a mother and son should talk about," I say with a light laugh and a shake in my head as we start walking to the water's edge.

For the most part, it works. We talk about what we see – a banana boat throwing holiday-makers around in the sea, no fewer than five men around my father's age also conked out asleep, a team of maintenance men near the beach toilets being bossed around by Jake although he doesn't see us – and she asks me about my bike rides with Dad, questioning if he's pushing himself too hard. Ma then gives me another lecture about my physical health and doing too much exercise, about being careful of any possible lasting effects from the scooter accident, in response to which I start singing *The Hills Are Alive* from *The Sound of Music* and she promptly shuts up.

We find the ice cream stand and each get a cone with mango sorbet, and my following her choice of flavour makes her irrationally delighted which both irritates and pleases me, another reaction I can't make sense of. We start our walk back in silence, licking our ice creams as they melt quickly in the heat that is soothed by a fresh ocean breeze. But it doesn't last.

"So, your degree," she says. I admit, it's not a topic of conversation I specifically forbid, but her hesitant tone and my raised shoulders in response indicate we both know she's pushing her luck.

"What about it?"

"Are you looking forward to going back in September?"

I think about what Jenna and I discussed on the deserted beach yesterday. "I'm not one hundred percent certain I will go back," I say.

"Why would you not go back? You should finish your degree. You don't want to throw it all away."

"I only did a year and a half, Ma. And it served its purpose. I learnt a lot. I got to experience college life, and I got to live with Arnie and..."

"But you're so smart, Aiden."

"So? I can be smart and working in a kitchen too."

"You can't work for Dermot forever," she says.

"You're right. And I don't plan on it. I've got more than enough experience to apply for a role elsewhere now."

"With an unfinished degree?"

"A decent head chef isn't going to give a flying fuck about that. All I've got to do is get in front of the right person, show them what I can do, get some sound references from Dermot and Craig," I say referring to my uncle's head chef. "You know me, Ma. People can't resist me when they meet me."

"Apparently not," she says under her breath.

"Would you really be that disappointed if I didn't go back?" I ask. "I'll pay you back the college fees."

She shakes her head. "You know we don't care about the money. Well, we care enough that we want you to understand the real value of it, but you don't need to pay us back your fees. The credit card debt we paid off, yes, you need to pay that back but there's no rush. I just worry a lot about your whole life being a restaurant. It's a stressful environment. You said yourself so many times in the past that there's a lot of drinking, and sometimes drugs. Isn't that just too much temptation?"

I want to launch into the same speech I've given her many times before. About how the jury is still out if I'm actually addicted to alcohol and drugs, rather than they just became my crutch, my coping mechanism, my escape. But I know I'm walking on thin ice if I dare highlight this now. I also can't deny how being sober has helped me, and over the last few days, since Jenna, it's never felt easier or better.

"It seems whatever I do and wherever I go, I end up doing things you don't exactly approve of," I say in a quiet voice.

"What do you mean?" She slows and turns to look at me closer.

"Well, Jenna. You don't approve of her," I say coming to a stop.

Ma points her cone at me. "You said we weren't allowed to talk about her!"

"You're right. We're not. My point is, you may not always agree with some of the choices I make, but not all of them are because I'm fucked up, if that makes sense. I'm sober now and still doing things you'd rather I didn't. And I'm not just talking about Jenna, but also college, because I don't think I want to go back. So maybe... Maybe you just have to get used to me doing things you aren't always going to like?"

She sighs so hard her shoulders sink as we start walking again. "Aiden, you're twenty-four. I don't think I have any say on what you do with your life," she says, and it sounds like surrender. "But as your mother, I just want you to be happy and healthy. That's it. That's all I want. Happy and healthy and safe. And before, it seemed like those things couldn't co-exist."

"And they didn't. I did make stupid decisions and do stupid things..."

"And this isn't a stupid thing?" Ma blurts out.

Stunned, I stop walking again and stare at her, feeling the sorbet melt down the side of my hand. But I make no effort to lick it off.

She turns to face me but doesn't quite meet my eyes. "Of course, I'm not saying Jenna is stupid..."

"But I am?" I ask.

"No, Aiden, no, you're the smartest kid I know," she says and her hand twitches like she wants to reach for me.

"I won't share that with Maeve, but thanks, I guess." I look up and over her head at our sun loungers up ahead.

"You know what I mean. You're smart, but... but you don't always think things through. Going off like that after Arnie died. It was all so spontaneous. Even with Arnie, you two happened so quickly. The travelling, the relationship... and when he got sick, you just gave everything else up for him."

"Because I fucking loved him! I did all of those things with Arnie because I loved him. Is that so hard for you to understand?" I shake my head, only partly conscious we're putting on quite a show for other people on the beach.

"I know you loved Arnie," she says. "I'm not saying you didn't. I'm just... It was just all..."

"You found it hard to accept," I say sounding as bitter as I feel.

"You know I don't have a problem with your sexuality." She steps forward so she can whisper-shout that sentence.

"Funnily enough, yes, I do know that now because even when I want to be with a woman, you're against it."

"An *older* woman," she hisses. "Is it because of me? Is she like a mother substitute or-"

I back away then, holding my hands up. "That's it, Ma. We are done talking about this."

I march back past our loungers and keep going until I see a bin. I shove my cone in it, then I head to the sea to wash my hands in the water that laps around my feet. Standing up again, I turn to look at our loungers and see Mum is already there and she's sitting next to Dad, crying, with his arm around her. My shoulders drop at the sight, but then I see Maeve stand and walk towards me with a bemused look on her face.

"So, what was it this time?" she asks.

"She went too far." I can hear how angry I really am. I turn away from watching Dad comfort Mum and walk back to the water's edge, letting the waves crash up against my ankles.

"Our mother? Surely not." Maeve stands next to me.

I huff out a quick laugh. "She's never been completely comfortable with Arnie and me. And now-"

Maeve interrupts me. "Did it ever cross your mind that it has nothing to do with you being bi and more to do with her just not being able to cope with what happened. And I'm not just talking about the last year or so. I'm talking about the last three or so years, really. You leaving home and travelling with Arnie for all that time was hard for her. Then when you came home, you went straight to university, moving in with Arnie rather than living at home like you originally agreed. Then he got his diagnosis and you dropped out. It all happened so quickly, one thing after another. And when he passed, she thought she would get you back, but she didn't."

"I'm twenty-fucken-four," I say. "I'm an adult."

She leans in and nudges my arm then. "I mean that's debatable, but yes, I get what you're saying. But here's the thing. You're her favourite, her first. After Dad, you're her favourite human in the whole world. And you know

Dad's great, he loves her to pieces but he's hardly the best person in the world to talk to. Likewise, her friends are fine and all, but she doesn't open up to them. You were the one she spoke to, Marty. You were like her best friend growing up. I'm not saying that's right. It's probably a bit fucked up on many levels, but that's how it was. Until it wasn't. And she's not accepted or adjusted to losing that yet."

I sigh, not because Maeve's words enrage me but because they ring true and yet I still feel great resistance. Or maybe that's exactly why I feel it.

"She needs to learn how to adjust because things change, whether we want them to or not," I say without looking at my sister. The sudden wave of heavy grief that hits me out of nowhere is so intense it feels miraculous to still be standing.

"I know," Maeve replies. "And I think Mum will adjust, eventually. But it will take time. Just don't cut whatever thin thread of a relationship you have with her before she does."

We stand side by side for a long time, watching the water roll up to our feet and away again, my hands in the pockets of my swimming shorts and her arms folded over her chest, her phone nowhere to be seen. When I finally feel able to talk again, I reach over and push her arm, making her stumble to the side.

"What the fuck was that for, gobshite?" she says as she straightens up.

"When did you became so fucken emotionally intelligent? I am feeling very intimidated by it so I just needed you to know I'm still your big brother and can kick your butt." I glance back to see Mum and Dad sitting side by side on a lounger together. Dad's arm is still around her, but she's not crying anymore. Out of Mum's eyesight Dad gives me a thumbs-up, which I appreciate. I nod back at them and am even more relieved when I see Mum return the gesture before I look back at my sister.

"Wanna go ride a jet ski together?" I ask.

"Fuck yeah, but I'm driving so hope you're ready to look like a complete tit again," Maeve says before she turns and races to the water sports hut.

The Fourth Sunset

"It's almost impossible to watch a sunset and not dream."
- Bernard Williams

Chapter Thirty-Two

Jenna

Robert's parents were stuffy and predictable, but they were pleasant enough and had decent taste in restaurants so I could easily survive meeting them for dinner once every few months. So while I'm experienced at having dinner with the parents of someone I'm fucking, I'm not exactly well-versed in doing it with the parents of a man who is thirteen years younger, and I am definitely not even close to being prepared for having dinner with a mother like his.

This is why, after a quick walk to the resort's shop, I pass my afternoon sunbathing and doing very little other than scrolling on my phone, wondering what I should wear, how I should do my hair, and whether red lipstick is appropriate or not. These thoughts are interrupted far too often with mad dashes to the bathroom as my stomach reminds me just how nervous I really am.

In the end, I choose the fitted mid-length black dress I was saving for my last night and a possible dinner with Jake. I pin my hair up in a French twist and opt for a nude shade of lip gloss instead of anything bolder. I get to the restaurant thirty minutes early and am busy talking to Eric the barman, when I see my brother fly out of the kitchen carrying four plates like the silver service pro he's been since his first job as a waiter at the four-star hotel down the road from our childhood home.

My eyes follow him as he places plates on a table, a slightly manic grin wrapped around his face. It's only when his hands are empty and his back is turned to the customers that a frown returns.

"Jakey, what's up?" I ask as he approaches me.

"Our chef has got the flu. Like how is that even possible in this heat? Anyway, he's off and I've made two of the serving staff jump in to help in the kitchen, meaning my pert backside is running around like Manuel in Fawlty Towers."

"Well, you make it look good."

"Just wait until the end of the evening. We have a late booking for a group of twenty here for a family reunion, and as luck would have one of the teenage daughters was stung by one of the wasps in the nest we finally removed today, so I could really do without this tonight as I want to impress and make it up to them, but we shall see just how spectacularly it all goes wrong."

"Oh, Jakey, I would offer to help too but I'm about to have dinner with Marty and his family."

My brother's jaw drops. "What the actual fuck? Did I just miss out on six months of dating? Was there a time warp and I wasn't notified, which would be criminal because you know how I feel about that musical number!"

I chuckle despite the churning in my stomach. "No time warp, just a holiday fling that took a wrong turn."

"Or a right turn?" He gives me one of his best pouts before realising where we are. "And what are you doing behind my bar, Peggy Mitchell?"

"It's Marty's birthday present," I say.

"Oh, that's right. He's like eighteen today, right?"

"Ha-di-ha."

"But seriously, what are you doing?"

"I'm making him a mocktail. I wanted to get him something for his birthday but as charming as it is, what would I get him from the resort shop? A two-day-old *Sunday Times*? An inflatable slice of watermelon? A book of sudoku puzzles? No offence but it's a bit short on exciting gift ideas. But I know he likes his mocktails so here I am."

My brother opens his mouth but pauses a moment before he speaks. "So, what's in it?"

"I'm not quite there yet, but I know it's going to be fruity but not too sweet, a little fizz, a little heat and of course, very colourful."

"Wow, you almost sound like you know what you're doing," he says.

I'm blushing because it's true. All that scrolling of recipes was the most productive thing I did all day.

"Oh, God. Are you falling in love with him?" My brother asks, which promptly wipes the pink right out of my cheeks as I freeze, arms and chest tight.

"Jake, I barely know him..."

"All the more reason why it's entirely possible. I never fall in love with people I know well. In fact, that seems to make me fall out of love rather quickly, so I try to avoid it at all costs."

"Let's have a conversation about that one day, please," I say. Although we have before, many, many times.

"Don't dodge the topic. State your case that I'm not speaking the truth," he says.

I sigh. "He lives in Dublin. I live in London."

"Let the parish council minutes reflect she neither confirms or denies the accusations."

I pull my eyebrows together. "Parish council meetings are not places for accusations, Jake."

"You clearly have never been to a parish council meeting. Vicious gatherings." He leans over the bar and his voice is lower and softer when he practically whispers in my ear. "You know it's okay to fall in love with him."

"It's been three days, Jake," I tell him but I'm talking to myself, especially the already simmering hot waters that swim in my gut whenever I think about any of the moments Marty and I have shared.

"And so fucking what? Please tell me you believe in love at first sight? You of all people should."

I'm about to answer but he's pulling a ringing phone out of his pocket.

"Sweet child of my straight ex-boyfriend, it's reservations again. That's the third call in an hour," he says.

"Problem?" I ask and he answers, shaking his head at me.

"Jake speaking." He's all charm, even if the frown crinkling his brow remains.

I go back to taste-testing my third attempt at making the perfect mocktail, dipping a straw in what I just mixed. It's good but not quite right. Something's missing. I bend down to look in the juice fridge another time.

"But that will mean the resort is full?" I hear Jake say, all his calm replaced with shock. "For five weeks!"

He turns around to face the restaurant, rubbing his forehead. I follow his gaze towards the kitchen where one of the usual wait staff is manically gesturing at Jake while wearing a chef's shirt and trousers about five sizes too big. My brother gives him a wave back that could easily mean, *Come here*, *Stay there*, *Piss off*, or all three.

"Okay, well, do it," Jake says into his phone, turning back to face me, a little dazed. "And then we need to start looking at optimising where everyone goes so we have more availability. Put a freeze on the free upgrades for the foreseeable future and send me an updated bookings schedule for the next two months before you log off for the day. Please." He hangs up but keeps his eyes fixed on his phone.

"That sounds like you're about to get very... busy?" I say tentatively.

He looks at me, still bewildered. "Something has happened. We've completely packed out the resort for the next month and a half. We've taken more new bookings in the last two days than we have all year. After the Bouras' told me I had to increase positive organic reviews by 300%, I was confident that would get a few more bookings but not this many, and not this quick," he says when his phone is back in his pocket. "I wish I had time to look into it, but I need to get back in the kitchen."

"You're doing amazing, Jake. It's probably all your hard work already paying off."

"Maybe." Jake's thoughts drift elsewhere for a moment but then he snaps back to me, his nose wrinkling with a quick sniff and his eyes narrowing. "Oh my Greek Orthodox God, can you smell burning?"

I don't have time to reply before he's halfway to the kitchen in a very nimble jog. I smile after him and make a mental note to go help him out with washing up or serving customers as soon as this meal is over. Then I turn my attention back to what I'm doing.

Three batches later, I have it perfected, or at least perfect enough. It's fruity with a little fizz that tickles the tongue and a little spice that warms the throat. It's so very, very Marty and I hope I don't have to explain the reasons why in front of his parents.

I thank Eric after he helps me prepare five glasses of the drink, leaving them in the fridge to stay cool. He then pours me the glass of white wine I suddenly need more than I care to admit. After quickly looking at the reservations list, Eric points to a table that I walk over to. Then I sit down and wait.

As it happens, I don't have to wait long. I barely have two sips of wine, muttering, "Everything's going to be okay," to myself a handful of times, before I'm watching the tall, striking figure of Marty walk towards me. He's wearing faded but fitted black jeans and a baby-blue polo shirt that's tucked in, accentuating his narrow waist and broad shoulders. His hair looks like he's just stepped out of the shower, which conjures up the best recent memories, and I catch a glimpse of his naked ankles in his Birkenstocks. He's never looked sexier, and maybe older even, like I really wouldn't have said he was just turning twenty-four. But if I'm honest, I'm past even caring about this. What I care and am delighted about is that he's alone.

I stand to take a step toward him but he's already there, jogging the last few metres and pulling me straight into his orbit as his hands cup my face and he takes a long deep kiss from my lips.

"Fuck, I missed you today," he says, completely unfiltered and genuine, and I should have put more chilli in that mocktail because the amount I settled on now feels very under-representative of the instant fire in my chest and between my legs.

"Happy birthday, again," I say, and I stretch as far as I can up on my toes and rub his nose with mine. "Are you surprising me and saying your parents got a better offer?"

"You sound far too hopeful," he says, and his hands slide down to hold my waist against him. "But I'm sorry, no. They're on their way but I had to come early and do this."

He kisses me again, this time with enough force that I almost stumble back, and I feel an uncomfortable twinge in my neck from the angle he moves me in. That is why I'm a moment late in realising that his hands have slid lower, grabbing a substantial handful of my butt in each palm and pushing my stomach against the place where Marty is growing hard. I'm starting to think it could easily be criminal that he's that big, hard and ready for me already and we have to wait hours before he can slide inside me, but then we hear a loud, intentional cough.

"Would you please extract your tongue from my sister's mouth?" I hear Jake say from somewhere behind Marty. Obeying, Marty pulls back, and we both turn to him.

"Jealous, Sweet Cheeks?" Marty asks with a grin that is much too cocky, even feeling what I'm feeling against my belly button.

"Of a meal with a lover's parents who are possibly closer in age and cultural references to me than the man who's dicking me? No, thank you very much. Believe me when I say I can handle a lot of drama but even I couldn't cope with that."

"Thanks for the vote of confidence, Jake," I say as I step back and find my chair.

"Didn't have your down as a bottom, Resort Manager. But good to know." Marty winks as he also sits down.

"Everything okay back there?" I jump in just as I see Jake's mouth open to reply with something equally inappropriate.

"Not in the slightest," Jake says with a pained smile. "We're down to our last ten scallops - which is easily our most popular starter, and we have another fifty covers coming this evening - and unbelievably someone just burnt soup, so am pretty sure I'll have aged ten years by the time tonight is over."

"You're a man down in the kitchen?" Marty couldn't look more interested.

"Two men down now. Our head chef is off with flu, and I've just had to send our commis chef home for sneezing a little too close to our dessert station. I refuse to take any chances."

"Jesus, that's a fucker. How can I help?" Marty says standing up again.

I am too stunned to protest - the horror of even imagining having dinner alone with his parents and sister grips me - but I don't have to thanks to my brother.

"And leave my poor sister to get ripped to pieces by parents who are no doubt as quick-witted and dry in the sense of humour department as you? You must think I don't actually love the only living family member who gives a monkeys about me? Sit your admittedly cute backside down and take good care of her, please."

"Sir, yes, sir." Marty gives a quick salute before he sits down.

"And please ensure nobody orders the scallops!" Jake declares before marching off.

"Love you, Jakey," I say to his back.

When it's just us, and after a quick scout of the entrance to check his family aren't on their way, I lean towards Marty.

"How are you doing, birthday boy?"

"Me, I'm fine. The question is how you are, and if you're ready for this? It's going to be an absolute shit show, you know. My mum has had plenty of warnings today, but so far she's ignored every single one."

"What's the worst that could happen?" I ask, both as a joke and because I'm now a little worried what the answer could be.

"Tears? A tantrum? A mental breakdown? And that's just me, I haven't even considered the possibilities for my mother. Now, are we sitting in the right seats to get the best view of the sunset?" he asks.

I lean over and rake my fingers through his hair. "Yes, that was my first thought too." I brush his lips with mine. My intention wasn't for it to be more than that, but he's quick to nudge my mouth open and find my tongue with his, and I'm too enraptured with how he's stroking my neck and how he smells – sun cream, cinnamon, lemon and fresh air - to stop it deepening, which it does until we are jolted apart from the loudest, most severe throat-clearing noise I've heard in my life.

Please be my brother. Please be my brother. Please be my brother. I beg the universe as I open my eyes.

It is not my brother.

Chapter Thirty-Three

Jenna

Smiling at us with an undeniable glint in his eyes, I see Marty's father. Again, I notice how his features differ from his son's – a more subtle nose and fairer colouring - but he has a similar presence, the same strong and straight-up physique. Apparently, he also has the ability to make quite the noise when coughing on purpose.

Standing next to him, almost a foot smaller, wearing an elegant floaty chiffon dress in a canary yellow that accentuates her tan, Marty's mother seems to occupy just as much space. Her scowl pulls at features which would otherwise be classically beautiful - dark eyes framed by brows that have a natural arch, rosy-pink lips and high cheekbones. Now I see them side by side, I can tell she and her husband differ in age, and I fleetingly can't help but wonder by how much. Maeve then steps up to join them, her head bowed over her phone, and the screen lights up a face that I can now see mimics her father's, even despite the artistry that is her hair and make-up. Her outfit, a skin-tight olive-green dress, makes her eyes pop and accentuates just how long and lean she is.

Marty's relaxing in his chair and chuckling to himself because of course that's his default reaction to being interrupted mid-snog by his parents. Meanwhile I am busy touching a hand to my mouth as if to remove any evidence as I also pray for the ground to swallow me whole.

"Should we give you a minute?" his father asks, but all the same he moves to the table, placing his phone down. Then he steps to the side and pulls out the chair opposite Marty for his wife to sit in, which she does, her expression no softer.

"Not necessary." Marty shuffles his chair forward as I attempt to meet his mother's eyes and smile at her. She suddenly becomes deeply invested in unfolding her napkin and placing it across her lap, looking at nothing else. Marty's father sits at the head of the table.

"I'll sit myself then," Maeve says, and she drops her phone to the table with a loud thud. She flops down in her chair – the one opposite me – with a huff. "It's not like I'm already experiencing my perpetual third wheel PTSD from this dynamic."

"You can't get PTSD from that," Marty says.

"It certainly feels traumatic at this point," Maeve mutters.

"Actually, Maeve has a point. Loneliness is an epidemic," I say and am now trying to catch any of his family member's eyes to prove I'm more than just an older woman who chews Marty's face off.

"Oh, fantastic. It's killing me too as well as making me a social pariah," Maeve says, but then she catches my eye and gives me a wink I could describe as life-saving.

"You're a lot of things, Maeve, but lonely is not one of them. Not with 800,000 followers on TikTok," Marty adds.

"960,000 actually."

"How many?" I gasp.

Maeve just shrugs. "And here I am, date-less, while my social media inept brother has managed to pull someone while stone cold sober and practically bankrupt."

Marty does a mini bow over the table towards his sister. "It's a natural talent. I can't teach it."

"Jenna's right," Cynthia says suddenly, and all our heads twist her way. She's still playing with the napkin on her lap, eyes downcast. "I've read about it in the *Independent*. We don't have the same sense of community anymore. We used to live together - multi-generational families all under the same roof - and now families are separated by more distance and have much more disconnected lives with online connections replacing real life contact. And the research suggests that loneliness does indeed kill."

"Yes, that's very similar to what I've read," I say. I am ready when Cynthia looks up, nodding at her with a small smile she doesn't return.

"Well, at the risk of exposing myself as the emotionally-underdeveloped man that I am," Marty's father says after a much quieter throat clearing. "Could we maybe rewind the conversation a little from such a heavy topic and start again, also pretending that obscene French kiss hadn't happened?"

"French kiss? Jesus, Da. What year are we in?" Maeve spits out.

"Yes, I'm sorry about that," I say, wiping my mouth again, this time with my napkin.

"Jesus, we were just shifting. It was hardly obscene," Marty mutters.

"Tell that to my stomach contents," Maeve retorts, her phone back in her hand.

"Shifting?" I ask inquisitively.

"Snogging, lobbing the gob, eating face, póigín, getting off, kissing," Marty lists and I swear out of the corner my eye I see his mother flinch with each word.

"It's good to see you again, Jenna," his father interrupts loudly.

"You too," I say, following his lead. "James, right?"

"Correct. Good memory. And I believe you've already met my wife Cynthia," he says in a way that teeters between innocently cheerful and deliberately cheeky. I can see where his children get that from now.

"Yes. Nice to see you again too, Cynthia," I say the name somewhat intentionally because while I am ready to prove to an extent that I'm not too old to be her son's date tonight, I equally want her to know that I am definitely too old to call her Mrs O'Martin.

"Hello, Jenna," Cynthia says, finally looking up for more than a moment. The similarity between her eyes and Marty's stuns me briefly. Holding my gaze, she swallows. "I want to firstly say that I'm sorry for this morning. I shouldn't have said some of the things I said."

It's a real, genuine apology and it lands with me as exactly that.

"Thank you, Cynthia. I appreciate that although I do understand why you may have some reservations." I feel Marty's hand clamp down around mine which actually makes my body jolt as much with desire as shock at this very

281

sudden display of affection. As if that wasn't enough, he pulls both our hands over to rest on his thigh and the heat from him travels up my arm.

I'm not sure if it's because of my hand on his leg or despite it that Cynthia grabs hold of what I just said and continues. "Well, yes, I do and it's ever such a worry, considering the year we've all had. Aiden's had a very hard time."

"I know." I squeeze Marty's hand while smiling at her in a way that I hope is both sympathetic and reassuring.

"Jenna knows all about that, and me, and well, everything." Marty leans towards his mother now. "You already gave her an unnecessary lecture this morning. It doesn't need repeating, or that just makes your apology worthless."

His words have a bite I haven't heard in Marty's tone before and it startles me, as does his mother's reaction when she shrinks back into her seat.

"Water, anyone?" James calls out, a bottle in his hand ready to pour.

"Thank you." I nudge my glass forward. Marty and Maeve do the same, but Cynthia doesn't move, except to cross her arms over her body as if she's suddenly cold.

James quickly adopts the role I suspect he's going to play tonight, Chief Conversation Topic Coordinator. "Tell us a bit about yourself, Jenna. Aiden says you're a writer."

I have an answer prepared for this question. "Yes, a columnist. I've been writing for newspapers and magazines now for around fifteen years. Mostly freelance but I have done some stints as a staff writer before."

"Jenna writes about sex and relationships," Marty adds, and I swear his stare is on his mother, gauging her reaction with a mischievous look in his eyes.

"Oh, really?" James' eyebrows are skyward. "That sounds err...interesting."

I steal a quick glance at Cynthia, who has her hand flat on her chest as if to check her heart is still beating. Her jaw is clenched, again emphasising her resemblance to Marty.

"Do you like, give sex tips and advice?" Maeve asks, her phone discarded, and there's something in her question that tells me she's actually very interested.

I suck in a deep breath and take a few seconds to consider how to respond. I comfort myself with the knowledge that I'll never see these people again. I am not filtering myself for them. "Yes, I have in the past, but I'm trying to now shift my focus to more research about intimacy, sexuality and relationships. I'm really interested in the psychology of what makes people have fulfilling relationships and satisfying sex lives...or not."

My eyes are first drawn to Marty's father as he chokes on a mouthful of water. Out of the corner of my eye I then see Cynthia's hands grip the arms of her chair. Finally, I look back at Marty whose smile has narrowed, and I see him swallow, hard.

"Wow," Maeve mumbles, as she sits back in her chair holding her phone. "You do pick 'em, Marty."

"Excuse me." Marty's father continues to cough and starts banging his chest.

"That does sound very interesting," Cynthia speaks up with a slight wobble in her voice. "Who do you write for?"

I shift my weight in my seat. "Actually, I'm not working right now," I say. "But I'm hoping to start writing a book soon."

"You are?" Marty sounds surprised.

"I've always wanted to write a book," I say to Marty. I then turn back to his mother. "I've got some possible angles I want to explore, and I think when I go home I'll be ready to do some research and write a plan."

"But how can you afford not to work?" Cynthia asks as she picks up her glass of water. "Do you not have a mortgage or rent to pay?"

She looks curious, and not necessarily in a judgmental way. I'm about to answer her but Marty steps in.

"That's a bit of a personal question, Mum. Does it matter?"

"I was only asking-" Cynthia puts her glass back down without drinking from it.

"You don't have to answer that, Jenna," Marty interrupts, turning to me and for the first time since I met him, I am not fully enamoured with the shape of his smile or the dimples it creates.

"I don't mind. It's a fair question." I squeeze his leg again but this time it's so I can then slide my hand away from his grip. "I do have a house, yes, but it currently doesn't have a mortgage. I was lucky to pay it off early, as I inherited some money when I was younger that helped pay a large deposit."

"Jenna's mother died when she was fifteen," Marty butts in and I have no idea why he says it, especially in such a pointed way.

I blink but keep talking. "And I have some decent savings as well as the money I got for his share of the house when my ex and I divorced." I turn and smile at Marty then, but he's not looking at me. His eyes are suddenly fixed on the cutlery in front of him.

Cynthia is as still as a statue, her mouth slightly open, and I know immediately what word will come out of her mouth next. "Divorced?"

I hold onto my smile. "Yes, we split up about a year ago now," I say, as heat soars up my neck. I can physically feel how much of a test this is for me to own this part of my story.

"Didn't mention that, Aiden," Marty's father says quietly.

"Because it's not a big deal," Marty snaps.

At the same time his sister speaks up, her phone still in her hand. "So what?"

I definitely owe Maeve a drink.

"I understand if your parents have questions." I pick up my wine glass. "It was amicable. No cheating, no foul play. We just changed a lot and fell out of love with each other."

Cynthia nods as if she's absorbing what I'm saying. But when she speaks, I realise she was just planning a different approach.

"And how old were you when you met your husband. Sorry, ex-husband?"

My smile gets harder to hold onto. "We met when I was twenty-four."

Cynthia nods to herself, then leans forward to pick up her glass again. She takes a long sip, her eyes darting from Marty to me and back again, not realising how much more power she holds when she says absolutely nothing.

"Oh, this is actually getting interesting now," Maeve says sliding her phone down on the table, screen down. "I wish I had a drink already."

While I don't like Maeve's new dark interest, I am relieved she's throwing me a cue to stand and leave.

"Yes, drinks! If you'll excuse me, I will go and see to that," I say. I'm barely three steps away when I hear Cynthia speak.

"She's divorced!? Why on Earth didn't you tell us that, Aiden?"

I roll my eyes. Looks like it's going to be a long night.

Chapter Thirty-Four

Marty

"I'm not going to talk about this with you, Ma," I say.

"Why does it even matter?" Maeve says. "Marriage is such an outdated, problematic institution. Divorce is basically inevitable."

"It's not such a big deal," my father says to my mother, who still looks like she's glitching. "Both my brothers are divorced, Dermot twice, of course, the hopeless eejit that he is with women."

"I don't really care that she's divorced," Mum says although the way she says the word - all hard consonants and forced syllables - contradicts that statement. "I care that you didn't tell us."

"Why would I tell you? You want to know her bra size too?" I shoot back.

"36C," Maeve says without hesitation.

"Pardon?" I glare at my sister.

"She's a 36C," Maeve repeats. "Or maybe 38B. Either way. Lovely boobs. And those hips... She's a true hourglass. You're definitely punching above your weight there."

My father's head is shaking as it hangs in his hands and he tries to swallow his laughter. My mother is still open-mouthed and looking lost.

"Maeve," I say and intend it as an admonishment, but I start chuckling too.

"Just in the interests of avoiding more shock and awe, is there anything else we should know before this dinner continues?" Dad asks as he straightens up. "Does she have kids? A police record? Is she a member of a religious cult?"

"As far as I'm concerned, there's nothing shocking about Jenna," I reply but I'm looking at Mum. "Divorce, age, whatever. They are hardly skeletons, but so what if she did have one or two in her closet? We all have things in our past that we may not be proud of, but that doesn't mean we are bad people."

Much to my surprise my mother nods at this. "You're right, Marty, and I'm sorry," she says in a voice so soft and quiet it's practically a whisper, and that along with her apology is so unexpected it silences me.

I'm still staring at my mother waiting for her to throw in a "but" when Jenna comes back with a tray filled with tall glasses, and under her arm is a stack of menus.

"So," she says as she hands me the tray, and starts handing out menus. "The restaurant is a little short-staffed so I'm going to be our waitress tonight. Here are your menus, and also a special welcome drink I personally prepared earlier."

Jenna hands the red and pink drinks around and I notice my mother give her the smile I always describe as "try-hard" but it prompts me to downgrade my Mum Terror Alert to a Hot Amber rather than a Lava Red.

"Oh, Marty, you're going to enjoy this," my father says, his head stuck into the menu before I've opened my own.

"Oh, yes," Mum chimes in as she reads.

It's Jenna's turn to cough now for our attention, so I don't get a chance to look at what's on offer although my curiosity is piqued. I've had four days away from a kitchen now and I'm starting to miss it. But I'm suddenly intrigued by what Jenna's doing as she raises her glass and holds it aloft in the middle of the table.

"Maybe we could toast the birthday boy? Would you all raise your glasses and-"

"Wait!" Mum calls out, and she wrinkles her nose and sniffs with her glass under her nose while mine, Dad's and Maeve's are all held aloft.

"Jesus, Mum, it's not alcoholic!" I say loudly, and if I had a hand free, I would probably slam it down on the table.

Mum's neck almost breaks the way it swings her head towards me. "I know, Aiden. I was just going to ask if it has pomegranate in it because Maeve is allergic."

"Oh," I say and then mutter a hasty apology.

"What was that, Marty?" Jenna's head turns to me to, her eyes flashing, daring me.

"Sorry, Ma," I say a little louder.

"It doesn't have pomegranate in, Maeve," Jenna says with a smile at my sister.

"So, back to a toast," Dad says, lifting his drink up higher.

"Yes, I'm afraid this is my only gift for you, Marty," Jenna says. "It's a mocktail named The Marty Party. And well, thank you for letting me share your birthday with you. I hope you enjoy. Happy birthday, Marty!"

"Happy birthday Marty!" Everyone choruses and then takes long sips on the straws in their drinks. But I'm too stunned to move, keeping my drink in front of me.

"Wait, what is this?" Maeve asks. "It's amazing!"

"Not bad." Dad smacks his lips. "A dash of rum wouldn't go amiss, but not bad at all."

"It's delicious." Mum finally changes posture, literally loosening up. "You need to try it, Aidey."

"You made me a mocktail?" I turn to Jenna. "That's like the best present in the world."

"Don't thank me before you've tried it."

I take a sip. Immediately the layers of different fruits hit me – watermelon, apple, raspberry, all delivered with the fizz of a little lemon and lime bitters, but a beat later the sweetness dies down to reveal cinnamon, fresh mint and possibly a hint of chilli, the heat of which stays on my tongue.

"You like it?" Jenna leans closer to me, while Mum and Dad discuss the menu and Maeve is back on her phone.

"It's perfect. Sweet but not sickly, a little zing and heat, and very, very memorable."

Jenna blinks once before she speaks, drawing my eyes to her honey-brown pupils and the long lashes that frame them. "Now you know why it's called The Marty Party."

If hearts could swell up large enough to burst through rib cages, that's exactly what mine would be doing right now. I hold her eyes and hope she can read what I want so desperately to say to her, words that are suddenly at the tip of my tongue but it's not like they've had far to travel. They've been knocking around my mind all day.

"Thank you," is what I manage to say instead, but I do bend down and kiss the top of her shoulder, while still holding her gaze. When I pull back, finally able to give the menu my full attention, I catch Mum's eyes on us. It's an undecipherable look, but it seems to have a question mark rather than a hard full stop or loud exclamation mark.

"Wow," I say, when I finally turn my attention to the menu.

"Fuck yeah!" I whistle as I read the starters.

"Jesus," I whisper when I'm done considering the mains and sides.

"Bugger me," I exclaim when I read the dessert options.

"This menu is fucken class," I say in conclusion.

A perfect blend of Greek and Cretan dishes mixed with modern Mediterranean cuisine, it's fun and playful but it still has the power to impress without being too pretentious. And from a chef's perspective, I can imagine it's a challenging but satisfying mix of technically advanced innovation combined with classic cooking.

"Well, order away, son," Da says leaning back and catching a server's eye. He's no doubt going to ask for that shot of rum. "It's on me tonight."

Maeve grunts. "This whole week is on you," she says, fingers tapping on her phone. "Otherwise, we wouldn't be here."

"Thank you, Maeve, for always humbling me back down to Earth with a bump," Dad says, and I see him catch Mum's eye and wink. I don't know why but that also helps melt some of the tension inside me.

A hurried-looking member of the service team rushes over and indeed is given an additional drinks order by my father with input from everyone else. Me, I'm more than happy to savour my Marty Party and drink water so I can focus on the flavours in the food. When I say this the server barely conceals her sigh of relief as she stashes her pad and pen in her apron just before her attention is

pulled to a neighbouring table who are calling her. When she looks torn about
what to do, Jenna stands and waves the waitress away to deal with other tables,
saying she will take our food order, which she proceeds to do, using her phone
and then walking over to her brother who is on the phone by the bar. I watch
them for a while and then find my eyes turn the other way towards the kitchen.

"You're missing being in the kitchen, aren't you?" Ma says to me, and I
realise it's the first time tonight she's said something to me that doesn't feel like
an argument.

"I am," I say to her with an easy smile.

I am already enjoying tonight more than I expected, despite some foot-in-
mouth moments by Mum, and admittedly myself too. I knew I'd enjoy spending
the evening with Jenna and I can't help but recall the countless times Arnie
joined my parents and I for dinner. I always liked the idea of having a boyfriend
or girlfriend for the obvious things - good sex, good fun, good companionship -
but I never imagined how grounding and affirming it would be to then be with
that person and your family. Before the last year, I'd always gotten on great with
my parents, and would consider our relationship a relatively good one. Arguably
it was at its peak when Arnie and I were together before he got sick. We'd all
drink together, eat together, laugh together, and they would all spend far too
long taking the piss out of me together. The love I would feel in the room when
this happened always floored me. And now, fraught conversations and tense
moments aside, I'm getting a glimpse of it again.

When Jenna is back sitting by my side, she smiles at me and gives me the
quickest wink. I return it but then feel Dad's stare on us. I'm about to give him a
questioning look, but he quickly starts talking to Jenna.

"So, aside from work, tell us a bit about yourself? How do you like to spend
your time?"

Jenna takes in a deep breath that I suspect only I can hear because her reply
is flawless. "You mean aside from picking up younger men in holiday resorts?"

There is barely a beat of silence before Maeve bursts into laughter and Dad
and I are not far behind. I risk a look at Mum and while her eyes are wide and
unable to focus, the corners of her mouth hold a slight curl.

"Sorry," Jenna says. "I lean on my often-inappropriate sense of humour to diffuse potentially awkward social situations."

"Why does that sound familiar?" Maeve says under her breath.

"But seriously... how do I spend my time?" Jenna turns back to Dad. "Well, I read a lot. It's partly because of my work, yes, but also, I love books. Always have, always will. Fiction, non-fiction, I'll read anything and everything."

"Like Arnie," Mum says and when I look over at her, I see her remembering him with a soft smile.

"Yes, you said he studied English Lit." Jenna turns to me and her fingers land on my forearm which she strokes as she keeps talking. "I secretly wish I'd done English Lit too. But anyway. No regrets. My other hobbies include lifting weights, the theatre, seeing friends for park walks and pub lunches, and board games. Gosh, I love a good board game."

"You do?" I twist to look at her. "How did I not know this?"

"Well, we only met a few days ago, Marty, I think there are still a few things we don't know about each other."

I ignore the noise my mother makes when she hears this.

"Which board games?" I ask.

"Oh, anything and everything. But my brother and I have been known to take Cluedo far too seriously, complete with costumes and character accents. You should hear his Professor Plum."

"Ha! I can imagine," I say, and I almost forget my parents are there as I drift away into memories I haven't thought about in months but now suddenly want to share with Jenna, even though they still threaten to slice up my insides as I do. "I love board games. Arnie and I... we used to play a lot. When he was on a chemo cycle or towards the end... in palliative care. Board games were like a manageable distraction he could almost lose himself in."

"Oh God!" Maeve exclaims, leaning in. "Do you remember that marathon Monopoly game you had?"

"That's right!" Da says. "That was madness! How long did it last? Like two weeks or something?"

"Eighteen days," I say without thinking about it.

"I thought it would never end," says Maeve. "You were both so serious and invested in it. Didn't you create like bank loans for it as well? Just to keep it going."

"Yeah," I say, rubbing my chin as it all rushes back to me. "We even printed off contracts that we both signed. After about a week we also added a new player each and pretended they were our partners. Then our couples would have kids, so we'd add a few more players, and hand over streets and properties as gifts for birthdays and the like. God, it got really complicated. I had a spreadsheet to keep track of it all."

"That's amazing," Jenna says, and her face beams in one of her eye-dazzling smiles that emphasise the heart-shape of her face.

"Who actually won in the end?" Mum asks, and she too is smiling.

I sigh then, almost certain the tears will come but I really don't care if they do because I'm still grinning widely. "Nobody. Or, rather, we both did. We decided my boot and his Scottie dog would get together and have a polyamorous relationship with our other partners. So, we pooled all our money together, turned all our properties into a socialist commune where nobody had to pay rent, essentially shunning capitalism and disrupting the whole point of Monopoly."

"Oh, Jesus, you two were something else," Dad says shaking his head while quietly laughing.

"So ridiculous." Maeve gives another loud snort, then picks up her phone again.

Jenna reaches over and wipes away the only tear that was too heavy for me to keep hold of. She does so with the kindest, warmest look in her eyes, like she actually loves it when I talk about Arnie. Is that even possible?

"You okay?" she mouths, and I nod back at her. When I look back at the table, Mum is studying us again and I see it's with a new expression, her head slightly turned to the side, her eyebrows pulled together and her lips twitching like they can't decide if they should smile or frown.

Our starters arriving pulls my attention away from my mother's odd look and helps the conversation naturally switch to the food we all enjoy, which then prompts me to share more than a few war stories from my uncle's kitchen. Seeing as my dad and uncle Dermot are little more than a year apart — giving almost far too much accuracy to the term Irish twins - he too has some stories about his childhood, all of which I've heard countless times but there's something about Jenna hearing them for the first time that makes them funnier tonight. At one point after our mains' plates are cleared, while Dad and Jenna are deep in conversation about a London restaurant Dad went to on a business trip recently, Maeve gets up and whispers something in Mum's ear, and a second later they're excusing themselves. The relief that lightens my shoulders in Mum's absence is noticeable and unwanted, replacing one discomfort with another.

"Everything okay over here?" Jake says as he appears at my shoulder a moment later. His hair is flopping all over his face. His suit jacket is off, and he has his sleeves rolled up and two buttons undone on his shirt. The colour of his skin is akin to mine after a ten-kilometre run.

"Everything's grand," my father says.

"Dad, this is Jake, Jenna's brother, the Resort Manager." They shake hands. "Is everything okay with you?" I then ask Jake.

Jake straightens up and addresses my father first. "Mr O'Martin, I ask that you kindly avert your ears for what I'm about to say next, or failing that, I pray you have the same sense of humour as your son." He turns back to me. "No, Marty O'Martin, I am not okay. The kitchen looks like it's been bombed. My staff is currently rotating crying breaks in the pantry every thirty minutes. And my smartwatch keeps buzzing me because my heart rate hasn't dipped below 120 beats per minute in the last two hours. But truly, as long as you are all enjoying your food and drink, then everything is absolutely dandy."

"Will you just let me come and help?" I say, moving my napkin off my lap and pushing up to stand, but Jake has his hand on my shoulder forcing me back down.

"Nope, not going to happen. Your place is here, ensuring my sister doesn't deepen that mid-brow frown. It undoes all those expensive facial treatments I buy her for her birthdays." Jake darts up as straight as an arrow. "Okay, must go. It's my turn for a crying break."

Dad is like me, chuckling and shaking his head. "Your brother is a hoot," he says to Jenna.

"Absolutely. He got all the good genes," Jenna says, and I feel a rush of joy when her hand curls around mine.

"You did alright," I say looking at her. The colour of her hair has changed, the gold shining brightly, almost like embers. I don't have to turn my head to know where it comes from. The sun is starting to fall lower in the sky.

"I'd agree with that," my father says. He looks past us, presumably to check my mother isn't close by. "Jenna, I know it's been a bit wild, meeting Cynthia and all, but for me it's been a real pleasure. It's clear to me you and Aiden here really do enjoy each other's company, and it's been very good for me to see my son smile like this again... and without a drink in his hand too. Miracles will never cease."

"I smile, Da," I say and lean back in my chair, bringing Jenna's hand with me.

"Not like this," Dad says. "You haven't smiled like this since we lost Arnie."

I am left speechless by him saying that. A ball of emotion shoots out of my stomach and fires up my throat, burning up any words I may have had.

Luckily, my mother and sister arrive back at the table filling the silence.

"I don't care if it happens all the time," Mum says as she pulls her own chair out quicker than Dad can stand up. "It's not appropriate. In fact, if it happens all the time that just makes it worse."

"Ma," Maeve says throwing herself in her chair, arms folded. "It's what happens when you do the kind of work I do. I can't stop people sending me messages like that."

"Maeve, that wasn't a message, that was pornography."

"It was just a man asking me out on a date."

"A Greek man! From Crete!" Mum shouts, then leans low on the table and adopts a voice that is part-hiss, part-whisper. "And he was saying indecent things about what he wanted to do with Maeve."

"Sorry, what's going on?" I lean forward, suddenly concerned.

"Someone figured out where I was on my Live on the beach this afternoon." Maeve groans, loudly. "They could see the villas in the background, and they left a comment with the name of the resort. I've gotten really good at not sharing my real-time location and I didn't think anyone would figure it out, but hey, I fucked up, so now all of my Greek followers have been going crazy and a handful of men have messaged me asking to meet up."

"That was not someone asking to *take* you out, Maeve, that was someone asking to *eat* you out," Mum snaps back.

I'm fairly sure Jenna, Maeve and I all shudder in unison while Dad freezes and goes very pale.

I shake the words and potential visuals out of my head, suddenly alarmed. "How do you even know this, Ma?"

"Maeve asked me to record some video of her, in the nice golden minute light."

"Golden hour, Ma." Maeve rolls her eyes.

"And I was doing that when this notification popped up with half a message showing and it was... it was smut."

"Nothing wrong with a bit of smut," I hear Jenna say and I can't help my chest from tightening. I love her sex-positive attitude, but it would be helpful if it had a filter when I'm trying to establish if my sister is at risk of a sexual predator.

"I mean, when it's consensual and safe. Research shows people who read erotica-" Jenna continues.

"Are you really saying this in front of my parents?" I turn to look at her and the playful spark in her eyes makes me drop the stern stare I was trying to give her and just laugh instead.

"I think your mum can cope with it," she says, taking a sip from her drink.

"I can indeed," Mum says reaching for her glass. "What that man said was nothing I haven't read before. It was almost tame, in fact, compared to what I've read."

Maeve and I both sigh together, practically in a melody. I turn to Dad.

"Don't look at me!" He holds his hands up.

"God, no, if it's not a crossword answer, your father's not writing it. I'm talking about the books I read. They're often described as smut."

"Oh, you like erotic romance?" Jenna stretches towards my mother. "Who are your favourite authors?"

"Well, I'm quite partial to..."

And this is precisely my prompt to push my chair back, which I do, saying, "I'm just going to the little boys' room." I walk away as my mother and Jenna continue to share author recommendations and book names, and did I really just hear the words "kitchen counter cunnilingus" leave my mother's mouth?

When I'm done in the bathroom, I find myself slowing my pace as I cross the entrance to the kitchen. I can almost feel the energy emanating from it, feel the heat of the chaos I know is inside, and sense the weight of the pressure. It reminds me of how challenging cheffing is, and how the harder it is, the more rewarding it can be. I've always been someone drawn to risk, and that's something I get to play around with every night in a restaurant kitchen when there are always deadlines, always things out of your control, and always multiple things to think about at any one time. But now, glancing back at our dinner table and seeing my mother and Jenna's heads practically touching as they look at something on one of their phones together, I realise I'm a risk-taker with my heart too.

First, Arnie with our friendship that our relationship could have nuked had it all gone wrong.

And now, Jenna. The risk is massive - she is older, she lives in a different country, she may well decide she wants an older, more successful and more financially-independent partner - and the stakes are high, but the reward - having her, holding her, loving her and having her love me - it's undeniably worth it.

With this thought erasing all others, I walk around the outside of the seating area and find a spot at the walled viewing platform that gives a slightly different view of the sunset to the one in the beach bar or Jenna's villa. From this more elevated position it feels a bit more like I'm eye-to-eye with the sun and the effervescent copper glow it casts across the sky. Our table in the restaurant isn't going to let me see the sunset's final minutes, but from here I can see it all, all the while warmed by the sun's buttery glow. I sit sideways on the wall, and watch.

For the second time that day I feel almost paralysed with the hopeless desire to have Arnie there with me. This thought is not out of the ordinary, but the reason I want him there possibly is. I want him there to ask his advice. How do I tell Jenna how I really feel? How do I find out if she wants to also give this a go after this week? How do I tell someone I've known for only three days that I think I'm falling in love with her?

As ridiculous as it sounds, considering who he was to me, I know that Arnie would know. He would know how to do all of that.

Arms wrap around my chest and a warmth presses against my back.

"Hey," I say as I lean back against Jenna.

"You're not wearing your sunglasses," she says.

"I'm not looking directly at it."

"But then you won't be able to look for the green light."

"You know," I say. "I think you can believe something is there, even if you don't see it."

"That was profound, Aiden," she says after a few seconds.

"What the fuck are you doing calling me Aiden?"

I feel her body move in a shrug. "Just testing to see if you prefer it."

"God, no. I'm Marty to you."

"But your parents call you Aiden."

"I'm Aiden to them. And that's okay. I want to be Marty to you," I say.

"What was Arnie's real name?"

"How do you know Arnie wasn't his real name?"

"Well, first of all, I don't know many twenty-something-year-olds with the name Arnold. And secondly, I assumed Marty was originally his nickname for you, and so you must have had one for him."

My chest gives as I exhale. "You're right, but it's not much of a story. We were kids playing rugby together and nobody was called by their first name. O'Martin was my surname. His was McArnold. Marty and Arnie. It was easy."

"Yeah, zero points for creativity." Jenna chuckles.

"I think for two eleven-year-old boys it was pretty creative." I sigh and slide my hands up to keep her grip on me. I suddenly feel like I'm about to cry. The one thing that stops me is the silence that we share as we watch the sun continue to sink lower. Her chin is on my shoulder, her hair tickling my cheek. I feel safe and I feel loved. I can't help but wonder if it's her love I feel, or Arnie's.

Or maybe, possibly, both?

"You miss him so much it hurts, don't you?" she whispers in my ear.

I nod. "Pretty much feel like it might kill me sometimes."

"I loved hearing you talk about him at dinner," she says, her hands stroking my chest. "I know doing so must hurt, and I see how being with your family is also like a near constant reminder, but please don't stop talking about him, Marty."

"I want to keep talking about him," I say, and my tentativeness is so audible in my voice. "Can I keep talking about him with you?"

Her exhale moves my body. "Of course."

"We only have one more sunset here together after this," I say and saying it feels like a new sharper knife piercing a new fleshier part of my heart.

"Marty," she says. "Let's not talk about this now."

"But we could have more sunsets somewhere else?" I ask, ignoring her warning.

"We could," she says but I struggle to hear the certainty in her voice. I feel her head move, her eyes now face down in my shirt.

It's not the answer I want, but it's not the answer I feared most. And more importantly, I've started the conversation.

The sun has all but melted into the sea when we hear a click behind us, and our heads turn in sync. My sister is there holding up her phone.

"That is the kind of photo that could launch your social media career, Aidey, just in case you need something to fall back on," she says. "Also, we need you at the table. It's cake time."

The cake is indeed there on our table and Jake is standing beside my mother, looking even pinker and more harassed than before, but I know she won't notice as she chats away, touching him lightly on the arm. I take Jenna's hand as we walk back to the table and choose not to mention how the shoulder of my shirt is now damp, because even if she was crying, she is smiling now.

Back at the table, I admire the cake – a layered strawberry and cream creation - and dutifully sit there grinning while Jenna, my family, her brother, surrounding tables and a handful of equally harried-looking serving staff all sing Happy Birthday to me. It's more people than I expected to be celebrating my birthday this year, and while there is one voice I miss with every note, I can't help but feel buoyed by their singing. I blow out the candles with far too much gusto and fanfare, which I hope covers up the fact I made what feels like one of the most important wishes of my life.

Chapter Thirty-Five

Jenna

When all the candles are blown out and Marty has served us all up a piece of cake, he puts the knife down without slicing one for himself.

"Right, that's enough of this celebrating horseshite. I thank you all for being here with me and behaving, for the most part," he says with individual looks at us all. "But now I want to treat myself to a little extra birthday fun."

He stands and looks around the seating area. He catches my brother's eye, who is seating that group of twenty and looking like he's not going to make it back to the pantry in time for his next crying break.

"I'm off to go save this kitchen and fucken enjoy every second of it." Marty stands and walks off before any of us can say anything.

Feeling both incredibly proud of him and relieved for my brother, I am also pinned to my chair in panic now that I have to eat cake and make polite conversation with his parents, alone. Maeve is fully absorbed in her phone again so will be little help. But after one mouthful of the cake - a decadently light and moist sponge with fresh cream and strawberry filling - I decide to persevere, knowing it will make Marty happy.

We make small talk about the cake, the resort, and how lucky we are with the warm weather, and I am relieved when Cynthia asks me more questions about my work and asks if I can recommend some books about grief and loss.

"I have tried to get Marty to read one or two, but he says he doesn't have the attention span for them," she says.

"It's possible," I say. "Grief can often manifest in periods of restlessness with an inability to focus."

"I'm not sure that's the grief," James adds. "That's just Marty. He's not a sit down and read kind of lad. He's like me, feels better when he's active or busy."

"Maybe I could suggest one or two audiobooks to him," I say. "Maybe he could listen to them on a run or in the gym."

"Could you?" Cynthia looks stunned. "That would be fantastic."

"What about books on sexuality?" Maeve pipes up and the three of us turn to her. I'd assumed she was busy on her phone and not listening. She doesn't hold any of our gazes. "For all of us, I mean. To try and support Marty better with that."

"I can recommend some books for that too," I say, and I make sure I have Maeve's eye before I continue. "I know some great websites too that can help you understand different types of sexual identities."

Maeve shrugs and looks back on her phone. "Sounds good."

"I'd like to see them too," says Cynthia as her eyes flit between the two of us.

"Oh, for feck's sake, I'll even have a look. Is metrosexual in there?" James says, and that makes me laugh while Maeve groans.

I am about to ask Maeve about her work, when I spot my brother charging for our table.

"Your boy is a chef's version of Superman," Jake starts collecting our empty glasses. I'm not sure if he's talking to me or Marty's parents but still my cheeks warm. "He's whipped the whole team into shape, he's attacking orders like a Riverdancing ninja, and I have finally got a server back. Also, did you know he likes to listen to ABBA while working?"

His parents' laughter fills my ears.

"Oh, God, does he still do that?" James asks.

"I'm afraid that's my fault," Cynthia says, dabbing at her eyes with her napkin. "I like to relive my youth when cooking. He grew up listening to far too much Seventies pop. I used to play it every evening as I made dinner."

"No apologies necessary. He's literally saving my life tonight, so I don't care what he listens to," my brother says then he leans towards me and whispers in my ear. "But my God, he cannot dance. I think that rhythm is his kryptonite."

I am quick to turn my head so only he can hear. "Oh, his rhythm is just fine."

My brother's eyes close and lips flatten as he gathers his composure, straightening up.

"Needless to say, your meal is on the house tonight," he says to Marty's parents.

"Oh no, that's not necessary." James now has his wife's hand in his and I find myself smiling as I watch his fingers stroke hers.

"It absolutely is," Jake says. "Do you need anything else? Some coffee or tea? An after dinner drink?"

"Well, if you're offering, I'll take a whiskey." James smiles. "Irish, of course."

"And I'll have a mint tea," Cynthia says, leaning forward. "And could I also ask you a quick question?"

"Certainly." Jake comes to stand beside Cynthia again.

"What kind of security do you have here?"

"Oh, Jesus, Mother." Maeve slams her elbows on the table and her head in her hands.

"Maeve, it's a valid question if there's a Greek sex pest out there wanting to find you."

"I'm sorry?" His attention grabbed, Jake tilts his head to the side.

"Maeve is getting some unwanted attention from local men who know that she's staying here," I try to explain as quickly as I can. "She's a social media influencer. Nearly a million followers on TikTok."

"Yes, and I stupidly revealed my location earlier today while I did a Live on the beach," Maeve says and it's the first time I've seen her look anything but cool and composed. Suddenly I see her youth and her vulnerability, and it surprises me that I want to rush over to hug her tight.

"That was you!" Jake practically shouts.

"What?" Maeve asks.

"You're the reason my ass may actually survive until October!" Jake's delight is palpable.

"I am?"

"You've been sharing videos of the resort?"

"Yes, but I didn't say I was staying here. People figured it out during my Live and I was a bit slow with the damage control." Maeve still looks frustrated.

"Oh, God, there's been no damage. At least not for me. People have been making bookings all day. The resort is practically full for the next two months. Headquarters are already talking about extending the season. You have literally turned my career around in the last twenty-four hours."

"Well, that's great to hear." Maeve smiles.

"So do you think you could tell your security team to be extra careful about any strange men coming onto the resort?" Cynthia interrupts.

"Oh, yes, absolutely," my brother says, defying forces of gravity as he balances the full tray in one hand while reaching to pull his phone out of his back pocket with the other. "You're in Villa 12, right? Well, extra patrols and checks for you tonight."

"Oh, thank you so much," Cynthia says, leaning back with a smile.

"It's totally unnecessary. I doubt they're sex pests," Maeve says.

"It's really not a problem," my brother says pushing buttons on his phone. "I will personally handle all the sex pests myself."

He stops as James snickers, and I bite down a smile.

"Forget I said that," Jake says, and he spins around and goes, keeping the tray perfectly level as he presses the phone to his ear.

"Maeve, I know you don't think anything of it, but you really have helped my brother." I lean towards her.

"Well, it was Marty too."

"It was?"

"Yeah, the video of him and I jumping in the pool the other day was the one that went viral and got me thousands of new followers and traction with the algorithm."

"Oh, God, you two were cackling with laughter doing that," James says.

"I thought there would be no more water in the pool by the time you were done," Cynthia adds, giggling.

304

"He did a video with you?" I ask.

"Yeah, you want to see it?" Her eyes are sparkling again.

"Yes, please," I say, and Maeve moves over to sit in Marty's chair. She starts scrolling through her phone and before I know it, Cynthia and James have stood up and moved over to crouch behind us. I catch a whiff of Cynthia's perfume - it's soft, floral, with vanilla undertones. It's the kind of motherly smell I find instantly comforting and homely. I wish I could remember what my mother smelt like.

We all watch the video together and it's hilarious. Marty and Maeve take it in turns to throw themselves in the water adopting positions that text pops up to describe. There's running, sitting at a desk, yoga positions, cooking - which Marty naturally excels at - and each one gets more ridiculous than the last. I glance at the side of the screen and see there are over three million views, over a million likes and nearly 10,000 comments. My mind boggles at that many people casting their eyes on Marty. After we watch it three times, we end up scrolling through a few more of Maeve's videos until my brother brings James and Cynthia's drinks and an update about an extra security patrol. Marty's parents turn to thank him profusely while I talk to Maeve.

"You're very talented," I say.

She pulls her head back to look at me. "You think?"

"Yes." I nod. "Your videos are fun and creative. There's lots of variety, but each one lines up nicely with the others. People know they're going to be entertained, informed or inspired by what you post. As someone who's also in the creating content game, I know this isn't easy to do."

"Thanks, Jenna," she says, almost shyly.

"People don't tell you that very often, do they?" I ask.

"I shouldn't need to hear it." She shrugs, avoiding both a direct answer and my eye contact. "But doing this already doesn't feel like a 'proper' job and I do nearly all of it on my own, so I sometimes doubt myself and if I'm actually contributing anything."

"Sounds like impostor syndrome to me," I say and sink the last mouthful of my wine.

"Yeah, I think I get that a lot," she says.

"A lot of talented and successful people do," I say and when she looks up at me, she returns my smile.

"Marty's got his own hashtag now." Maeve turns her phone's screen off. "#MaesHotOlderBrother. Please don't tell him. He'd be insufferable if he knew."

"Oh, I won't tell him," I say. "I don't want to have to put up with that either."

To my surprise, Cynthia chimes in as if she'd been listening all along behind us. "That boy and his self-confidence. He always had it. Even as a kid."

James guides his wife back to their seats. He swirls his whiskey as he sits. "He's not as confident as you think, Cynthia. I've always said that."

I find myself nodding but stay silent, looking down at my hands in my lap.

"I think that's what hurt the most." I hear Cynthia speak and when I look up I see her seeking out my eyes. "The way his confidence and optimism were shattered after Arnie. Marty always had a very rose-tinted view of the world, until Arnie died. And when he lost that, he sort of lost himself."

I feel my forehead wrinkle when I see a tear seep out of the corner of her eye.

"As somebody who only met Marty a few days ago," I say, leaning towards her. "I can say that your optimistic and confident son is still very much there."

Another tear leaves Cynthia's eye.

"She's right, Ma," Maeve says, and I turn to see a contemplative look on her face. "I mean, you'd have to be ballsy sort of guy to shoot your shot with Jenna."

"I'd rather not thinking about my son shooting his shot," James says before knocking back the glass.

"It's an expression, Da!" They laugh together, and I see their physical similarities in sync - bunched-up cheeks, narrow light eyes that almost disappear with their surprisingly broad smiles.

I feel the need to say something in order to deflect the comment or attention, especially when I see Cynthia's gaze is back on me, but this time it makes me feel soothingly warm rather than uncomfortably hot.

But before I have the right words to say in my mouth, I see Marty bounding over towards us and after bending down to kiss my cheek, he straightens up and talks animatedly. "I'm having the time of my fecking life!"

I try to ignore how good he looks in chef's whites. I wonder if it would take one or two goes to rip that shirt off and make the buttons go flying.

"Aiden, you should take it easy," his mother says, rubbing away at the corners of her eyes. "You don't want to overdo it."

"Oh, Mum, don't piss all over my parade. Not on my birthday, and when I'm doing a good deed." His fingers are dancing on the back of the chair he was sitting in earlier, the high energy pouring out of him.

"I just worry..." Cynthia tries again.

"Seriously, enough!" Marty's stare at his mother is stormy and his words sound like thunder. "We just survived the world's most awkward dinner. Why don't we quit while we're ahead?"

"Marty," I say.

"Jenna, can I stay at yours tonight?" he asks loudly and suddenly enough for everyone to catch every word.

I cover my eyes with my hand but still I nod.

"Ma, I'm staying at Jenna's tonight. And I'm sorry, Dad, I won't make our bike ride tomorrow. Jenna's only got one more day before she goes home, and I want to spend every single second with her."

James says and does nothing, but Cynthia shifts in her seat. "Aiden, you should think-"

"No, Mum. No!" Marty is shouting now. "Whatever it is you're going to say, no. I can do my own thinking and my own decision-making. And that's what I am deciding for the next twenty-four hours."

"Marty, you don't need to shout," I say.

His dark eyes are on me. "Sometimes I do. Because sometimes people don't listen to me," he says as he turns to his mother.

"That's enough, son," James says, and his hand finds his wife's again.

"Come on, Da. You know what it's like. What she's like. I'm twenty-four years old now. I've not been a kid for a long time."

"No, you're not, which is all the more reason you should be behaving more respectfully." James' voice is very different now. All the warmth is gone.

"I'll start being respectful to her when she shows *me* a little respect," Marty seethes, and I pull my eyes away from how sharp the edges of his jaw are.

"You're embarrassing yourself in front of Jenna," his mother bites out.

"Jesus," Marty laughs in disbelief. "I'm not the one embarrassing myself, you are! Tell her, Jenna."

I find myself needing to groan as I exhale. "Honestly, Marty. You are a little bit," I say.

"What?"

"I know you're all high on the energy in the kitchen, and I know there are a lot of things going on in your head and heart right now, but you do need to calm down. Just take a breath," I say.

"I do not need to... I'm fed up of being treated like a child!" he exclaims.

"I understand that." I keep my voice low, hoping he'll do the same as nearby tables are looking at us now. "I understand how it feels."

"Do you?" Marty says, turning that angry tone on me. "Do you really? I mean, it's not like you've had to answer to a parent for a long time."

His words pull my shoulders back and make my back straighten, uncomfortably so.

"Okay, I'm done." I stand, picking up my bag. "I have really enjoyed this evening, for the most part, but I don't need to be involved in someone else's family drama tonight. And Marty, I think you should think about that too. Just go back into the kitchen and enjoy yourself, and then come and see me... tomorrow."

"Tomorrow?" He looks horrified.

"Yes, tomorrow, Marty. We'll have the day together, but I think tonight I need to be alone," I say even though it feels like a lie. I step closer to him, rise and kiss the corner of his mouth and stroke his cheek. "Good luck tonight. Thank you for helping my brother out." I turn again to his parents and sister. "Thank you so much for dinner tonight. It was a pleasure to meet you."

I turn and walk away in something like a hurry, however it's not fast enough.

"Look at what you did, Aiden." I hear his mother say in that hard-edged critical voice I've heard one too many times.

And just like that, I'm not done. I swivel back and step to the end of the table. All their eyes land on me but I am looking only at his mother.

"Just so you know, Cynthia, Marty is one of the most mature men I've met. I don't know if it's your parenting or the experience he had with Arnie, or both, but I don't think he lacks maturity. Or self-awareness. It's my impression that he really does know what he wants in life and with all due respect, I think all your lives would be much easier and simpler if you learned to trust in that, to trust him. You should be incredibly proud of him. You raised a brilliant young man."

Cynthia's eyes fill with tears again and I suspect her lips are pulled into her mouth because she wants to stem their flow.

"Thank you, Jenna," Marty says, and I can see his chin is lifted now, his shoulders squarer.

"You're welcome, Marty," I say, turning my body to his. "But while I'm dishing out unwanted advice, I also have some for you. Please stop being a dick to your mother. It's not a good look on you, and she doesn't deserve it."

And without waiting to see how the shock settles on Marty's face, I turn around and walk to my villa without looking back.

Chapter Thirty-Six

Jenna

It's three hours later when I hear my doorbell ring. I open the door and see him in the clothes he was wearing earlier, although his shirt is considerably more rumpled, and his jeans have splatters of dirt and stains on them. I smell the food on him too. It's not unpleasant, but it's not the fresh air Marty smell I have come to crave.

"Hey," he says. His face looks weighed down by exhaustion, his skin sallow and grey in the moonlight. Dark circles puddle beneath his eyes and his mouth can only hold his dimple-free smile in one corner.

"Hey, Marty Masterchef," I say. "Thank you again for saving my brother's arse tonight."

"Man, I know I'm tired because that's the perfect set-up for a joke about your brother's arse and yet I can't get the words in the right order."

"Come in, you need a shower." I put my hand on his shirt ready to drag him inside. "And bed."

"Wait." he doesn't step forward. "I need to say something. I'm sorry for my behaviour at dinner."

"Thank you for apologising, Marty," I say, and I mean it. I didn't know how much I needed that apology.

"You were right. I am being a dick to my mother."

I nod and pull him towards me, closing the door behind us.

"I don't even know why I do it," Marty says as he kicks off his shoes. I take his hand and lead him to my room.

"I can't stop it sometimes, no matter how hard I try," he says as we walk into my bathroom and I sit him down on the shower bench.

"And other times, I don't want to stop myself. I just let rip at her," he adds as I lift his T-shirt off his body.

"It used to make me feel better, even if just for a few seconds, you know, but recently, it all makes me feel like shit," he says as I undo his jeans and nudge for him to sit up so I can slide them and his boxers off his body. I step away and turn the shower on, keeping my hand under it until the temperature is right.

"I know she loves me. I know she wants the best for me. I just can't help feeling angry sometimes," he says as I go back to him, hold out my hand and pull him up.

I shuck off my robe and throw it outside the shower just before we stand under the spray. It feels right we're together under the water again in the place where we first saw each other naked, when he first filled me up, when I first felt what I now know was more than just lust for him.

But now is not a time for love-making, at least not in the sexual sense. Now is a time for me to wash him clean, which I do with copious amounts of shower gel, my hands going anywhere and everywhere. When I get to between his legs, he swells in no time, but I don't do anything to tease that into something more. His touches on my body are the same, tender, giving, not at all taking. It still readies my body for him, but it doesn't send me spinning with desire. I am tired too.

I switch off the spray and lead him back to sit on the bench. I get us some towels, feeling his eyes on my skin as I move. There's a stab of pain in my gut when I realise how much I will miss that feeling every time I'm naked in the future.

Wrapping my towel around me, I secure it under my arms before I take the other one and start to dry him off, limb by limb, before standing between his legs and rubbing the towel over his hair, making it stand up on end.

"Jenna, you look after me so well," he says as I help him to stand and wrap the towel around his waist.

"Shh," I say and then lead him out of the bathroom and into my bedroom. I throw back the covers and pat the bed, telling him to lie down, which he does as I go to the kitchen to get a glass of water and some paracetamol which I bring to the bedside table next to him.

When Marty's eyes land on the glass and two tablets, he bursts into tears, his face crumpling in directions I've never seen it fold in before.

"Marty?" I climb on top of him, pulling his body into my arms.

He heaves with sobs, and I want to know what it was that set him off, but I realise it doesn't matter; he's allowed to be upset. Either way, he doesn't need questions. He needs answers, one particular answer.

"Marty, it's okay. Everything's okay." I repeat this until the crying slows and he moves back creating some space between us.

"Jesus, I'm sorry." He rests back in bed, rubbing his eyes with his fingertips.

"It's okay," I say again, staying where I am, my legs straddling him.

He nods to the side table. "It was the water and painkillers. It's what my mum always does for me. Whenever I'm having a bad day or if I'm a little under the weather," he says. "Fuck, I've been such a shit to her."

I nod. "But she's not been easy for you either."

"No, that's true," he says with a light laugh, and it's good to see his dimples again.

I slowly lift myself up and get under the covers with him, throwing the towel onto the floor once my body is covered by the duvet. "You know, I don't know what it's like to be a mother, or even have a mother into adulthood. But as you know I've thought a bit about becoming a mother over the years and do you want to know what I think being a mother really means?"

He nods once and I lift my head to see his eyes are hooded and glazed with the tears he just cried. He looks just as beautiful like this – vulnerable, soft, exhausted – as he does when he's fucking me hard, licking honey off my fingers, or chasing me down the water's edge of an old Cretan fishing town.

"I think it means loving someone so much you can forgive them almost anything, over and over again. From what I've read and studied, I'm not convinced there's such a thing as unconditional love, nor that there should be.

313

But I strongly suspect the love a mother feels for their child is the closest you can get to unconditional love. What I mean to say by this is, you and your mother are going to be okay. Truly."

He tilts his head to the side. "I believe you. I never questioned her love for me in all of this. I guess I'm sad because now I'm questioning mine. I get so angry with her, and so quickly."

"I understand. But you know being angry, that's part of grief, right?"

"Yeah," he sighs, "I know."

"Maybe you just need a better place to direct your anger?"

He nods again and then slides his body further down the bed.

His hand finds my thigh and I feel it glide up towards my centre, probing. I look over at him and see his eyes are fully closed now, his breath slow and even. I find his hand and hold it still, more on my inner thigh now than my pussy.

"You need to sleep," I say to him and then I reach back and flick the light switch on the wall, plunging us into darkness.

"Hmm," he mumbles. "Can you say it again?"

"What?" I say as I lay down on my side, facing him. There is a magic in this moment, the first time we are in bed together, going to sleep together, without making love. It's just as intimate and satisfying than if we had made each other see stars with orgasms.

"Tell me that Mum and I will be okay. Tell me that it will all be okay."

"You and your mum will be okay. Everything's going to be okay," I say slowly, I take his hand off my thigh and bring it to my mouth to kiss his fingers. I love how heavy his arm is; he's completely surrendered to his fatigue. I can feel the same pull come for me as I knit our fingers together and burrow my head into the pillow, closing my eyes. I take lots of long deep breaths, trying to keep at bay the ache that reminds me how little time he and I have left together.

"What about us?" he says in the darkness. "Are we going to be okay?"

"We're going to be okay too," I say, and I believe this even though I don't know what it really means, let alone what it will look like.

Then my head finds his chest, my legs open for one of his, my arm circles his waist, and I drift into a sleep that is so deep, I wake in exactly the same position.

Chapter Thirty-Seven

The Next Day

Marty

I wake before Jenna and do everything I can not to move, wanting her to stay asleep after I woke her in the night. Her face is tucked into the side of my chest, so I can't even watch her sleep, but instead my mind is busy remembering the kitchen last night. The way I got straight to work, commandeering the speakers' aux plug with my phone, and quickly re-allocating duties and buddies. I'd trouble-shooted the urgent issues and then I'd got to work on the long list of mains. I'd checked in with everyone as often as I could and invited people to dance or sing whenever they felt the stress bubble up inside them, and I was as surprised and delighted as anyone when some of them actually did this.

Then after service, I turned the music up a little louder, poured a round of shots for those who wanted one, and we got to work scrubbing the kitchen spotless. In the last six months I've started to think cleaning has gone from being the bit I disliked most to one of my favourite parts of the job. Maybe it's because I no longer rush through it, desperate to top up the post-shift beers with something harder at a local bar or club, or maybe it's because now I'm sober, I can appreciate the satisfying sheen on stainless steel, the quiet sense of achievement, and the calm in the room as I switch the lights off and leave.

Calm is also what I feel as I lift my head up and look down to catch a glimpse of Jenna's eyelids twitching in her sleep. I can't stop my hand from brushing Jenna's hair off her face. I can't stop my other fingers from finding the leg that is draped over mine. I can't stop the way they massage into her smooth flesh that feels so solid and yet so soft. I love that about her body.

When I feel her eyelashes tickle the skin on my chest, I stop moving. But when she lifts her head up and gives me a gentle kiss, I start again, this time sliding my hand further up to her hip. When she pushes up with her hands, I can snake my fingers around and grip her right butt cheek. It is never-ending under my palm. No matter where I grab, what I take, there is always more for me to enjoy.

As Jenna lifts up, I see her eyes are barely open, but there is the smallest smile on her lips. I take my hands off her and give her space to move and am neither surprised or disappointed when she moves further under the covers and comes to rest her pussy perfectly on my hardening cock. She straightens up, pushing the covers off us, and while her eyes are still heavy, her mouth is stretched into a wide smile.

Naked like I am, Jenna shimmies around until my hard cock is flattened against my lower belly, and she sits down on it, starting to move, back and forth, so very slowly as she wakes up. When her pace picks up, I go to grab her wrist, to tell her I need to get a condom, but before I speak, she nods at the bedside table. I open the drawer and find a new unopened pack lying next to a bottle of lube and two sex toys I would like to have a closer look at, but I am distracted when Jenna's mouth moves down and sucks on one of my nipples.

I grunt and thrust up against her as I take the condom packet and make such a mess of opening it that she takes it from me, opens it and retrieves a condom with far too much grace for a woman who's just woken up. The only way I can show her my thanks is by gliding my hands up her thighs, her hips, over the arc of her waist and taking her breasts in my palms, I squeeze them hard enough that she rolls her head back while the now-empty condom foil is still between her teeth.

Still without a word passing between us, Jenna lifts onto her knees, creating cold empty space between us, making me ache for her warmth again as she grips the base of me with one hand and positions the condom at my tip, rolling it down a little too slowly for my liking, and to let her know this, I pinch her nipples.

She hums in response, her teeth biting her bottom lip. Then she leans forward, and her breasts are close enough I can flick my tongue over her nipples.

She sighs as she moves my dick, positioning me where she wants me, and then she finally opens her eyes wide for the first time and locks her gaze on me at the exact moment I feel the warmth of her entrance kiss the head of my cock.

As Jenna sinks down, I move my hands back to her hips, my fingertips grazing the peak of her buttocks. I sigh when I feel her sit firmly down, and I suck air straight back in as her muscles squeeze me. Her left eyebrow raises upon hearing that, and she does it again. I shake my head at her as I smile and then I have had enough of her taking this slow, I move quickly wrapping an arm around her waist and putting my other hand down to steady myself on the bed so I can lift her up and swing her around so she's lying on her back, looking up at me, and I'm still blissfully deep inside her.

We have talked a lot during sex. Like yesterday, when we said our names to each other, over and over. I loved that. And I love how she tells me what she likes, what she needs. So I'm not sure why we're not talking now, but I'm not mad. I want this. This silent love-making that is only punctuated by our sighs and moans, my grunts and her gasps.

This is also why I don't fuck her. At least not yet. I take it slow, grind into her as patiently as my hips will allow, feeling every centimetre of her surrounding me. Looking down at Jenna, I watch her top lip arch when I push her knees up to her chest and go as deep as I can go, giving her a gentle twist up.

God, she's beautiful.

As I watch her wriggle underneath me, I find myself feeling the same kind of satisfaction I felt with Arnie, that unique kind of satisfaction that satiates while also creating a constant craving. This desire is what satisfies me the most. Always wanting more is a headspace I am comfortable in.

Jenna interrupts my thoughts and my quickening pace, by reaching across the bed, grabbing a pillow and shoving it under her hips. I'm not sure if she did it for me or for her, but it lets me go a little deeper and makes her squeeze me a little harder. I throw my head back as a soft growl leaves my lips. Her hands come to my backside and she squeezes, digs her nails into me, grasping at the muscle there and searching. I smile about where she's going, and I spread my legs a little for her so she can play with me. Moving me up her body a little, my head is now slightly higher than hers. Her eyes flicker closed as I realise this has probably put more pressure on her clit and so I start to roll my hips around in a circle and then a figure of eight, just as she starts to apply some pressure exactly where I like it.

I wait for Jenna to open her eyes again and then I lift my eyebrows, checking she's okay. She starts to nod with me as we rock together.

When I start to thrust again, slamming myself harder and faster inside her, the nodding of her head picks up pace, whimpers leave her lips, and I know she's close and I so badly want to watch her come before I do, but her finger, my arsehole, her cunt and my cock are all in a world of their own and I can't stop them. So I don't. I thrust into her again and again, harder and harder, pushing up on my hands so I have more strength and more space. Just as my spine tingles and balls seize up high, I look down and I see her eyes are arrested on me, staring at me like she needs me more than oxygen, like I am more than I am, and that tips me over the edge.

Surging waves of pleasure wash over me, and each one feels like it can't be beaten but then more tingles, more warmth, more relief comes with the next. When they finally slow down, I open my eyes again and watch her as she comes. She gasps, she sighs, and then she opens her mouth wide and breathes out the daintiest short scream once, and then again. All the time her eyes are on me and mine are on hers and I have never felt so sure that I am exactly where I am supposed to be.

As my breath returns, I shift my weight down so I am right above her face and can look down at her. Her face has smoothed out from the orgasm and she looks up at me and we both smile. Her eyes then start darting around my face as her hands come up to smooth out my hair, before cruising down the bump on my nose, cupping my cheeks, stroking my chin. I keep my eyes on hers, wondering what she sees or what she's looking for. When her pupils settle on mine again, I feel relief because whatever it was, I see she's found it.

And then I go and break the silence, and possibly both our hearts, when I open my mouth and say, "I love you, Jenna."

Chapter Thirty-Eight

Jenna

I don't freeze because I'm surprised by what he says. I feel it too, emanating from his skin and mixing with the post-orgasmic oxytocin rush that washes over me as my insides stay moulded to him.

I freeze because I am instantaneously both proud that he was brave enough to say it first, and ashamed because I wasn't.

I am the one who has studied love. I am the one who has written about it extensively. I am the one who champions love for all. I am love's greatest advocate and yet, I've been fighting it, ignoring it, holding it back in myself.

And so I stop fighting it.

My ears pull back as I smile wide. My eyes rest on his and I push up and touch my nose to his before lying back down on the pillow.

"I love you too, Marty," I say softly.

When he dives his face down into my shoulder and starts covering my neck and collarbone with kisses, I know that he didn't expect that. He was prepared for a rebuttal, for me to rebuke and challenge him. He was prepared for me to dispute and dismiss his love, and him having that expectation is almost as heart-shattering as if I had actually done that.

"I love you so much, Jenna," he says into my hair. "I can't believe this happened. I can't believe you happened."

"I love you, Marty," I say again. I slide my hand up his strong back and feel disproportionate disappointment when he slides out of me.

He pulls back and tells me he's going to deal with the condom, insisting I stay where I am, and I don't have the energy to argue even if I wanted to. I don't know if it's the incredibly intense sex we just had, the declarations of love, or just the last four days catching up with me, but I am abruptly weighed down with exhaustion.

That's why I'm in the same position as a naked Marty walks back to me. I start to smile but that quickly evolves into giggles when Marty picks up his pace and jumps over me, landing sideways next to my body with a loud "Bam!"

"What was that?" I chuckle.

"That is how I feel right now," he says, and he pulls me closer to him. I reach for the duvet and that gets tangled up with us too. "I feel like I could jump as high as the moon! Like I want to shout out from the rooftops how fucking happy I am right now!"

"Oh, Marty," I say before I erupt into laughter because he starts tickling me. This continues until I am trying to hit him through the duvet that wraps around me. "Stop!"

And he does stop the tickling, letting me roll onto my side away from the duvet. His body lines up next to mine and before I know what's happening his lips come down on mine, kissing me so hard I feel like he already wants to go another round. When I feel his dick hardening against my thigh, I know I have to pull away.

"Okay, okay, enough! I need to pee and wash before that happens again," I pant out, pushing his body away from mine but still keeping my hands on him. I always want my hands on him. "Do you still want to spend the day together?"

"Try and fucking stop me." He starts to rut against me. "I'm not going anywhere."

"Jesus, you're like a puppy that is yet to have the snip," I say but I hold his face in my hands so he can see all the affection I have for this fact.

"That feels like a compliment," he says, and thrusts harder.

"Stop, Marty! I also need coffee, and food, and I want to ask you something. Something important," I say, and I do. I nearly asked earlier, but I was scared. Scared to break the perfect dream-like state I was in as we made love without words.

His movements halt and he looks across at me. "What is it?"

"After Ibiza," I say slowly. "Did you get tested?"

"Like STIs?" he asks after a beat.

"Yes," I say.

"Yeah, like twice. I went once by myself. Then my mum dragged me there herself because she didn't trust the results I showed her."

"I'm sorry she did that," I say.

"I'm sorry I gave her reason not to trust me." He sighs. "You probably don't believe me, but I was actually quite careful in Ibiza. I did a lot of stupid things during that time, but messing with other people's health, and my own, wasn't one of them. At least not in *that* way."

"I believe you." I place a hand on his chest, playing with the sparse hair that's there, feeling the solidity of his muscles under smooth warm skin. "And no problems?"

"None, I've been clean and celibate since then," he says.

"I'm also clean, and until you, celibate since my divorce."

"You got tested?"

"After my divorce, yes, I was quite keen to move on. Have sex with others, and so it seemed like the right thing to do, as well as continuing to take my pill. Honestly, I also considered it research. The whole process has changed quite a lot since my own youth. It's easier now."

"Oh, yeah, it's quite a laugh really. The nurses love me," he says.

"I bet they do." I smile and shake my head.

"Why did you want to ask me about that, Jenna?" he asks, but his tone tells me he already knows why.

I pull in a breath. "Because, I want to feel you. All of you."

His eyelids pull down, almost closed. "Fuck, yes," he whispers, and he presses against me again, not thrusting this time. He bends to give me a kiss, which I take but don't deepen.

"Just not now," I say against his lips.

"What?" He pulls back.

"I need coffee and breakfast, and to pee, and to shower and brush my teeth. I'm not sure what order I need those things to happen in, but I know I need them all."

He bends down to flick his tongue over my nipple. "Really? That's what you need?"

I moan with pleasure but still move away.

"Do you trust me, Marty?" I say as I stand up and look down at him over my shoulder.

"I'm questioning it right now, but yes," he says, stroking his cock now and that nearly undoes all the resolve I have. I'm going to make him do that for me at least once today, fist himself until he comes, preferably all over my breasts or my tongue.

I close my eyes, shutting off the temptation at the source.

"Then, let's wait. You'll be amazed how good a little anticipation will feel." I walk to the bathroom.

Minutes later, I find Marty in the kitchen, making us both coffees. He's wearing the other hotel robe and my smile is impossible to hide. When he goes to sit outside at the table next to the pool, exactly where I was going to suggest we have breakfast, I feel giddy with the synchronicity even though it's not an impossible coincidence he would want to sit there too when the sun is still low in the hazy blue-pink sky and the air still has that clear, calm smell. As I pick up the phone to order us breakfast, I glance at the clock and call my brother, requesting another favour, which he doesn't even hesitate to agree too.

"You don't even sound tired," I say to him once my request and the breakfast order is placed. "But you must be. Yesterday was a long day."

"This job is just a series of long days. I am high on adrenaline and success right now," he says with a yawn. "Can you thank Marty again for me? He really did save me."

"I will. Do you need me to send him somewhere for lunch today? I think he'd love it."

Jake yawns then, but there's a bounce in his voice. "No, thank you. I have stand-in staff coming today. Besides, aren't you spending the rest of the day shagging each other's brains out?"

"Something like that." I sigh.

"I could always try and extend your stay," he says with a leading tone. "I'd have to downgrade your accommodation now we're going to be booked up but I'm sure I can find something."

"Yes, about that. Are the Bouras' pleased with the new bookings?"

"Delighted! They even mentioned my favourite B-word?"

"Boner?" I guess.

"Okay, second favourite B-word. Bonus! I may actually get a bonus this season!" Jake's delight makes me smile.

"You absolutely deserve it," I say.

"And you deserve Marty. So why not bunk up with me in my off-site shack for a few more nights?"

"No," I reply. I need to affirm out loud what I've been telling myself. "I think it's right I go. No matter when we say goodbye it's going to hurt."

"But you will see each other again, won't you, Jen? That Irish rogue is infatuated with you, and I don't think I'm far off the mark when I say you feel the same."

I look at Marty leaning back in a chair, gazing lazily at the horizon and hugging his coffee mug. "I feel the same. And he knows it."

"Just promise me when you get married you come back and do it here? Hopefully, I'll still be the manager and it will be a successful business again and I can source the most epic marquee to blow Hospital Tent Gate completely out-"

"Jake. Nobody is getting married. Certainly not me. Now can I ask a very depressing question? Can you check my car is booked for tomorrow?"

"Already did. It will be here at 9:30. You need an alarm call?"

"No, thank you. I will have another reason to wake up early," I say, my eyes still on Marty.

Jake groans. "You're testing my ability to stay at a healthy thirty per cent jealous of you both."

"And you're wasting too much of your precious energy on this phone call. Thank you for breakfast plus extras. I'll message you later."

"It's a pleasure. It should be with you in about thirty minutes," Jake replies. "And Jenna, enjoy today. I am so happy you found him or rather, that my arse found him for you."

"Me too, Jake." I smile as I replace the phone's handset.

"Breakfast is on its way," I say as I rejoin Marty. I place a quick kiss on his head before moving to sit on the other side of the table.

"Grand," Marty says. "So, what are you doing in July or August?"

I don't say anything, but he doesn't seem to notice as he keeps talking.

"I should have enough money then for flights to London. I figure I can get the cheapest ones possible, hand-luggage only, and just take a backpack because it's not like I'll need many clothes," he says with a wink.

I hope I swallow my wince before I speak. "Marty, we don't have to talk about this now."

"I *want* to talk about this now. I want to know when we'll be together again."

Despite our declarations of love earlier, and what I felt in that moment - what I still so fervently feel - I keep freezing every time the concept of us 'together' after this holiday is presented to me or arises independently in my own mind. I am doing my best to be curious about why I feel strangely ill at ease about making plans. It's not because I don't want to see him again - having a date in the diary for when we could hold each other close again is possibly the one thing that would take the edge off the dread at saying goodbye tomorrow - but more because when I told him I loved him, I accepted that came with a certain set of responsibilities.

Because I love him, I want to do the right thing by Marty.

"What does it look like to you? Us being together?" I ask.

"It looks like us single-handedly propping up the London-Dublin airline routes. It looks like us having romantic weekends spending far too much money on fancy dinners in London, and cosy pub lunches in Dublin. It looks like us spending weekends in other places too."

"Don't you work weekends?" I ask, the thought popping into my mind.

"Sometimes, but the restaurant can survive without me now and then," he says with another Marty-wink.

I nod. I know I'm causing more problems than I'm solving by resisting him right now, but the truth is I can't dive into these waters with him, not yet. And I need to figure out why.

"Marty, I love you," I say.

His fist pumps out above his head. "God, I will never get bored of hearing that."

"Well, I do love you, so please don't forget that. But because I love you, I want to be honest with you."

His smile drops. "Jenna, please don't say what I think you're going to say."

"What do you think I'm going to say?"

"That you don't want us to see each other again. That we'll just stay the most epic of holiday romances, so epic they will have memes, and GIFs, and a Wikipedia page about us. Don't you dare say that that's all this is. No way. I want to drag this into the real world, Jenna. I want us to try and make it work. So don't tell me I can't," he says, and then he pauses, eyebrows heavy and pulled together, pleading. "Please."

It's not just his words that puncture me. It's the way his hands grip the cup of coffee, paling his knuckles. It's the way he stares at me like I hold his whole future in my hands, a burden I would be honoured to have but am also uneasy about being given.

"Marty, I will never tell you that you can't do anything. You're one of the few people I've met in my life that I believe can do anything they want. But I am feeling very overwhelmed right now. Not in a bad way, but in a way where I worry these kinds of conversations will eat into the beauty of today."

"You're scared?"

"Fuck, yes, I'm scared. But that only proves my love. Love *is* scary. So I want to ask you to help me with this. Give me today. We have almost exactly twenty-four hours until I leave. That's more than enough time to figure out what happens next, but I don't want to spend the whole time doing that. I want today

327

to be today. I want it to be ours. Not tomorrow's or the future's." I force my expression to become more jovial. "I mean, don't we owe that to the Wikipedia page?"

He gives me a quick, gentle laugh but then his expression falls serious. "Just promise me this doesn't end when you leave tomorrow. I don't want that goodbye to be goodbye forever."

"Marty..." I begin.

"Just promise me this doesn't end tomorrow," he says again, eyes dark and fixed.

I nod as I consider my reply.

"I think I can promise you that," I say, and I reach my hand over the table and sigh with something like relief when his fingers touch mine.

Chapter Thirty-Nine

Marty

When I go to open the door to room service, my heart leaps. Balancing on top of the tray of covered food, I see an instantly recognisable red and green box.

"You sneaky little fucker!" I bellow at Jenna, then turn back to the man carrying the tray who looks thoroughly shocked. "Sorry, not you. Come on in. Give me all the food, and that board game!"

He walks in and sets the tray down outside where Jenna is after taking a quick shower, dressed in another beautiful sundress, this one a soothing shade of lilac.

"You got us a board game!" I say.

"Oh, it's Scrabble. I wasn't expecting that. Seems Jake needs a little help with his understanding of board games."

"Is there a board? Is it a game? Am I going to kick your beautiful butt playing this?" I ask grabbing a slice of watermelon and shoving it in my mouth.

When the man is gone, Jenna moves around to grab my robe and pull me close, kissing me, her tongue sliding into my mouth and swirling around my top teeth.

"I just wanted to taste that watermelon on your tongue," she says and then she moves away as my fingers twitch with indecision about what to reach for first; Jenna, the food, or Scrabble.

Instead, I sink down into the nearest chair and groan as I watch Jenna start plating up food. "Today is going to be the best day of my life, you know that, right? Board games, room service food, sunshine, and you. You, Jenna, you!" I pull her into my lap.

And she stays there as we eat. She stays there as we drink more coffee. She stays there as I tell her about Arnie's favourite board game (The Game of Life) and mine (Mouse Trap) and she admits that Scrabble is the one that has a soft spot in her heart because she would play it with her mum. This makes me wonder if that's why Jake chose that game, and prompts me to ask her more questions about her mother.

Jenna talks about Cathy in a tone that is careful and tender, like she doesn't want to betray her mother's memory, but she also doesn't want to pretend it wasn't hard or that her mum didn't struggle. She talks about what it was like when her mum slipped in and out of depressive episodes, and how the last one, the one that finally took her life, was after a good stretch of a month or so where her mother was truly present, out of bed most days and doing the things Jenna and Jake didn't always have in preceding years; daily home-cooked meals, help with their homework, clean clothes folded and put away in their rooms, after-school conversations over cups of tea in the kitchen. I find comfort in the way she talks with both sadness and happiness, the balance somehow just right. I know the situation is completely different, but I hope one day I can talk about Arnie's diagnosis, his worst rounds of chemo and the last few days before he passed like that, with sweet fragility and even something like nostalgia. Most of the time, I can't even think about those days, especially not the end, without still feeling like my heart is rotting inside my chest.

"Did she look like you?" I ask, desperate to know.

Jenna stills in my lap and I wait, wondering what she's thinking. When she still doesn't speak, I put my hand up and turn her face towards me. There's a tear slipping down her right cheek.

"Oh, Jenna. I'm sorry, I didn't want to upset you." I kiss the tear away. I want to kiss all her tears away.

"I'm not upset. Just remembering," she says, and she nestles down into me, sitting back to look at the horizon again. "It's been a long time since I cried about her, it's almost nice."

My shoulders sink as I wrap my arms around her, bury my own head in her back.

"One day, you'll feel the same. About Arnie."

I nod into her body and we fall into a thoughtful silence again. I'm not good at silences, at least not with people I don't know. But with people I love, I think maybe silence is how I say the most.

"Wait here," Jenna says after some time. She then gets up and walks back into the villa.

When she returns, she's holding out her phone and showing me a photo of an old printed photograph taken on a sandy beach. The sun is shining, and the sea's blues meet those of the clear sky above. In the forefront of the image, there's a young girl, possibly around the age of six or seven, with a heavy fringe and impossibly big brown eyes. She's wearing a bright pink fringed T-shirt and denim shorts, weirdly an outfit I could imagine Jenna rocking right now. She's holding a young woman's hand - a woman wearing a long smock-style dress and oversized sunglasses - and both of them are grinning at the camera like their faces are incapable of anything else.

"You have the same smile," I say, but after looking more, that's actually about it. Jenna's mother has darker hair and smaller features, and by the looks of it, not the same height or curves as her daughter now. But that full smile that stretches out of nowhere, morphing her plump lips into the warmest reward of a grin, I would recognise that mouth anywhere.

"I look more like my dad, or his mother to be specific. Jake looks more like my mum, but he got dad's light hair and colouring. It's really strange to think Mum is a few years younger than me here."

"How old was she when she died?" I ask, taking her phone from her so I can zoom in and look closer at this adorable child version of Jenna.

"Forty-two," she whispers.

"That's no age," I say and then I move my eyes to Cathy's feet, catching the faintest line of gold on one foot; Jenna's anklet. I say nothing but reach out my hand to hold hers.

"No, it's not. I feel like her life was just about to come back to her too. Jake and I were getting older and were mostly independent. She would have had more time to do the things she enjoyed..." Jenna shakes her head suddenly. "Thank you for letting me talk about this and share with you. I haven't looked at this photo for a long time." She takes her phone out of my hand.

"Fuck, now I want kids with you." I reach for her again, she turns to straddle my legs, and I take her mouth.

"Marty," she says to break the kiss. I expected a denial, but the way she just said it sounds more like an invitation.

"Have I waited long enough? Can I fuck you now?" I move her hair to the side and suck on her neck.

"First Scrabble," she says.

"Are you fucking kidding me?" I lower my head to her chest all the while she rolls her pussy on my thighs.

"You have no idea how horny word games make me. I am a writer, after all," she says into my ear before sucking the lobe into her mouth.

"I feel like I have a lot of words now and none of them belong on a Scrabble board." I grab hold of her arse cheeks, unsure whether to use my hands to stop her or help her roll harder.

As soon as I deepen my grip and rock with her, she jumps up.

"Come on, O'Martin." She adjusts her dress. "Whoever wins decides what position."

"I don't give a fuck about positions, cupcake," I say with my best smirk.

She narrows her stare on me. "Okay then, whoever wins gets one of my toys... wherever they want."

My eyebrows shoot up. She knows I saw them. I pause only for a few seconds before I leap up, not giving a crap that my boner is probably pointing right at her, because I'm busy setting up the Scrabble board.

*****

Just over an hour later, I'm howling with laughter, having put down a seven-letter word on my last go, winning the game beyond any doubt. CARROTS. It's not elaborate or sophisticated by any stretch of the imagination, but it moves me to nearly 100 points in the lead. With a pout, she folds by knocking her tile holder over and putting down the pen she was using to keep score.

"Well played," Jenna says with the smallest, cutest scowl. "What's so funny?" she asks when I don't stop laughing.

I shake my head before I try to explain. "He's such a... he always said... oh, fuck. It's Arnie."

"What?"

"It's Arnie doing his guardian angel shit he promised me he'd do." I rest a hand on my chest. "I've never really believed he would or even really felt him much in this way, but right now, I know it's him. Here I am thrashing you - a professional writer - at Scrabble with a crappy food-related seven-letter word, and what do I get for winning?"

Jenna's giggling with me now.

"A dildo up my arse! He's stepping up when I need him most."

Jenna stands up to tidy up the letters. "You know I would have done that for you, win or no win."

"I know but let me have this," I say, laughing some more, as Jenna packs the game away. "It feels good to feel him close, and for it to not be when I'm sobbing and eating my own snot. Even I can't make that look sexy."

"Some people find crying a turn-on."

"Are you serious?" I straighten up my robe. I really should have a shower and get dressed.

"Dacryphilia," she says, as she walks around the table and picks up our now-empty coffee cups.

"Well, if it's got a Latin name, it must be real."

"Greek," she says with a side smile. "It's a Greek word."

"It's all double fucken Dutch to me," I say as I grab her and pull her between my now open legs. "How about we talk instead about what turns you on."

"Or I deliver on our deal?" Her smile turns wicked.

I can't stop myself clench with excitement. But then I remember our conversation earlier and impossibly, it's like the light in the sky brightens a little.

"Your pupils just dilated at lightning speed," she says as her hands come down to rest on my shoulders, close to my neck.

"I just remembered what we spoke about earlier," I admit. "No more condoms."

"I have been thinking about it non-stop. You're going to feel so good inside me, skin on skin."

That snaps the tight piece of elastic that was keeping me off her. In a single movement, I stand up, lift her by her waist and haul her up so she can wrap her legs around me. She doesn't feel as steady there as I would like, but we don't have far to go. I just need to get her to the bedroom where I am going to devour her body.

Chapter Forty

Jenna

After throwing me on the bed, he stops. Probably to catch his breath, possibly to think out his next move, maybe to take the sight of me in and commit it to memory, which is exactly what I'm doing looking up at him.

"I need a shower," he says.

"I don't care," I say in a hurried breath.

"I care," he says finally. "And I want to make you wait, like you made me wait."

"Marty," I say, and I think I'm going to laugh but it's more like a strangled, desperate plea.

"Wait," he says with a long-pointed finger I suddenly want in my mouth. "Don't move. And don't you dare touch yourself."

I throw my head and body back on the bed with a grunt.

"I mean it, Jenna," he says, his stern voice moving away from me.

He's a quick learner. The anticipation of knowing he is in there washing his body, touching skin I want to touch, is almost too much to bear. The heat between my legs starts to throb and ache. My nipples push against the fabric of my bra and I know without looking they'd be visible through the extra layer that is my cotton dress too. My breathing is no slower or deeper and my fingers literally shake with the urge to touch myself, but instead I just fist the bedsheets. I don't need to put my fingers anywhere near my pussy to know I am already very, very wet.

When I hear the shower turn off, a tap starts to run and then there's a gentle electric hum. I realise he's using my toothbrush and that little intimate detail somehow turns me on even more. I throw my arm over my eyes and laugh at how undone I am. I'm drowning in the kind of desire I dreamed of for years and I am delirious with joy that I am experiencing it again.

The stretch of time between hearing the toothbrush switch off and the moment when the bedroom door opens is the longest minute of my life. And the only thought I have during it is, how will I go days, weeks, or months without his touch when I can't even survive seconds without feeling like I'm losing my mind? But I quickly bury that conundrum as soon as I see him, standing again exactly where he was when he told me to wait and not touch myself. He is wearing nothing but a towel, and my eyes shoot straight to his waist to see if he is hard for me, but his hand is in front of what I want to see.

"Waiting isn't easy, is it, cupcake?" he smirks.

"Marty." I start to pull my dress up my legs, forcing his eyes in that direction. "I will happily wait a very long time for you."

"Happily?" He arches an eyebrow. "You don't look happy. You look... needy."

"I am. And we're running out of time, aren't we?" I ask, the dress now halfway up my thighs.

"In some ways, yes." He steps closer to me, his shins hitting the bedframe, but he doesn't flinch. "But in other ways, we're just getting started."

The dress is above my waist now and I let my legs fall open.

"Jenna." He exhales. "You're not wearing any underwear. Have you been like this the whole time?"

I nod. "Now do you want to make me wait?"

He doesn't reply, at least not with his voice. Instead, he falls to the ground and dives his head between my legs. With one strong, firm lick he glides his tongue up, parting me. With another, he finds my clit and flicks the tip of his tongue there back and forth, back and forth.

My hands go to his hair, and I hold him there for a while, rocking up into his licks and kisses, but when he starts to suck, I use my grip to move him away.

"No, Marty," I say. "Not yet. I want to come with you inside me."

"You can, you will," he says, placing gentle kisses and bites on my inner thighs and trying to nudge my hands away so he can go back for more.

"And I promised you one of my toys," I remind him.

He lifts up to look at me. "I don't want that. I mean, I do but not now. I will cash that win in for sure, but all I could think about in the shower was your pussy. This is all I want, right now. Like this," he bends to lick my clit, "and then like this." He pushes two fingers inside me and strokes my front wall. My belly convulses. "And then I want to feel it all with my dick, all of you." His fingers go deeper, and they scissor from side to side.

"Yes, that's what I want. But please fuck me," I beg, riding his hand. "Please, I love you, please."

His mouth goes back on me as his fingers keep caressing me inside and I give up begging for his dick because this is just as good. Fuck, no, this is possibly better because I am so much more aware of where his tongue is, what his digits are doing, and where they're stroking me so deep, so very, very deep and...

"Oh, shit," I say, and I clench my thighs around his head.

"What?" He jolts back and I relax my legs.

It's just how it was the last few times this happened. Times when I was on my own, with a toy or toys, plunging one inside me, vibrating another around my clit for long, long minutes, taking my time and discovering myself. It's exactly the same now as it was then; I really do feel like I'm going to wet myself.

"You okay?" Marty says, and his voice is clearer because his lips are off me although his fingers keep thrusting gently and deeply inside me. I squeeze my muscles to stroke them back.

"So good," I reply, and I throw my head back and surrender, only the smallest part of me worrying he won't like it. "Stay deep, just like that."

He does as he's told, his fingers completely hidden, penetrating and probing deep inside me. His mouth is back too and the slick warmth of his tongue finding a perfect rhythm circling around my clit is everything I need.

"Marty," I gasp as my hands grip his head again and I rock myself into his mouth as the pressure builds and that feeling returns. I fight the urge to resist it and instead I even push a little, actively releasing all the delicious pressure that's building and... "Fuck!" I squeeze my eyes shut as my orgasm hits.

It's hearing it that tells me it happened. A light tinny tinkling sound as my cum hits Marty's face, once, twice. I take this confirmation with me as I shudder through my orgasm, the pleasure making me twitch and shake. As the waves die down, I release my grip on his hair and cover my face with my hands, laughing and a little embarrassed, but mostly, mostly elated.

Only when my giggles subside do I dare a quick look at Marty and see him straightening up and wiping his face with his left hand, and then put all four of his fingers in his mouth, sucking. That's when I realise his right hand is still inside me. And that makes me cover my face again, now because I feel blinded by how much I am feeling in this moment.

"That was fucking epic," he says.

"I haven't..." I try to speak but I can't. I'm still out of breath and totally spaced out from such an overwhelming orgasm. "It's been a long time since I've done that. I didn't know I still could."

"I feel like I have a new life purpose. To make you do that again, and again, and again." He kisses my knee. Then he pulls my leg straight up against his chest, finds my gold anklet and kisses that too.

I go back to being a wordless lump of flesh as I let myself consider his words.

"Jesus, Jenna. Look at you," he says. I lift my head and look at my pussy still rocking against his hand, my nipples hard and hungry, my leg on his chest and body completely open to him. "You're a brilliant, beautiful mess for me."

And he's right, so very right.

Then I see him rising above me, his towel gone and his cock long and hard and pointing to the sky.

"Still want me?" he asks.

"Always," I reply.

He nods his head in a way that I know means I need to move further up the bed. After shuffling back, I open my legs again and he lies himself down between them.

Marty has one hand near my head, holding his body up, and the other is guiding himself towards my opening.

"So wet," he says as his head touches me.

"So soft," he says as his crown fills my opening.

"So warm," he whispers as his mouth comes close to my ear, his chest pressing down on mine, and his cock drives up and in.

"Yes," I hiss and feel new bubbles of pleasure burst inside me.

"This feels better than how I imagined," he pants out as he thrusts into me again, long and slow. "And I imagined it would feel like heaven."

So very suddenly my lust is muted with the bone-deep urge to cry, and I give into it immediately. I give in to all the things I've tried to put off thinking and feeling today, and maybe over the last few days too.

How unfair it is that we are not closer in age. How hard it feels that we live in different countries. How difficult it will be when he is there, and I am somewhere else. How wrong it will feel to say goodbye to him tomorrow. How insurmountable all these obstacles feel right now. And by consequence, how bleak the future looks no matter what we promise each other today, because we won't be together on an island in the sun anymore.

The only good thing about crying right now is that it keeps my next orgasm a little further away, so I can focus on the way his body rides up above me, every single one of his muscles flexing tight. How his eyes are firmly closed, and his top teeth are clamping down on his bottom lip. How there's an almost strained expression hardening his jaw and making his Adam's apple bob when he swallows every few thrusts, thrusts that are now speeding up.

But then his eyes flicker open and he sees my tears and whatever pained expression I have on my face.

"Shit." He stills, his pupils darting left and right. "I'm sorry. Is it too hard? Did I hurt you?"

I shake my head profusely. "No." I sigh and lift my hands to stroke his cheeks, his stubble rough against my fingers. "I'm just sad about tomorrow. I've been trying so hard not to be, but I am. I can't help it."

I feel the breath of his exhale on my nose and mouth.

"I know," he says. "I'm sad too."

"But don't stop," I say, wrapping my legs around his waist. "Please don't stop."

"Are you sure?"

I nod. "I may not come, because I'm not great at separating my emotions from my orgasms, but I am still enjoying every second. I want this. I want you."

I'm not sure if it's because of my tears, or because he wants to be gentler on me, but he lowers his body again so it's flat against mine and he starts to rock into me rather than thrust. He lies his forearms flat on either side of my head and he dips his head to kiss me, a slow, unhurried kiss that has more fragility than hunger and is more calming than craving. It's what I didn't realise I needed. A reminder that we still have time, albeit not as much as I would like. A prompt for me to hold space for feeling sad but to also make plenty of room for also feeling so very happy at the same time. An invitation to enjoy loving him as much as I cherish feeling loved by him. A reminder that while this will all stop tomorrow, at least we had it. At least we found each other for these blissful five days.

Feeling soothed, if not resolved, there is space again for my desire to burn bright. When he moves his mouth away to kiss my cheeks, my eyebrows, and at my temples, I grip his butt cheeks with my hands and push him into me deeper, applying a little extra pressure on my clit. Responding to my grip and the way I roll my hips up towards him, he makes his strokes longer, harder.

I swallow a moan at how good it feels.

"I lied," I whisper.

"What?" he says, leaning back to look at me.

"I am going to come," I say. "And soon..."

"Good." He almost grunts and starts to move his hips in a circle. "Because I want to watch you come."

"Are you close?" I somehow manage to ask in a breathy exhale.

"Close enough."

"Oh, Marty," I say as I feel myself slip past the point of no return.

"Come for me, Jenna." He speeds up a little, still fully in control, which I realise I need in this moment. I need him to fuck me, for him to be the one in charge.

"Yes, like that, don't stop," I mumble, closing my eyes.

"Come for me, Jenna," he says again. But it's his next words that undo me. "Give me something to remember you by when we're apart."

I do as he says. Panting and moaning and saying his name, my body convulsing, and small high-pitched gasps leaving my lips when another strong surge comes out of nowhere. When I finally open my eyes, a warm glow spreading through my body, I watch as the strain is back on his face and in his arms and chest. Lifting my head, I graze my teeth over the bump in his nose like I did the first night we met.

"Come inside me, Marty," I say. "Make me never forget you."

And he does. Pushing up on his hands, he starts thrusting in earnest and a few seconds later, I feel the heat and the force of him spilling inside me once, twice, three, maybe four times, all the while swearing and cursing and saying my name. When he slows down gradually, rocking into me still as if he can't stop himself, I feel the familiar crescendo of another orgasm build and I can't stop my hands from pushing him down on me with more force.

"Oh, God," is all I can manage to say as I come again. I close my eyes, feeling him watch me, feeling him smile at me, feeling him love me.

Eventually, Marty collapses on me and his weight brings me back down to Earth. I know I should pee. I know I should clean up. I know I should try and stay awake so the day isn't wasted, but I can't. I can't do anything but pray that he never gets off me.

"I'm fucken shattered. Will we have a short nap?" he whispers in my ear.

I don't have the energy to reply. I don't even have the energy to lift my own body and get under the covers, so when I feel Marty move off me, and then gently lift my torso and move me so my head hits the pillow, I let him do it all. The only things keeping me awake are the fact Marty is not in bed next to me, and that there's a new dampness seeping out of me, but a few seconds later, I feel a warm wet towel between my legs and a kiss on my belly button. Marty is cleaning me. Moments later he slides into bed beside me, wrapping an arm around my waist.

And then I fall asleep, still not wanting to squander my time with him, but also knowing this is anything but wasted time.

The Last Sunset

"Sunsets are proof that endings can often be beautiful too."
— Beau Taplin

Chapter Forty-One

Jenna

We sleep for longer than I would like, but when I open my eyes, roll over and see his face at rest, blissed out, relaxed, it's worth it. I stroke his chest as it rises and falls. I kiss his shoulder and put my nose to his skin and inhale it.

We are so animal when we love. It's all about smells and touch and what our gut tells us is right. It's not perfect or logical, but it's instinctive and real. It's not an exact or predictable science, but a heady mix of chemicals and magic. There is only so much logic that can explain why I feel the way I feel about him, and it's that missing element of sense that makes it all so enchanting. It's that part of the equation that I want to excavate and examine under a microscope, but also happily let it be wild and unwieldy.

My thoughts and gaze have drifted far away from this moment and by the time Marty stirs under me and my gaze lands back on his face, it startles me that his eyes are open and fixed on mine.

"Hey," I say.

"Hey," he says.

"You want to go swim? Take a jacuzzi? Play another round of Scrabble? Or cash in your bet from earlier?" I waggle my eyebrows and he laughs.

"I want to do it all." He reaches for me, pulls me to him as his arm goes around my waist. "What time is it? Do we have time to do it all?"

I glance at my watch. "It's nearly three. We have time to do it all, but we do need to make sure we fit something else in. Something more important than anything."

"More important than board games and butt fun? What else could that possibly be?"

I chuckle and put my head on his shoulder. "Take a guess."

"The sunset."

And I kiss his skin in response.

Yes, the sunset. Our last sunset.

Somehow, I don't dissolve into tears. I manage to sit up, pull him with me and get us a bottle of water each and some peanuts from the mini bar and make him play Scrabble with me again under the shade of a parasol.

I focus so hard on the game, it helps me win. Then we lather up our bodies with sun cream and go about doing the most ridiculous jumps into the pool, completely naked. I make him do all the poses that he did for Maeve's video, and he then barks out new ones for me to do – playing rugby, whisking eggs, cleaning a toilet - and again I choke on water from laughing so hard. I do the same for him and we take it in turns taking photos on our phones, photos I already know I'll look at hundreds of times in the future.

After he pours me a glass of wine from the mini bar while he grabs a Coke, we get into the jacuzzi, still naked, where our hands are ready to roam each other again and we both rush through our drinks and drying off so we can make our way to the bedroom and the fun that lies ahead there.

And what fun it is.

It is exploratory sex at its best. Rooted in trust and love, we give each other parts of our bodies that aren't easy to share, but are rewarded with surprising sensations of pleasure, and the right kind of pain. We dive into it all so deeply that when we emerge from it, sated and sore, the sky has already changed colour.

I make a quick phone call for room service - two burgers, fries and virgin mojitos - and then we get into the pool, him naked but me in a swimming costume as I need to let room service in. This time, I position him facing the sunset, his arms resting on the infinity edge of the pool in almost exactly the same place he fucked me two days ago, and I stand behind him, wrapping my body around his, looking at the view over his shoulder.

We don't speak much, and I'm glad. Words are now scary things, because they risk taking us to places I am not yet ready to go. Instead, I turn to the recent past and the one question I feel I still need an answer to.

"Marty," I say softly after kissing his back. "I need to ask you a question."

"Okay," he says, and I feel his torso tense.

"The motorbike accident in Ibiza? Was it an accident?"

His sigh is heavy and hollow. "The truth is, I don't know. I can't remember that day. None of it. Even the day before is sketchy. I hit my head pretty bad, and the doctors said I had severe concussion so short-term memory loss wouldn't be surprising. I only remember waking up in hospital." He sighs again, this time in more of a rush, like he's desperate to say something. "I know what the witnesses said. I know what it must have looked like. I mean, I'm not the world's best driver, but even I know not to accelerate into a brick wall. I know I was pretty low at that point, but I don't know if I wanted to end it all. I certainly don't think I was planning on it or thinking about it for weeks or days before. And I definitely know that when I woke up in hospital, and was told how badly I was hurt, well, I remember so clearly how that made me feel. I remember so vividly the first thought I had..." His voice trails off.

"What was it?" I prompt after a few seconds.

"Like I was so close to touching Arnie again," he says with an audible smile. But a beat later, it's gone. "Like he was right there, and I got so close, but I blew it. I couldn't even get that right."

It feels like my heartbeat stops and an ice cold breeze finds me out of nowhere.

"But then the nurses told me my parents were on their way and I knew just as certainly that I wasn't ready to leave this life. I mean, you know if I'm excited to see my parents after I'd basically disappeared for six months and I knew that they were going to roast the living shit out of me, then I had some lust for life left in me."

"You wanted to live?"

"Yes, I wanted to live. I wanted to get better. I wanted to remember Arnie in the way he deserved to be remembered, and I wanted to honour his life in a way he deserved."

"Marty, I think you do that," I whisper, resting my forehead on his back. "I think you will always do that."

Silence returns and I lift my eyes a little to find the sunset again, almost ready to watch our last one together on this island. It's many minutes later when Marty speaks again.

"I don't really believe in the afterlife or spirits or even fate much." His voice is dry and deep, and it cuts through the air like it's everywhere. "But if I *was* one to believe in that stuff, if I was someone who really believed in angels for example, I would have some questions for Arnie about what happened the day I met you."

I don't reply, can't reply, but I push my head a little harder onto him. I wish I could disappear into Marty's body, bury myself in him and stay there just to carry some of his grief for him.

"Would you hate it if I thought Arnie sent you to me? Would you think that was batshit crazy?"

I shake my head again and finally, finally feel brave enough to raise my head and move my body so I can look at him. He turns too and cups my face.

"I'll never replace him," I say, because that's the most important thing to say. I should have said it sooner.

"God, no," Marty says, and his voice also sounds choked. "But I think that's one of the reasons I love you, Jenna. You don't take away from my love for him."

I crash my mouth onto his, smearing my suddenly wet cheeks against his, and I use the kiss to slow my breath and my tears. I kiss him until I stop crying and I feel him harden against me. Then I reach down, move my swimsuit to the side and slide him inside me. We don't fuck, we just line up and stay joined together, and we stay like that for many silent minutes.

Finally, Marty speaks. "I should have money for flights to London in a few weeks," he whispers in my ear.

"Marty, I don't want you to bankrupt yourself to come and see me," I say, pulling back to look at him.

His shoulders sink a little. "I owe so much money already, you could say I'm already bankrupt."

I open my mouth, but Marty continues to speak. "Please don't offer to pay for them. Or say you'll come to me. I still live with my parents. That's not going to be a good look no matter how much I suspect they may like you now."

"It would bother me if you were struggling to pay for flights to London," I say simply. This much is true, and he deserves whatever truth I can give him.

"You made me a promise." His jaw tightens.

"I did?" I blink.

"You promised me tomorrow wouldn't be goodbye forever."

"I did," I confirm.

"Please don't break that promise," he says, his voice low.

"I love you, Marty."

"That's not answering my question."

"Didn't I also promise you something else?" I put my fingers in his hair, run my nails all over his scalp.

"What?" He bends into my touch.

"That everything will be okay." I push up to kiss the firm edge of his chin.

It takes longer than I expect but he finally melts a little, leans into me and eventually, finds my mouth and kisses me back. I don't know who starts to move first, him or me, but together we rock our bodies in a rhythm only we know until I'm squeezing him and he's filling me, and I close my eyes to the future.

After, when he slips out of me, we both sigh and he tightens his arms around me as if to compensate. And that's how I stay until the sun has sunk so far down that when I finally open my eyes, the world is a completely different colour.

Chapter Forty-Two

The Next Day

Marty

It's the first morning I beat my dad. And I don't just beat him. I thrash him. I'm racing up our climb and speeding down the descent like my life depends on it, which feels entirely plausible considering I am approaching my final few hours with Jenna. I enjoy the muscle burn, the views of the island and of the beach where Jenna and I had our day together, but I also regret leaving her side. When we're about five kilometres away from the resort, winding around the zig-zagging coastal road, I look back at Dad and he lifts his hand and waves me on, and I hope he knows how grateful I am.

I didn't want to go on the bike ride, but last night, after our sunset swim and then a long hot shower, she told me she was too exhausted to pack and that she would need time in the morning to do it, so she suggested I get up at the same time and do my ride with Dad. She had the alarm set before I could convince her otherwise, and I wasn't about to spend our last night together arguing with her. Not when I could lie in bed, sniffing her hair and feeling her stomach rise and fall under my hand as I drifted off to sleep.

There is relief when I burst into our villa and Mum only says hello as I rush to get showered. I smile when I come out of the shower and find a cup of coffee and a pastry waiting for me by my bed where she usually leaves a glass of water. They taste all kinds of wrong after I've cleaned my teeth, but I hastily gulp both down.

"Thanks, Ma!" I call out as I pull on clean underwear, shorts and a T-shirt.

"I'll see you later," I say as I charge to the front door.

"Good luck!" Mum calls out.

"Say goodbye from us!" Maeve yells.

Goodbye. Goodbye. I don't want to say goodbye. I'm not going to say goodbye. Because this is not goodbye.

And those are the first words that leave my mouth when I'm finally at her villa and she's opening the door to my incessant banging.

"We are going to see each other again. We are going to make this work." I stare down at her.

Jenna is smiling, and she has never looked better. She's wearing jeans and a white T-shirt, the kind of casual, normal-life outfit I'm yet to see her in and I love how good it looks. It boosts my confidence that our love can also carry on in our normal lives, and that I will get to see her in any number of other outfits in years to come; winter coats, Christmas pyjamas, evening dresses, sexy lingerie...

"Come in," she says. "I have about half an hour before I need to head down for the car."

"We," I say. "We are heading down together. I'm coming with you in the taxi."

"Marty, you don't have to. It will take over two hours to get there and the same again back. That's a waste of your day."

"Don't argue with me, Jenna. I've made up my mind."

Her shoulders lower and her expression softens as she acquiesces. "Fine," she says. "You know what you want and who am I to stand in the way of it?"

That right there is why I love her. Because she trusts me to make my own decisions.

"Are you all packed?" I ask.

"Yes," she nods to where her luggage stands.

I can only look at her suitcase quickly before putting my eyes somewhere else. It hurts more than it should.

"I still can't convince you to stay two more days?" I ask.

She shakes her head slowly. "There's no room in the inn," she says. "Thanks to Maeve. My brother needs all the available villas he has thanks to her."

"There's plenty of room in my bed." I step closer, needing to hold her while I still can.

"And that would be a sure way to stop any growing fondness for me that your parents may have. You know I make a lot of noise," she says with a soft wink and I'm filling my shorts a little more at the reminder.

"Do we have time for a quickie?" I push my pelvis against her.

Her eyes roll back in her head as she looks up at me, her mouth in that dangerously delicious pout. "I think we need to talk, Marty."

I nod. I've been wanting to talk with her for days but felt her resistance too many times to push harder. She promised me she wouldn't end it, and I remind myself of that as I keep hold of her hands and take us further into the room. I perch on the sofa arm and she stands between my legs, meaning I am looking up at her for a change.

"Okay," I say. "I'm listening."

"Marty," she says, and her hands are on my face, her eyes bearing down into me as they fill with tears. "Shit, I had this all figured out. I even practised a handful of times. It all sounded so good."

"I don't need a speech, Jenna, I just need to know I can see you again," I say.

"Yes," she says. "Yes, you can see me again."

"Thank fuck for that," I say, grabbing handfuls of her butt and pulling her closer.

She places a flat palm on my chest, directly over where my heart beats for her.

"But not for five years," she adds in the quietest, most devastating voice.

"What?" I feel like I've been shot. Straight in my heart. I flatten my palm against her hand on my chest, like the pressure will stem the flow of pain that's there.

"Five years?"

"Yes." Her tears spill over and slide down the freckles on her cheeks, but somehow she holds onto a smile.

"Why?" My head is spinning. It makes no sense.

"Marty, I love you. I am in love with you. I want to be with you. But I don't think it will work if we try now. You are so young..."

My spine elongates. "No, Jenna, no. Please don't play the age card."

"It's not a card to play. It's the truth. You *are* young. And you've been through so much the last few years." Her fingers are stroking me through my T-shirt. It feels like both heaven and hell.

"All the more reason why I need this," I say. "Why I need you."

She pauses, swallows, and looks down at our hands. "I don't want you to *need* me, Marty. I want you to love me and have me as your partner. Not your crutch."

"Is that what you think you are to me?" My mouth falls open.

"No." Her eyes are back on me – dry again, and more serious. "I don't think that at all, but I worry that's what it *could* be."

"I would never, Jenna, I..."

She's quick to interrupt. "And I worry you would become the same for me. I'm still healing from my divorce too. I still have things I need to figure out and work through."

"Why can't we do it together?"

"How, Marty? With trips here and there? With you working a lot of weekends, it's just not sustainable. It will get stressful very quickly, and you don't need stress in your life right now. I don't want to be a source of stress to you."

"You are the literal opposite of that to me," I begin.

"Right now," Jenna interjects. She glances up and her eyes rest on the view through the double doors. "In this little paradise, away from the rest of the world. But we can't live here, Marty. The real world is waiting for us. You will change, I will change. Whatever we feel now, it will change. Like I said, I don't want to play the age card-"

"Then don't," I interrupt.

"But I've been here before. I had all this magic and spark and joy and sex - all the wonderful sex - and the connection, and it faded away when things got hard and I needed space to grow. And honestly, I don't think I can survive this spark dying because you didn't have space to grow."

"Who says it has to?"

"It's what happens. Of course, you don't know this yet."

"I asked you not to say shit like that." I grit my teeth. I feel dangerously close to losing it, but really, I know it's more dangerously close to losing her.

"And I am asking you to not play the youthful magic card. I know you see the world differently, with all its shine and possibility, and in some ways that's the thing I want to protect by doing this."

"But five years..." It's an eternity. I was still a teenager five years ago. Arnie and I weren't even together. I didn't know who I was.

"One for every sunset we've shared..." Her voice is so full of pain I can't bear it.

"Jesus, Jenna!" I have a sudden urge to pull out of her grasp but I daren't. I worry if I do, she won't let me back in. Instead, I hang my head low and heavy on her shoulder. "It's such a long fucking time."

"I know," she says, her voice breaking. It's only a small comfort to have her fall apart with me.

I decide to level with her. "You know you're doing the one thing I thought you'd never do. You're telling me I don't know what's best for me. You're trying to make that decision for me."

"Marty, no," she begins but the protest drops from her voice quickly. "Well, actually, yes. You're right. That is how it sounds, and I can understand that's how it may feel, but this decision isn't about that. It's about what I think is best for me too. I am also vulnerable and scared and fragile right now. I've not had anything like the loss you have but I have had a huge life change and I still feel lost and I don't know what I want my future to look like. I need some time and space to figure that out. And the way I feel about you... Oh, God, Marty, the way I feel about you. It's not for the faint of heart. So, I want to make my heart stronger. I want to make myself stronger. I want to be the best version of myself for you."

"But I love you as you are, right now," I say, lifting my head and digging my fingertips into her flesh at her waist. "Why not five months? Or just one year? Bollocks to the symbolism of it all."

"I think it has to be longer. It has to be years," she says slowly, her hands now smoothing out my T-shirt on my shoulders. "You're still very deep in your grief about Arnie. I have to figure out my career and I want us to have all the time and energy we need to tackle both of those things. Even if that wasn't the case, you are just twenty-four. When I think about who I was at that age and who I was five years later, it's not the same person."

"I don't think you would expect me to stay the same person. I certainly don't expect you to never change."

"That's true, and I love that," she says. It's almost patronising, except there is too much kindness and love in her eyes as she looks down at me.

"I don't think I can do five years," I say because honesty is all I'm capable of.

"Maybe it will go quickly. If we both stay busy..." she says but there's nothing certain in her voice, it just sounds like air.

"It's forever. I've only had five days with you!" I pull her back into me, but her body feels a lot more rigid now.

"I'm sorry I'm hurting you." Her arms come around my waist and I feel her stroke the my back. Her touch is so gentle and intentional that for a few brief moments, I exhale and relax into it, but immediately that peace is tinged with the sadness when I remember that nobody touches me like her. And nobody will for five fucking years.

"And we really won't see each other?" I ask, my mouth back in her hair. "Can we talk? Can I text and call?"

She shakes her head against my chest. "No, I don't think so."

"But why? If I'm not seeing you then it's still time apart."

"I want you to explore other options," she says quietly. "Other lovers, or partners."

"What the fuck, Jenna!?"

Her whole body sighs. "I'm not saying this because I want that to happen, but I do want you to be as happy as you can possibly be, and if that's with someone else, Marty..." She takes another breath. "Well, I'd never be able to forgive myself if you missed out on that."

Her words are so cruel and yet so deeply laced with love. It makes no sense and yet I know there's truth there. "How can you even think like this?"

"Because..." She pauses and I wait. She doesn't have an answer for me and instead continues talking like I never asked. "After five years, if you still think what you feel for me can go the distance, we'll give it a go."

Swallowing, I feel how heavy the lump in my throat is. "I can't have nothing. I can't just go from this to not hearing from you again. In five years, you'll have forgotten about me."

Her smile shrinks into a very knowing pout as she shakes her head looking down at me. "You have to trust me when I say I will never forget about you, Marty."

"I need something to hold on to," I say. "I need to know I can contact you if I need to."

She sighs but there's no impatience in it, only fatigue and sorrow. "You can have my address. And if you want, you can give me yours."

"I want," I say although it feels like begging for crumbs.

"But we make no promises to each other. I don't expect you to get in touch. I don't expect letters, or anything."

"Oh, you'll get letters. I've never had a pen pal before," I say, and my first attempt at a joke in this conversation lands as miserably as it's delivered.

Her pulling back is instant. "No, not pen pals, Marty. Just, if you need to get in touch with me for an important or urgent reason, then you can, but it has to be by post. That way you have to think about it before, during and after you do it. Texts and emails are too easy and quick."

"You want me to have time to stop myself contacting you?" I hold her elbows and give her a little tug as if to pull her back in, back into reality, maybe, but she doesn't move, not an inch.

"Yes and no," she says. "Like all of this, it's yes and no."

This is when I start to tell myself things to try to make myself feel better. I don't want to spend any more time arguing with her. She still has a flight to catch after all and I don't want to waste a single second with hostility. This is why I tell myself that I will agree to her suggestion, but I will keep in touch. I will send her notes and letters and make her realise that I cannot be without her, that I will wait however long I need to and then we will be together. Unless...

"What if *you* meet someone?" I ask. "What if you meet someone and you fall in love and you have those babies you maybe want."

"I still don't really know how I feel about kids," she says. "But I know you are not ready for them."

I nod. That much is true.

"But these are your years for it." It chills me to my core to think of her having children with someone else, but the idea of her missing out on it, that would hurt me too.

"They are," she says. The corners of her eyes and mouth fall and for a second, I think she's about to cry again. "But honestly, I'm not even thinking about that right now."

"But you might meet someone," I say again.

She shrugs. "I might. And *you* might," she adds with more emphasis.

"This sucks so fucking much!" I turn my head and shout out to the room.

"Yeah, it does." She is crying now, so I stand up and pull her back into my chest and we wait like that for her tears to dry and for my brain to formulate a plan to keep her close.

I am not losing this woman. I am not losing her.

I am not losing another person I love, especially not now I don't have to.

Jenna breaks the silence by sucking in a deep breath. "I really do want you to try and meet other people. Take other lovers. Give yourself to them."

"Do I get a say in this?" I ask sounding everything I feel; angry, sad, disappointed, scared, frustrated, hopeless, and yet still, despite it all, hopeful.

"Of course," she says quietly. Her hands grip my back and I can feel how many of her silent tears have soaked my T-shirt.

"You think I haven't felt like this before. You think I'm all high on how good this feels, but I'm not. You forget I have been in love before. Arnie and I fell in love slowly and awkwardly, with lots of stops and starts and mistakes made along the way. But this, this was so quick and oh-so-fucken easy. This feels more real, more mature, more solid, which makes no sense considering he and I had nearly

358

a decade of friendship before we even kissed, and we've only had five days, but I trust how it feels. I trust how I feel about you now. I... I..." I cough, swallow down the solid ball in my oesophagus one more time. "I thought Arnie was forever, and maybe he would have been if it had played out differently. It wasn't my love ending that stopped our forever, it was his life on this planet ending. None of us are guaranteed forever, Jenna. I just want as many days as I can have with you. I don't want to waste a single day."

"They won't be wasted days," she replies. "Not if we live them with love."

She leans back and searches my eyes for a few seconds before resting her forehead on my chest again. My chin automatically falls to the top of her head, locking her in place.

"I don't want anything to happen to you and for me to not be there," I say in a quieter voice.

Her laugh is small and weak. "Now, I know I'm old, Marty, but I'm not that old. As far as I know I have many more years left."

My exhale is one of defeat. "And what then, in five years?"

Jenna turns her head to look out of the door, at the swimming pool we made love in, jumped in naked, held each other in as the sun sank into the sea that stretches further than we can see. "How do you feel about coming back here?"

"In five years?"

"Five years to the day," she says. "How's that for romance?"

"I fecking love the romance of it, but the five years part scares the shit out of me. You're asking a lot of the man who doesn't even know what he's doing next week."

"I don't know that, either, Marty," she says, still staring outside. "That's why I'm asking for this time so we can both get a better handle on our lives and make plans for the future."

"Didn't someone famous say 'life is what happens when you're busy making plans'?"

"John Lennon," she says, kissing me once, twice, her hands in my hair. "But he also said 'a dream you dream alone is only a dream. A dream you dream together is reality'."

"Now who has an answer for everything I say?" I whisper into her lips.

I feel her tears on my cheek as she speaks. "I don't mind us being a dream, Marty. It will be the sweetest dream of my life."

"My dreams torture me," I say, my words full of tears. "I dream about Arnie and then wake up to remember he's gone."

"Well, give yourself the gift of this dream." She holds me tighter as we both shake with crying. "If you want this dream, it's yours. It's ours."

We stay like that until our sobs ease and our tears slow. I am the first to pull back and speak again. I feel she's carried the conversation enough and it's my turn. It's my turn to be strong.

"So, five years, back here? You and me?" I ask, gripping her upper arms firmly.

"I think I would like that." I see her trying to smile, my beautiful, brave Jenna.

"And then..."

"And then... then we take it day by day."

"Sunset by sunset?" I offer, feeling the smallest, thinnest, most threadbare piece of hope. I'm not sure it's big enough for me to hold on to, but I know I have to try.

"Sunset by sunset." She turns her head to bury her nose against my ribcage again and I close my eyes as I feel her leave kiss after kiss after kiss there, and tear and tear after tear.

Chapter Forty-Three

Jenna

I know I'll never forget the taxi ride to the airport.

The way Marty interlaces his fingers with mine and holds our hands against his solid thigh. The way I feel each pad of his fingertips on my skin, and how sweaty our palms get but neither of us lets go. The way he looks out of the window for long minutes until something seems to snap his attention back to me, and he studies me in such a desperate way I wonder what it was that prompted him to look. The way, as our car weaves across the island, I put more and more of my body weight against him until my head is resting on his shoulder and the peace I feel doing that is almost reason enough for me to tell him I didn't mean it, I take it back, we should try and make it work, now. The way that, conversely but comfortingly, I have moments of calm, knowing any other outcome would have me worried, panicked, fearful, more uncertain. The way I use these moments of calm to commit today's date to memory, hoping he's done the same. The way I hope there is traffic around every corner to slow us down, only for my heart to break all over again when there isn't.

Then there's the way I ask him not to come inside the airport with me, to instead take the taxi straight back. The way he protests a few times, but when I turn my head and kiss his neck and he feels new tears there, he stops. The way neither of us say another word to each other the whole journey. The way that both shatters my heart but at the same time, somehow, starts the slow process of sticking fragments of it back together, albeit in a completely different arrangement to how my heart was before I met him.

Once we are at the airport, the heat and the crowds confronting me as my door opens, I let out a heavy breath before swinging my legs out of the car.

But I'm stopped by Marty who keeps my hand firmly in his, pinning it down to his leg.

"Promise me this is not goodbye forever," he says. "Because I just can't believe that it is."

"I don't want *you* to promise *me* that, Marty," I clarify.

"Promise me," he says and the tinge of aggression and pure passion in his voice dissolves my insides.

"I promise you," I say.

"And..."

"And everything will be okay," I say with much less hesitation. In fact, this is what makes me climb into his lap and kiss him long and hard, while other doors slam shut and car horns beep and people wheeling their suitcases make noises outside. When I know I'll never be ready to stop this kiss, I break it, lifting my lips to wrap them around the bump on his nose, grazing it with my teeth.

"I promise everything will be okay," I say, my lips moving against his skin. "I love you."

"I love you," he says into my neck and then I slide off his legs and move to the door, my limbs as heavy and stiff as stone.

I gift myself one last look at him before I close the door, reach for my suitcase, and walk away.

Chapter Forty-Four

Marty

I manage to sit in the taxi the whole way back and not cry. I manage to walk out of the car and climb the path up to my villa without shedding a tear. I manage to unlock the door, make my way through the villa, ignoring my parents' voices and not looking up when Maeve stands to greet me, and still not sob. I get all the way into my room, gently close the door behind me, and collapse into bed and then I finally give myself permission to cry. Permission to sob, permission to moan, permission to howl out my pain.

But the tears don't come. It hurts too much.

I curl into a ball, make a fist, lodge it between my teeth and do the one thing that I have been so scared to do since Arnie died. I stay still and feel my pain and my sorrow. I don't try to stop the chaos I feel.

And it fucking hurts.

It's instant vindication for my past decisions. Of course, I chose to drink and fuck and get high rather than feel this. It's understandable I filled my life with noise rather than the emptiness of nothing that only exists because someone you love can no longer fill it with their laughter, their words, their body.

But with the pain, there is something else, although it is formless and nameless. It's not a comfort as such, just a tender, almost hopeful, awakening as I realise it's happening. I'm still here. The pain feels all-consuming, but it hasn't actually consumed me. Not in this moment.

Maybe, everything really will be okay.

I don't hear a knock if there is one. I don't hear her steps or words if there are any. The first sign of my mother is her hands placing a glass of water and a strip of paracetamol tablets on my bedside table. Then the bed dips as she sits beside me, and I feel her hand come up to my shoulder.

"Marty, sweetheart," she says.

"Ma," I say as I push up. "She's gone. She's gone, and I don't know if I'll ever see her again."

"Oh, Marty, my wee boy," she says, and she pulls me in, holds me close. "I'm so sorry she's gone. But it will all be okay. I promise, it will all be okay."

And I don't know if it's because those are the last words I heard Jenna say or if it's because it's her, my mother, the one I know will always love me, will always be there for me no matter what, but I finally start crying, sobbing, really heaving the pain out of my body, and I let her words and her embrace be a balm to my crushed heart.

Chapter Forty-Five

The First 365 Sunsets

Marty

I send my first postcard the day after I get back. I purchased it from Dublin airport - a cheesy postcard with a pint of Guinness in one corner, the Ha'penny Bridge below it and next to them a dated photo of The Temple Bar pub – and had the message written and a stamp on it that night. I then got up early the following morning for a ten-kilometre run in the rain and posted it at the first post-box I saw. Even though I had it tucked in the back of my shorts and boxers, a fact I painfully wished I could have shared with Jenna, the Irish drizzle still managed to get at it and the first few lines were blurred with droplets.

JENNA, IT'S BEEN 48 HOURS AND I THINK I'M DYING. IF I DIDN'T LOVE YOU SO MUCH, I WOULD HATE YOU FOR DOING THIS. BUT I DO LOVE YOU. SO MUCH. P.S. THE SUNSETS WERE SHITE AFTER YOU LEFT.

The second postcard is also from Dublin. This time, a shot of Trinity College I chose and posted on a whim one surprisingly warm evening in September. I'd just watched the sunset during a long bike ride with Dad that took us out in County Wicklow, and we stopped at the corner shop at the end of our street to pick up milk at Mum's request. Since the last one I sent went unanswered, I'd been trying to put off sending another, but the sunset had been too beautiful and my mind was always so full of her, I couldn't wait any longer.

JENNA, IT'S BEEN THREE MONTHS AND IT STILL FEELS LIKE I'M DYING. YET I'M STILL HERE. I SACKED OFF UNI FOR GOOD AND WORK FULL-TIME AT DERMOT'S. THEY ADDED THE MARTY

PARTY TO THE DRINKS MENU. IT KILLS ME IN THE BEST WAY WHEN I SEE PEOPLE DRINKING IT. I LOVE YOU, MARTY.

I send my third postcard from France on a Christmas ski trip with my parents, Maeve, my uncle Dermot and his kids. It's not the worst trip in the world but I miss both Arnie and Jenna in equal measure, thinking how Arnie would shit himself on the black runs and how good Jenna would look with ski gear gripping her curves. It feels like a true achievement when I make it through the week without a drink, but I realise part-way through I have my sister to thank for that as she drinks Diet Coke with me and helps me carry our drunk father, uncle and cousins home most nights.

JENNA, THE SNOW IS FUCKING BEAUTIFUL. TWO SEASONS HAVE GONE BUT MY LOVE FOR YOU HASN'T. I THINK ABOUT YOU ALL THE TIME. I WISH THIS WAS EASIER. BUT MORE THAN THAT, I JUST WISH I COULD SEE YOU. LOVE, MARTY.

The fourth postcard I send is in April on my first holiday with friends since Ibiza. It's a slightly more civilised long weekend playing golf in the Algarve, a sport I am categorically shite at, but the sun shines and the sunsets over the Atlantic take my breath away. I play the Dead Boyfriend Card so my mates join me for them and they stay respectfully quiet and contemplative as we sit back and watch the ocean claim the sun. Little do they know I'm sitting there thinking about the other love of my life as well.

After, they let me choose a restaurant that serves more than burgers and chips, and then they get to drink their bodyweight in Sagres beer while I return to the hotel and think about Jenna, cry about Arnie, or sometimes call my sister or mother and let them distract me with their ramblings.

JENNA, I WATCH THE SUNSET EVERY NIGHT HERE. I DO IT TO FEEL CLOSE TO YOU, AND ARNIE. I GOT A PROMOTION AT WORK AND AM HELPING DESIGN THE SUMMER MENU. I WISH I KNEW YOU WERE OKAY. LOVE, MARTY.

The fifth postcard I send when I'm away in Ghana, teaching at a summer rugby camp for three months. It was a last-minute decision to go, what with work going so well, but Dermot gave me the final prod when I told him about it. I'm there with lads from all over the world who are five or more years younger than me, and it shows. Immature jokes, inappropriate comments about sex or women or queer folk that I pull them up on, not to mention hygiene habits that have me learning to breathe through my mouth whenever I'm in the dorm room. But I'm outside all day. I'm meeting and playing with kids who teach me more about life than any adult ever has, bar maybe Jenna or Arnie. And I'm reconnecting with a sport I love.

I also spend a handful of nights kissing Veliane, a strikingly attractive woman who works at a bar in town, where we go occasionally to play table football and dance terribly, much to the locals' amusement. Veliane has the most impossibly straight teeth, the daintiest hands, and an elegant arch in her back. She is a Christian and doesn't want to have sex before marriage, and the relief I have when she tells me this is felt from my head to my toes. She and I have easy conversations and sweet end-of-the-night kisses once the bar is closed, but all too soon she has to return to Accra for university.

JENNA, IT'S BEEN A YEAR, ALMOST TO THE DAY. I'LL NEVER FORGET THAT DATE. I HOPE YOU WON'T EITHER. RUGBY CAMP IS CLASS, BUT AS WITH MOST THINGS I JUST WANT TO TELL YOU ABOUT IT. PLEASE BE THERE IN FOUR YEARS. I LOVE YOU, MARTY.

Chapter Forty-Six

Jenna

I give myself two weeks. One week to stay in bed and cry as much as I need to. And another week to stay at home, on the couch, in my pyjamas and with only the TV as company. Then I try getting dressed again. I tidy up, and eventually I leave the house. A few days later, I start thinking about what I want my future to look like, searching for ways to ease the pain. Ways to feel less lonely. Ways to feel okay being alone.

And I do. I create a schedule for myself; lifting, walking, yoga classes, reading time, writing time, evenings for socialising, weekends with friends or watching movies that make me laugh, *Dumb and Dumber* being top of that list. I also go back to my therapist and tell her about Marty. I only bristle a little when she asks me if I think I'm self-sabotaging. When I answer that it's possible, but more likely that I want space to heal and to give Marty time to heal, I think her fleeting smile could be described as proud.

At some point, weeks into this routine, and almost out of nowhere I get an idea for a book and I start researching for it.

It's not the book I thought I'd write, but it's the book I now know I can write. I work hard and it consumes the parts of me that thoughts of Marty do not. When I can't work, I go to the gym. I'm there three times a week, focusing on a new eating programme and having regular check-ins with a PT who talks more than I'd like, so whenever he spots me I don't have the brain space to remember what it was like when Marty did it on that sunny morning in Crete.

When I start going out more - to the library, the theatre, to see friends, or just on long walks by myself - I find my eyes looking for him even though I know he is in Dublin. I know this is just part of the mourning I need to do. I don't blame or punish myself for it. I accept it for what it is, but I don't do any less searching for him as the days roll into weeks and the weeks pass by, blurring into months.

I dread the end of summer, but once autumn is here, I am reminded how beautiful it is seeing the streets of London bathed in autumn sunshine and falling golden leaves. It gives me a new appreciation for the predictability of nature and this is one of the many smaller things that help my days feel a little easier, sometimes even hopeful. I email a few old colleagues who have published books and I ask them to recommend agents and imprints, and slowly, alongside a fast-growing draft, I also build a list of people who could help me publish my book.

When winter comes, my brother moves in for his downtime between seasons. He is exhausted and depleted, and I take my duty of managing his rest and relaxation very seriously. I cook for him, take him on gentle strolls in Alexandra Park, and insist he comes to yoga with me each Sunday morning, even though he spends most of the time winking and pouting at Jorge, the instructor. Together we paint my bathroom (a green called Stormy Gale) and the guest bedroom (a soft terracotta pink heartbreakingly called Sunset Coral), and we spend more hours than is necessary building the flat-packed furniture I buy to finally replace what Robert took. When I need to, Jake lets me talk to him about Marty, and he holds my hand when that results in tears.

For Christmas, my brother insists we go and see our father and it's not the disaster I think it will be. Their dachshund dogs are hilariously contrary, and they leap into any puddle they can find. Their splashing makes me think about Marty and Maeve's pool antics and it takes willpower I don't know I have not to download a certain app and find her videos in hope of just a quick recent glimpse of him.

On the second-to-last day of our visit, my father's neighbour asks me out for a drink with a blush so deep, it makes my own cheeks warm. There is no spark, but there is good conversation and the gentle stroking of my battered ego. On the train back to London, I reactivate my dating profiles then gaze out of the window as I think dreamily about getting a dog and how strange it is that I don't even know if Marty is a dog person. There really is still so much I don't know, and may never know, about him.

Thanks in large part to a string of terrible first dates, January and February drag in a way that makes me question everything, not just the decision I made about Marty, but everything else. It proves a useful emotional experience for my book, but disastrous for my self-confidence which is possibly why, three days before my thirty-eighth birthday, I end up going for dinner with Robert. After rejecting his offers to meet up for over two years, I am left stunned and more dejected than ever when, over medium rare steaks and salad, he tells me he's met someone and he hopes to propose in the summer. He asks me if I've met someone and I say yes, but other than his name – *Marty, Marty, Marty* – I don't say much. I simply tell him I'm in love, because I am.

Spring comes, and I pause the disastrous dating to focus all my energy on work. As well as writing my book, I return to freelance work, contacting editors and explaining with tentative authority how I can now write about divorce and break-ups. By the end of April, during the same week my brother returns to Crete, I have completed several commissions and have a May meeting with a possible agent lined up.

I collect and treasure each one of Marty's postcards. Each one feels like a miracle I am both living for and don't deserve. I give myself hours to read and hold them. I wonder if the water marks on his first were his tears and I lift those blurry words to my lips hundreds of times. I wonder how he survived the family ski holiday. I wonder who he watched the sunset with in Portugal. My pride in him not going back to college, getting a promotion at work, and doing a rugby camp in Ghana sits heavy and happy in my heart for a long time. Keeping them under my pillow, I reach for the postcards on sleepless nights, and then I tuck them away and reach for myself, remembering the things he did to me and the things I did to him on a Greek island I wish I'd never left. I always think of him when I come. Always.

Maybe that's why I go back to Crete and spend a week at my brother's resort again. I know it means the world to my brother, who has another fully-booked season ahead of him. At my request I'm in a room at the other end of the resort from the villa I was in the year before, but it does little to mute the pain I feel being there without him. I drink too much on the first few nights, cry almost constantly and hide in my room, even though there is no private pool to cool down in this time as the temperature climbs.

My brother intervenes on the third day and drags me to the gym, where he makes me do one of my workouts while he files his nails and moans about Lionel's Greek boyfriend. I can't figure out if my brother is jealous of Lionel or the boyfriend but it is a good distraction for the remainder of my time there. With less alcohol and sobbing in my system, I read nine filthy novels, write five chapters of my own book, and laugh so hard my sides hurt after my brother and I get roped into Greek dancing at a restaurant in the village.

A year to the day I celebrated Marty's twenty-fourth birthday with him, I write and send him a postcard from the resort.

Dear Marty, Happy 25th Birthday! The sunsets here miss you and your Marty Party. I promise you. Everything will be okay. Jenna x

I kiss his name twenty-five times.

Chapter Forty-Seven

The Second 365 Sunsets

Marty

My sixth postcard to Jenna is another one from Dublin and it boasts a picture of the Molly Malone statue, a landmark I have walked past a thousand times but never looked at closely. Until, that is, one October afternoon, when I'm standing opposite it while waiting for the first date I've arranged via an app I hesitantly downloaded a week before. As I wait, I find myself studying the bronze statue. Her side profile is frighteningly like Jenna's - demure nose, full lips, and yes, a cleavage that demands attention. Needless to say, I'm distracted and thus a great disappointment to my date who is a softly-spoken young lad from Belfast who has sparkly grey eyes and curly blond hair on his forearms, but an alarmed reaction to my sobriety and an aversion to eye contact that I am probably wrong to inwardly scorn. I'm walking back to the bus stop when I see the postcard of the statue in a tourist shop and I write and post it immediately, Jenna's address long etched into my mind.

DEAR JENNA, I KNOW I'M MISSING YOU BAD WHEN I SEE YOU IN STATUES OF FISH-WIFE PROSTITUTES. I REALLY BLEEDING HOPE YOU TAKE THAT AS A COMPLIMENT. IF NOT CONSIDER IT PUNISHMENT FOR PUTTING US THROUGH THIS SEPARATION. I LOVE YOU, MARTY.

My seventh postcard to Jenna is one I buy, write and post in Paris in March the following year. I'm there for a three-month pastry course Dermot arranged and it helps pass a long, cold winter. The city is just as beautiful as I have heard, and the people I meet there aren't hard on the eye too. Despite my minimal

French and making very little effort to meet people, I fall into dating easily while there, but it's still a shock of an adjustment when I find myself in a French woman's bed and she is undressing me. She couldn't be more different to Jenna – she has long dancer's legs and a frame so slender I'm scared to touch it - but she's passionate and enthusiastic about me in a way I'd forgotten lovers could be. She's also firm about what she wants - a depressingly short list - and firmer still about what she doesn't like - a catastrophically longer list. We enjoy a handful of nights together, but then she explains she's been dating someone else and there's more of a connection so she's going to pursue him instead. I am shocked and sad at first - the ease of comfortable, predictable sex treated me well - but an hour later as I head home on the Metro, I'm laughing to myself, realising how quickly I would have become bored. I remember what I said to Jenna about vanilla and I curse the fact we didn't have more time to explore other flavours together.

DEAR JENNA, I DON'T KNOW IF YOU'D LOVE PARIS OR NOT BUT I'D GIVE MY RIGHT NUT TO FIND OUT BY WALKING ALONG THE SEINE HOLDING YOUR HAND ONE DAY. I STILL FUCKEN LOVE YOU, MARTY.

The eighth postcard is the one I'm most anxious about sending, because it's from London. I'm here on a foodie trip with my uncle as he finally caves to my nudging him about opening a second restaurant. He has the funds, and I have the energy and the ideas for it, now he just needs to visualise the potential. We head to London to try and get inspired.

Every minute I'm lost in London's grey, grizzly bustle, I'm thinking about how close I potentially am to Jenna. I don't just think about it, I feel it. Every time we visit a new restaurant or notice a landmark, I'm checking the map on my phone to see how far away I am from her address which is starred on the app, as it has been for over a year. It's only because we're so busy meeting restaurant owners in all corners of the city that there's no time for me to jump on the Tube and take myself to her street. Instead, I send her a postcard of the London Eye.

DEAR JENNA, IT FEELS BOTH GOOD AND BAD TO BE CLOSE TO YOU. THE ONLY THING KEEPING ME AWAY FROM YOU IS DERMOT DRAGGING ME AROUND LONDON'S CULINARY

**OFFERINGS, MY SECOND FAVOURITE THING ABOUT THIS CITY,
AFTER YOU. I REALLY HOPE YOU'RE OKAY. I LOVE YOU, MARTY.**

In the summer I finally have the money to move out of my parents' house
and rent a small studio apartment on the other side of town. It's cramped but
cosy, gives me the freedom I've been craving for so long, and is a welcome refuge,
albeit one that unsettles me because I'm not naturally good at being alone. I
think momentarily about telling Jenna my new address, as we agreed, but my
parents aren't going anywhere, and she hasn't sent me any letters or notes yet
anyway, so I don't do it.

I try to be proactive about filling the silence and emptiness of living alone.
Three years to the day that Arnie died, and three days before my twenty-sixth
birthday, I get a dog from the Dogs Aid shelter in Dublin; an undeterminable
mixed mutt with short stumpy legs and pointy, expressive ears, and I call him AJ
after the two people I love and miss most. I question the name at first, wondering
if it is too morose and depressing, but within weeks I know it suits him well and I
enjoy hollering it out loud whenever he fails to keep up with me on walks,
distracted by the possible scent of food somewhere. AJ keeps me company,
covers me in sloppy kisses and gives me begging eyes whenever I have food in
front of me; his love for me is almost as good and grounding as the love I felt
from them.

Chapter Forty-Eight

Jenna

The rest of summer isn't terrible. I soak up the good weather when we are blessed with it, join an outdoor CrossFit gym to try something new and I end up going for coffee and sometimes beers with the men I meet there. Some of them catch my eye, and I see I catch others' attention, but sadly they don't quite align.

When September brings a modest but decent enough offer on my book, there's now a deadline to complete the first draft. I welcome the extra pressure and pour all my energy into it. I find some purpose in my life and welcome the ease that brings even though the work itself exhausts me, not least because it requires me to get closer and closer to the core of what I feel – what I still think I feel - for Marty.

Triumphant after another successful season in Crete, my brother keeps me company again during the cold winter months and before I know it, we are once again on the train up to Scotland to be with Dad and Carol for Christmas. It's a welcome break from work that I use to rest, read and daydream about what Marty might be cooking for Christmas dinner. As soon as we get back, I open up my book's draft and start work again and I practically stay like that – head in a book or over my laptop – until late March when I send the most nerve-wracking email to my new editor with a 140,000-word draft attached.

In late May, I board the plane to Crete with another man's hand in mine. It fits well, not perfectly, but well enough. Everything about him fits well enough. From how we met - the only people swimming in London Fields Lido on a sunny but chilly spring morning - through to how well we slotted into each other's empty lives. Chris is a good kisser and a proficient lover. He makes me laugh in a way that may not surprise or bedazzle me, but it does placate and reassure me. He is the comfort I need after two years of heartache.

But on the first sunset there, as we sit at a table he reserved specifically for sundowner drinks after I had told him misty-eyed about how beautiful the sunsets were, I can't stop my eyes from travelling over to the stack of sun loungers. My pupils then practically burn a hole in the spot where Marty and I sat two years ago, where I sank my teeth into a beautiful broken nose. As the bottom curve of the sun kisses the horizon and Chris reaches for my fingers, I feel my heart break all over again when I look down and see his hand is not Marty's.

I retreat into a safe place inside myself for the rest of the holiday, moving through the motions Chris expects and it doesn't kill me to perform because he is a kind man whose company I enjoy and I hope he will be a friend in years to come. I break free on the fourth day, excuse myself for a walk alone to the resort's shop, buy a postcard and write it while drinking a Greek coffee that is still too strong and bitter for me.

Dear Marty, Happy 26th Birthday! The sunsets still miss you. And I still promise you. Everything will be okay. Jenna x

I kiss his name twenty-six times.

Chapter Forty-Nine

The Third 366 Sunsets

Marty

The ninth postcard I send to Jenna is from Dubai where I'm visiting Maeve who is there as part of a three-month contract with an influencer agency. Sitting by the swimming pool in her hotel on a warm November day, I don't hide when I'm writing the postcard to Jenna.

"You still love her," she says, looking over my shoulder.

"Fuck yeah, I do," I reply.

DEAR JENNA, DUBAI IS A WEIRD FUCKEN PLACE. MAEVE'S WORKING HERE. GOOD TO GET SUNSHINE THOUGH, AND THE SUNSETS ARE DECENT ENOUGH. I WISH I'D KNOCKED ON YOUR DOOR IN LONDON. LOVE YOU, MARTY. P.S. MAEVE SAYS HI!

"I do not!" Maeve exclaims, looking over my shoulder.

"Well, it's rude if you don't."

"Fine, I say hi, but more than that I want to ask what the fuck are you two doing? Are you really going to see this through?"

"Abso-fucken-lutely," I say as I fix the stamp on the card. "I'm almost halfway there. I actually think I can fecking do it."

"I can't tell if this is the stupidest idea or the most romantic sappiest shit I've ever heard of."

"Probably a bit of both," I say and not in the least bit embarrassed by it.

"But what if she meets someone else? What if you do?"

"I'm pretty sure that's not going to happen, at least for me."

A week later I meet Matthew in the restaurant. After over a decade of working for my uncle, I've managed to not get tangled up with colleagues for anything more than a few drunken snogs when I first started, but the moment Matthew walks in, I know I'm fucked. With dark hair, light blue eyes, and sculpted arms that belong on an athlete, he is the new restaurant's front of house manager and the way he takes his instant nickname of Door Bitch with a suggestive pout and eyebrow raise directed at me tells me I wouldn't be barking up the wrong tree if I decide to bark up his. The surprising thing is, after a few weeks dancing around him in the kitchen - smelling his cedar, evergreen scent - and watching his tight buttocks march around the restaurant - I realise I do want to.

So I do. I do what I haven't done since Jenna. I flirt aggressively with him. I practically chase him down with my banter. And I then apply for a new job elsewhere so we can do more without it posing problems for either of us. In some ways it's the push I need. I've been professionally ready for a change of scenery and a new challenge for a while, but mentally and emotionally, it is now time to cut the cord on my attachment to my uncle's restaurant, a place that saved me when I needed it.

Matthew meets me after my first shift as Deputy Chef at Kaiteki, an Asian-fusion soul food restaurant near St Stephen's Green, and we get the bus back to my place. That night we talk our voices hoarse and drink green tea until our bladders can't take anymore. With AJ snoring at our feet, we fall asleep on the couch, both semi-clothed and semi-erect, promising ourselves we'll make up for it the next day. And we do.

We make up for it most evenings for the next seven months and every night I feel myself inch closer to falling for him, so close that I don't see the signs he's not as keen as I am. He doesn't want to meet my parents. He isn't interested in going away with me, or spending Christmas together, and when I mention throwing him a birthday party, he makes excuses. A couple of weeks later, I realise I haven't heard from him for a few days so when I meet my uncle for coffee at his restaurant, I ask how Matthew is, and Dermot tells me he has moved back to Cork. It stings. It hurts me, that people could treat someone that way.

Then I get angry. Angry that he doesn't realise how much pain already exists in the world even when you do love someone, let alone when you are trying to love or be loved. But after a few weeks I stop torturing myself about it and realise I got lucky to know the truth before I did actually fall.

Maybe because I'm still a little heartbroken, I agree to go on holiday with my parents again, just the three of us as Maeve is working in the USA. So it's from a seaside hotel near Biarritz that I send my tenth postcard to Jenna, written the day after an embarrassingly pitiful accident.

DEAR JENNA, I BROKE MY FUCKEN ARM SURFING SO THAT'S WHY IT LOOKS LIKE A 5-YEAR-OLD WROTE THIS. WORK ARE GOING TO KILL ME, BUT IT'S NOT SO BAD RIGHT NOW AS I SPEND MY DAYS IN THE HOTEL SPA. BY THE WAY, YOU HAVE RUINED SHOWERS WITH SEATS FOR ME. I LOVE YOU, MARTY.

Chapter Fifty

Jenna

I wait three more months before I break-up with Chris, wanting to give it a chance once we're back in the real world, wondering if it was just being at the resort that tainted it for me. But it doesn't work. He doesn't want to be friends and that is upsetting, but not as much as being loved by someone who isn't Marty.

Still waiting on my editor's feedback, I find myself volunteering at Battersea Dog Park two afternoons a week, and training for an amateur weightlifting competition that I get a PB from but no awards. Then, as summer fades into autumn, my manuscript is sent back to me and long hours of research and edits help me count down the weeks until my brother's season ends, and he moves in again.

It's on his second visit to the dog shelter with me that Jake points out a Jack Russell mix with what he calls Bi Dick Energy and he practically insists on me adopting him and calling him Marty. I succumb to one of those requests and take home the little troublemaker a few weeks later, but I keep his name as Rocky because I can't bare the idea of hearing Marty's name even more times than it already echoes through my mind. That little hyperactive dog and I break up my relentless days of edits by going on long daily walks. I find myself welcoming the change of season, and almost feeling excited about heading up to the Edinburgh for Christmas and watching Rocky terrorise my dad's dogs, which he does at every opportunity.

I think about Marty often - every time I catch the sunset, whenever I hear an Irish accent, and solidly for weeks and weeks when I'm editing the chapter on grief for my book - but slowly and surely I start to notice that he's no longer my first active thought in the morning, nor is he always who I think about when I glide my hands over my own body.

It's back in London on New Year's Eve, tipsy on expensive champagne bought by my brother and his wonderfully eccentric friends, when I realise that I am halfway through the five years. We are halfway there. I search for the pride I should feel, but it's out of reach, and so is Marty, by at least two and a half years.

The next day I stay in bed until midday, trying to cry away my hangover, and when that doesn't work, Rocky and I walk eight miles to Hackney Marshes and back before picking up supplies for the most epic dinner for my brother and his friends. As their laughter fills my house for the second evening in a row, I feel full and happy and like maybe I am doing okay.

That is how I spend most of the rest of winter - walking and cuddling Rocky, cooking for Jake, and keeping my house and mind as full as possible - and finalising my book edits.

I hand over the updated draft the day before my fortieth birthday in March and to celebrate these two milestones, a week later my brother and I head off to the Maldives for two weeks to a resort he gets generously discounted.

I start as I mean to go on by doing next to nothing apart from an hour in the gym each day. That is until the fourth day when the gym manager asks me if I'd like to go snorkelling with him, just the two of us. Intrigued by his jet-black eyes and a little dizzy from his thick, defined quads, I push aside the sting that comes from remembering my snorkelling date with Marty, and I go with him. We see turtles, manta rays and baby barracuda sharks. Then he takes me off the resort to a private beach on the other side of the island that the staff use on their days off. Drinking cocktails out of plastic bottles with straws, we sit on the smooth white sand and watch the sunset while the sea water dries crisp and tight on my sun-tinged skin. A couple of hours later, he licks the salt of it off my body before we take a shower together, an experience that brings Marty's image so vividly to my mind when I close my eyes, until the gym instructor's hairier chest jolts me back to where I am. I pull the man in front of me closer and I take and give pleasure as much as I possibly can. And it is good - he ravishes me and caresses me in equal measure. He takes instruction well and surrenders his body to my touch in a way that reminds me of Marty but not in a distracting way, more as encouragement. It's bittersweet having that reassurance; that sex can still be good after Marty. If it has to be...

I only get two postcards from Marty this year, but that makes them even more precious. I read them just as often as the others and they are dog-eared and creased in no time.

Because of that Maldives trip, and my brother's resort being booked out a year in advance, I wasn't going to go to back to Crete this year, but then he has a cancellation and I get a phone call from Jake telling me that he may or may not have slept with someone he shouldn't have and he needs me there. The next thing I know, I'm on a plane to Crete again.

Four days later, I send Marty a postcard.

Dear Marty, Happy 27th Birthday! I look for the green light every time the sun sets. I promise you always. Everything will be okay. Jenna x

I kiss his name twenty-seven times.

Chapter Fifty-One

The Fourth 365 Sunsets

Marty

I write three postcards but don't send any of them.

There are two reasons. One, it's been over three years since I last saw Jenna and I've sent her ten postcards and I've not had a reply to one. I know that she forewarned me about this. She told me she was going to give me a lot of space and she has proved true to her word, but it still hurts. That said, it's a pain I have some control over. Some. Because I can stop sending her postcards. I can stop putting my heart on the line like that. I can redirect my energy and attention elsewhere.

That is one of the reasons I decide to cycle the West Ireland Way with my father to raise money for a teenage cancer charity. I pour all my free time into planning it, training for it, involving Arnie's family in the process and towards the end, working closely with the charity to raise as much awareness as possible. Turns out if you're a semi-attractive bisexual man who looks good in Lycra and you had a boyfriend who died at the age of 22, the media will quickly show up with a camera or two. I don't love the attention, but I am proud of how much money we raise in the build-up, thanks in large part to Maeve's own efforts on her social media.

The postcards I get but don't send are ones I pick up along the way as Dad and I cycle through wind, rain, sleet and occasionally spring sunshine. Despite aching muscles, the sorest arse in the world and suffering my father's teasing whenever he manages to creep ahead of me, it's the literal ride of my life.

I'm grateful for the silence my father and I share that lasts hours, as it's in these long quiet moments that I find my thoughts taking me to places I know I've been avoiding despite years of therapy. I can cry on the bike without Dad seeing, the wind swiping my tears away as soon as they emerge. I can release my sadness that Arnie suffered so much before he died, and that he died so young. I relinquish the anger and hurt that I feel at Jenna for not giving us a go, for testing me and my love. And after a few days of doing that, I find myself starting to think about them both without visceral physical reactions.

The second reason I don't send the postcards is I meet Ciara.

She works for the charity we raise money for, and we bond over the most depressing thing; we've both lost people to leukaemia. Ciara's older sister died around the same time as Arnie did, and when we share our stories, it's the first time I feel seen and validated since Jenna. They are totally different in many ways. Ciara is more fragile, her sense of humour more delicate but just as sophisticated, and where Jenna is full and curvy, Ciara is short and slim. And yet I can't help but believe they are made of some of the same stuff - empathy, kindness, and generosity. The sensuality is there too, if not a little bit more buried under the surface, but after taking it slow, enjoying dates of all kinds, I have fun teasing it out of Ciara and it doesn't take long for my heart and stomach to flutter when I think about seeing her. It doesn't take long for me to insist she moves in when the contract on her place is up for renewal. It doesn't take long for me to feel like maybe Jenna was right all along and I could maybe feel more with someone else. Maybe.

We travel a lot together, to Milan, Bologna and Florence on a road trip, around Thailand's Andaman coast, a week in Costa Rica, and then to Mykonos where we spend my twenty-eighth birthday together. Even though it looks and feels nothing like Crete, it still takes me back in time. The Aegean Sea is the exact same colour as the water Jenna floated on as my fingers brought her to orgasm. The rich and fresh flavours in the food are just as promising and delectable as the dishes we tasted at my birthday dinner. And the sunsets are easily among the best I've experienced since Crete.

Like Jenna, Ciara holds space for me to feel Arnie by my side as we watch the sun close out each day, but perhaps unlike Jenna, she has more questions about the different shapes of my love as she rarely asks me questions about our time together, more about how his death affected me. Ciara wants more reassurance about my sexuality too. It's not an overbearing problem - she talks from a place of love - but I don't always have the words she wants to hear, or the patience to explain the same thing over and over again.

It's different. But why? *It just is.* But how? *Just because.* Don't you miss it? *Dick? No, I have one.* Marty, be serious. *I am serious. I don't miss anything when I'm with you.* I don't understand. *You don't have to. You just have to trust me.* I do. *Then why do you worry?*

Sometimes it's impossible to avoid comparing, but it's never with men or Arnie. It's with Jenna. I didn't appreciate what Jenna's age gave her that women closer to my own age lack; self-trust, confidence, a hunger for life and love that only comes when you are aware it's not going to last forever. But then Ciara will cook for me on the days I want to be nowhere near a kitchen, play with AJ like he's her own dog, and she will melt her body into mine so exquisitely, peacefully, lovingly, I feel safe and so close to whole with her.

More than all of this, I love that we have the one thing Jenna never gave me; time. Time to figure it out. Time to grow together. Time to just be with one another.

Chapter Fifty-Two

Jenna

My book is published the week before my forty-first birthday and despite the pride and the long-anticipated milestone, I feel bereft. And I don't really know why.

I'm proud of my book. I love how much of my heart and soul I poured into it. I cherish how writing it helped me heal from my divorce. I treasure how every day I worked on it, something I wrote or read would make me think about Marty. I love how, when I hold it in my hand, my skin tingles because I truly believe it will help others look at love differently – more forgivingly, more generously, more hopefully.

Because that's exactly how I look at love now.

So why am I not overjoyed? Why am I not celebratory? Why do I wake up on the book's launch day wanting to sob?

My rational brain is quick to explain; because I am drained after working and focusing so hard on a project that is now completed. Because I had to be my most vulnerable self for this book, and now it's going to land in the hands of others, and I have no control over how it will be received. Because my book was my focus, my saviour, my lighthouse as I navigated life after Marty. And now it's done. Gone.

My irrational brain is just as eager to have some input. Because I miss Marty. Because I want to be with Marty. Because I would love nothing more than to celebrate this moment with him. Because I still love Marty.

I take breaks from crying only to do more nervous poos than I have all year. I spend practically all day in the bathroom holding my cramping stomach while my brother slides Imodium under the bathroom door and talks to me so I'm not alone.

Although I appreciate his presence, I send him out with some friends because I'd rather be alone. Even though I'm emotionally wrecked and can almost feel my insides exit my body, I am okay. I am not lonely.

I miss Marty, yes, but I am not lonely without him.

In fact, I don't get lonely very often anymore.

The next day I don't just feel better, I feel a sharp lucidity that explains why I don't feel lonely at all these days. Because the pain I felt yesterday was love. And it wasn't just my love for Marty, it was the love I now have for myself. It was the same love I nurtured while healing from the divorce, writing my book, and yes, even missing and wanting Marty from afar, because giving myself permission to feel the ache of my love for him was, is, self-love. I love who I am. I love what I do. And I love who I love.

With this reckoning comes more clarity that I relax into. I know I won't be able to move on until I've gone to see him next year. This hope, as delicate and transparent as it feels, is what gets me out of bed on the days I need to do book launch events or radio interviews. Each time I do the latter, I wonder if it will get aired in Ireland somehow. I also ponder whether he ever Googles my name and if he knows about my book. This curiosity mixes with my hope, making it a more solid, opaque thing I can use as energy. It gently propels me forward as I fill my days with work, lifting weights and walking Rocky, and my evenings with house-decorating, good books and dinners with friends who have no idea that I am just over a year away from the biggest, riskiest adventure of my life. It's what makes me book next year's holiday at Iliovasílema Villas eighteen months in advance, and what makes me ask my brother to ensure I get assigned the villa I had the year I met Marty.

Jake does what he can to make sure this happens next summer, but he will not be there himself. He spends the winter with me talking about needing a change and feeling restless. He's already committed to one last season at the resort, but he sets off in April with a resignation letter in his luggage and the promise that I will be there just over a month later.

Jake wants me there as I have been every year since he started, and I can't deny that I want to go to the place where I will possibly return to Marty in twelve months' time. I want to send him one last postcard, even though I haven't received any from him in over a year. I want to remind him of my promises to him. It was not goodbye forever, not from me. And everything will be okay, because even though I want it to be okay with Marty, I also know it will be okay without him. I needed this time apart to know that that truth is what will make it so much better *with* him.

Dear Marty, Happy 28th Birthday! I think I saw the green light in a sunset tonight, the 1458th sunset since our last one together. I promise you. Everything will be okay. Jenna x

I kiss his name twenty-eight times.

1826 Sunsets After Their First Sunset

(aka Five Years Later)

Chapter Fifty-Three

Marty

I broke up with Ciara two months ago.

It was a joint decision. Communication was breaking down and neither of us had the energy or desire to battle it out when walking away and being respectful was an option. While I've had my doubts in the last few months, I'm finding more peace with it. The fog of sadness I was waking up with now lifts by the time I've had my run and my second coffee. When I'm at work, I find I can forget how she snorts a little when she laughs and how she never gave me a cup of tea without a biscuit. Sometimes, when I'm walking AJ, I even feel happy for her that she can now go on and meet someone else who is ready for marriage and babies and giving her all the things she wants.

And now, on a bright late May morning, on a bike ride with Da, I finally feel like it was the right decision.

"You look like you've been sleeping more," Dad says as we wheel the bikes into his garage. I stayed over last night, went to the pub with a few friends, and today Maeve is coming over for lunch before she flies off to Paris for another work trip. I'll be working tonight, but it's good to know I now have a day of relaxing, eating Mum's roast dinner and irritating my sister ahead of me now our exercise is done.

"Yeah," I say. "I've been going to bed a bit earlier, when I can. Last night helped too. Never thought I'd sleep so well in my childhood single bed that is almost a foot too small for my lanky arse."

"And to think you shared it with Arnie many a night." Dad chuckles.

My eyes widen. "You weren't supposed to know about that."

"Oh, I didn't at the time. It takes me a long time to catch up with what's going on, but when I know, I know," he says, tapping his nose. "Come on. Let's go inside and annoy your mother until Maeve gets here and then we can piss her off too."

"Sounds like a plan. But I call shotgun on the shower!" I race off, my cleats clip-clopping on the driveway.

After I'm showered and dressed, I go to the kitchen and make a coffee. I call for AJ as I slip on my trainers, getting ready to take him for a walk.

"I've already taken him," Mum says when I reach for his lead on the kitchen counter.

"Serious? Thanks, Ma," I say giving her a peck on the top of her head. "How's the bird doing?"

She follows my nod to the oven where a chicken is roasting. I can smell all the right things; garlic, lemon, rosemary and thyme.

"Grand," she says. "Marty, could we sit down and have a wee chat?"

Mum moves to the circular kitchen table and sits. It's then that I see she has something in her hands. With AJ on my heels, I go to the table and sit, feeling both curious and alarmed.

She sucks in a deep breath, then starts talking.

"You're either going to hate me or love me for this. Maybe it will be both, if I'm lucky, but I have thought long and hard about this many times over the years and I still stand by my decision."

I open my mouth to speak but she doesn't give me a chance.

"What you've done and achieved and experienced in the last few years, Marty, it's really quite remarkable. And you did it on your own terms. And I'm not talking about your work achievements or your travel and life experiences, more who you are, who you've grown to be. Marty, that's the real success."

"Ma," I say, my eyes narrowing on the things she holds in her hands. They're postcards. Postcards from a sunny place with blue seas and skies.

She inhales, exhales. Her hands are shaking a little. "Jenna sent you a postcard from Crete every summer for the last four years. I'm assuming her brother was still working there, or maybe she just went back because it was... it was where she met you."

My mouth is open but there are no words. There isn't even much air moving in or out.

"You weren't here when they arrived. You were always somewhere else, travelling, or you'd moved out. You were just living your life. And then you met Ciara and I thought maybe it wouldn't help to see them. I thought after the first few, she would stop. Jenna, I mean. But no, she sent you a postcard every year, on your birthday."

I dig my fingernails in the flesh of each palm and bite down on the flesh of my cheek. Staring at the postcards in my mother's hands, my tongue lies limp in my mouth.

"And I know this summer is when you said you'd reunite, back in Crete."

"It's next week, Ma," I say. The date has been ingrained on my brain for five years. I have no plans to go but that doesn't mean I've not been thinking about it.

"I know, son," she says. She flattens her hands on the table, over the postcards which are face up. I see then there's something else with them; an envelope. "I think you should go."

"Oh, do you?" I splutter. "I have your permission?"

"It's not like that." My mother holds my gaze, doesn't shrink like maybe she would have once. "Not at all. You can do what you want, but I want to give these to you now."

"Why now?" I say my throat dry and hoarse. It's a miracle I'm not shouting. That or the years of therapy finally paying off. "Why not a few months ago? Give me more time to think and make plans, for Christ's sake."

"You'd only just broken up with Ciara. You needed to heal."

"This could have helped!"

"That wouldn't have been fair to Jenna. You would have been rebounding."

"I don't think hiding her post to me for five years is very fair to her, Ma." My voice is louder but still I'm not shouting. Now the shock has worn off, I know yelling won't help. I just want to read Jenna's words. I want to touch something she has touched. I want to have whatever scraps of information I can about her, and about how the last five years have treated her.

"That's probably true," Mum says. "But I *am* telling you. Aren't I? I always intended to tell you."

"So now you want me to go to her? Why, Ma? You hardly encouraged it five years ago."

"You were younger, and you were grieving. And Jenna... when she said she wanted you to take this time, I think it was the right thing to do."

"Well, that only makes two of you." I feel something like pain flood back. It doesn't sting or ache as such, it's more muted or softened than that. It's almost nostalgic, like I am tapping into a painful memory that still means something and while it's not comfortable, it's not totally unpleasant.

"And you survived," she says. "Look at you, Marty. Look at what you've done and enjoyed in the last five years. Ciara may not have worked out, but you had happy times together. That counts for something."

I rub my hands over my face, my beard scratching my fingers. "Can I... can I just read the postcards please?"

Mum coughs, clearing her throat. "There's something else," she says.

"Jesus, what now?"

"It's a letter," she says, and her voice is lower, her gaze more earnest. "From Arnie."

Whatever breath I have in my lungs evaporates now. The wobble in my chin and the heat in my eyes come from nowhere.

"He wanted me to give this letter to you, when you had fallen in love again," she says.

I hold my hands up in a stop action when I see her fingers twitch. I'm not ready for this. Not yet. I need to gather my emotions and my thoughts, even if my tears are now a lost cause.

"Why didn't you give this to me when I was with Ciara?" I ask as steadily as I can. "Last year, when we moved in together?"

Mum nods and there are tears in her eyes too. "I nearly did. When you took her to Costa Rica, I thought maybe you were going to propose, but your father told me to wait. He didn't say why, but now I wonder if he knew all along it wouldn't work out."

"Dad's as bad as you," I say, trying to smile but failing.

"Your father thinks you should go to Crete."

"How? I don't have flights. The resort will be all booked up. I have AJ to think of."

"We'll have him, you know that."

"What about work?"

"You give that place everything, they can give you something back," she says. "Call them now and tell them."

I flatten my hands on the table, close my eyes for a moment just to pause and breathe. "I don't know how I feel about Jenna anymore. And she probably won't even be there."

"There's only one way to answer those questions, son," Dad says from behind me. I turn to look at him, his hair still damp.

"We just want you to be happy and have the love you deserve," Ma says, her eyes almost as moist as mine.

And then she slides over four postcards and a letter.

Chapter Fifty-Four

Hey Fuck Face,

So you finally found someone else foolish enough to fall in love with you? How the fuck did you manage that?

I had all these ideas for letters to write to you after I pissed off to The Other Side. A card for all your future birthdays (stopping around 65, of course, because nobody who drinks like you will last much longer than that). A letter for when you finally graduate, if you manage to pull your finger out of your arse and finish that degree (P.S. I think it's okay if you don't). A congratulations note when you open your first restaurant (because I know you will). A card to go with flowers when you get married or maybe when you get a kid (FYI it might be helpful if they're with the same person but not essential, I guess). But honestly, I can't be arsed to do it. Not when I am the very definition of time-short and I have all these TV series to watch and books to read before I kick the bucket. You already take up too much of my time with your incessant talking and board games and desire to reminisce with travel memories I have long forgotten but am secretly so very pleased you remember.

But I did want to make you sob like a baby with at least one P.S. I Love You style letter (still not forgiven you for making me watch that, by the way), and so I decided the best time to surprise you and fuck you up a bit would be when you finally fall in love with someone else. I know it will happen. How could it not? Have you seen your arse in a pair of jeans?

I don't know who they'll be but I know they'll be fucken awesome. At least, I hope they are and if they're not I'll get to haunting them pretty fucken quickly so they get the message and clear that space for someone else who is worthy.

Because you deserve to have someone, Marty. And not just anyone. You deserve someone who wakes up every day and knows how fecking lucky they are to have you. You deserve someone who would step up and look after you the way you stepped up and looked after me. You deserve someone who matches your razor-sharp banter, your insatiable appetite for sex, and your filthy, filthy sense of humour. You deserve someone who knows when you need a hug more than a shag, even when, or maybe <u>*especially*</u> *when you don't. You deserve someone who makes you laugh half as much as you make me laugh, so you can experience what it's like to have far too many laughter lines at a young age.*

I hope I don't need to say this because we talked about it enough, dickhead, and I'd like to think you remember some of the things I tell you, but I give you my blessing. I give you bucketloads of the stuff. In fact, I command it. The only thing that makes me smile on my darkest days is the knowledge that you will keep on living and loving. This world is a better place because it has you doing that, Aiden O'Martin.

I'm not sure where I'll end up. I like your theory of coming back as a gay penguin or a fly in Harry Styles' house so I can listen to his conversations with Louis, but I'm not sure I'll be that lucky and it's important you know why. Because the thing is, I feel like I've cashed in my own share of luck during my time on Earth, mostly thanks to you. I know everyone feels sorry for me dying so young. I feel sorry for me sometimes too - it's fucking shite! - but really, there is nothing sad or pitiable about my short life. I had the best friend in the world growing up, and then I fell in love with him. And after some gentle persuasion that night we watched Pirates of the Caribbean and I experimented with eyeliner (Jesus, that night, Marty. Do you remember how amazing that night was?) we travelled the world and he fell in love with me too.

My God, your love is a hurricane of good things. I knew it would be, but even you exceeded my expectations, because you're you and you do things in the extremes, even love. So that's why it's no tragedy I'm dying young. I'd rather have that and die at twenty-one with abs and taut asscheeks then die at one hundred with saggy balls and never loving or being loved by you, Marty.

And now I'm fucking crying, which is only fair I guess as I bet I've made you cry a few times since I've been gone. Yeah, I really am sorry about dying. It was a dick move. I hope whoever you love now sticks around longer. I hope whoever you love is there to put an arm around you when you need to cry. I hope whoever loves you now takes great care of you. I hope whoever it is, that they are prepared to take risks for you, be brave for you, show up when you need them to, just like I know you will.

And thank you for loving me so good. I'll love you forever, you fuck face fantastic man.

Arnie x

P.S. Keep looking for me in the sunset, I promise you if I can be anywhere, it will be there.

Chapter Fifty-Five

Jenna

While he's not here himself, Jake is the only person who knows where I am. He's managing a larger, high-end resort in Morocco and while I miss him, and his absence throws me because this place is so deeply connected to him, I am relieved I don't have to talk about what I'm doing with anyone more than I already did on a rushed phone call to him in the airport before I boarded my plane two days ago on Marty's twenty-ninth birthday.

"I just don't want you to be disappointed," he said.

"I'll be disappointed if I *don't* go," I replied. "So if that's how I'll feel anyway then surely it's worth trying."

"But have you even considered how you'll feel if he doesn't come? It's an awful lot of money and effort just to get your heart broken. I mean, I could possibly talk to HQ about getting you a refund or credit for next season..."

"Jake!" I said, his name a single staccato noise on my tongue. "I know what you're doing. You're trying to protect me from pain. But life is full of pain. Some of it we can't control or avoid, and other kinds of pain are a more conscious experience, and one we maybe risk experiencing knowingly because the risk is worth it."

"I'm not really sure what you just said." He sighed. "But it definitely gave me a bit of a headache."

"I'm saying, I'm ready to feel the heartache of him not showing up. But I'm not ready to ignore the possibility he will be there."

There was a pause. "It's been five years," Jake said in a gentler voice. "When I think about how much I've changed in that time...what I've done and how I've grown. You too, Jen. Look at where you're at now."

"That's exactly why I wanted to give him that time," I said in little more than a whisper. "And myself. I needed the time too."

"But you never forgot him?" Jake asked. "You never stopped loving him?"

"No." The word hollowed me out. "I never stopped loving him."

"Well, when you put it like that," Jake said. "I just pray he shows up."

I took in a deep breath then. "You know, if he doesn't, that's okay too. In some ways, that will help me move past this whole chapter, if I have to. So either way, if he's not there in two days, then at least I'll know he's happy without me."

"Or dead," Jake said without hesitation.

"Jesus, brother! That isn't helping."

"Have you never looked him up?"

"A few times in the first few years but he's not his sister. There wasn't much to see. And then it didn't make me feel good, so I stopped."

"I wish I could stop doing things that don't make me feel good. Sorry, did I say *things*? I mean, *men*. I wish I could stop doing *men* that don't make me feel good."

"Jake-"

"No, not now. No time to discuss the tragedy that is my love life when you are literally living out the climax to an early 2000s rom-com, airport and all."

"Yeah, speaking of which, my flight's boarding now. I'll miss you in Crete," I said starting to collect my belongings.

"I'm going to ask all the staff and Matthias to keep an eye on you," he said.

Matthias is the manager of the neighbouring resort - a tall, silver-haired German with piercing grey-blue eyes. It's his third season working in Crete and we'd met a few times before.

"Please don't," I said. "I don't need looking after."

"We all need that, Jenna. Isn't that why you're doing this? Because part of you wants to look after Marty and part of you wants him to look after you."

"Well, now who sounds like he knows what he's talking about?" I laughed before hanging up.

After arriving at the resort, I spent many minutes walking through the villa looking at, touching and reliving the places Marty and I made love. When that made me so horny and dizzy I could barely breathe, I focused on unpacking, and then went to the gym for an hour before I swam and sunbathed. I passed the next day in much the same way.

Today has been different.

All day I've been looking out for him. In the gym, on the beach, in the lobby when I had to dash to the bathroom for my fourth nervous poo of the day. I look for him on my way back to my villa to get ready, and after on the way back down to the bar where I can't help but feel pulled to be. I look for him as I think about how familiar the sun's warmth is on my skin, how I can smell sea salt in the air like I did five years ago, how there are the same uneven tiles underfoot and I am wearing the same style of Birkenstocks on my feet even though they're a newer pair, this time patent white. As I wonder if he still wears sandals like this, I feel a wave of sadness crash into me, slowing my stride. What if I never find out?

What if he doesn't come?

I haven't heard from him in two years.

He probably isn't going to come.

This is what I'm telling myself as I walk into the bar.

This is what I tell myself as I sit at the only available table and peruse the drinks menu, not really looking at the words, only keeping my eyes busy so they don't do what they really want to do which is scour the crowd for him, for Marty.

He probably isn't going to come.

This is what I tell myself as I order a virgin mojito because I will save drinking alcohol for when he doesn't show up and I can numb the sharpest edges of my pain.

This is what I tell myself as I sip my drink alone and almost can't bear how beautiful the sunset is. All clear skies that idyllically display the blue to purple to pink to copper red ombre shading of the sun's descent. I feel the magnetic pull for Marty blast through my bones. He should be here. He should be here. But he's not.

He's not coming.

This is what I tell myself as I order a second drink, a cocktail now because the pain is already here. It's because the sun is so low in the sky, and he wouldn't leave it this late. He would want to see the whole thing.

This is what I tell myself when Matthias comes over and asks to sit next to me. Out of nowhere, I recall my brother mentioning his divorce has just been finalised and he looks lonely. I can relate.

Before I agree to let him sit next to me, I do the thing I have forbidden myself to do for the last twenty minutes of waiting. I turn my head and survey the space behind me, to the side of me and hopelessly, in front of me. I take my time. I search the space once, twice, but Marty is nowhere to be found. I sigh as my heart sinks into my stomach and then I smile at Matthias and shift over to make space for him.

After five minutes of pleasant enough small talk, Matthias narrows his gaze on me. "You know, I'm still curious about why you're here, alone, when your brother works somewhere else?"

"It's a long story," I say, hoping that will put him off wanting to hear it. I glance at the sun now. It is so very close to melting into the horizon.

"I have time," he says, and the sun's butterscotch glow emphasises his tan. He's an attractive man. He's not Marty, but he's an attractive man.

I pull in a breath before I speak.

"Well, five years ago I met a man here," I say. "And we had the most amazing five days together and we fell in love. But then... Then he went back to his home and I went to mine. We agreed to meet up in five years' time and watch the sunset together, right here. Today."

He blinks at me. "And that's what you're doing? Or rather... you're waiting for him?"

I grit my teeth to slow the onslaught of tears. "Yes," I say, my voice cracking in too many places for such a short sound. "I'm waiting for him, like I promised I would."

410

"Why didn't you try to make it work? Five years ago?"

"That is an even longer story," I say with a small smile.

Matthias leans back. "It's my night off. Like I said, I have time." He lifts his drink as if to toast me.

I let myself do it once more. I crane my neck in every single direction, looking for Marty, searching for a sign he is close by but there's nothing but the golden light of the sunset illuminating strangers' faces.

He isn't going to come. It's already too late.

But our story will always be what it is. The greatest, sweetest love story of my life. While not easy, loving Marty from afar hasn't been hell, it's been the closest thing to true love I've ever experienced. It's a love that has stayed with me as I grew and changed and evolved. Loving him regardless of what he's doing, where he is, who he is loving, it's been humbling and honest and raw. It's been the most human thing I've ever done, and I have no regrets.

I take a sip of my drink, a deliciously sweet and juicy Sex on the Rocks, sink back into my chair, then I watch the last minutes of the sunset as I tell my story. Marty's story. Our story.

Chapter Fifty-Six

Marty

I should have come a day early. Of course my flight was going to get delayed but at least it gives me time to call Maeve and ask her to sanity-check what I'm about to do.

"You smile a lot," she says. "Like way too much if you ask me. But not all of your smiles are equal, and I've only ever seen you smile like you did with Jenna with one other person."

"Who?" I ask wondering if it was Ciara or Matthew.

"Arnie," she says. "Whatever you felt for Jenna that week in Crete, it's about as close as what you felt with Arnie, so I think it's worth going to find out if she still makes you smile, and feel, like that."

"Jesus, Maeve," I say. "I thought you were going to talk me out of it, be a voice of reason."

"How is what I said not reasonable? I want you to be happy. I know I don't always act like it, but I do want that for you."

"But what if she's not there? Fuck, I don't even know if she's still alive."

There's a pause before Maeve replies. "She's alive, Marty."

"How do you know?" I demand.

"You should Google her. You may get more answers than you expect if you do that."

Heat prickles up my back. Not looking up Jenna's name over the last five years has been one of the hardest things I've ever done.

"Go be happy, Aidey," Maeve says.

"What about yourself, Maeve? When are you going to do what you need to do to make yourself happy?"

"Gotta go! Someone else is calling," she says. I know it's a lie, but I let her go.

After I look up Jenna's name – and read the title of the book she published last year *Falling: How We Fall In and Out of Love (And Why Both Are Good)* - I let myself go too, boarding the plane with determination and purpose despite the long delays, time I passed by looking at the videos I recorded of her jumping in her pool, and staring at the photo Maeve took of us in the restaurant at sunset. Not that I needed to have it in front of me. I've looked at that image for so long over the last five years, it's forever imprinted in my mind.

The delays only start to stress me out when I'm arriving at my hotel down the road and see that the sun is already sinking low in the sky. Tumbling out of the taxi, I estimate I have about half an hour before it's gone completely, and considering I've been sweating buckets since the first of five delayed announcements in Dublin airport, I am not exactly thrilled about not having time to take a shower. Jenna will just have to take me as I am, sweaty balls, clammy palms, and stinky pits.

Jesus, will she still want me?

Fuck. Will she even be there?

I think about the postcards. "I promise you." Written on each one. That has to be what she was promising me, right? That she will be there.

I quickly throw on a crumpled but clean T-shirt and change my jeans for shorts, and then I'm rushing down the street as quickly as I can.

My Dublin body isn't used to the heat and it doesn't take long for the perspiration to make my T-shirt stick to my chest. I also don't run as much as I used to and that makes me wonder if she is there, will she mind the small belly I have now, or the beard I've grown which has the faintest dusting of grey hairs. Something tells me if she's there, if she's still the same Jenna I fell for, then she won't mind in the least. Eager to find out, I pick up my pace and sprint along the waterfront path, and with each step, the pinks and oranges in the sky taunt me, telling me I'm late.

When I see the first sign for the resort, despite my heaving lungs and pounding pulse, I feel a sort of peace wash over me. It's the kind of peace I get in the kitchen. It's a peace that comes through intention and focus, just like I experience on a busy day at work. As I pump my legs, use my arms to drive my body forward, I feel like I'm doing exactly what I'm supposed to be doing. It doesn't matter if Jenna is there or not, I owe it to myself to try. Hell, I owe it to Arnie and his letter to try.

I slow down as I approach the resort's security gate. Awash with nostalgia at the sight of the walnut trees at the entrance, I quickly explain to the guards why I'm there - dropping both Jenna and her brother's name into the conversation - and I am let in after singing my name and giving my telephone number on a guest registration form. I wait until I've cleared their line of sight and then I'm off sprinting again, down to the lobby bar. It all looks and smells and feels so familiar. Was it really five years ago I was here last? I have a brief moment walking through the building's entrance where I tell myself that even if she's not there, some good can come of this. I can relive where we were, where I was when I fell in love with a wonderful woman.

But that thought is obliterated when I take just one step into the bar and see her. Or at least her side profile. Her hair is in a different style, but her nose is the same and her lips are still unbelievably plump and pink. Her skin is still tanned, or maybe she's been here already a few days so has topped it up, and I itch to get closer to see how many more freckles she has on her face and body.

The one thing stopping me from rushing forward and finding out, is that she's sitting with someone else, deep in conversation. And that someone else is a strikingly handsome white-skinned, silver-haired man who is approximately the same age as Jenna.

If my eyes weren't so delighted seeing her, they would look away because it kills me as much as it thrills me to see her there looking happy, but with someone else. Because she does look happy. My brain can't quite make sense of why she would be here with someone else on the day we are supposed to meet, but my heart is busy absorbing the way her cheeks still bunch up as she smiles, how she still talks with her hands, and even perversely, the way the man stares into her eyes like he's getting sucked into something he never wants to leave.

I know exactly how he feels.

I'm going to wait a minute. I'm going to wait and see if she really is happy. I'm going to memorise her looking this happy and then I'm going to walk away and let her live the rest of her life. And I will try to do the same.

That's when my phone rings, loud enough that it can be heard by people close by despite the DJ's music. It's a foreign number I don't recognise. Curious, I press answer and lift the phone to my ear.

"Marty O'Martin," a voice I recognise says.

"Sweet Cheeks," I say back, my words shaped by the smile growing on my face.

"A little birdie told me you showed up. Are you with my sister?" Jake asks.

"Not yet," I say. "But I'm looking at her."

And I am. Jenna must have heard my phone ring, because she's standing up and facing me, a sunbeam of a smile on her lips. A smile of surprise, wonder, and hope. She takes a step towards me and then she stops, as though she's suddenly terrified, and her hand comes to rest on her heart.

"Thank you for showing up," Jake says in my ear with audible sincerity. "I hope you can keep doing that for her."

"I hope I can too. I know I want to try."

"Marty, you're losing your touch," he says. His voice back to the playful tone I remember. "You've said maybe four things to me and none of them have been filthy innuendo."

"Suddenly feeling a little serious right now," I say and I am. I can't take my eyes off Jenna. I want to throw the phone in the sea and run to her. I want to tell her I love her. I want to tell the world I love her. Because I do. I still do. As I realise this, I also know that deep down, I never stopped.

"I hope that passes for you. Sounds uncomfortable," Jake says.

"So is my growing boner, if I'm being honest," I say quiet enough only he can hear. And I'm not lying. My body is ready for Jenna. My body apparently will always be ready for her.

"And there he is," Jake says with a soft laugh. "Go get her, Marty O'Martin. I'll see you soon, I hope."

He hangs up and I slide the phone into my pocket. Out of the corner of my eye I see the man Jenna was sitting with stand and touch her shoulder, she gives him a quick, kind look but her eyes snap back to me as he walks away. She opens her mouth and I can see her hands twitch as if to move towards me again, but I am quicker. I take great strides to practically jump my way over to her. Even then I don't scoop her up in my arms because I want to look at her more first.

With just inches between us, I soak in how Jenna both looks exactly the same and very different. Her hair is the same length, but she has a fringe now and part of it is grey-white, in just one corner. It looks distinguished and frames her chestnut eyes beautifully. Her cheeks are still painted with a galaxy of golden freckles and while there is more softness in her chin and more lines in the corners of her eyes, they seem to add something, not take anything away. Looking down, I see her body is a little more toned than before – her arms more defined and her waist narrower – but her arse, noticeable even from the front, is still there and I nearly fall to my knees there and then to give thanks for that. I see the same gold chain around her ankle, and I feel a rush of love for her, and for her mother, who I hope is watching her daughter take this next step into a life filled with love.

"Jenna," I say.

"Marty," she says and it's upon hearing my name in her silky warm voice that I know she feels exactly the same way I do.

"I hope you weren't looking directly at the sun," I say nodding at the sunset but keeping my eyes on her.

"No, I wasn't," she says as her smile deepens and her eyes lock with mine. "But I am now."

Epilogue

361 Sunsets Later

Jenna

When my breathing slows and my belly stops quivering, I release my grip on Marty's head. As I open my eyes and see how the light in the room has changed, I gently tap my fingers to get his attention. He stops kissing my thigh and licks his lips as he locks in eye contact with me. And just like that, I'm ready for more. I think I will need a chapter in my next book about how tall, bearded Irish thirty-year-olds have the ability to restart my libido in half a second.

"Look outside." I nod towards the nearest window, which overlooks our small garden. A green space that is thankfully well covered by trees and shrubs so nobody can look in on these spontaneous love-making sessions of ours that are a near daily occurrence.

He looks then sits up completely. "Do we have time?"

I glance at my watch. "Yes, easily. You get the leads." I stretch forward, pushing my skirt down and bending to press my lips to his, letting my tongue roam, licking all traces of me off his beard.

Then we move. Him getting his keys and the dogs' leads, and me quickly grabbing my cardie and running to the toilet as I call for the dogs who come running instantly.

When I'm done, he's standing at the open front door, holding out my bag and positioning my Birkenstocks in a way I can just slip into them.

I hook my hand in his arm as we wander down the path, my other hand holding AJ's lead. A moment later Marty gets yanked forward by Rocky.

"Jesus, Rocky, slow the fuck down you fecking terrorist eejit dog!" he yells then turns to his left. "Oh, Mrs Dougal. Didn't see you there, good evening!"

I blush and bite back my laugh. She's one of the very few people who have given us some form of hostility to our relationship - namely gossiping very loudly in her garden about 'the handsome young lad and that much older woman who have shacked up next door' when we bought the place six months ago. So I am definitely not going to prompt Marty to apologise for his language in front of her.

We walk briskly up our street and then take a few turns before we are in Marlay Park, a generous stretch of grass and woodlands with the rolling hills of County Wicklow in the background, and on days like today, when the sky has been unusually clear, a beautiful view of the sun sinking behind them.

Not needing to say where we want to be, Marty and I head to the Dog Park and let Rocky and AJ off their leads. On the way we pass plenty of evidence others have been enjoying the park for a few hours already – they're drinking beers, lying out on picnic blankets, or enjoying portable BBQs they're not really allowed to - all soaking up this early summer sunshine that is so very welcome.

I've not hated living in Dublin for the last ten months. I've enjoyed it very much, but the weather has bamboozled me. It's not like it's different to London - the greyest city in the world - but the rain always feels wetter, the cold a bit chillier, and winter felt longer and bleaker than any I'd experienced before. That was what was going on outside our four walls, but inside was a different story.

Inside was perpetual summer.

I came back to Dublin with Marty after four days and another five sunsets together in Crete and in between seeing his parents and sister again, meeting everyone at his work and watching him move around a kitchen like he was dancing - whether ABBA was playing or not - we talked about where we would live together. We gave ourselves time to think on it when I returned to London for a few weeks, but the answer was already clear in my mind.

London had lots of positives for Marty from a work perspective, but Dublin was where his family is, and I was more ready for the upheaval of moving than he was. I'd spent most of the year before our reunion mentally preparing myself to leave London for him, even hoping it would happen, while Marty had spent most of his five years falling back in love with his life there. I wasn't willing to make him leave it so soon. My work could be done anywhere, and he agreed there was more he wanted to achieve in Dublin before he went elsewhere.

"Thirty tomorrow," I say as I slip my hand around his waist. We're standing still now, facing the sunset, both of us taking it in turns to quickly check if AJ is sniffing out treats from someone else's pockets or Rocky has bolted to the other side of the park.

"I know," he says and runs a hand through his beard. "I'm so fecking old!"

I lightly hit his stomach. "Piss off."

"I'm glad to be thirty," he says. "I know it doesn't work like this, but it makes me feel like I'm almost catching up with you."

"You're right, it doesn't work like that. But it may stop some of the raised eyebrows I get as I can now say you're thirty-something rather than twenty-something."

"Then what would we have to laugh about?" He bends to kiss the top of my head. "Actually, don't answer that. We never run out of things to laugh about."

And we don't. We laugh every day, many times a day.

"If you could be older or I could be younger, would you want that?" I ask Marty, the question suddenly popping into my mind although I suspect it's been hiding there in the shadows for some time.

He stares ahead at the sunset and I know he's thinking about it. Taking his time. Searching for the true answer rather than what I want to hear or what he thinks is the right thing to say. He does this a lot now, thinking before he speaks.

"Honestly, yes," he says. "I wish we could have been different ages when we met so that we could have had those five years together."

I nod, my eyebrows pull together with a pang of sadness.

"But I also wouldn't change anything about where we are now. And if who we are now is dependent on every single day we have each lived, every single step we've taken to get to this point - together or apart - I wouldn't change a single thing."

My frown flattens out.

"How about you?" he asks.

I wrinkle my nose and look at the lush green of the trees on the horizon contrasting with the tangerine orange sky. "I wouldn't mind you being a bit younger. You were fucking hot at twenty-four," I say.

His hand reaches down and slaps my arse with now oft practised precision, making me squeal.

"I'll kiss it better later," he says. "After twenty more lashings."

I shiver. "You better. Now, can I tell you what your present is?" I ask, unable to wait any longer.

"A day early? What have I done to deserve that?" he asks.

"Well, besides what just happened at home," I say, and look up at him with a side smile. "I think I've made you wait enough for things in the recent past..."

He laughs as I hoped he would. He hasn't always laughed about it, and sometimes he's been downright angry with me - usually after a good day together when he demands to know why we had to forsake years of potentially good days - but there have been just as many times when he looks at me levelly and I can see what he's thinking. That maybe we are as good as we are now because of that time apart.

"I'd do it again in a heartbeat, and you know it," he says as he stares.

"Well, surprise, that's your birthday present, another five years apart!" I tease, pulling my arms off him and rummaging in my bag.

"Feck off, Jenna! No way. No fucken way you're prepared to do that, not when I now have a sexy-ass beard and know how to cook all your favourite foods!"

It's true. He knows exactly how to keep me close but what he's talking about is just the tip of the Marty-sized iceberg I love.

"No," I say, pulling out an envelope. "It's this."

"What is it? Another postcard my mother will intercept?"

"Ha! No." I hand it over. "Open it."

We both watch his hands open it and retrieve two printed pieces of paper, one with details for a reservation at a resort in Morocco and another for two return flights to Marrakech. On a small postcard of Dublin I've written:

Dear Marty, Happy 30th Birthday! How about seven sunsets in Morocco with me? I promise you. Everything will be okay. Jenna x

His mouth falls open.

I smile at him. "Seven sunsets at my brother's resort. A room with a jacuzzi and sunset views. I booked time off with the restaurant already. We leave on Saturday," I explain. "Maeve is coming to house sit and look after the dogs and your parents are giving us a lift to the airport because that's apparently a thing that close families do."

He's smiling so wide as he skims over the pieces of paper. "A holiday... The first in a year."

Marty wanted us to buy the house together. I kept my house in London and rented it out and the monthly income from that would have covered a decent chunk of our Dublin mortgage, but it was not what he wanted, and I know better than to argue with a determined Marty. He's been working extra hours and avoiding any additional costs for the last year to match me sum for sum on the repayments and any other outgoings. My first book did well, I have two new regular columns and now have an easier time pitching the pieces I want to write, all of which has helped me have a steady income as I now work on my second book, tentatively titled *The Importance of Being Patient*, a more personal story about Marty and our relationship.

"Thank you," he says as he pulls me into his body.

I turn my head while there, facing the sunset and look at how the sun's radiance fills the whole sky as far as my eyes can see. A moment later I feel a thud against my ankles and look down to see AJ trying to squeeze his fat body between our legs while Rocky runs circles around us. Smiling I turn my head back to the sunset.

"No, thank you, Marty," I say.

Thank you for living your life. Thank you for waiting for me. Thank you for coming back for me. Thank you for loving me.

"And thank you, Arnie," I whisper so quietly because I don't want Marty to hear. I know he often feels him close, but I haven't yet told him that sometimes, I do too.

Marty

It doesn't make any sense, but I have never felt closer to Arnie than I have this last year with Jenna.

Five years away from Jenna taught me how to be my own person and how to love that person, but that hasn't stopped this year either. I keep going to therapy, if not as regularly. I cry when I need to, which again is less often. I keep trying to be the man who would make Arnie proud.

A year with Jenna and I am still getting to know myself, I'm just doing it through the eyes of someone else at the same time. And fuck, is it a beautiful reflection. I also have all the things I really missed most about Jenna. Yes, the sex and the intimacy and the humour, but more than that I have someone who I can share the more mundane things with like work problems, interior décor decisions and Mathew McConnaughey rom-coms, although she begrudges me the latter. I now have someone who can share life with me. I have someone who will not only grow old with me but will *grow* with me.

I asked Jenna to come off the pill three months after she moved to Dublin. I am curious about having a child with Jenna. I want it enough to try, but not too much that I think it will ruin us if it doesn't happen. When I put it like that, she agreed. I think if we had more time, she would have wanted to wait, but we both know we don't always get what we want when we want it. It doesn't break my heart that Jenna hasn't got pregnant yet, mostly because I see it not breaking her heart. I see her happy and full of life. I see her giving her new life in Dublin her all. She has yoga and coffee with my mother once a week - their blossoming friendship the biggest and most bizarre surprise of the year - a gym membership she uses every other day, a workspace where she goes a few times a week to write and meet other creatives, some of whom are slowly becoming friends. Jenna says she didn't give up much leaving London to be with me, but I know she misses her friends, and her brother who now stays with someone else in London during the winter months, and I never want her to think I don't appreciate what she gave up coming to Ireland.

Our life has become wonderfully normal and brilliantly boring, complete with a full but satisfying routine of work and play, our daily dog walks together in the early afternoon before I start my shift and she takes a break, and then, more often than not she wakes up when I return from work and we shower together. Sometimes, she washes me down like she did that night in Crete after dinner with my family, occasionally taking an orgasm from me as she does. Other times I use up whatever energy I have left taking her, tying her up, fucking and loving her until she's the one that needs to be washed down and put to bed. But always we fall asleep together, our bodies still damp and drying as they find one another.

Every morning we wake to our dogs scratching their paws against our bedroom door and we turn to each other and smile. Then I go for a run with Rocky and his buckets of energy, or a bike ride with Da and his still unfading competitive spirit, while Jenna makes breakfasts and takes AJ and maybe Rocky too for a short walk.

It's during those mornings of exercise that I talk to Arnie most. I tell him stories from the night before at work, and I tell him how good it is having Jenna with me in Dublin. And I thank him. Thank him for leading me to her on that first sunset in Crete with a little help from a mysterious cat, and for taking me back to her five years later, with a little help from my mother.

That's why, as I hold Jenna in my arms, her present still in my hands, a holiday that we both need and deserve, I feel the urge to do something I've been thinking about for a long time.

Just as the last slithers of the sun are sinking into the green hills of County Wicklow, I fall to my knees. Then I prop up one leg, and find Jenna's hands, hold them close in mine as her mouth opens wide.

"Jenna, I know you don't want to get married again, and you know I couldn't give a flying fuck," I say as she looks down at me, her eyes widening. "I don't have a ring, but I do want to be with you forever like I have been this last year. I want that to be my life, our life. So, I wonder if you will *not* marry me, but instead promise to stay by my side for a lifetime of sunsets?"

"Marty," Jenna says, and her hands are squeezing mine, so very tight. She glances around her and out of the corner of my eye, I can see people stopping and turning our way. I can hear their hushed murmurings, but I don't turn my head away. It's possible there are some phones recording this, but I don't care. I am only looking at her, wondering for the millionth time how I survived those five years without her, but believing that our love is the strong glorious thing it is now because I did.

"Promise me?" I prompt her again. She is no closer to forming words, but her features are settling into a smile that makes her eyes sparkle.

"A lifetime of sunsets?" Jenna tilts her head to the side and gravity pulls a tear out of her left eye. But still she smiles.

"Yes," I say and there are tears in my eyes too, and I fucking love it.

"I promise you a lifetime of sunsets," she says. "I'm not going anywhere, Aiden O'Martin. Only wherever you go."

"Thank fuck for that. I need someone strong to carry all my emotional baggage." I grab hold of her hips and pull her down to sit on my knee.

"No, Marty, you don't. You do that just fine yourself," she says.

And I find myself wanting to nod in agreement. I think I do okay too.

"I love you, Jenna." I wrap my arms around her waist, wobbling as I find some balance and slide her closer to me down my thigh.

"I love you too, Marty. But I am going to crush you if I stay sitting here much longer," she says as her lips linger above mine.

"It will be a grand way to go," I say and then I take her mouth and ignore the cheering and the clapping I hear, I close my eyes and focus only on her kiss and her hands on my face and our two mad dogs jumping up and bumping into us as I thank fuck I am still here for this moment. I thank fuck that I am here and get to spend the rest of my hopefully long love-filled life with her.

THE END

THANK YOU!

Thank you so much for reading Five Sunsets. I really hope you enjoyed and fell in love with Marty and Jenna as much as I did.

If you're not ready to leave their story yet, you can receive a bonus two chapter scene when you sign up to my newsletter, https://geni.us/FiveSunsetsSignUp. (You definitely want to go to that link if you want to know what happened when Marty cashed in his Scrabble bet!)

There follows an Author's Note about some of the topics I wrote about in this book, and after the Acknowledgements you can find a recipe for the Marty Party mocktail that Jenna made for Marty.

And if you'd like to leave a short review or rating, you can do so at the following links:
Amazon: https://geni.us/FiveSunsetsBook
Goodreads: https://geni.us/FiveSunsetsGoodreads

I am busy working on more steamy AF romcoms, so if you want to know more about them, or you'd just like to keep in touch, here are the best links:

Join my newsletter: https://geni.us/FiveSunsetsSignUp
TikTok (@francesmthompson): https://geni.us/FMTTikTok
Instagram (@francesmthompson): https://geni.us/FMTInstagram
Twitter (@FrancesMTAuthor): https://geni.us/FMTTwitter
Join my ARC team here: https://forms.gle/YyHUwesEhPprZ8D58

Author's Note

Shannon from Home Away was where it all began for me. Shannon, played by Isla Fisher, was my first crush on another girl. But while I felt that crush, I didn't translate it as meaning anything for my sexuality. At the time it wasn't fathomable to me that girls could fancy other girls, and if they did, well, that wouldn't be me.

It wasn't that I thought it was inherently bad - I was raised better than that - but as a sensitive teenage girl with an overactive imagination who struggled with her self-esteem and confidence, I didn't want to be any more different than I already was. All my adolescence I wanted to fit in. I craved popularity as validation. I obsessed over my appearance and wanted to look more like my friends or celebrities. I assumed therefore that my obsession with a character from a soap opera was an extension of this. I didn't want to kiss her, I wanted to *be* her. At the time, I also poured far too much energy into having crushes on boys - fictional and in real life – and because I was busy enough with that it seemed implausible I could squeeze in fantasizing about girls too.

But I did fancy girls back then. I always have fancied more than just one gender. And I suspect I always will. However, for many different reasons I didn't admit this to myself in earnest until my mid-thirties, and I was thirty-eight when I told those closest to me that I was, am, proudly bisexual.

It's so heart-breaking to me that I closed off this side of myself for so long, especially when I wasn't raised in a homophobic environment, and indeed I had long considered myself an ally to the queer community. And yet there are reasons why this happens. Misogyny, heteronormativity, biphobia are all things I could write several essays about but that's not what this note is for. This note is to explain why, as a bisexual woman who has struggled with her sexuality over the years, in the first romance novel I write, the main bisexual character is a man.

But first a step back. A step back to a small promise I made myself, and my future readers, last year. All my romance novels will feature bisexual characters, and nearly all of them will be one or both of the main characters. My goal in doing so is very simple; I want more representation of bisexual love in the world (and when I say bisexual I very much mean to include all multisexual or polysexual identities including but not limited to pansexual and omnisexual people). I want different kinds of bisexual love to be explored and discussed and understood and appreciated for what it is; love. I am quite certain had I had more examples in books (and other media) in my youth, I wouldn't have denied my sexuality to myself for so long. Even now, whenever I hear about a bisexual person finding love, I feel joy. I want to read books that bring me the same warm tingly feelings, and don't the mythical they always say "write the book you want to read". So that's what I'm doing and Five Sunsets is hopefully just the start. Also, if you've read even just a few romance novels, you'll know they're just as much about the characters falling in love with themselves as much as they are about finding a HEA with a love interest and I want to read about that in bisexual characters too. That brings me so much happiness and hope, and for good reason.

When research shows that bisexuals are more at risk of mental health struggles than straight, gay and lesbian people, this is not just a whimsical personal wish, this is also something I think our community needs desperately. Until very recent years, representation of bisexuality in media has been, at best skewed for comedy ("indecisive characters who can't make up their minds", "quirky eccentrics who are going through a phase" or "greedy people who want it all") and at worst, it has been exploited to add extra layers of evil to villains (the "depraved bisexual" uses their sexuality as a control mechanism to get close and harm indiscriminately, and yes, I'm looking at you Hannibal Lector, arguably the darkest of villains in modern cinema) and while things are changing, there's still a real lack of positive representation of bisexual men. Furthermore, where are all the FM relationships with bi-men where that man's bisexuality isn't a plot point or a problem for the woman?

It's these two short-comings that I wanted and really do hope Five Sunsets goes some way to address and resolve.

Furthermore, bisexual men come across some of the vilest forms of biphobia, and often by both "sides" of monosexuality. Bisexual men are shunned by gay men for not being queer enough, while straight women are suspicious of their monogamy and promiscuity. Bisexual people of all genders are often assumed to be more likely to cheat or to be going through "a phase". Furthermore, bisexuals are frequently not taken seriously - i.e. their bisexuality is not real, it's seen as a phase, or quite nastily, it is regarded as a call for attention - and while I'm the first bisexual disaster to play up to the bisexual disaster stereotype, it's not helpful to have any of these narratives be the whole story. Again, there are valid reasons for biphobia and bi-erasure in our culture and society, and very few are any one individual's fault, unless of course you are presented with more information and choose to ignore it.

A different narrative is exactly where Five Sunsets comes in. I wanted to depict bisexuality as a beautiful thing, something that is ultimately rooted in love, and I hope Five Sunsets does that. I also wanted to create a bisexual man who wants what we all want - love, validation, companionship, ABBA Greatest Hits on repeat - and I hope through Marty that has been achieved. While yes, it's true that Jenna's professional experience no doubt influences her attitude towards Marty's sexuality, and her deep respect and admiration for his love for Arnie, it was important to me to not have her fetishize him or his sexuality, something bisexual people of all genders experience. It was therefore my intention for her to appear mostly neutral about it but when it boiled down to it, when it came to both his sexuality and his love of Arnie, because they are part of Marty, they are things she also came to love and celebrate. While this acceptance and celebration should be the norm, I am only too aware they are not which is why there is the brief mention of Ciara's concerns and also a hint at some struggles in Cynthia's own adjustment to learning her son's sexuality. That said, I didn't want this book to be a heavy and loaded presentation or analysis of biphobia. More than anything I wanted it to be a love song to bisexuality, and specifically a serenade to bisexual men because they are both so sorely needed.

As for bisexual women like me. Well, I may just be working on that love song right now.

Thank you again for reading Five Sunsets.

Frankie x

P.S. Isla Fisher, if you ever read this, I never got over my crush, so you know, call me.

P.P.S. I also like to donate a percentage of each of my book's profits to charities or causes that are touched upon in the story. For Five Sunsets I will be donating 0.25 Cents from every book sale to the Irish Cancer Society.

Acknowledgements

Five Sunsets was my most collaborative book yet, and so lots of people are owed cake and thanks.

Niamh, my developmental editor, thank you for your enthusiasm for and embracing of Marty and Jenna, and for getting the story in a much better shape than it was before we met. I thank you also for ensuring the O'Martin family were convincing enough as the Irish legends they are and for teaching me more Irish swear words and slang than I never knew I needed. Any mistakes in this department are all mine.

My thanks to Sophia for being such a sharp and thorough copy editor and steering the happy couple closer to their HEA with considerably fewer sighs.

My gratitude is also owed to Crystal who fit me in her busy schedule to proofread and sanity-check Five Sunsets at almost the last minute. I'm so glad TikTok introduced us to each other.

Thank you to Teju who worked tirelessly to create the stunning cover and character illustrations. Teju, you were a joy to work with and nobody else could have brought Marty and Jenna to life as vividly as you did. Teju's work on Instagram is breath-taking too so please do go and check it out @tejuabiolaart.

My thanks to M Designs for doing the final touches on the cover again, and for helping with some of the formatting dramas that shaved years off my life in the final weeks before release.

Thank you to my friend Tabi for their road cycling knowledge to make sure I didn't sound like a complete idiot. And thank you Helen for confirming the weights Jenna was pulling wouldn't kill her. Credit for the yawning trick in Chapter Twenty (aka the BKGY) goes to Brandon Kyle Goodman, whose Messy Mondays on Instagram (@brandonkylegoodman) start my week in exactly the right way. I hasten to add that any mistakes relating to cycling, lifting weights or blow jobs are all my own. (That's a sentence I thought I'd never write.)

Huge thanks to all my ARC readers for their reviews and encouragement for this little big book. You all took a chance on this newbie romance author and it has been a true delight to hear that risk paid off for you all. I have loved getting to know you all better.

Now for those who keep me going in real time away from my desk. To Beth and Cat, phew, you did it again. You helped keep me sane, keep me feeling loved and keep me focused on this writing dream of mine, even when the days were long, hard and blurry for us all. There are often occasions when our Whatsapp group is the only thing that gets me through to bedtime and I don't think any acknowledgments I write will ever exclude you. Thank you for being my best ones.

Jhanelle, my baby-girl. For a woman with few books, I'm truly honoured your collection includes mine, and I'm forever grateful for your friendship and presence in my life. Love you long time.

Janneke, my favourite Dutchie. Thank you for your friendship and constant support on my writing journey and in many other areas of my life. My boys love their Tante Tjompi and so do I. I also hope this one delivers in the steamy scenes for you! Ik hou van jou.

Sarah, rediscovering our friendship has been one of the biggest joys of the last few years and I hope you know I'm never letting you go again. Thank you for your love and support of me as a writer and a human. You, Marius and Ella have taught me more about love in the last few years than anyone. I love you all so very much.

Jenny, do you know how grateful I am that we met in the snowy arse crack of nowhere in Austria nineteen years ago? Nobody "gets" me quite like you do and I will never take that for granted. Thank you for supporting me in ways only you know how. I love you.

To my parents, I really do hope you skip this book but whether you do or not, please know that the first things I learnt about love, I learnt from you. Aside from making me want to write Happy Ever Afters for love-crazed fools like Marty and Jenna, love is what guides me through everything in life, and you both planted that seed in me. Thank you.

To my kiddos, O and JJ. You are the reason I do what I do in life, and often the reason I don't do as much as I would maybe like to do of it! Thank you for understanding Mummy needs her writing time and being forever curious about the books I write. Whoever you end up loving in the future, I hope it is as beautiful, fun, and affirming as the love I write about in my romance books. I love you both with every fibre of my being.

My partner Mark deserves more thanks than I can write in a few sentences. Monster, I only hope my actions show you how grateful I am for your support, your enthusiasm and your love for me and my writing. Thank you for taking me and the kids to Crete last year where this story first took shape in my head, thank you for "talking" through the logistics of some of the scenes in this book(!), and thank you for spending an evening getting The Marty Party just right. I love you like you love Mai Tais and I love Pina Coladas. I am so happy we get to do this life together, sunset by sunset.

And to my left inner ear. Ha, you thought you could stop me. Well, nope. Not this time. Now sit down and behave while I work on Jake's and Maeve's books. Please.

Recipe for Marty Party

If you'd like to have your own Marty Party one time, here's a short but spicy and sweet recipe to recreate the mocktail that Jenna makes for Marty. If you're like Marty's dad and want to add a bit more of a kick to it, try adding in a shot of vodka, rum or brandy.

Ingredients

1-2 Spoonfuls of Crushed Watermelon (whack it in a blender or mash it up with a fork)

1-2 Spoonful of Raspberries (or you can blend or mash them too)

Apple Juice

Lemon & Lime Bitters

Fresh Mint

Ground Cinnamon

Ground Chilli Powder

Lime (optional)

Method

Making this mocktail works best when you blend the watermelon and raspberry together, and if you have a few ice chips to throw into the blender too – winner! For a really smooth drink you can throw all the other ingredients in too, but this is not a necessity.

If you don't have a blender, you can crush up the fruit and mix it with the apple juice in a cocktail shaker or simply in a glass with a long spoon or fork.

Once the fruit is blended or crushed and mixed together, add lemon and bitters to taste (depending on how fizzy you like your drinks).

As you mix it all up, add half a teaspoon of cinnamon, some chopped mint leaves and a dash of chilli powder. (You can skip this last part if you're not keen on chilli/heat.)

Serve on ice with a sprig of fresh mint or a slice of lime, or both! Cheers!

About the Author

Originally from UK, Frances M. Thompson (she/her) lives in Amsterdam, the Netherlands, with her partner and two young children. Please call her Frankie if you ever cross her path because nobody calls her Frances unless she's in trouble or you work for the tax authorities.

The author of three short story collections, a book of poems called Lover Mother Other and the London Killing series of suspense thrillers, Frankie is also the author of steamy romcoms and runs the semi-successful, but oft neglected travel and lifestyle blog, As the Bird flies. All of Frankie's books feature Bi+ main characters because that's what she needed more of growing up.

When not reading or writing, Frankie can be found dancing in her kitchen, cycling around Amsterdam, faffing with her many house plants, swearing her way through freezing open water swims, and squeezing in as many sunny or snowy holidays as she can.

Follow Frankie on Instagram or TikTok as @francesmthompson, or on Twitter as @FranceMTAuthor. You can find Frankie and all her books on Goodreads and Amazon, and you can listen to the playlists for her books on Spotify under her username "frankiebird".

Keep in touch with Frances M. Thompson:

Join my newsletter: https://geni.us/FiveSunsetsSignUp
Join my ARC team here: https://forms.gle/YyHUwesEhPprZ8D58
Frances on Goodreads: https://geni.us/FMThompsonGoodreads
TikTok (@francesmthompson): https://geni.us/FMTTikTok
Instagram (@francesmthompson): https://geni.us/FMTInstagram
Twitter (@FrancesMTAuthor): https://geni.us/FMTTwitter

Books by Frances M. Thompson:

The Moon Also Rises (Sun, Moon & Stars #2) – Coming 2023

The Way We Were (London Killing Thriller #3) – Coming 2022

Five Sunsets (Sun, Moon & Stars #1)

The Weaker Sex (London Killing Thriller #2)

The Wait (London Killing Thriller #1)

Lover Mother Other (Poetry)

Nine Women: Short Stories

London Eyes: Short Stories

Shy Feet: Short Stories About Travel

Printed in Great Britain
by Amazon